ALSO BY ANDREA BARTZ

The Herd
The Lost Night

WE WERE NEVER HERE

WE WERE NEVER HERE

A NOVEL

ANDREA BARTZ

BALLANTINE BOOKS

NEW YORK

Copyright © 2021 by Andrea Bartz Inc.

Published in the United States by Ballantine Books, an imprint of Random House, a division of Penguin Random House LLC, New York.

BALLANTINE and the HOUSE colophon are registered trademarks of Penguin Random House LLC.

LIBRARY OF CONGRESS CATALOGING-IN-PUBLICATION DATA
Names: Bartz, Andrea, author.
Title: We were never here : a novel / Andrea Bartz.
Description: New York : Ballantine Books [2021]
Identifiers: LCCN 2020052249 (print) | LCCN 2020052250 (ebook) |
ISBN 9781984820464 (hardcover) | ISBN 9781984820471 (ebook)
Classification: LCC PS3602.A8438 W4 2021 (print) | LCC PS3602.A8438 (ebook) |
DDC 813/.6—dc23
LC record available at https://lccn.loc.gov/2020052249
LC ebook record available at https://lccn.loc.gov/2020052250

Printed in Canada on acid-free paper

randomhousebooks.com

2 4 6 8 9 7 5 3 1

First Edition

Book design by Victoria Wong

For Jen Weber, my travel buddy and ride-or-die

WE WERE NEVER HERE

CHAPTER 1

Kristen trotted to the patio's edge and crouched, long arm outstretched. Her fingers groped along a vine, lifting leaves, exposing the tender stalks beneath. I pictured her tipping over and tumbling off, there and then not there, the afterimage of her silhouette still hanging in my vision. I don't know why. For a wild moment, I pictured pushing her.

Instead I half stood from the table. "Kristen, don't," I called. The wooden patio perched on stilts above the vines below and we were alone, as we had been almost everywhere we'd stopped this week. Empty restaurants, empty markets, empty tourist information centers. An occasional cluster of other visitors standing or sitting nearby despite everyone having all the space in the world.

A snapping sound and Kristen stood, holding up a blob of green grapes. She popped one into her mouth and chewed thoughtfully. "Not bad. Catch."

I missed the toss and the grapes bounced onto the glass tabletop. I glanced around, then tried one—it burst bright and tart on my tongue.

"He said their yield sucks this year. You didn't need to take an entire bunch."

She sank into her chair and lifted her pisco sour, lime green and frothy. "I'll leave 'em a few extra pesos on the way out. I was hungry." She nudged her glass against mine. "You'd rather see me steal some grapes than get low blood sugar, right?"

"Fair point." Hangry Kristen could cut to the core.

A man with a bandanna looped around his head was watching us from far out in the fields, just before the grapevines bumped up against a row of bushy trees. Beyond that, braided hills cut a jagged horizon. Kristen waved at the worker and he nodded.

I let the last of my drink linger on my tongue. We'd been sipping these daily: lime juice, powdered sugar, and the yellowish brandy the Chileans swore predated Peruvian pisco. I felt the swell of yet another one of those well-isn't-this-nice moments, one blissfully free from the fear that'd prickled my brain nonstop for the last thirteen months. Here I was, on the trip of a lifetime: seven nights in South America, exploring the rough mountains and the ripe valleys between with my best friend of more than a decade. A cocktail so bracing and sweet, it tasted like stepping into the surf. And we still had two nights to go.

Kristen made everything better, her confidence like a bell jar of security in a strange and gnarled world. When we'd hugged at the airport almost a week ago, tears of relief had coated my eyes. I hadn't seen her in a year—a year pockmarked by panic attacks, nightmares, and screaming into my pillow or the shower or occasionally my fist. But in Santiago, as we'd picked up our rental car and driven north on barren highways, Kristen was her usual boisterous self. She whooped when the Pacific came into view; she honked at a clump of plush alpacas by the side of the road. She pointed and gasped at roadside fruit stands, rippling cornfields with laser-straight rows, fat fields of vegetables growing bushy in the sun. And sky, sky, so much blue sky, almost crackling in its crispness, the way it shot down into the ocean on one side and the crinkled peaks on the other. Her presence was like a calming scent, aerosolized Xanax, and I allowed myself to relax.

We spent the first night in La Serena, where we carried leaky ice-cream cones around a leafy town square and stayed in a hotel with bright colors on the walls, where paintings of saints watched us as we slept. Too touristy, we decided, and the next morning we drove inland. In Pisco Elqui we took a yoga class from a woman with bowed knees and hip-length hair; as we stood in Mountain Pose, our chests puffed out, she announced, "Your smile powers your *corazón,* your heart." On the second night there, three college-age guys from Germany cornered us in a bar, and the panic came roaring back like a panther lying in wait. Kristen had taken the lead—she was charming, could talk to anybody—and when she'd noticed the fear in my eyes, she politely disentangled us from the cocky trio and led me back into the night.

"It's okay, it's me, I'm here," she kept murmuring as we walked the dark streets back to our hotel. "Kristen's here." Her voice was a balm; her words a weighted blanket. We'd packed up and left the following day.

And this morning we arrived here, in Quiteria. At first, I'd been alarmed by its emptiness. We'd parked in a lot and wandered the hilly streets, our suitcases trailing behind us like dejected toddlers, for what felt like hours before we found an open hotel. There I scored the keys to a small suite, the duvet damp despite the dry mountain air. The sun was sinking, and I realized the city's vacancy would be an asset: fewer men to bother us, two women walking the streets at night. You know what they say about women traveling alone.

Kristen swallowed the last of her pisco sour. "You know what we should do? Birthday wishes."

"My birthday's not for two weeks."

"I know, but I want to do it in person. And it's a big one!"

It was our tradition, telling the other what we hoped would happen for them that year. I'd had the idea after I read about two best-friends-slash-business-partners who wrote each other's New Year's resolutions.

"I'll go first," she said, turning toward the grapevines. "My birthday wish for you, my darling Emily . . . is that your company gets its head out of its ass and gives you the promotion you deserve."

"That would be nice." I'd thrown my name in the hat for a director-level position months ago, but my employer, Kibble, was disorganized and putzy and dragging its feet. I liked my job there, though, promotion or not: project manager of a start-up that shipped raw, organic cat food to pet owners with too much money. I had hip young co-workers, including my work wife, Priya, and cat photos literally everywhere.

Still, I didn't tell Kristen that my secret wish, whenever I saw a shooting star or caught a dandelion fluff or spotted a clock at 11:11, was to land a great partner, settle down. It felt too antifeminist, too needy to put into words. But with Kristen halfway around the world and all my friends getting married (hell, having kids), my patience was wearing thin. And maybe I was finally headed in the right direction . . .

"He said they're gonna start interviewing candidates this month," I told her. "It's funny, he acts like there's no time to even *think* about the open position. Like he's too busy saving the world, one feline digestive tract at a time."

"Cat people are the worst people. I say that as a card-carrying cat lover stymied only by allergies."

"I think his devotion is kinda sweet!"

Kristen snorted. "It's an entire business predicated on people being obsessed with a disinterested animal."

"Russell's cat isn't disinterested. Mochi loves him back. I've seen the videos." Kristen rolled her eyes and I leaned forward. "C'mon, I like my job."

"Sorry, sorry, sorry." She waved a hand. "Okay, now you go."

"Right. My birthday wish for you, a full four months early, is that, hmm." I tapped the stem of my glass. *That you realize you hate Australia. That you move back to Milwaukee. That we go back to the way things were.* "I hope you get your stupid boss fired and your job gets a million times better. Or you find a new job that makes you happy."

"No fair, you just copied me!"

"This is what our thirties are all about, right? Vaulting forward in our careers. At least we *have* jobs."

"True. And thank God we put that disposable income to good use." She swept her arm out across the vines, whose pristine rows narrowed in the distance. Behind them, rumpled mountains reddened in the dipping sunlight. A bird landed on the edge of the distillery's deck and uttered a squeaky trill. A cute sierra finch, yellow as an egg yolk—I recognized it from some idle research I'd done at my desk in Milwaukee.

Nearby, a thumping sound. It was probably a woodpecker, but before I realized that, the memory flashed before me: *Stop. Stop. Stop.* Kristen's eyes wide as she stepped back, blood speckling her shoes. The moment that changed everything, when life cracked neatly into Before and After.

Kristen slid up her sunglasses and gave me an indulgent smile. I grinned back.

I'd been wrong to worry. Even the incident with the trio of Germans had been harmless. There'd been no strange men hulking in corners, their eyes following us hungrily. No drunken dudes who'd stood a little too close or followed too few steps behind us on darkened streets. No cause for alarm.

I gazed at Kristen and felt a rush of warmth.

Everything had gone perfectly.

A fat bee bumbled around our glasses, and Kristen waved her hand, fearless.

"Feels like we're the only non-locals for miles," I said. The isolation was both thrilling and unsettling.

"It won't last. My guidebook says all the tourist buses arrive on Saturdays." She stretched her arms, recrossed her muscular legs. Kristen had gotten into CrossFit in Sydney, and sometimes her limbs still looked off to me. Tawny and taut, like they belonged on another body.

Kristen had moved to Sydney eighteen months ago; her market research firm opened up an Australian office and her boss encouraged her to apply. To my dismay, she'd complied, murmuring about how she was over Milwaukee—her hometown—with its smallish size and polarized communities.

Kristen in Australia: It'd seemed like a whim, fleeting and outlandish. I didn't know adulthood without her, from when we became friends as fellow econ majors at Northwestern to when we both found jobs in Wisconsin and shared a ramshackle apartment off

Brady Street. Together we fumbled through our postgrad years, through bad dates and good job news and rough nights and even rougher mornings, until we emerged, fresh-faced and triumphant, in our late twenties, me with my very own apartment in the Fifth Ward, her a few miles away in Riverwest. We spoke casually of how we'd someday be each other's maids of honor, how she'd eventually be my future children's "auntie." I'd grown to love Milwaukee by then, with its broad lakefront and myriad festivals and friendly little art-and-music scene, all of the talent and none of the pretension of larger cities. I'd tried hard not to take her digs at the city personally.

I'd been happy for her, of course, but almost glowing with self-pity: left out and left behind and left, left, left. I dipped into depression in her absence, forcing myself through life as if there were a layer of dust dampening every moment. But we kept up a tradition we'd kicked off in Milwaukee: annual trips to someplace exotic, far-flung places most people never put on their lists.

I'd only been to popular international destinations (London, Cancún, Paris . . .), so each vacation with Kristen felt like slipping into a wormhole and appearing in another dimension, dizzy with sounds and smells and sights. Vietnam had been first, Hoi An and Hanoi, exploring tube houses and night markets and elaborate temples, more colorful than a field of poppies. Then Uganda, all our savings poured into once-in-a-lifetime experiences that piled up like snow, miraculous at first and then oddly normal: staring into the marble eyes of gorillas in Bwindi, boating past Nile crocodiles and bloats of fat hippopotami, clutching each other from the back of a jeep as a lion regarded us during a game drive in Kidepo Valley.

The third trip—Cambodia—was when things had gone awry. It was our first time meeting up from opposite corners of the globe, and I couldn't wait for all that concentrated face time, the kind we took for granted when we both lived in Milwaukee. I never imagined it'd take a turn for the terrifying, become my own personal horror movie. But Kristen, as always, had helped me, saved me, taken care of me. And here we were, with our final hours in Chile's Elqui Valley dwindling like the flame of an old candle, and everything felt gushing and good between us.

Kristen plucked a grape from the bunch and tossed it into the air, catching it neatly in her mouth. She grinned as she chewed.

"Open your mouth, Em." She held another up, like a dart.

"No!"

"Let me try! I have really good aim."

"I don't trust you."

"Hey, you're talking to King of Kings' three-time basketball MVP. Here, throw one in my mouth." She unhinged her jaw.

"This is not going to end well," I warned, giggling as I pitched a grape her way. It bounced off her chin and landed, rather miraculously, in her empty glass, and we both stared in quiet awe.

It'd taken a few hours to find our rhythm here in Chile. On the long drive up from the Santiago airport, I'd been grateful to bask in Kristen's aura again, her casual confidence and glinting wit. But my nerves had hardened and sparked when she'd crunched our rental car onto the dirt in front of an empanada stand. We ate lunch leaning on the car's hot hood as the cook, a stout lady with leathery skin, looked on. A woman out here all alone, nothing but stubby trees and choky dust for miles—I tried to give her a friendly smile.

Packed inside each doughy triangle was an entire hard-boiled egg and seasoned ground meat, and without thinking, I lifted my phone to snap a photo.

"What are you doing?" Kristen swallowed her bite and raised her eyebrows. "Did you forget?"

"I wasn't gonna post it," I muttered, blushing.

"Hand it over." The sun beat into Kristen's open palm. UV rays shooting onto each crease in her palm, each groove of her fingertips. I didn't move and she flicked her wrist. "You know the rules."

A breeze sent the bushes and shrubs around us hissing. The woman glanced up from the counter, where she was rolling out dough.

I dropped my phone into Kristen's hand and grinned. "Digital detox commencing now."

It hadn't come up again. Our phones were in our purses now, there in case of emergency, but turned off, dead blocks of metal and glass. Our Cambodia trip had involved a no-phones-allowed two-night yoga retreat at the beginning, and we'd both agreed to keep it up. And then the decision had served us so well. So much luck, so many incidental details lining up to bring us here: alive, safe, free.

"So where should we go next year?" I asked.

Kristen rolled a grape between her fingers. "Turkey's still high on my list. And didn't you say you'd heard good things about Georgia?"

I shook my head. "Georgia, the country? I don't know anything about it."

"I could swear you were talking about it." She narrowed her eyes.

"Well, Turkey could be cool," I said. "Istanbul's supposed to be super vibrant."

"I was also thinking Morocco. Haggling in bazaars and riding camels in the desert and whatnot."

A thought cropped up and I swallowed it just in time: *Aaron went to Marrakech a few years back*. He and I had been on four dates, after months of casual banter at the coffee shop where he worked. Apparently four dates was just enough for him to hijack my mind, my daydreams floating out like bubbles toward potential coupledom.

I hadn't mentioned him to Kristen yet—not after she'd dismissed my "Met any cool guys lately?" on the first night with a scoff and a no. Kristen hadn't had a serious boyfriend in all the time I'd known her, and she'd gotten rid of her dating apps six months into Sydney, disappointed to learn that mate-seeking was just as frustrating there as it was stateside. It wasn't like I didn't *want* to tell her, I just hadn't wanted boy talk to dominate the week, drowning out the conversation around our dreams and plans and inner worlds . . . and I'd sooner die than rub my dating luck in her face. Aaron was the first guy I'd felt this excited about in years, and I didn't want to jinx it. I'd even set up a stupid, secret test: I'd turn my phone on sometime soon and see if he'd bothered to text me. If he was still demonstrably interested, I'd tell Kristen about him.

I jumped—out of nowhere, the distillery's owner leaned over my shoulder. He scooped up both our glasses. My fingers tingled from the cortisol spike, such an outsize reaction.

"Do you like anything else?" he asked. "We are closing now."

On the way out, Kristen extended her hand and asked for his name again. "Thank you so much, Pedro," she repeated, and behind her I stamped the air with a few more *gracias*-es. We'd joked about it on the drive from Santiago—she read out every road sign the American way and I threw on my best Spanish accent, my tongue flitting the way I'd learned in grade school: "That's *Chigualoco,* and I'm glad I can repay you for your chauffeur services with my terrible translation services."

Kristen had beamed, her honey-brown hair fluttering from the open window. "You know you never have to repay me for anything."

CHAPTER 2

We hiked in silence back up to our hotel, on a serpentine mountain road flanked with abrupt drop-offs and the occasional barking dog. The region was known for its stargazing, so streetlights were nonexistent and porch lights were hazy orange.

"What should we do for dinner?" Kristen asked. She paused to sniff a bough of fuchsia flowers. "No smell."

"I'd go back to where we had lunch." I fished in my bag for my inhaler; the steep walks and thin air didn't bother Kristen, but I wasn't in excellent shape like her. "Your quinoa bowl looked insane. And—I never thought I'd say this—I'm kinda sick of empanadas."

"Oh God, same." She paused at our hotel's driveway. "I was hoping you'd say that. I'm gonna shower before we eat."

"No rush." I pulled the keys from my purse and fumbled with the gate. In the dark, we squinted at the brick path. The hotel had an odd setup: rooms clustered in four separate buildings, with doors that opened to the outside, motel-style. It was fancier than the hotels we normally chose, and pricier, too, but Kristen had insisted on picking up the tab, ignoring my objections as she handed over a wad of cash.

Kristen was wealthy in a way that'd intrigued me in college, prodded at my bubble-wrapped middle-class mind. She didn't talk about it, but I began to catalog the evidence in secret: While I made my bed with a striped comforter from Target, Kristen spread a creamy duvet, bleeding from teal to cobalt like pliable art. My standing lamp was a cheap plastic thing with limbs sprawled out like Medusan snakes, while an elegant torchiere stood in Kristen's corner. She mentioned trips to exotic places, their names like something out of a sci-fi paperback (Ljubljana, Brno, Zagreb, Baku), but never name-dropped, never alluded to her background with showy pride or even showier humility.

The key clunked and we tumbled into the suite with that instant release of making it in from the outside world. I dropped my bag on a chair and Kristen closed herself in the bathroom. We'd been upgraded to a suite for some reason—either because we were the only people there or because it was the only room left, per my mediocre Spanish comprehension. I could usually piece together whatever we needed to say, but my mind went blank when a local responded, mumbling at high speeds like a rock tumbling down a hill. No matter how much I begged them to slow down (*"lentamente, por favor, palabra por palabra"*), they repeated themselves at the same tempo, then smiled expectantly. Kristen would stare at me, too, everyone waiting for my sluggish brain to work as I grew more and more exasperated with myself.

In here, we only had to speak English. I plopped on the couch, a horrific aqua thing, and glanced out the window: During the day it was a glorious vista, brown mountains with a few colorful houses sprinkled across its base, but now there was just star-spangled sky, the land below it a jagged blank. I listened to the rush of water on tile coming from the bathroom, then pulled out my phone and connected to the Wi-Fi. A long string of texts from Priya recounting a hilarious moment I'd missed at an all-hands meeting. And three texts from Aaron: the kookiest Milwaukee news stories he could find.

A smile stretched across my face. He'd passed my test—I'd fill Kristen in on him this evening, when the time was right. She'd understand why I hadn't mentioned him; she'd appreciate that I hadn't wanted to spend the whole week analyzing dates. Of course, I wouldn't mention the other reason I'd stayed mum: Kristen, with her sky-high standards for me, tended to be critical of my love interests. She picked up on the red flags I missed, the warning signs I didn't want to see. Thank God Aaron had passed my test—Kristen's scrutiny would almost certainly be harsher.

Still, Aaron, shock of shocks, really did seem to be one of the good ones. Our meet-cute was a movie cliché: We chatted as he made my daily oat-milk latte at Café Mona, just down the street from my office, and over time I learned he was recovering from a breakup. Then, last month, I was slack-jawed when he asked for my number.

I liked going on dates, but things never seemed to go anywhere with the men I met on apps or through setups. And then a year ago, I'd sworn off dating completely, every male hand reminding me of the one that'd threatened my life and bruised my skin that night in Cambodia. So I surprised myself by agreeing to a first date with Aaron: clapping to polka tunes at a homey concertina bar. I entered the night with friend vibes and finished it with a crush. He was patient, never making me feel bad for not being ready to veer beyond make-out territory. (That was when the panic flared, *Stop. Stop. Stop.*) And he was weird, with his tortoiseshell glasses and dark floppy hair and manic, beat-poet energy. Not my type. And yet . . .

Aaron was nothing like my college beau, Ben; maybe that's what I liked about him. I kept seeing shades of Ben in men from dating apps: a sighing superiority, obscure pop-culture references and I'm-too-good-for-this overtones. Aaron had an openness that struck me as refreshing. He completed colorful graphic-design projects in the middle of the night. He'd grown up in the area and liked to wander through old-school museums on his days off, like the Pabst Mansion and the slightly creepy *Streets of Old Milwaukee* exhibit at the public museum. He was interested in everything, but especially in me.

Kristen came out of the shower, framed in steam. She pulled a dress from the wardrobe and then sat in front of a mirror, carefully applying her foundation, a few swipes of mascara. I wasn't sure why we kept doing this: We weren't sharing photos of ourselves, after all, and Kristen didn't care much about impressing strangers. I imagine she was used to looking beautiful, with her caramel-colored waves and wide hazel eyes.

"I CAN'T BELIEVE this is our second-to-last night," Kristen mused as we strolled into town.

"I know. Soon we'll be back in our *cubicles,* ugh." I glanced at her. "We need an action plan for dealing with Lucas." She hated her boss, a heavyset Swiss expat who, as Kristen told it, had begun disliking her the minute the firm forked over $1,500 for her work visa. "What do we know about managing up?"

"That it's impossible if you're a scapegoat." She shrugged. "The branch isn't hitting its quarterly goals, and I'm the only manager who's not part of their C-suite boys' club. I think they're afraid of me."

"Afraid of you?"

"Just in the way all men are afraid of women. Deep down." She ran her fingers through a jungly vine hanging over the street.

"You think men are afraid of us? I feel the opposite. Then again, I'm not all CrossFit tough like you." Was this how she experienced life? I envied men's indifference to personal safety—how they could amble through a dark alley without thinking twice.

"Of course they are. It's why they're so cruel. Men with batshit manifestos and access to assault rifles."

"Why would we scare them?"

"Because we know things. We see things—*sense* things they miss." She stepped over a pile of horse poop. "After all, we're the ones who ate the fruit from the tree of knowledge."

"*Biblical* references. Old-school." Were all women masters of detection? Kristen could be observant, reading implications and people and rooms in a shrewd, cerebral way. But I was more sensitive than her, more thin-skinned and porous. It meant the sight of a bird dying on the side of the road could fill me with sorrow, but there were advantages too: Whenever a butterfly whiffled by, my eyes brimmed with joy, as if we shared a secret.

We turned from the narrow street onto a cobblestone one and gazed at the cute vegetarian restaurant anew: A treelike fern was plopped in the center of the patio, with colorful dream catchers and a worn Tibetan prayer flag strung between nearby trees. Kristen's and my excitement over new cities borders on orgasmic. When we'd stumbled upon this spot earlier, we were both so overcome by its loveliness, we fell into a spontaneous, giggling hug.

Kristen loved telling people how we met, as if we were a long-term couple still astounded by our luck. Sophomore year, we were the only women in our Statistical Methods in Economics seminar. A couple guys, mostly seniors, had boxed us out of the discussion, rolling their eyes at our questions and regurgitating our own points with almost comical smugness. As we filed back into the hallway, I'd smiled shyly at Kristen.

"So that was . . . interesting."

"We should study together," she replied. "Ruin the curve for all those assholes. I'm Kristen."

I shifted my books to shake her outstretched hand. And then I felt it, a decentering, a wobbling motion like when you've just stepped off a boat: Some part of me knew this was *important,* that things wouldn't be the same.

I hadn't had that feeling since I'd met Ben at a party junior year of high school, when he, a cute prepster from the all-boys school, ambled over and said hi, his ice-blue eyes holding mine. Within the month, we were officially "going out." Sophomore year of college, by the time Kristen's hand grasped mine, Ben and I were decidedly not in love anymore. But I still loved him, because we'd been together for years. I took a behavioral economics approach to it: All the time and space and knowledge and feelings we'd already invested, the future we'd envisioned back in Minneapolis, where we were both from—it felt like a done deal, inevitable. Sunk costs, sunken hopes.

I had so little context back then. No ability to take a step back and see things clearly. *He takes care of you,* I told myself, because he made it clear that he was smarter than me. *He only wants the best for you,* I told myself, because he disliked my more boisterous college friends, hated when I drank, and turned nearly apoplectic when I tried pot. *He wants you to be your best self,* I recited like a windup doll, because he wanted me to learn about esoteric Russian literature and art-house cinema and snob-approved music. Plus, there was a certain coziness to our dynamic, to knowing how he took his coffee and which restaurant we ate at before a movie and how everything would end. A peek at the future, like flipping to the last page of a mystery before the narrative gets too intense.

And then I met Kristen. She and I were almost instantly inseparable: We discovered our mutual love for nerdy wordplay and stupid brainteasers and whipped up our own secret language, our world for two. We'd meet all over campus to study together, and the location inevitably came through texted clues—a treasure hunt with our togetherness as the prize. Over in the dorms, we'd leave cryptographs on the whiteboards on each other's doors, coded complaints of being SEXILED AGAIN or invitations to DINNER AT HINMAN. The stealth, hiding secrets in plain sight, gave all our interactions an electric current. Who doesn't love getting away with things?

An ironic thought, I supposed, after what happened in Cambodia. Blood on the floor in a widening pool.

In college, the high of prancing around with Kristen threw into stark relief just how small and tense I felt around Ben. Kristen had been the first to question it—to ask the just-right questions, until slowly, slowly, I came to recognize the manipulation, the criticism, the subtle gaslighting. I began to hold my ground with Ben and call him out on things. Question why our postgraduation plans were really *his,* with me as set dressing, a prop. Hers was the apartment I rushed to at two A.M. when, senior year, Ben and I got into the Argument of the Century, yelling and flailing.

He and I almost never fought, our resentment building instead, and so it was one of those moments when a part of you splits off and hovers over you like a drone: *Will you get a load of this? Can you believe this is really happening?* He whirled away and I reached for his shoulder, *look at me when I'm talking to you,* and he turned so suddenly that the back of my skull connected with the wall behind me before I could figure out why or how.

"I wasn't trying to hit you," he said, glowering, in lieu of an apology. I pushed past him and ran to the door. After a multiday standoff, Kristen went over to Ben's and my apartment and filled a suitcase while he looked on, jaw set. We never had an official breakup.

I'd wanted to see him again, pathetically; I wanted to scream and cry as he held me, because his arms were almost as familiar as my own. But Kristen knew better. "Screw '*closure*,'" she said at the time. "You're not wasting another second on this loser. Now he can find someone new to try to cram into a tiny, suffocating box, and you can be the badass you are."

Now Kristen strolled over to a waiter and held up two fingers. "*Una mesa para dos*," she said. She always was a quick study. He let her choose a table and she gave me the nicer seat, facing the interior; her view was of me against the wall.

"This has been such a fun week." She reached out and squeezed my forearm. "So laid-back and magical."

"Exactly what we needed," I agreed, unfolding a napkin. "I haven't been this relaxed in a long time."

Stop. Stop. Stop. Blood trickling like paint down the metal pole. Kristen's eyes wide, amazed. Blood mottling her hands, her wrists, her shoes.

"It's like no time has passed," she said. She snapped open a menu. "We can pick up right where we left off, like nothing has changed. And that's how you can tell we're true friends."

CHAPTER 3

What happened was this: A man attacked me in Phnom Penh, Cambodia, and we killed him in self-defense.

He was a backpacker, a South African dude with a big blond beard and huge hairy arms, freckled and tanned. He'd turned to us in a dank bar—to Kristen, casually gorgeous in her elephant pants and tank top sans bra—and asked how we were liking Cambodia. He was what we called a "duder," fratty and loud, but cute. After a few minutes, he stuck out his hand ("I'm Sebastian, by the way,") and Kristen told him her name was Nicole. It was something we'd done in college: tossing out a fake name to indicate how little the interaction mattered, how sure we were we'd never see this guy again. After Ben, it'd kept me from jumping back into anything too quickly—something Kristen warned me about. And during our trips, using aliases gave nights a thrilling, what-happens-in-Vegas undertone.

I played along, introducing myself as Joan. But Sebastian the South African was actually funny. And in the way it sometimes does when I feel like the less-desirable friend, my wit flipped on like a light, zapping and sparking with impeccable speed and timing. Kristen didn't seem to mind; he was more my type anyway, and she did the appropriate wingwoman things: fluttering around, chatting with strangers.

The hours dwindled; the air cooled. First the bar died down, then the streets outside followed suit. The roar of passing motorbikes softened to a purr, punctuated by occasional shouts from drunk tourists. I touched Sebastian's rough bicep when he made me laugh, and he pressed a palm on my waist when we moved to let a waiter pass. "Nicole" bought us another round of Angkor beer and, as we toasted, shot me a knowing grin.

Talk, inevitably, turned to "getting out of here." He was staying in a hostel even crummier than ours, renting a bed in a room packed with bunks—so Kristen, the saint, insisted she wanted to hang around this dead bar for one last solo beer. "I'm sure I'll be back at the hotel by . . . midnight?" she proposed, and Sebastian and I nodded gratefully, and it was all very clear to everyone.

Kristen grabbed my elbow on the way out and asked it one more time: "You're good?" And I hesitated. I didn't know this guy, after all. My one-night stands and third-date hookups back in the Midwest (ranging from fun to regrettable to maaaybe not really what I wanted but I went along with it because I'd stupidly found myself in bed) had had a pall of familiarity around them—neighborhoods I knew, a cellphone and three digits I knew by heart. This was different. Neither Kristen nor I had had a vacation fling. But then I beat back the unease, the kind that so often creeps up when you're a woman moving through space, because this guy was funny, and hot, and he wanted me.

I think about that moment a lot, when I patted Kristen's arm and turned away. How it changed the course of our lives, Kristen's and mine. How our path forked off and veered, leaving behind so many untouched threads funneling out of the center like a lace doily. One where I gave into the wariness and changed my mind, and Sebastian huffed off into the night. Or I rerouted on the spot and we made out in the bar or on a jungly street corner instead.

But as it was, on the knotted thread I followed that night, Sebastian and I left. As we were heading out, a camera's light flashed the world away, and when we blinked through it I couldn't tell who'd taken the shot—one we'd unintentionally photobombed in the little bar. I think about that picture sometimes, too, how someone has it likely locked away in the Cloud, unaware it's of a missing person in his final public moments. It could be very, very bad if the right person came across it—connected the dots, turned it over to South African authorities. Who knows what else is unwittingly documented in people's phones and hard drives and dusty photo albums, background noise that would swell with meaning to a different audience?

Sebastian and I walked together through the mosquito-choked air, hand in hand, and his palm slipped down to squeeze my ass as we got to the hotel's front door. The on-duty employee was asleep on a lobby sofa, and Sebastian's thumb stroked mine as we waited to be let in. Heat building in my groin, a sexy full-body kiss as soon as we were shut into the room.

The making out was hot at first: I discovered he liked to mix pleasure with pain, catching my lower lip in his teeth, raking my hair back with a sharp tug. Not my thing, but it was a turn-on to feel a bit like prey, so desirable he could barely contain his animalistic urges. And I'd had enough sex education over the years—quizzes in magazines and wine-fueled talks with friends—to know that the way to Blow His Mind, to Be His Best Ever, is to show that you're into it and read his nonverbal cues. So I gave his blond hair a yank. Turned a neck kiss into a bite. Ran my fingertips over his bare back and abruptly curled my fingers, ten tiny scratches, and smiled against his lips when he moaned with pleasure.

But then—something changed.

And that's where my brain wants to haze out, switch to another channel. *Stop. Stop. Stop.*

The sensation of his mouth on my nipple tipped into pain. I gasped and pushed at his cheek, and he moved to kiss me again. Then his fist closed around my hair and tugged so hard tears pricked my eyes. I was surprised and dim, "Hey, not so rough."

He smiled again, his movements still smooth. "C'mon, we're just having fun." His teeth found my earlobe, bit down until I yelped.

I sat up against the headboard. "You're hurting me."

"You're so fucking sexy."

"I'm *serious*." I swatted his hand away from my breast.

He moved as quickly as a Venus flytrap, snatching my wrist in his palm. "You're going to make me work for it, huh?"

"We're done." I clambered off the bed. "I think you should go."

His eyes hardened. "You've been leading me on all night."

A tear snaked from my eye, but I kept glaring, kept acting tough. "You need to leave."

But then he reared back and slapped me. "Or maybe this is how you like it?" Shock crystallized on my cheek, the pain like the peal of a bell.

An icy plunge as lust turned to fear, survival mode, fight or flight. I pushed him away, blindly, desperately, and my hand caught his jaw—an accidental punch. Nostrils flaring, he shoved me against the wall by my throat—*thwock,* a clang against my skull—and my fingers flew to his knuckles, trying to peel his palm back from my neck. His other hand reached down and yanked my underwear to the top of my thighs. I felt an odd pulse of shame, like the moment in a dream when you realize you're naked.

His hammy fist encircled my wrists and jammed them against the wall over my head—like I was a witch tied to a pyre. I remember this moment in impressions: his hips pinning mine against the wall, his dick pushing up against his shorts. The smile on his sweaty face, the cruelty in his eyes as I started to scream. His free hand lifting in slow motion, then flying up against my mouth. The back of my head slammed into the wall again, harder this time—the same sharp crack from that time with Ben, eight years earlier—and I saw a flash of fuzzy white.

He paused then, and I stopped struggling. Scuba diving—that's where my mind went, zooming off as if underwater. Kristen had wanted to try it in Vietnam years earlier, and I'd said no because I'd read once that divers die not from running out of oxygen, but from disorientation—they panic and remove whatever's in front of their nose and mouth. That's what I thought of as Sebastian concentrated all his weight into my jaw: something in front of my mouth, something I desperately wanted to rip away, but I knew I was screwed either way.

He's going to kill me.

"Emily!"

We both froze. He turned to look at the door, and though I couldn't turn my head, I felt the pressure ease. Anger surged as I parted my lips and bit down on a knob of calloused flesh, harder and harder until the tang of iron hit my tongue.

"Fucking bitch!" He released my wrists and stepped back, clutching his bleeding palm. The lace of my underwear cut into my thigh as I brought my knee up, and I surmised from his groan that I'd hit my target. He grabbed his crotch and fell onto me.

A clanging sound and his body moved again, and I scrambled out from under him. Kristen stood above us, chest heaving, teeth bared, a real-life Buffy the Vampire Slayer. She was clutching a heavy standing lamp like a bat, and as I scooted back on my butt she swung it again, and with a sickening *thunk* it connected with Sebastian's back. He collapsed to the ground, his head thudding against the floor an inch from a leg of the metal bed frame.

I saw my fury echoed in Kristen's gaze; for a moment, we locked eyes. Then I detected motion before I could even process it.

"Stop. Stop. Stop."

I see it in flashes, as if through a strobe light: Sebastian's head up against the bed frame. Three kicks, four, blood staining the metal leg and pooling into the cracks in the laminate floor. I grabbed Kristen and dragged her away and into a hug. We leaned against each other, shaking.

We stayed like that for a while. Seconds, minutes, possibly hours. Motorbikes streaked past the cheap drawn curtains, a flash and a roar. Sebastian was still. It was Kristen who pulled away first. Her eyes were clear now, narrowed. Her voice was strong.

"We have to get out of here."

She thought aloud, walked us through our options. She floated the idea of calling the cops: This was clearly self-defense, after all. But our guidebook had brought up the difficulty of working with police here, and I knew from that time with Ben that reporting assault—a move I'd considered then and several times in the months afterward—is more complicated than most people realize. The last thing we wanted was to wind up in a Cambodian jail cell, passports confiscated, accused of murder. We'd seen *Brokedown Palace* and read about Amanda Knox.

I was shivering and incoherent, but Kristen was magnificent. She checked for a pulse and, finding none, made a plan. Preposterous luck amid an otherwise unlucky night: The barely manned front desk hadn't looked at our passports when we'd arrived, and we'd prepaid in cash. The bartender had overheard a "Nicole" and a "Joan." Sebastian had been traveling for nine months, on an open-ended vagabonding tour—and like us, he was proud to eschew social media or regular phone calls home.

We'd weigh down the body, she announced, and heave it over a nearby cliff into the rushing river below. Cover our tracks. Leave Phnom Penh before anyone knew anything was wrong. I felt numb, the tingly kind, as if someone had hooked me up to an IV of Novocain. Kristen and Emily would never dispose of a body, but somehow, Nicole and Joan could. They *did*. The ensuing hours were a movie montage I will my mind to never, ever cue up. They were grueling and cruel, leaving me sore for a week, but Kristen was tireless, her jaw set, her expression determined. I did exactly what she told me, and miraculously, it worked.

When it was done, we took a bus to Laos, silent and sleepy the whole ten-hour ride, and spent the last few days keeping a low profile in a two-star hotel there. I don't remember the flight home, the cab ride from the airport, the sleepless night before I returned to work. I kept seeing Sebastian's skull, dented where it'd met the bedframe's leg, blood forming an oval like a ruby-colored speech bubble.

I was a mess. My brain felt fuzzy and opaque, coated in black mold. At night I fell into gnarly, restless ten-hour sleeps, and during the day I burst into tears at random. Some mornings I slept through my alarm and wandered into work midday, my eyes puffy and unfocused. I went entire days without eating, then woke in the night with my stomach cramped and empty. My manager warned that if I didn't get it together, they'd need to let me go. I stared at him blankly, too broken to care.

Sebastian shouldn't have died: I didn't support the death penalty and certainly didn't fancy us vigilantes, taking justice into our own hands. It was an accident, self-defense that went too far. But I didn't regret getting rid of his body instead of calling the police; I'd come to believe it was our only choice. I did a deep dive on Americans who'd been arrested overseas—across the board, their lives were ruined. A woman from Oregon spent years awaiting trial in Argentina for fatally pushing her pickpocket into traffic. A jailed spring breaker from Virginia insisted he had nothing to do with an attack on a restaurant hostess in Acapulco. So many travelers battling to get home or whiling away their youth in dingy cells. Horror stories, the sickening thrill of *that could have been me*. But though the stories took the edge off the guilt, they didn't relieve the trauma, the unfairness of it all. Why had the universe wedged *us* between Charybdis and Scylla's sharp-toothed barbarity?

Shortly after we'd returned home, I told Kristen I wanted to talk to a therapist. Patient-client privacy, I reasoned. I knew she'd talked to a therapist as a kid, after her parents' death, which made her the only person I knew who'd seen a shrink. I liked the sound of a paid, impartial, sympathetic ear. I was having nightmares, panic attacks, painful echoes of the helplessness, the all-consuming fear.

"I'm so sorry to say this," she'd told me, the call tinny from its nine-thousand-mile journey. "But I don't think anyone should know the connection between us and that guy."

"Even if I lie about where and when and . . . and how it ended, obviously?"

A very long silence. "That's not really how therapy works."

"Didn't it help you, though? When you were going through something . . . traumatic?"

"I was a kid—I'd lost my parents, and my grandparents had no idea how to talk to me. So Dr. Brightside helped me, like, learn some coping mechanisms. But you're resilient, Emily. You're strong as hell. I know you."

A long silence. Finally: "Was her name really Brightside?"

She snorted. "So on-the-nose, right? Looking back, that must've been a nom de plume." When Kristen spoke again, her voice was soft. "I just want you to be happy. And healthy. You should do whatever you need to do to make that happen."

But I did see her point. "I know you're right. I can't think straight. I'm still processing."

"It will get easier, I promise. And until then, I'm totally here for you, anytime, day or night. I wasn't sure if you wanted to talk about it, so I didn't bring it up, but I'm here." Bubbles back in her voice: "I can totally be your Dr. Brightside."

"How does nothing get under your skin?" I tried to say it playfully but landed somewhere between hurt and jealous.

"I don't want you to think I'm not listening. I hear you, I swear I do." She infused the words with urgency, and I found myself nodding. "I've been struggling since then too. Of course I have. But what always grounds me is knowing you've got my back, no matter what. And I've got yours. We're here for each other. Right?"

I didn't yet know how much she meant it. How, in the weeks and months that followed, she'd call me every single evening—her morning, before work—to check in, to ask how I was feeling, to talk me down or champ me up or catch me off guard with something so funny I couldn't help but feel like me again. On weekends she stayed on video calls with me for long stretches—once her entire night, a full ten hours—and watched movies with me, ordered food for me, sent services to pick up my laundry and clean my sad, sticky kitchen and do all the things she'd do in person if she could. I knew if she were there she'd be spooning the udon down my throat, tenderly washing my hair and clipping my nails. When she said she'd be my Dr. Brightside, I didn't yet grasp how she'd save me, piece me back together yet again.

But I knew that she meant it—that she was there for me, come hell or high water. A sob rose and I cleared my throat. "I don't know what I'd do without you," I told her, tear-stained and almost catatonic in my darkened living room.

She chortled. "Let's hope we never have to find out."

CHAPTER 4

"So I've been meaning to talk to you about something." Kristen set down her fork and leaned her elbows on the table.

I took a sip of my Carménère, grassy and dark. Chilean wine was consistently delicious. "Oh yeah?" Funny—I was just about to tell her about Aaron.

"I didn't want to bring it up right away. I wanted to . . . feel you out first, I guess. But I'll just come right out and say it." She spread her palms and I watched them, slow-motion, how her fingertips flared. My innards compressed. *It has to do with Cambodia.*

Then she pierced the dramatic pause: "I think we should travel the world for six months. Starting this summer. *Your* summer."

It didn't sink in. Like she'd spoken rapid Spanish and now stared expectantly. "'Travel the world'?"

"You have tons of money saved from your cushy cat-food job," she went on, "and I was thinking of taking a sabbatical at work. My sublet runs out in June. I'm totally serious, Emily. We could do this."

I shook my head. It was strange enough to imagine Kristen on the underside of the globe, the lilt of her sentences morphing, a thick "roight?" peppering her speech. But Kristen was a trailblazer, an adventurer. I, stable, dependable Emily, simply paid her exciting world the occasional visit. Could I really put my life on hold now, when I was about to turn thirty and finally, finally seeing someone I liked?

"Don't take this the wrong way," she said, which people only say when they're about to insult you, "but what's keeping you? You're not tied down—you don't have snot-nosed kids and a boring husband or a career that feels like your calling or a family you're close with. Right?"

I bit my lip. She was mostly right: no siblings, a mom and step-dad in St. Paul, a dad and stepmom in northern Iowa, all out of touch for months at a time.

Kristen and I had bonded over this in college: While all our class-mates seemed to call their mothers once a day, at minimum, we rarely spoke to our guardians. Around then, I started to realize why—I noticed how casually cruel my parents could be, dismissive and self-centered. Kristen's grandparents, Nana and Bill, had raised her after her parents died when she was twelve, and though the cou-ple always seemed nice enough when I met them, Kristen claimed Bill was a tyrant and Nana a ball of anxiety.

Kristen glanced around the restaurant and then hit me with a sparkly-eyed smile. I caught her exact meaning, best-friend telepa-thy: *This could be our lives.* Traversing the world together. Discover-ing wild corners of civilization, bathing ourselves in landscapes so surreal they belonged in space operas.

But: Aaron. Not that I should plan my whole life around some-one I'd only been on four dates with. But.

She leaned forward. "I remember back when you and Ben broke up, you were like, 'This is it—now my life can be huge. As expansive as I want it to be.' " Her hands shot out. "But . . . I know it's different for me because it's my hometown, but is Milwaukee really where you want to be?"

"I love Milwaukee. Unlike you, I really do love living there."

"But *you* were the one who made it sound like an expansive life meant leaving the Midwest."

"Hmm."

The waiter appeared and Kristen asked what beers they stocked, and I tugged at a thread coming loose from my placemat.

The breakup with Ben: a knife in my psyche's tenderest flesh. Banished to Kristen's apartment, discombobulated and glum. At the time, my friend Angie, a plucky redheaded linguistics major I'd met in chess club, had shared the burden of nursing my broken heart, stepping in with ice cream and sympathy when I needed a break from Kristen's screw-him MO. When, a few weeks after the split, Angie suggested it would be nice to go home for Christmas and have my mom "dote on me," I burst out laughing.

"When I told her we broke up, all my mom said was 'Huh, I was just starting to like Ben.'"

Angie's jaw dropped. "She didn't, like, ask what happened?"

"Why would she?" My folks, who'd divorced when I was a teenager, had met the physical requirements of Acceptable Child Rearing to a T and, come college, seemed relieved they no longer had to attend to my comings and goings.

Angie considered. "Well, I don't know what she's talking about—we all hated him."

I stared at her for a moment. Angie's verdict—something I'd known for weeks—still burned, the secret everyone at school had been keeping from me practically since freshman orientation. Everyone but Kristen.

At home the next week, my scalp prickled with wonder as neither my mom nor my stepdad mentioned Ben on day one, day two, day three. The topic of my long-term boyfriend grew shy and conspicuously quiet in my mind, like an empty cemetery. Kristen and I spent the next two Christmases on our own in warm places: Fort Lauderdale, then Puerto Rico. The trips were Kristen's brilliant idea, sunsplashed jaunts that cemented her spot on my personal family tree, the one that matters: the Family You Choose. *Your folks don't give a crap about your feelings,* she'd pointed out. *Why do you owe them your time?*

Kristen selected a Chilean lager and sent the server on his way. She folded her hands. "Think about it, Emily. You said yourself that all your friends there are married and having kids."

But I want that. Tears pricked at my eyes, several strands of frustration fusing into one: annoyance with myself for pathetically wanting a boyfriend; shame that I couldn't be all carefree like Kristen, couldn't drop it all for six months of wanderlust.

"Oh my God, don't cry!" Kristen's hand flew down to mine,

threaded through my fingers. "I'm sorry—I'm saying this all wrong. I just mean . . . so many people would *kill* to have your freedom. All our college friends are lugging around diaper bags and burp cloths now, right?" We both chuckled. "I just thought . . . hey, we're turning thirty. Isn't now the perfect time to try something new? And I got excited thinking what our lives could be like on the road. Like it used to be, only better, because we're grown-ass women now." She sat up straighter, still clutching my hand. "You know I love our trips. But seeing you once, maybe twice a year isn't enough. I miss you like crazy." She looked down at the placemat. "And . . . and last year, when you were having a tough time, I felt *awful* that I couldn't be there for you in person. You're the most important person to me, you know?"

This time last year. My stomach flipped, picturing last spring, post-Cambodia: how I'd floated through work in a stupor . . . on the days I managed to make it in. How I swung between deep, spastic sobs and wild, thrashing panic, a single thought like a subtitle: *I'm going to die.*

"It's not just that, though," she went on. "I miss watching Netflix on the bed when we're too lazy to go out. I miss discussing a single topic over the course of days or weeks and not, like, mentally organizing a life update with bullet points for one of our three-hour calls. I dunno. Just me?"

I shook my head and laughed. "Yeah, no, me too. It's just—it never crossed my mind. It's not something I ever imagined doing." I sat back, took a sip of wine. "Kristen Czarnecki. You crazy bitch."

She laughed. She had the nicest laugh—full and musical. "We can totally do this. Why not? Other people do it all the time. Hell, we meet them on our trips, and I'm always jealous. We could be the people everyone else is jealous of!"

She stared at me then, smile broad, her eyes pleading—the same look she gave me whenever she was trying to convince me to go on an adventure with her. *Climb into this abandoned cave with me; follow these strangers to a speakeasy in another neighborhood.* Her cajoling always paid off, always led to the most magical and memorable pieces of a trip, so I never regretted following her fearless lead.

Look how things had turned out the one time *I'd* tried spontaneity on for size.

Stop. Stop. Stop.

I wouldn't think of that now. I met Kristen's gaze over our empty plates, bits of avocado and quinoa speckling the surfaces. All that was behind us. This week—this proposition, which flipped and frothed inside me—proved it.

"Please tell me you'll consider it," she said.

"I'll think about it." She squealed and clapped and I felt myself blush. Okay, another delay in telling her about Aaron—I wasn't going to ruin the moment now. I'd see how I felt in the morning.

Back at our inn, we followed a twisty stone staircase to a plateau, where an oval pool winked up at the sky. We lolled on its lounge chairs, batting leaking from their seams, and counted shooting stars. I saw five; Kristen, six.

OUR LAST DAY had that misty, prematurely nostalgic air, bittersweet as we sucked in each sight and experience hungrily, willed it to last. I woke up early to visit the town's pretty church, with its cerulean ceiling and simple stained glass, its outside the friendly white of a chipped diner mug. Kristen—once a devoted Protestant, now vehemently opposed to organized religion in any form—didn't want to hear about it, and instead greeted me in the hotel lobby with the just-right shade of milky coffee and a proposed plan for the day.

We rented bikes from a kiosk and tottered over the winding road, stopping to gaze at the mountains in silence, as if saying goodbye. We pulled on bathing suits and plunged our toes into the hotel's frigid pool, then reclined in the filtered autumn sun, sharing a bottle of Chardonnay and reading our books in amicable silence. The hotel's whistling custodian clambered up to a shed and gave us a wave before digging a rake from a tangle of tools inside, and Kristen jumped up and asked him to take a photo of us with my camera. I got us both massages at a tiny, green-walled spa, where we lay on musty massage tables while thick-limbed women rubbed our backs with more speed than precision. It was a perfect last day. Kristen didn't mention the backpacking pitch, but I could feel it between us, the possible future hovering like a shared memory.

I was torn. Though she was still right next to me, I already missed Kristen. I'd sunk back into the salve of her devil-may-care sense of humor, her constant championing of me—she saw me as strong and smart and competent, and she always had a pep talk at the ready. As other friends in Milwaukee paired off and married and had kids and drifted further, farther away from me, ripples in a pond, Kristen remained more loyal than a sister, more loving than a doting mom.

But . . . part of what made our time together special was that it *was* limited. And stuff was maybe, finally happening in Milwaukee—there was Aaron, the thought of whom set off small fireworks in my chest. Plus the possible promotion at work, the job I genuinely liked.

I broached the topic while we paused for an afternoon coffee. I loved this part of a travel day, the predinner *ahh*. We were on a bench in front of a shipping-container-turned-café that sold coffee and Chilean pop (Bilz and Pap and other excellently named soft drinks) from a sawtooth window.

"So, I've been thinking about what you said. About traveling for the rest of the year."

"Oh yeah?" She slid back her sunglasses and beamed at me. She'd asked for her coffee over ice, *café sobre hielo,* to which the server frowned in confusion and scooped some cubes into her steaming cup.

"I'm truly honored that you asked me." My rib cage tightened—I hated conflict, hated letting someone down. "You know you're my number-one travel buddy. My ride-or-die."

"But?"

I sighed. "It's not a good time for me to leave for six months. Things are happening at work and—and I'm interested in someone, which I'll tell you all about . . ." I paused to giggle at Kristen's delighted gasp. "I just want to give it a chance. You know? But I still really like this idea, and there's no one I'd rather do it with than you. Can we maybe try to make it happen next year?"

She was quiet for a moment, staring into her coffee.

"Kristen?"

She licked her lip. "I'm taking it in. A part of me *really* wants to try to convince you."

"I'm sorry."

"No, it's okay. I just . . . wow, I really thought you'd say yes." She nodded, slowly at first and then with fervor. "I'm bummed, obviously, but I'll deal with it. Hey, tell me about this guy! There's a guy?!"

Her smile was big and brave and try-hard, and it snapped at my heart like a rubber band. Still, I smiled back, feeling a blush creep up my cheeks. "His name is Aaron," I began, "and we've only been out a few times."

"And you didn't mention him all week? Is there something wrong with him?" she joked, smacking me playfully.

"I mean, who knows if it's even anything. And dating is, like, the least interesting thing we talk about." I snickered. "I didn't want to be the girl who can't shut up about a guy she barely knows."

"Don't worry about it. I know you've always had issues around self-esteem with dudes." Her eyes widened, like someone else had said it. "Oh my God, that came out wrong."

It stung, but I shook my head. "No, it's true. You know how hard it is for me to be vulnerable with someone I like. And how even *liking* someone happens sooo rarely."

"Totally. Well, and you have this nasty habit of picking guys who are one one-millionth as awesome as you and don't treat you like the queen you are." She grinned. "So tell me about him! Does he kiss the ground you walk on, like he damn well should?"

I laughed and felt my shoulders loosen. "Not yet, but I think he might actually be a good one?" And so I told her about him, glancing away whenever my smile felt too big for my face. What a relief, feeling this secret I'd been carrying soften and dissolve. Kristen listened,

eyes sparkling, pressing her palms together and occasionally punctu-
ating my patter with quick, happy claps. So supportive was she, so
encouraging and excited, that I forgot to make a point I'd vowed
earlier to state outright: *I'm not choosing him over you.*

IT WAS A Saturday, and restaurants that'd been dark the night before
were flicking on lights, sweeping off decks. We selected a cozy café
with bean stews and hearty corn casseroles. Kristen's guidebook was
right: Our waiter confirmed that cheap buses rolled in from Santiago
and Valparaiso and the Atacama Desert weekly, and we watched as
new visitors streamed past. Two shiny-haired, bird-boned women
sat in the corner with their enormous backpacks next to them, like
canvas stand-ins for dinner dates. There was a bustle now, movement, energy matching our own. Kristen was still acting normal—
bouncy and ebullient—and I felt dizzy with relief. The thought of
disappointing her filled me with a fireball of anxiety and guilt.

Out on the street, she clutched my arm and pointed at the sky:
stars as bright as fireworks, layers and layers of them, like someone
had cleaned off the glass separating us from the heavens. I gasped
and gave her a side hug.

"That's us." She pointed just above the horizon. "See those two
little stars? You can tell."

It was goofy but somehow perfect; they were equal in size, close
together, and just a smidge above the mountaintop. "Which one is
you and which one is me?"

We both squinted and then I spoke again: "You're the one on the
left, the pinkish one."

"I was going to say the same thing! You're totally the greenish
one."

"I think it's bluish."

"That's so green-star of you to say." We watched them giddily,
these two bright-burning peas in a pod light-years away. Warm and
together, just like us.

"Let's go get a drink," Kristen suggested, and off we went.

A whole new swath of places were open tonight: dark lots transformed into leafy patios where string lights clung to latticework and vines. We ordered bottle after bottle of cheap Chilean wine, Syrah and Cabernet Sauvignon and Chardonnay. We danced to pop tunes, both American and regional, and ate endless bowls of spicy corn nuts, licking our fingers when we finished each refill.

I went off to the bathroom and got waylaid for a while—first to hunt down toilet paper from a harried-looking employee, then to find someone to hold the stall door closed for me, then to carry on an enthusiastic conversation with the helpful stranger, who wasn't a complete stranger, it turned out: She was one of the two tiny black-haired backpackers I'd spotted at the restaurant, and she was from London, and we liked each other ever so much.

I made my way back outside and stared in confusion: There was someone at my table. But was I looking at the wrong table . . . ? No, there was Kristen across from him, nodding with her chin in her hand. He had a five o'clock shadow and dark hair pulled into a small ponytail, and skin so tan it glowed amber in the dim light. Like embers in a campfire.

I crossed the patio and stood over them, and suddenly everything was wrong. I could feel it instantly, on her face, her posture, the stiff line of her back. My chest froze over, icicles on the inside.

"Oh, this is Paolo." She cut him off midsentence. "He's from Spain. He was just telling me how he's spending a year backpacking across South America."

He smirked and flicked his chin toward me. "I thought maybe your friend Nicole was doing the same thing, traveling around by herself." He shrugged. "But for women, it's much safer with a friend."

Not icicles—something sharper, like a head-freeze to my entire body.

"This is Joan," Kristen said. She swept her palm my way, never took her eyes from my face. "She's the best friend a girl could have."

CHAPTER 5

I breathed hard and chastised myself for feeling upset: Kristen was allowed to flirt with a cute backpacker. Not just allowed—I owed it to her, after all she'd done for me in Cambodia. And after I'd dropped the bomb of Aaron's existence? Of course she was seeking a little romantic validation. As long as she didn't ditch me for him, it was fine. It was a selfish thought, but one I hoped she'd pick up on: I didn't want to be left alone in an unfamiliar city after . . .

I watched the two of them banter and rearranged my face into an attentive smile. I'd just wait it out, and at some point he'd step away to buy more drinks or she'd head toward the bathroom and I could tell her, make sure she understood I needed her company.

But an hour passed, then two. There was another code Kristen and I had used throughout our twenties: a finger point, plus, "Doesn't he remind you of [a random male friend, real or imagined]?" Inevitably, the man would tell us he had "one of those faces" and got that all the time, but we knew what the comment really meant: *I'm done talking to this guy; an escape hatch, please.*

She didn't invoke it, her get-out-of-jail-free card, so after a while I interrupted and said it myself: "Kristen, doesn't Paolo look like my friend Dennis?"

Kristen's brow pursed in friendly confusion. "You think? I don't see it at all." Then she turned back to him and smiled conspiratorially. "You're much more handsome."

So it was on. I steeled myself, moved around the patio, made more chitchat with the British girls, breathed deep to slow my racing heart. *It's just an hour. She's been having terrible dating luck. Don't be such a chicken, not to mention a cock-block.*

"Nicole" announced she wanted to show Paolo the crystals she'd picked out at the market, and I gave her one more out: "You're sure? You know we have that flight tomorrow?" She brushed me off, so I recited my lines: They should go, I wanted to finish my drink, but I was sleepy so (*yaaawn, streeeetch*) I'd probably be back in forty-five minutes. Paolo lifted his gigantic backpack, and Kristen touched her palm to my cheek gratefully as they slipped past.

I hoisted myself onto a stool at the bar and pulled out my book. I strung my purse over the back of my chair and tried to read, tried not to think about what was happening in our suite a few blocks away. *I envy her,* I realized suddenly. Sex had been stripped from my list of acceptable activities for a full year now, to the point where it was wearing my new love interest's patience thin. And here she was having a spontaneous vacation hookup. As if nothing bad had happened the last time one of us gave that a go.

But there was more to it than that, and I sat quietly, waiting for my thoughts to snap into place. Aha: I envied *him,* as well. A week with Kristen had reminded me how I felt braver around her: more capable and resourceful, more cavalier and fun. *Chosen.* Kristen could do that, her attention like a tractor beam, now trained squarely on Paolo. On our last night, no less.

But that was just my own insecurity—I was happy for her, her and this handsome Spaniard. I had Aaron waiting for me at home, and more travels with Kristen to look forward to. Maybe we really could pull off that backpacking stint next year, when things were more settled with Aaron and Kibble and my life in Milwaukee. The thought cheered me, and I ordered a beer.

Thirty minutes later, I swallowed the last of it, then asked for a bottle of water. Thirty minutes when I was blissfully unaware that panic was about to go off like a grenade. Alone in a leafy bar with cigarette smoke and the barks of desperate dogs wafting past, I noticed nothing. I reached for my purse and half registered that it was unzipped. Stuck my hand inside, felt around, slowly at first and then with mounting alarm. I slid from the stool and searched the floor around my feet. Patted my hips, as if my sundress had suddenly grown pockets, then tore through my bag again.

"Someone took my wallet," I gasped at the bartender. I forgot every Spanish word I'd ever learned.

"*Mil*," he repeated, then pointed at the bottle of water. "One thousand pesos."

I shook my head and opened my purse wide, as if to show him. "I don't have any money. Someone took it." My voice cracked and he made a sympathetic face, then whipped the bottle back behind the bar. I hugged my bag against me, unsure what to do next.

When had someone taken it? I picked back over my minutes alone at the bar like this was a puzzle I could solve, rooting around for the instant my subconscious had picked up on something wrong. The way some faraway part of your brain snags while you're leaving your scarf on a bus: a momentary *something's not right*.

Nerves popped along my neck. Someone had watched me from across the bar, noticing my bag hanging limply as I curled over my book. Plunged their fingers inside just inches from my hip and strolled away with fifty bucks in local currency, my driver's license, and a few credit cards. I loved this wallet—green leather, a relic from a flea market date with another ex, Colin. *Stupid*. I'd let my guard down in a foreign country—and I'd been violated.

I took a step toward the exit; Kristen would know how to handle it. It hadn't been forty-five minutes yet, but I'd knock and knock, giving them time to cover up. She'd hug me tight and know what to do. She always knew what to do.

But then I sank back into a seat. *I should wait.* Barging in on them now would just be selfish.

Another decision that changed everything. What if I'd run straight back? Banged on the door, interrupted them just a bit sooner?

It was time—I rushed off, making my way uphill in the dark, and rapped on the glass door to our suite. In the second that followed, I knew something was wrong: a gasp, a clang, a strange, strangled groan.

"Kristen?" My heart beat wildly, the wallet forgotten. I tried the handle, then fumbled in my bag for my key. "What's going on?"

I slid the door open and slapped at the light. It blared on, blue-white and hideous, and I froze.

Kristen sat crumpled on the floor, crying. Her tears mingled with a spray of blood across her jaw, and there were smears of it on her palm and forearm.

"What happened?" I asked, my voice almost a whisper, and she lifted her eyes to me. Something came into focus behind her: two legs, poking out from beyond the aqua couch.

"Emily." She reached for me, a toddler who wants Mommy.

My pulse was so loud it was an ocean, surf pounding against the inside of my skull. *Whoosh. Whoosh. Whoosh.*

Like a sleepwalker, I took a step forward. Then another, and another, past Kristen, whose face dropped back into her blood-spattered hands.

"He attacked me."

Another step, another. Then the sight blasted through me like a sonic boom, shaking all my cells: the bottle of wine, streaked with red. Blood on the tile floor, forming a strange amoeba shape. His eyes open and vacant, and just to the right of them, the dent in his skull.

I shrieked and sank to my knees.

"He attacked me," she repeated, struggling to stand. I met her gaze across the room. "You have to help me."

I let out a sob and turned back to Paolo.

"Emily." I heard her walking toward me, toward us, one living person and one dead one. She paused, and her palm found my shoulder. "We have no choice."

CHAPTER 6

The room disappeared as panic pulled me in like a riptide. I squeezed my eyes tight while gravity reeled around me and I begged, begged, begged the churning tugs to be a wormhole, a passage out of this nightmare.

Eventually the spinning slowed. I cracked my eyes open and the scene filled in, like a Polaroid developing: bright reds and yellows and oranges and greens crisscrossing the darkness, and people swarming around me, parting like I was a rock in a river. A night market—I was standing in the Phnom Penh night market, lanterns dangling in every direction and hawkers in a line selling noodle soup and cheap Cambodian magnets and jewelry dripping with sparkly stones, all bathed orange from the artificial light.

But where was Kristen? I looked out at the stalls and cook smoke and hubbub that unspooled into infinity. Then someone was touching me from behind, stroking my left arm with increasing urgency, and I jumped and whirled around, but no one was there.

"*Emily*." Kristen's voice strained with concern. But where was she? My heart thundered as I looked around, completing a full circle as people bumped past me, as hawkers shouted in Khmer, as teenagers horsed around and two backpackers argued in French and someone grabbed my arm again and I turned to try to catch them and—

"Emily!" Kristen was kneeling above me, clutching my arm and shaking it like a tambourine. I looked at her in wonder.

"Are you okay?" She touched my cheek. "Oh my God, that was

so scary. You totally passed out. No, don't try to get up. Are you dizzy?"

I peered at her. We were in . . . Chile, that's right, in our suite. And that meant . . . oh God . . .

"Your eyes rolled back and you slumped to the side, it was terrifying. Stay here, I'll get you some water." She scurried off, and I saw the sight that'd knocked me out the first time: Paolo with his doll-like eyes and cratered, weeping skull. I scrambled up to a sitting position and backed away.

"Here, drink this." She thrust a cup toward me. Her hand was trembling so hard that a patter of drops sloshed over the side.

I took a sip. Thoughts pinged: *We could still call the police. How did this happen? What is it about us that this horrible thing happened twice? There's no way we'll get away with this a* second *time. What's her plan?*

"Kristen," I whispered. "What do we do?"

Her expression drooped toward the floor like melting wax. She crawled over my knees and toward the bathroom, and the retching sounds were so loud, I thought crazily that the noise might wake the neighbors. Never mind the deadly battle I imagined these walls had just absorbed.

I gathered my limbs and climbed to my feet, swaying for a second before following her. I willed my own nausea to freeze in place as I rubbed her back.

"Oh, Emily, I was so scared," she wailed into the toilet bowl. "It was so sudden, he was being too rough and—the look in his eye . . ." She gave up trying to talk and I swiped at the tears surging down my own cheeks, hot and raw. I knelt to hug her, our torsos shaking in tandem.

The realization was like a car tearing toward me on the road: *You have to step up. You need to pull it together. We haven't got much time.*

"Okay." I skated my thumb across a tear on her cheek. "We need to think." I tipped my forehead against hers, exactly as she'd done for me that night in Cambodia. "We could . . . we could call the police?"

Alarm blazed in her eyes. "Why would the police here be any better than the police in Cambodia? I'm not going to prison in Chile."

"We'll tell them what happened."

She glanced toward the living room—so much blood—and shook her head urgently. "They won't believe us."

"You don't know that."

"You could barely communicate well enough to get us checked in." Her eyes glistened. "The cops will throw us in a cell until they can figure out what's going on and . . . and . . ."

Something rushed up through me, a shriek or sob or bile. "Kristen, this is *insane*." My heart beat like a drumroll and my breath sprinted past it, tight and quick and too high up in my ribs. My lungs were on fire, squeezing like two fists.

Concern bloomed on Kristen's face. "Breathe, Emily."

Inhaler, I mouthed, unable to muster even a whisper. She bolted into the living room and returned with my purse, and frantically I dug until my fingers closed around the periwinkle plastic. I lifted it to my lips and inhaled the tiniest stream.

Ten seconds. Nine. Eight. Exquisite relief as the vapors worked their way into the air sacs. Seven. Six. An internal release, like a tourniquet loosening. I finished the countdown and took another eager dose, puffing my chest and noticing Kristen's worried expression, her hand on my arm. Rust-colored speckles mottling her skin. We locked eyes as I counted down a second dose, time frozen for ten infinite seconds until I exhaled again, loudly.

"I'm okay." I pulled away from her. "I don't understand. How could this happen again? Wasn't once enough?"

"I don't know, Emily. I don't know." She shook her head. "Are you . . . do you think it's something I did? That I was asking for it somehow?"

"No! No. That's not what I meant." My thoughts were all jangly, coming out wrong. Still, it tugged at me: Were we somehow attracting this kind of awfulness? Putting something out there to lure in the quick-tempered and dangerous? I didn't think it was Kristen's *fault*, not at all. Yet the coincidence couldn't be ignored. "Are you sure we shouldn't call the police? I can . . . I'll walk to reception, maybe someone's still there."

"No one at the hotel speaks any English." She touched her fingers to her chin, smeared the blood there. "How will we explain it? What happened?"

I fished around for the words, but my brain was blank. *Kill, die, attack, rape*—the only translation I could pull up was *sangre*: blood.

"We'll act it out," I said, "show them your injuries." My palm crept to my neck, where eggplanty bruises had sat swollen and angry for weeks after Phnom Penh. I looked at Kristen's throat and saw nothing but Paolo's blood on her alabaster skin. "What *did* happen?"

"He attacked me," she said again. She shrunk inward, hunched her graceful shoulders. "He . . . he got handsy and I told him to stop and then he pushed my shoulders against the wall and I said, 'Hey!' and he said, '*Cállate, puta*' and . . ." A tear leaked out. "He shoved me again so that the back of my head crashed into the wall. And I was fighting back and he started to close his hands around my throat. And I was terrified, obviously. Afraid for my life. So I reached out and grabbed whatever I could find and my hand closed around a bottle of wine and I swung it, hard, to get him away from me. I swung it without looking—I wasn't aiming for his head."

"I'm so sorry," I said after a moment. "That's . . . that's self-defense."

She squeezed her eyes closed. "It was last time too. They won't believe me. No one believes victims. We're stupid Americans. And I'm wearing booty shorts and a tank top without a bra and we got drunk of our own accord and I took this guy back to our hotel. Willingly, *I* invited him to *my* room. We talked through all this in Cambodia, Emily. Do you think it's suddenly changed?"

I swiped my hand under my nose. She wasn't wrong—all those how-to-stay-safe-while-traveling articles warned us not to dress provocatively, talk to strangers, leave a friend unchaperoned, bring an unvetted man into one's room. Though I'd wrestled with the hornet-like thought after Cambodia—*Was it something I did?*—I couldn't let Kristen do the same.

Oh my God. How had this happened twice?

Her eyes popped open. "Remember what I said about Amanda Knox? Everyone attacked her—the media, the goddamn *Italian police*—because she liked sex and didn't behave the exact way they wanted her to after a tragedy. Now, she's a freaking pariah. Her name is synonymous with scandal. This would be a front-page story for months—it would ruin our lives."

Kristen was right. As always. The horror stories were still fresh in my head: the kid locked up in Acapulco, the woman imprisoned in Argentina. And this was my chance, my turn to protect her like she'd protected me after Cambodia. To finally repay her for what she did for me. I was so tired and confused, and Kristen seemed so sure.

She and I had gotten tattoos together in Vietnam, tiny lotus flowers on our inner ankles. It was her third tattoo but my first. In the second before the tattoo gun had stung my flesh, the artist had looked up at me: *Ready?*

I felt that same wild rush now, the dark finality. The weight of the moment's irreversibility.

"I . . . I guess we need to get rid of the body, then," I said. "And clean up here."

"Okay." She nodded slowly, pulled away from me. "Okay, let's think."

"It's dark." I leaned against the tub behind me. "That'll help us."

"You're right. That's good." She sat back. "Cover of darkness."

"We'll wear black."

"Good." She tipped her head back and closed her eyes. "But what the hell do we *do*?"

I reached out and flushed her vomit. We listened to the gurgle.

She glanced at me. "Can we drop it off a cliff?"

It. We'd both noticed the switch.

"Where's there a cliff?" I asked.

"Next to the main road—it's so steep."

"That's a drop-off, not a cliff," I pointed out. "They'll find him as soon as the sun comes up."

"You're right."

My mind had cued up a supercut, every disposing-of-a-body scene I'd ever watched. Noirs, reenactments, slick crime thrillers. "Isn't there a dam?" I asked.

"A dam?"

"Someone mentioned it in Vicuña. Where they dammed up the Elqui River."

"Oh my God, you're right." She chewed on her lip. "We could—we could weigh it down. Like in Cambodia. Do you know where?"

I shook my head. "No idea. But I could look it up?"

"We're not turning on our phones. Absolutely not."

"Why not?"

"Because we don't want anything definitively tying us here."

We were trapped off the grid at the bottom of the world, on a different plane from our normal existence. The thought was another clanging bell: *Shit, she doesn't know I connected to the Wi-Fi to check my texts.*

"The distillery." Kristen sat up straighter. "They were digging. All the dirt will look . . . freshly disturbed, so no one will notice if we . . ."

I frowned. "You think we should bury him?"

"You just said it can't be out in the open. There's . . . there's a reason people bury bodies."

The room lurched again, a quick spin on an emotional Tilt-A-Whirl. "Okay," I said, "but not at the distillery. They've seen us there, and they could dig it up in a second." I locked my arms around my knees. "Somewhere far from here. We get in the car and drive out to the middle of nowhere. Between towns. In the pitch-black."

"You're right. That's it." She was quiet for a moment, then struggled to her feet.

I stared at Paolo, whose vacant eyes watched the ceiling. After a long moment, I stood too.

CHAPTER 7

How to transport the body: That was the first challenge, the first of many, cropping up faster and faster, multiplying like cancer cells.

We'd use the car, obviously. But how to keep his blood out of the trunk's interior? Kristen first argued that we should steal a sheet, leave behind twenty bucks and a note apologizing for staining the linens with *la sangre de la menstruación*. But I pointed out that would only draw attention.

Then I had the idea of stuffing Paolo's head into his emptied backpack so that the waterproof canvas would trap the blood inside. Better. We emptied the huge sack and positioned it on the floor near his crown, then held our breath as we each grabbed a shoulder. We counted down, then lifted his upper body and shimmied the backpack down over his damaged skull, *Oh my God oh my God oh my God*. We got it over his shoulders, the best we could do, and then we yanked it to the side and lowered it onto a clean patch of floor, lest it fall into the pool of sticky blood. I covered my mouth and fought down burps; Kristen let out a strange, throttled laugh. On the tile, Paolo now looked like a surrealist painting: *Figure with a Backpack Head*.

But the clock was still ticking, South America swiveling back toward the sunlight. I began sorting through Paolo's things.

"What are you doing?" Kristen asked.

"Finding everything that makes him easily identifiable," I said. "So we can burn it." I felt surprisingly focused, uncannily alert. Kristen had come to my rescue when I'd been shattered in Cambodia, and now, I needed to do the same for her. Only one of us could fall apart at a time.

Kristen kept watching me, her hands clutched near her breast.

I sucked in a breath and reached into Paolo's front pocket. I almost cried out—I could feel his hip beneath the fabric. Finding nothing, I moved onto the next pocket, then his back ones, the weight of his ass bearing down on me as I yanked out a wallet, then a cellphone—shit, a phone wasn't good. I smashed it with a few hard stomps (*Stop. Stop. Stop.*) and added the shards to the burn pile, along with the passport and journal we'd shaken from his backpack. A journal—this set off a fountain of horror inside me. I couldn't read the entries, but the handwriting, squared-off and small, made him real.

I noticed Kristen by her suitcase, methodically shunting clothes inside.

"What are you doing?"

She looked up, wide-eyed. "Packing."

"Why?"

She shook her head. "Aren't we getting out of here?"

Equally bewildered: "Not—not now."

The argument was fierce and thrumming. She thought we should get out of town—throw Paolo in the trunk, pack our things, and leave a few hours early, burying the body at the loneliest stretch we could find along the way. But disappearing in the middle of the night when we'd requested a late checkout might prompt curiosity, perhaps a closer inspection of the room, even a bit of town gossip: *¿Qué pasó con las dos gringas?* We needed to arouse as little suspicion as possible.

"We'll bury him tonight and then check out tomorrow morning," I told her. "Like everything is normal. Think about it—it's our best option." She stared at me until I took a step toward her. "It's okay, Kristen. We're going to get out of this. You're safe now. I'm . . ." I hesitated. It was like I was reading her lines. "I'm here."

She swallowed. "How are we getting him into the car?"

In Cambodia, we'd simply dragged Sebastian, but that was out on an abandoned hill. I glanced again at the sheets. "We need to make some kind of sling."

Kristen's eyes lit up and she disappeared into the bathroom; I found her easing the shower curtain from its hooks. "And it'll be another layer of protection for the trunk," she said. I nodded, military-serious, and began unhooking the other side.

We pulled the door open and I dashed outside to do recon. I cocked my head, listening. The cold blackness boiled with insect sounds, screeching cicadas and rattling grasshoppers and katydids crooning together, a synchronous symphony. A breeze rippled the vines and trees, a fizzing, hissing sound coming from everywhere at once. Overhead, the stars looked on stoically. Far-off spotlights on our nightmarish tableau. No sign of other people—of witnesses—anywhere.

Two earsplitting beeps and the car's trunk hinged open. "Quickly," I whispered, pushing past Kristen in the doorframe. We'd spread the shower curtain along Paolo's side and now we stepped onto its corners and dragged his body and backpack on top. We picked up the curtain's edges, like two ladies folding linens, and counted to three.

Christ, it was heavy. Like we'd lifted a tarp filled with rocks. I felt it yanking away from me, back toward the earth, and thought wildly that this was weight I'd feel forever. The shower curtain tugged at our palms and we paused to make sure it wouldn't rip at the bottom and spill pooled blood as Paolo rushed back to the floor. After a frozen moment, I murmured, "Let's go."

The load was bulky, awkward, swaying and knocking against our knees as we shuffled and whispered and stumbled outside. Oh God, was that Paolo's head pushing against my shin, glued with blood to the inside of his backpack? My fingers cramped against the sweat-slick plastic, and the pain crept up my wrists, my forearms, my whole upper body tensing against the weight.

We reached the trunk and I almost cried out with relief. Another countdown and we lifted the bundle toward the back of the car—but Kristen raised her side too quickly, those toned arms like a lever, and for a wild second I thought we'd catapult him inside. My heartbeat scattered as we jostled the curtain, almost overcorrecting, but then we evened out and lowered him into the trunk. I dashed back inside and loaded my arms with his other clothes, whipping my head around to make sure I wasn't missing anything. A migraine surged behind my eyes as I hustled back into the cool air and dropped Paolo's clothes on top of him.

The trunk squealed as we pushed it shut, and we glanced around the small parking lot. No movement on the street or in the blackened windows of a nearby guest room. Of course, if someone was watching us from inside, we wouldn't be able to see them. We were staking so much on luck, on the gamble that I'd understood the hotel receptionist correctly, that most of the property was vacant.

"Shovels," I prompted, moving toward the stone steps. This was another reason we couldn't just pack up and leave: We couldn't dig with our hands, and borrowing and returning shovels from the hotel before dawn was another microstep in our gambit to remain forgettable, under the radar. A process that already felt painstaking and nearly impossible, like building a ship in a bottle.

Kristen followed me upstairs and to the end of the pool. The air up here had that cold, steely-clean smell, and it was oddly bright, as if the water weren't just reflecting the night sky but actually amplifying it. A shudder ran through me, guilt like a sprinkler: Paolo on the bar patio earlier that night, a flesh-and-blood being with secrets and dreams and loved ones and—

No. He was a bad man.

He attacked Kristen.

She was fighting for her life.

She reached the shed and ran her palms over the door's particleboard surface, then found the lock: a smooth padlock that hung from two strips of metal screwed into the door and the frame.

"Shoot." She gave it a tug. "It's locked."

My brain recentered, an auto-refresh. I nudged her out of the way and lifted the lighter I'd brought from the suite. My problem-solving instinct clanged on, the same knack that makes me so good at escape rooms and brainteasers and my job as a project manager. Maybe focusing hard on this simple problem—*door is locked; we need what's behind it*—would distract me from the larger and more horrifying issue on our hands. The stained backpack heaped in the trunk, and the pile of bones and organs and pooling blood inside. "Here, hold this."

As Kristen clutched the lighter, I dug in my pockets, then selected the tiniest coin—an octagonal one-peso piece. I eased its side into a screw that held the lock against the door, then turned.

She gasped. "It's working." She held her fist to her mouth as I rotated the coin.

My mind scuttled ahead. "We have to leave everything exactly as we found it," I whispered. "We should even mess up our footprints here." Everything would need to look locked, secure, untouched— nothing to raise suspicion. Hopefully *ever,* but at least long enough for the signs of our presence to grind down to nothingness, for the hotel suite and walking paths to move back toward their median condition. Like we'd never set foot here.

I plucked out the screw with a surgeon's care, then pulled on the still-locked padlock. The door swung toward me, and the hardware with it.

Kristen pushed in front of me. "You're a genius. Let's find those shovels."

I almost couldn't believe they were there: leaning against the back wall, caked in dirt and jumbled with rakes and hoes. Each tool looked like a deadly weapon, something meant only for pummeling human flesh. For a wild second, I pictured it: Kristen in Cambodia with the metal lamp held aloft, *sa-wing batter batter batter*. Her eyes as electric as a storm. The image flipped: Kristen in the same stance, but here, with a bottle of wine. I felt a brief swoop of fear and pushed it aside.

I grabbed a shovel from Kristen, and she ducked back into the shed, rifling around.

"Yes," she hissed, then held out two flashlights. "Let's go." She plunged back toward the stone steps, the spade slung against her shoulder. Like she was one of the Seven Dwarfs. *Hi ho, hi ho, it's off to bury a body we go.*

CHAPTER 8

Kristen squinted out the windshield, her shoulders buckled in concentration as we rolled out of the driveway and down the mountain road.

"Can you see?" I whispered. Her night vision was better than mine, as we'd discovered on a stargazing tour a few nights ago, when she had to guide me by the hand to the massive telescope the guide had set up. My astigmatism made the darkness staticky and dull. Astigmatism and asthma—small defects mostly sidestepped in the modern world. It was the big things that got you: bottles of wine, the metal legs of a bed frame. A lengthy plummet from the lip of a cliff.

"I can see enough," she replied. "I'll turn on the headlights as soon as we get around the corner."

"The last thing we need is to go over the side." A laugh rose through me, neon and hysterical. I turned it into a cough and Kristen glanced at me sharply. "I'm fine."

The engine seemed impossibly loud, a tank trundling through the silence. Of course, it had to work harder with a 180-pound man in the trunk. Another 40 with his backpack and belongings over and around him. We were lucky he had his bag with him, that he hadn't checked in anywhere yet. If he'd left all his stuff in a hostel, surely—

Kristen ignited the headlights, then slammed on the brakes. A creature sat in the road, about a foot long, with rippling gray fur and enormous eyes. A rabbit—no, a chinchilla. It fixed us with an accusing stare, then sauntered over to the shoulder. Kristen exhaled and took her foot off the brake. I watched it through the window until its outline melted into the charcoal night.

I kept feeling its obsidian eyes on me, judging, *seeing*. The incident in Cambodia had felt improbable, out-of-body, the kind of thing that happened in movies and true-crime podcasts but not to me. And yet here I was, blackened by a lightning bolt a second time.

In Phnom Penh I'd been useless, shaking and crying and chattering at the jaw so violently that Kristen had cloistered us in the bathroom with the shower running, the steam turning my cheeks pink and drawing blood back into my hands and feet as if hypothermia were the real problem. She'd pulled it together, because she needed to. Remembered the rushing water of Tonle Kak, the spooky stories of women filling their pockets with rocks before flinging themselves off a cliff, hoping for a riptide. A disappearance if we were lucky, a probable suicide if the body turned up. The plan was harried and haphazard, but it had to work. It *had* worked.

Now Kristen clung to the wheel, her chin strained forward, the same posture she adopted when she drove through a blizzard. The reel of horror stories looped in my head again, unlucky Americans locked up abroad, and a new thought sent terror up my arms: If someone connected this to Sebastian, we'd be doubly, irreparably screwed. We couldn't bring Paolo back to life, and just like in Cambodia, our priority must be making it home without leaving breadcrumbs behind.

Kristen hit the brakes in the middle of the street. I glanced around for a stop sign I'd missed. When I turned to her again, she was slumped against the steering wheel.

"This isn't going to work," she said, her voice muffled.

A stab of fear. "What?"

She looked up at me. "There are no trees, not even shrubs. We'll be totally exposed. There's nothing but red dirt." She tipped her face back down and a drip hovered on the end of her nose.

A rushing sound filled my ears and I felt cold again, my shoulders and jaw tensing. *She's right.* What the hell did I know about evading law enforcement, about ditching a goddamn body? It was hopeless; we were done for.

But then I looked at Kristen, sagging in the driver's seat, and tenderness sprang up in my chest. I knew how she felt; my brave, beautiful best friend had just been *attacked*.

I blinked hard. She'd done this for me in Cambodia—I could dig deep, channel her confidence. Be there for her like she'd been for me. "The nothing—that's why we're safe," I said. "There's nothing out there, so no one will stumble onto the spot where we dig. No hikers or, or campers with their dogs or farmers or alpáca herders or anyone else."

She wiped her silvery tears and nodded. The car began to move, imperceptibly at first and then with mounting assuredness, as if it, too, were growing in resolve.

There was only one road in and out of Quiteria, as well as all the towns before and after us, a twisty two-lane highway slithering through the valley like a lizard in the shade. I thought back to when we'd first trundled onto it, after a few confused loops around Santiago: flat, open road, how sunlight had beamed into the windshield, as cheery and charmed as the Latin pop Kristen found on the radio. Everything was blasting that day: the bass through the speakers, the sun through the windows, our zippy sedan down an endless road.

Neither of us remembered seeing any side roads up into the mountains—just sudden grids of streets when the road bloated up into towns and villages. Now we were in a barren stretch, with signs placing the next town at eighty kilometers away, and Kristen tasked me with looking for a swath of mountain we could walk out into, something remote and forgettable, and not near farmers' fields. It was hard work, not least because I was also keeping an eye on the clock: We'd been driving for a half hour, and we needed plenty of time to get back and return the shovels before the sun rose. It was already after one, and the sun would be up at seven. And though I'd never dug a grave, I assumed it would take hours.

"What about here?" I said, so quietly I had to clear my throat and repeat myself. Kristen eased the car to a stop and opened her window. The cold rushed in, eager and uncaring. Foothills loomed on either side of the road, ragged outlines blotting out the stars.

There were a few bushes near the road and a smattering of skinny pines, but no sound for miles.

"This could work," she said. "I'll drive down and see if there's a big curve ahead—we don't want another car appearing out of nowhere."

We hadn't seen another soul all night, but it was a smart thing to check.

"Go ahead," I said after a confused, waiting moment.

"You should get out here."

Cold splashed through my insides. "What? Why?"

"C'mon. Figure out which hill we should be climbing and make sure there are no signs of life—fencing or sheds or anything."

"You're going to leave me here alone?"

"Just for a minute. We're going to lose our sense of where to stop otherwise."

I stared at her, my heart thrashing.

"Emily, we don't have all night. Can you please just do this?"

Wind whipped around the brush and through her open window, a hushed, zipping noise. It mingled with the warmth of the car, and with the oxygen churning in and out of my body, my chest heaving as if I'd run a marathon.

Okay, I thought, then realized it was aloud. "Okay. Okay. Okay." I reached for the door handle and held my breath as I pulled. The dome lights flicked on, spooking us both. Kristen looked pale and childish in the sallow glow.

"I'll be right back," she murmured. "Aim your flashlight at the road when you see me."

I nodded and stepped into the frigid darkness. I swung the door shut and she drove off into the night.

I was alone. The space around me was like something solid, chilled air and night sounds and the cosmos pushing in on me, vibrating on my lips, my scalp, my eardrums. I felt a sudden instinct to pierce it all with a wild scream. Instead I squeezed my fingers into fists and watched Kristen's taillights shrinking in the distance. They hooked to the right, then disappeared altogether.

The cold air felt charged and fear mushroomed inside me, a huge desperate thrash. I'd be left alone forever; the whole world had evaporated and it was just me, alone in the Earth's wrinkled fold. The sky overhead was too bright, too high, too deep. I clicked on my flashlight and swept the feeble beam onto the soil behind me. I wished I had my phone—its light put this one to shame—but Kristen had insisted we leave them at the hotel; even in airplane mode, she said, a phone was traceable, chattering with satellites in the night sky.

Over the last few days, we'd learned what a strange swatch of land the Elqui Valley was: tropical trees and bright flowers on bar patios, fields of tender vegetables stretching from one mountain base to another, but beyond that, an arid moonscape, mountains coated in pebbly gray-brown. The streak of green narrowed in points, like here, where the valley oasis was only as wide as the highway and a few roadside shrubs; in every direction, I saw sloped hills covered in desiccated dirt and the occasional rock. *We'll have to cover our footprints,* I thought, and bent to find a bough that'd work as a makeshift broom.

Pinpricks of light in the distance, and my shoulders eased. Only now did I let myself indulge the hellish vision: me abandoned, wandering this mountain road as my tongue grew parched. Kristen speeding toward civilization, alone except for the body in the trunk.

I pointed the flashlight at the pavement, and the pale disc of light shook in time with my hand. Kristen rolled to a stop and climbed out of the car.

"Did you find a good spot?" She crossed to me and put her hands on her hips.

"What? Oh, not really." How long had she been gone? It'd felt like hours, like days, but I hadn't actually done any recon. "It's just sloping land in every direction. Did you see anything?"

"There's a curve up ahead so I followed it for a while. No signs of anyone using this area. If we're smart, we should be fine."

I turned to face uphill. "There are a few big rocks. If we dig right behind one, it'll be hidden from the road." I held a boulder in the flashlight's beam, and Kristen nodded and opened the car door. The shovels leaned against the back seat like awkward teenagers, and they clanged as Kristen yanked them out.

We set off on the crumbly hillside. One step at a time. One foot in front of the other. One task, then another, then another.

"It's just after one," I said. "If we want the car back at the hotel before sunrise, we have maybe five hours here." Car in the lot. Shovels in the shed. Padlock on the door, hardware screwed back into the frame. Our things folded in our suitcases, the hotel suite tidy, like we'd never been in that room, this valley, this country. This quivering, epic nightmare.

"It's enough time if we keep our heads." She hesitated on a stone, then pushed off.

My heart boomed. I could feel her listening, waiting for me to add something. "We're almost there now," I murmured. "This is almost behind us."

We climbed in silence, calves clenching, the ground sucking on our toes as we leaned against the pitch. My breath hitched from the hard work—the hard work and the horror.

It'd seemed easier in Cambodia. Or was that only in hindsight? I could remember scenes from that night, the hotel-room cleanup, the search for smooth stones to slip into his pockets. But I'd been numb, so numb. An abrupt cessation of feeling, like someone had switched off a lamp.

The real horror had come afterward, a cocoon of pain.

I froze and looked back toward the car. "Shouldn't we have brought him with us?"

"What?" Kristen gave her head a little shake. "Em, we'll find a spot and dig a hole. Then we'll go back and get the backpack and everything. It'd be awkward to drag all that weight with us."

"So we're just leaving him in the trunk and making multiple trips back and forth? Isn't that pushing our luck?"

"We're almost at the rock. Let's go." She squeezed my arm, gently at first and then hard enough to bruise, to break the blood vessels underneath. "Let's. Go."

I power-sighed, then turned my flashlight back uphill.

The rock was farther off than it'd seemed from below; in the darkness, I could barely make out the car now, or the road that snaked below it. Kristen reached the boulder first and pressed her palm against it gratefully. It was about her height, as wide as it was tall.

I stood the shovel in front of me and nosed it into the earth. Sucked in a breath, then set a foot on top and leaned my weight into it. The blade plunged into the crumbly ground and I lost my balance before rocking back and gouging out a silty chunk. My lats tightened and a sliver needled into my palm. I poked at the wound, then hurried to catch up to Kristen, who'd already cleared a small hole.

Crunch, hiss. Crunch, hiss. Over and over, we rammed our shovels into the arid ground and slid the dry dirt into a growing mound. It was hard work, but rhythmic, like paddling a canoe. We huffed as we raised each clump of soil and groaned as we tipped it onto the pile.

In, then out. My arms began to shake. Pain branched out from my spine, along my back and shoulders. Blisters sprang up on my hands, then popped, sending stinging blood into the cracks of my palms.

Down, then to the side. Sweat slid beneath my breasts and along my tailbone. The muscles around my wrists burned like they'd been doused with acid, and the shovel trembled so hard I had to focus to keep the soil from scattering off the sides. Terror threatened to rise up through my ribs but I funneled it into my muscles instead, glutes and quads screaming as we dug, dug, dug.

The sky was changing. At first I thought I was imagining it, but when I shined the flashlight on my wristwatch—the small movement painful in my overworked arm—I saw it was true. The stars were dulling, like they were all on a dimmer switch. Morning was coming. Not soon, but not that long now.

"We need to dig faster," I said, wheezing a bit. "We can't be carrying anything up here when people are driving to work."

"I think it's deep enough." She rested her palms on the shovel's handle. "There's room. Let's do it. It's never going to be perfect."

Was it deep enough? Or would it leave the body right up against the surface, awaiting the dog or wind or flash flood that would break through the crust on top? A sudden breeze ruffled past, nuzzling my sweaty body with a blast of icy cold. There was no time. I dropped my shovel with a thud. She did the same and we trotted down to the road, our heels kicking up clods of dirt. My back and arms were on fire. I was going to be so sore.

It took Kristen a moment to find the key and another to locate the open-trunk button. The trunk flipped up instantly, cheerily, yawning wide and then sinking halfway back down.

Paolo was still in there, a freaky, Dalí-esque sight: a colossal tan backpack with legs growing out of it. A rumpled casserole of clothes surrounded his ankles and shoes, forcing the feet into an odd disco pose. Thoughts tumbled before I could stop them: Had Paolo liked to dance? Run? Rock climb up cliffs or tear down them on a mountain bike? What had given him those knobby calf muscles, the swollen quads? My stomach lurched and something hysterical somersaulted up through me. I pressed my hands on the bumper and the cold metal braced me.

"We'll use the shower curtain again, yeah?" She peeled back its plastic corner. "Make sure all the clothes are here so we can carry everything at once."

I nodded. My body was cramping up from the dig now; my back throbbed, my fingers had stiffened, and hot pain unfurled along my neck. Most of Paolo's clothes were piled around his hairy legs, but a few items had slipped beyond the shower curtain, and I snatched them up and piled them on his lumpy knees.

This is a weird break from reality; you're about to slip into an alternate timeline and wormhole back when it's over. This is a project to be managed, a problem to be solved. Keep going. Keep going. Keep going.

I tugged my shirt cuff over my bloody palm and grabbed the shower curtain's corners. My forearms screeched in pain, begging me not to lift him. I tried to take a deep breath and it split into an asthmatic cough.

"You okay?" Kristen asked, and I nodded. She met my eyes. "Good. On three."

It hurts it hurts it hurts. Kristen led the way, shuffling backward, glancing over her shoulder like someone being followed. My arms gave out a quarter of the way up—hers too, the adrenaline unable to counter his weight—and we set him down and shook out our wrists. It was an eternity, perhaps thirty yards but the longest hike of my life, my whole body pulsing with pain, a giant bee sting. Kristen and I were unable to find a rhythm as we rushed and stopped short, like friends hauling a sofa up the stairs. When we reached the boulder, we were so eager and exhausted that we wobbled and tripped and nearly dropped him.

"Quickly, now." I helped her lift the shower curtain and tip its contents into the pit; we scattered the clothes around, cramming them into the grave's deepest edges. She picked up a shovel and I snatched mine from the grave's edge. This part was even worse, my only thought a screeching, looping *ow*. We groaned as we buried him, our cries carnal and pathetic as we pushed our battered bodies to cooperate. When we'd finished, she smoothed the dirt with the back of her spade. It was a gently curved mound now, a bump in the night.

We hurried down the mountain as the edge of the sky turned cerulean. Near the road we picked up branches and rushed back up to the rock, sweeping at our scuffs and skids.

We tumbled into the car and slammed the doors. For a moment Kristen closed her eyes, her crown tipped against the headrest.

"Do you think it'll look weird in the light?" I peered out the window. "Will the dirt be another color where we swept it?"

She was quiet for a very long time. "I don't know what to tell you, Emily. There's nothing else we can do." Her hand shot out and turned on the ignition, and then we began the long drive back.

The car felt so much lighter without Paolo in the trunk.

CHAPTER 9

It was almost six, the sky brightening with alarming speed. We passed three vehicles along the way, headlights like eyes in the early-morning murk: a truck, a sedan, and a pickup pulling a trailer with four men in the back, handkerchiefs clutched to their noses. Each time I stared down at my lap, willing us to be forgettable. Finally we turned into our tiny parking lot. It was still cold out, but mistier now, so the dampness had a bite. In the purgatorial light of predawn, we carried the shovels back up to the shed. Kristen grasped my shoulder when a window lit up nearby (in another guesthouse, I think?), but it darkened after a few seconds and I went back to screwing the lock into place.

Dew glistened on the sliding door as we slipped back inside our suite. With a stab, I pictured him there again: calves poking out from behind the sofa, the wine bottle smeared red but otherwise unharmed, having won the durability contest against Paolo's skull. It had to be One of Those Things—a centimeter up, down, or to the side and he could've been fine.

I looked over at Kristen and felt a wash of compassion. She was still being so strong—stronger than I'd been in Cambodia, certainly—and it had only been a few hours since Paolo had threatened her life.

"Help me finish cleaning." Kristen rummaged in the kitchenette, then held out a dish towel. We ransacked the rooms for cleaning products and, finding none, pooled our resources: makeup remover, hand wipes, soap, Purell. The day cracked open like an egg, sunlight nosing against the windows and then pushing inside with sudden vigor. We swiped and swabbed and dusted, silent and focused in our own personal hells. I scrubbed the shower curtain in the tub, body gel foaming brown and red on the colorful plastic, then strung it back up. Was it enough? Could we really expect to leave no trace when we lacked even proper cleaning products?

We touched a lighter to crumples of newspaper we'd piled in the fireplace. Once kindling and then a few logs popped and roared, I added Paolo's things one by one: passport, journal, wallet, phone. I coughed as they curled into a stinking mass; Kristen opened a window and fanned out the foul-smelling smoke. When Paolo's effects were a blackish chunk, I poured water on it.

"I'll take it," Kristen announced after the lump stopped sizzling. She wrapped it in newspaper and stuffed it inside an empty chip bag. "I'll toss it when I get home."

NORMALCY—WE HAD TO maintain it, had to load our suitcases into the trunk and then trudge to the lobby for breakfast. After all, we'd made it to breakfast every morning and the owner was so proud of it, their *desayuno delicioso,* and the last thing we wanted was anyone wondering where we were. There we stared at baskets of rolls and colorful fruit plates in quiet revulsion. We stopped at the front desk to turn over the key (they'd been very clear about this at check-in, *do not leave the key in the room*), and I suddenly realized everyone was staring at me, the only possible translator.

"*¿Cómo?*" I prompted, too out of it to recall the polite way to ask her to repeat herself.

"*¿Cómo estuvo su estadía con nosotros?*" she asked, too fast and too mumbly, and I blinked at her for a long time before the words unstuck themselves. How was our stay? Fine—the suite's romantic wood-burning stove sure had come in handy when we had evidence to destroy.

"*Muy bien.*" I forced a smile. "*Gracias por todo.*"

IT WAS A six-hour drive back to the Santiago airport, out to the sea and then south between the mountains and the water. Monotonous and brown, as ugly outside as the muck I felt covering my breast and brain, horror and disbelief clotting beneath my rib cage and skull. We'd driven the opposite direction this morning—was that just this morning, with all that dead weight in the trunk? Still, I found myself scanning the hills, watching for our footprints, probably smeared away but possibly more obvious than ever after our sweeping—like a giant arrow from the road to the grave. I was so sore that raising my hand to slide on sunglasses hurt. *Shattered:* The word lodged in my head, a skipping record. That's how I felt. My body, my life. Paolo's fragile eggshell skull.

A lookout point appeared, and Kristen swerved into it and threw the car into park. She stared straight ahead. Then, right as I was about to puncture the silence, her eyes went hard and she let out a scream. Not a scream—a roar, the way a little kid answers when you ask what sound a lion makes. It echoed around the car, buzzed in my ears, then stopped. She punctuated it with a single surprised laugh. Then she turned to me, as if she'd only just remembered I was there.

With a jolt, I heaved open the car door and dashed to the edge of the cliff. Nothing but tawny mountains, reddish in the morning light, as far as the eye could see. A wail poured out of me, mournful and low but powerful, too, until I squeezed the air from the bottom of my lungs and sputtered to a stop. Kristen appeared next to me and puffed her chest, and together we roared, our screams somehow in harmony, with the same uncanny intensity as a group *om* in yoga class. We listened to the echo and I pictured the sound waves rattling the cells of armadillos and vicuñas and Patagonian pumas miles from this place.

As if we'd triggered it, the sky bruised over and spat at us, at first a drizzle and then a steady tap.

Kristen smiled for the first time since last night.

"It'll wash away any sign that we were ever on the mountain," she said.

Or maybe it'll wash away the dirt we used to cover him. I lifted my face to the rain, then got back in the car. She gave my shoulder a squeeze before turning on the ignition and pulling back onto the road. Outside, the drops tickled rows of bushy vegetables and moss-colored shrubs. I watched rainwater spill together, a brownish vein working its way downhill.

I breathed deeply. I chose to believe her.

Maybe we were never here.

CHAPTER 10

At the airport, Kristen and I were almost silent, moving like automatons as we returned the rental car. There wasn't an inspection; we just had to push the keys through a slot. I checked again for any dirt in the back seat or ruby-colored speckles in the trunk. I searched and searched and searched, feeling the anxiety like an itch in the corner of my mind. *Will they catch us?*

In a long, twisty security line, Kristen stared off into space and I took her in, still beautiful despite the sleep deprivation, her tawny hair piled in a messy top bun, her contacts swapped with wire-framed glasses over her high cheekbones, somehow looking like a Hot Girl in Glasses and not a bespectacled woman. A key distinction I could never put my finger on.

"Oh my God." Just above her jawline was a dried speck of blood. Paolo's blood. I licked my thumb and swiped at it, and she batted me away.

"It's a *mole,* Emily," she snapped, covering her cheek. "What is wrong with you?"

Everything. Everything felt wrong. The soreness was stepping in to take the acute pain's place, and even reaching for Kristen's face had left my arm twinging. "I . . . I thought it was . . . never mind." We'd both taken quick showers before breakfast, scrubbing at the dirt and sweat. Of course there wasn't still blood on Kristen's face.

This will destroy her. My heart dropped and I turned away, blinking back tears. She didn't know it yet—she was still acting tough, keeping it together—but the attack would poison her psyche, as

Sebastian's attack had mine. My emotions swirled, fear and dismay and deep, bone-aching exhaustion, but this thought pierced through, a bolt of lightning in the storm: My strong and beautiful best friend was about to be broken. Cornered and battered and newly aware of her vulnerability, her fearlessness popped like a balloon. I narrowed my eyes. *Screw you, Paolo.*

Because he hadn't just hurt Kristen. He'd stolen something else— swept in right when I felt like myself again. When things between Kristen and me felt warm and safe and right. After the hideousness of Cambodia, this trip was deepening our friendship, making it like that night with Sebastian had never happened.

But now . . . well, how could I ever look at her without seeing the widening grave, the passport flopping in the fire like a living thing, Paolo's blood freckling her throat? How could either of us carry on under the crush of waiting to be caught?

Kristen, who'd risk her life for her friends. Kristen, who'd cooked lemon-chicken soup and let me sleep in her bed in college when I was newly single and alone in the world. Kristen, who put me back to-gether like a puzzle, who racked up hours and hours on the phone with me after Cambodia until I could finally unzip my sleeping bag of terror and tiptoe back into the world, had had the unthinkable happen to her. I'd been through it before—with Sebastian, with Ben—but now she knew how it felt to be punished for seeing the world as safe and kind and *yours.*

We collected our bags and entered another line for passport con-trol. Here my heart rate spiked—they'd see it on our faces; they'd know.

"What was the purpose of your visit?" asked the handsome Chi-lean border-control officer, though I'd already marked the form.

I choked on the word: "Pleasure."

He flipped past several blank pages to stamp my passport toward the back. "Have a safe flight."

A quiet moment in a bad coffee shop, and then it was time to part. Kristen hugged me tight, then held me out, hands still on my shoulders, looking deep into my eyes. I wondered if this would be our last trip—no Morocco or Georgia or Turkey. If the night before had bulldozed our wanderlust indefinitely.

"I love you," she said, lowering her chin. "Let me know when you get home, okay?"

"Love you too," I murmured, and she shuddered a bit as she nodded. Then she let me go, turned on her heel, and walked off without looking back. I was relieved, then intensely sad we were parting on that note, on my eagerness to let this nightmare end. I wished I could crawl back into last night, before anything went wrong, when we were pointing at stars and crunching on corn nuts and feeling the world was our playground.

It was a ten-hour flight to Atlanta and, in the second-to-last row, my body throbbed through all ten of them. It felt right, like my horror and guilt and sadness had taken physical form, swept through my muscles, bristled my nerve endings, turned my tendons taut. God, it hurt. Had it been this bad after Cambodia? No—I'd been so numb from being attacked myself that my brain hadn't let me feel it, the soreness, the misery. Kristen's body must have felt then like mine did now, all agony and aches. She never mentioned it. God, what a selfless friend she was, the crosshairs of her attention squared on me, my pain, my flailing attempts to cope.

After a short eternity, we slammed onto the tarmac and I rushed to check the news: still nothing about a missing backpacker. But that could change at any moment. This was my life now, forever waiting for not one but two shoes to drop.

I shuffled up the aisle, taking in the mess we'd made of the plane. One hundred and fifty feet of bedlam, of an aircraft in shambles as we ambled away from our titanic tin-can trash can. Blankets matted and crumpled, limp greens and errant cherry tomatoes mashed into the aisles, trash splattered like street art over every available surface. We're all disgusting, every single one of us. Making messes and then wandering away.

Except that Paolo paid for his sins with his life. What was this stupid voice rushing to pity Paolo, a bad man, a would-be rapist? Before I could stop it, I pictured his lifeless legs, the skin cool and knobby, sliding over bones and tendons as we rolled him onto the shower curtain. Was there a girlfriend he was cheating on back home? A friend somewhere else on the globe planning to see him a few months from now, wondering why Paolo was never on WhatsApp anymore?

I shoved the thoughts aside as I waited for passport control. WEL-COME TO AMERICA, a banner screamed. One more flight to go, but I'd done it—I'd made it out of Chile. I couldn't believe it, kept waiting to blink awake and discover I was still in the Santiago airport, feeling my heart beating in my fingertips.

At my gate, I sat in a worn fabric chair and peeled open a granola bar; it tasted like sand. My mind kept returning to the sudden desert rain, the way your tongue wants to push against a toothache. It wouldn't expose our shallow grave, would it? No one noticed Paolo chatting with us on the patio last night, did they? The two shiny-haired British girls, the bartender who saw me freaking out about my missing wallet . . . had we made an impression on any of them? The light blaring on in a window as we sealed the flashlights and shovels back in the shed—that was a coincidence, not a witness, right? Had we cleaned the floor of the suite thoroughly enough? We'd only seen it in the hazy morning light—what if the midday sun was like a spotlight on broad bloodstains we'd missed?

My phone buzzed and I blinked at the text for a minute before it made sense. Aaron, sweetly remembering my return date: "Safe travels today! Remind me when you get back?"

Discomfort buzzed in my hands and feet. The desire to see him, to kiss him, was visceral and thick, but . . . but what now? I'd always had trouble being vulnerable with guys: unwilling to let myself get excited about them, or—on the rare occasions I did fall hard—braced for things to fall apart. And now? How could I possibly open up and be *real* with this massive secret encircling me like a moat? Sure, I'd kept Cambodia from him, but by the time we started dating the attack was in the past, the scar tissue gnarled and delicate but *there,* atop a wound I didn't want to talk about. Keeping this—this fresh trauma, this clear and present terror—from him felt different.

Aaron thought I was just your average Midwestern gal, gentle and sweet. Could I really look him in the eye and pretend everything was normal now? I had finally emerged from the nightmares and panic attacks of Cambodia—and now Paolo had opened a trapdoor and spilled me back at square one. I was angry, and it was uncomfortable. Nice girls don't walk around with anger brewing in their chest. With blood on their palms and dirt under their nails from participating in their own late-night horror story.

Around me, everyone was too loud, too rambunctious—kids screeched and climbed, people brayed into their phones, teenagers giggled, a mom yelled. A screen was blasting the news, with no one watching it: wildfires in the Amazon, a drone strike in Syria. I'd heard once that TV news hits airports on a delay, so they can cut the stream if a story involves a hijacked plane or an active shooter in a terminal. Edit the feed to limit mass hysteria. Maybe something was happening in the air right now.

Edit the feed to limit mass hysteria. Was this something I could do, for internal hysteria? Somehow snip out the memories, one year apart, that threatened to send my world tumbling down? I wished there were a procedure, *Eternal Sunshine*-style, to erase the events' fingerprints on my brain. Maybe I could learn to compartmentalize. Pretend everything was fine around my co-workers, my friends. On dates with Aaron. Christ, I so badly wanted to be *normal* around him, to joke with him and hold him and kiss him and, yes, have sex with him like a regular person—not the broken, guarded, secretive woman I'd become. Doubly so now. My stomach tightened and I unlocked my phone.

"Hey you! Landing around 5 so it'll be a short eternity getting home in traffic," I wrote. "How's it going?"

Normalcy—we had to maintain it, had to behave like nothing was wrong. Like I hadn't pushed dirt on top of a goddamn body in northern Chile.

He started typing back right away. "Good! Excited to hear all about your trip. Have a great flight!"

I shot back prayer-hands and a smiley face and dropped my phone into my bag. I mashed my hands against my eye sockets, where a headache roared underneath.

A preteen soccer team jostled into the waiting area. One got out a ball and I stared stupidly as it rolled past my foot. Finally their coach yelled at them to settle down, and they sat in a large ring, blocking the flow of traffic and playing some sort of card game.

That damn voice again: Had Paolo played soccer growing up? ¿Fútbol? When would his mother notice he was missing? His friends? Did he have a ticket back to Spain, a one-way flight capping his year of wanderlust?

No. Paolo didn't deserve my remorse. Paolo was no different from Sebastian: a bad guy, one whose specter haunted me on dark street corners, and I wasn't sad to know he was no longer around. Sebastian had left me with bruises and scrapes—plus echoing fear, a geyser of terror I couldn't work through or discuss. My heart sank. Kristen had no idea what she was in for.

It was a short flight in a window seat that showed nothing but a blanket of gray clouds below. The man next to me jabbed my elbow clean off the armrest and I wrapped my arms tight around my chest. When we began our initial descent, my ears popping with faint fizzy sounds, I could have wept with joy. *Almost home.*

I hobbled off the plane and toward the exit, past souvenir shops selling cheeseheads and T-shirts with Milwaukee-centric slogans: THE GOOD LAND and DRINK WISCONSINBLY and WHOLESOME MIDWESTERN GIRL. Ugh. Aaron was calling and I silenced it as I jammed my way through the baggage claim. Then I heard my name behind me and twisted around.

My heart froze. Paolo was loping toward me, gaining ground as he weaved around luggage carts and bloats of people. *He followed me.*

He disappeared behind a pile of suitcases and I watched in terror, waiting for him to emerge from the other side. A flash of dark hair and skin, and then he looked at me head-on.

Relief pulsed through me, but then my stomach dropped.

It wasn't Paolo.

It was Aaron.

CHAPTER 11

I scooped up all my remaining energy and trained a smile on him. The act made me want to burst into tears—that it was fake, difficult, exhausting.

"What are you doing here?" I asked.

"I thought I'd surprise you," he announced. "I was already in Jefferson Park. I figured, who doesn't like getting a ride from the airport?"

I stretched my smile wider. "That is so sweet and so unnecessary. Thank you."

"Don't mention it. My car is this way."

He grabbed the handle of my suitcase and set off. I took in his rumpled brown hair, his plastic-framed glasses, his thin lips curved into a crooked smile. He was cuter than I remembered, more angular, as if the week away had sanded the edges off my mental image of him. I felt a ruffle in my belly: butterflies attempting to stir, tamped down by the events of the last twenty-four hours.

"So how was your flight?"

"Oh, fine—the first one was delayed but I had a long layover anyway, so."

We approached an elevator and he hit the call button. "I'm dying to hear all about Chile. But just a preview. You've gotta be dead tired—I'll take you straight home, don't you worry."

"Oh, thank God." I clapped a palm over my mouth and he chuckled. "Sorry, I'm so out of it. I didn't sleep on either plane."

The elevator doors opened and we shuffled in. "Are you sore? You're walking kinda funny."

"Right. We . . . went for a tough hike. Turns out I'm out of shape."
My sludgy brain shorted out as I stared at our murky reflections in
the brushed-metal door. I looked like shit—greasy skin, puffy eyes,
my hair a mess—but I was too tired to care. Too tired to panic too;
I just wanted to cry. *Aaron wants to hear about Chile:* It was an internal wail, a preschooler on the verge of a meltdown.

He grabbed my hand and smiled at my fingertips. "Must have
been a hell of a hike—you've still got dirt under your nails!" I tried
to twist away but he flipped my hand over, where fresh blisters dotted my palm. "Damn! What kind of path were you on?"

My heart pounded; asthma clawed at my lungs. I was a banged-
up mess, dirty and bruised from our all-nighter on the mountainside.
I yanked my fist back as the elevator doors opened. "Um, there was
some rock-scrambling, yeah. I definitely should have worn gloves.
I'm gonna be sore for a while."

Aaron glided ahead with my suitcase. "I dig a good rock scram-
ble. I have so many questions. What was your favorite part of the
trip? Best thing you ate, coolest thing you did? Weirdest thing you
saw? Oh, it's this way." A sudden swerve to the left.

The weirdest thing I saw: a wine bottle splattered red, as if the
liquid inside had seeped to the surface. A dented head, blood growing tacky on the floor. The jumbo canvas backpack with legs at the
bottom, hairy and brawny and still.

"I'm— God, I'm sorry, I'm so tired I can barely form sentences."

"Naw, I totally get it!" He hit a button and his car blooped and
blinked. He heaved my suitcase into the trunk and skidded around
to open the passenger-side door. Lord, he was taking such good care
of me, as if I were worth it—his kindness made discomfort yawn
open inside me.

"I brought you a croissant from the shop," he said, sliding into
his seat. "Should be by your feet. And there's water in the door."

"Wow. Thank you, Aaron." I tried to lower myself in carefully,
but my quads gave out and I dropped to the seat in a freefall. I
plucked a hunk from the pastry and shoved it into my mouth, but
my tongue still felt as dry as the dirt we'd carved up with our shovels.

Ben had behaved like this when we'd first begun dating; we were high schoolers then, raised on Midwestern politeness, and he stood out from the hooting masses by holding the door for me and paying for brimming waffle cones at a fancy ice-cream shop. I absolutely owed it to Aaron to be grateful, polite, charming. Instead I wanted to curl up in a ball and sleep for three to five days, at minimum.

He threw the car into reverse. "So Chile totally wiped you out? You had fun with, ah . . . Kristen?"

"Good memory!" I swallowed. I pictured her in the air right now, locked inside her own sore body. "Yeah, just lots of . . . running around." The sides of my mouth felt like they had boulders pulling them down, but I lifted them. "I don't want you to think I'm not happy to see you."

"But you'll be happier to see your bed. Let's do this." He stabbed a button on the dashboard and the speakers leaked classical music. "Google Maps says it's twenty-five minutes to the Fifth Ward. I'll wake you when we're close. Deal?"

"You're too good to me," I murmured, and I meant it. I thought I wouldn't be able to sleep, but within minutes, I was out.

In my driveway I thanked Aaron and gave him a peck goodbye, then staggered toward the front door like a castaway approaching shore. I could've dropped to my knees, kissed the welcome mat. Instead I fumbled in my purse and backpack, unsure where I'd stashed my keys.

Inside, I lowered the blinds against the afternoon light and was about to flick off my lamp when my phone rattled on the nightstand.

Kristen. Her name made my heart tick up—was she okay? Did she need my help? I squinted at her text: "Landed! You made it?"

"Just got home! Passing out now," I wrote back. I pressed my lips together, then added, "How are you doing???"

When her text came through, I almost dropped my phone:

"Great! Amazing trip. Miss you already. xoxo"

What trip had *she* been on? But then, as the goosebumps were still making their sweep up my sore neck and shoulders, it hit me: She was establishing a paper trail, maintaining normalcy. Making it clear to anyone listening in that all was well in the Journeys of Kristen and Emily. Ensuring we looked innocent. The text was a clever move, but it left me unable to nap.

Instead I stared at the ceiling and cataloged the details that would do us in. Each one hit me like a blast of cold, bright as a lemon, a strobe light's sudden burst: the crowded patio bar, the black-haired British women with their huge backpacks and wide smiles, the blood on the suite floor, the lit-up window near the storage shed, the torrential rain on our pathetic mound . . . there were too many gambles, too many loose threads to trust that the Fates would bless us a second time.

A *second* time. What the hell?

I'd done this after Phnom Penh, too, replaying our coverup operation in my mind and tensing every time my phone rang, every time I refreshed the news. Now I silently thumbed through *those* damning bits of evidence. The flash as Sebastian and I left the bar—someone would see the photo, know I had something to do with his disappearance. Or the body would break free from the stones and bob up to Tonle Kak's burbling surface.

Last year I also reckoned with the trauma of seeing blood gush from Sebastian's head: *Stop. Stop. Stop.* And the surreal gruesomeness of ditching Sebastian's body—in my milky memories, horror blipped out of the numbness like a voice through radio static. My hands had detached from my body, reduced a young man to an inconvenient bundle. *That really happened.* I knew it was him or me, that we were choosing the best worst option to keep ourselves alive and safe and free, but that primal horror stayed stamped on my psyche.

And above it all, like a drone whirring over a crowd, louder than a swarm of bees: After Cambodia, I couldn't stop replaying the terror of the *attack*. Even back in Wisconsin, I felt Sebastian's rough palm smashed against my face. I saw his clear eyes, blue and furious. The whole point of Kristen's plan was to preserve our freedom, but I felt caged and bruised, like he'd stolen my joy. After Phnom Penh, I was a shell of a human, waiting, begging for an hour when I felt like my old self again.

Kristen had taken me on as an unpaid full-time job—listening to me sob, distracting me with meandering stories. Finally, mercifully, a moment of relief had come five or six weeks later, when the two of us were several seasons deep into a shared rewatch of *Buffy the Vampire Slayer*. When the show triggered a funny high-school memory, I'd caught myself midsentence with a jolt: *Just now, you weren't thinking about The Thing*. It was fleeting but hopeful—if we could somehow evade notice and those periods between panic could lengthen like shadows in the afternoon, maybe someday I'd be okay.

And now I had to start that whole awful process again, from square one?

With shaking hands, I texted her back: "Miss you too."

Eventually I fell into a restless, jagged sleep, woke in the dark, and then lay awake the rest of the night.

KIBBLE'S OFFICE WAS in a skinny turn-of-the-century tower on Rogers Street, with an ancient, creaking elevator and an ancient, creaking security guy who never looked up from the front desk as people came and went, even as I said hello twice a day. The workspace lacked the techie, technicolor flair I associated with start-ups; instead it was a beehive of old desks all facing the same way, partitioned off by ugly gray cubicle walls. Still, there was iced coffee on tap in the kitchen and floor-to-ceiling windows and parquet floors that made coordinating supply chains and launching lines for feline urinary care . . . if not pleasant, certainly tolerable. And there was a democratic feel among the twenty-odd employees. The sole Kibble worker with an office was Russell, the founder and CEO, who was only a couple years older than me.

Normally I didn't mind coming to work after a trip—I looked forward to it, even. But as I rode the elevator up on my first day back, dread ballooned in my torso. I'd thought about calling Kristen before work, but it was the middle of the night in Sydney. How would I get through today without her quiet empathy, her reassuring confidence? And, jeez, how could I expect her to be there for me when *she* was the one who'd been attacked? She deserved a friend she could count on, the way I'd leaned on her after Cambodia.

As the elevator doors slid open, I paled. How was I supposed to sit at my scratched desk and poke at spreadsheets when Paolo's body was just . . . *there,* decaying under a thin layer of dirt, waiting for someone to find him?

"Welcome home!" Priya bounded over, ponytail shaking, and wrapped me in a hug. "I am *so* glad you're back."

I spread a smile across my face like frosting. Priya and I had met a couple years ago, volunteering at a fundraiser for a nearby animal rescue; though my landlord didn't allow pets, I loved ogling the shelter's adorable Instagram and decided to help out at a one-day event. An organizer had paired us off in the morning, and by lunchtime, we were friends. She'd been the one to tell me about the job opening here—she was Kibble's copywriter.

"I missed you!" I told her. "And I brought you something." A miniature bottle of pisco clinked in my purse.

"Was it amazing? It was amazing, right?" She accompanied me to my desk.

I widened my smile. I wanted to cry. Days later, the soreness from dragging and digging still hadn't let up its hold, and it matched the feeling in my chest: pain both broad and sharp. "It was unforgettable," I managed, "but I'm glad to be home."

I COULDN'T STOP poring over the news. I felt a jolt every time I refreshed CNN, like when you turn on music with the volume way too high. I scrolled and scrolled in search of any mention of a missing person. I knew I couldn't google it, not even in private-browsing mode, because last year Kristen had hissed that the function wasn't secure—anyone with your IP address could still track you down.

But nothing happened. Co-workers breezed by my desk to ask about Chile, but as is always the case with vacation recaps, they weren't all that interested. There was an e-commerce relaunch to jump back into. I could only devote maybe 20 percent of my attention to drawing up production schedules and futzing with budgets, but that was 20 percent on anything other than Paolo.

Has his family noticed he's missing yet? Has anyone raised the alarm?

THAT NIGHT I dreamed that Kristen and I were back at Northwestern, during the summer before senior year when we stayed in town and sublet a banged-up apartment on Clark. In the dream—as in my memories—we were sitting on the lakefill, gazing out at the black water and growing excited as the sky turned indigo and the stars began to fade. We said nothing, just watched in awe as the sun nudged through the watery horizon. Sunrise over Lake Michigan—we only managed to stay up for it three times during our tenure there, but it was always special, private, *ours*.

Then I opened my eyes, and the messed-up reality came crashing in.

I reached for my phone—the instinct to talk to Kristen was an itch, looping and loud, like when we lay in our tent in Uganda and felt the throb of dozens of tsetse-fly bites. Paolo consumed my thoughts and I craved a release, the chance to discuss it to death. *Do you still think we're okay? Is there anything we forgot? Can you believe that all happened??* But of course, I couldn't say any of that— Kristen wouldn't let us incriminate ourselves over the phone. I felt the secret pushing out of me, blowing up like a bubble and rising in my throat.

Another day of work. Somehow I sat through meetings and replied to emails and listened to gossip in the break room. Aaron and I texted throughout the day, the casual banter of the newly dating, and I clung to the dopamine spurt I got every time his name appeared on my lock screen. I waited in line for overpriced burrito bowls with Priya, taking in her patter of Tinder-date stories. All the while my id threatened to commandeer my throat, scream it aloud: *We buried a man soaked in his own blood.* It wouldn't even be the whole truth. Only half, one body of two.

Kristen and I scheduled a call for the evening. *Be careful not to mention The Thing, Emily, in case anybody's listening.* My heart pounded as I sat on my couch, earbuds in, waiting.

"Hey, Em!" So cheery. And what was whining in the background?

"Hi. Are you outside?"

"Yeah, I'm walking to work. Is it super loud?" The wind swelled, then quieted; a distant car honked.

"Uh, it's fine, I can hear you." There was something too casual about it, her multitasking on our first post-Chile call. "How are you doing?"

"Fine. Work is awful. I'm wishing we were still on vacation together."

I frowned and sank into the pillows behind me. "I'm so sorry work sucks. But how are you *doing*?"

"All right. So look, I know you said maybe waiting a year would be better for backpacking, but what if we plan it for *my* summer? If we start traveling right after the holidays, you'll escape the hellhole that is Milwaukee in the winter, and we could even kick things off in Sydney—January is perfect surfing weather."

I was glad we weren't on a video call, because I couldn't keep the shock off my face. She was acting so completely *fine*. I loved Kristen, would give anything to be physically with her right now as we processed our horror. But clearly, something about us together served as a beacon for very bad things. The two of us traveling alone were a magnet for violence. Why would we risk it again? And, hell, how could she *consider* globetrotting when she'd been attacked just days before?

"That's . . . something to think about," I said carefully. "I miss you so, so hard. But . . . I need a little time before I'll feel ready to travel again. Does that make sense?"

"Oh, that's fine," she said, too quickly, and changed the subject. We chatted for a few minutes more about anything other than Paolo, and then she arrived at her office. I hung up confused and sad.

And profoundly unsettled.

CHAPTER 12

Aaron and I made plans to meet at a cozy dive bar in his neighborhood. I found parking on a side street and stepped out into the dark, instantly reminded of Milwaukee's reputation as a patchwork of safe blocks and not-so-safe ones a few yards away. There was a man in a baseball cap leaning on a lamppost and I averted my eyes as I passed. But then I heard footsteps behind me and my heart roared, barbed adrenaline shooting through my limbs. I picked up the pace and darted across the street, then stole a glance over my shoulder.

It was nothing. He'd turned down another road. Just a guy going about his business, unaware that he'd set my nervous system on fire.

I thought back to a soliloquy I'd seen on TV about pain as women's birthright. It's not hard to catalog the dazzling torment life puts us through: childbirth and menstrual cramps and the suffocating heat of menopause. We do our best to avoid it, but men run toward it: war and wrestling and football that cracks their skulls, bruises the fragile gray matter underneath. Their bravado is just them manufacturing their own pain, trying to seem strong.

But *fear*—fear is at least as strong a motivator as pain. Maybe the TV show had it wrong; maybe men aren't out to experience pain so much as fear, the icy jolt of feeling alive. They crave it because they have no idea how miserable it is to feel that frigid blast a hundred times a day.

I heaved open the bar's door, grateful for the belch of warm, beery air that enveloped me. I breathed it in for a moment: people chatting and ordering PBR and munching on cheese balls brighter than a highlighter. Studding the wood-paneled walls were neon beer signs and dusty antlers and mounted fish, and I felt I'd slipped through a portal to a safer dimension.

I searched the faces around the bar and then headed for the back room, where a foosball table and old arcade games hulked between scratched wooden tables.

"Emily!" Aaron rose to kiss me hello. I liked how confidently he did it, like that was how we always greeted each other. "What are you having?"

He rushed off to get me a drink and I pulled out my phone. Kristen had sent me a photo from what I assumed was her office: its sweeping view of Sydney, the opera house twinkling in the distance. "Sure I can't convince you?" she'd texted, with a winky face. Wet concrete tumbled in my belly.

I jumped as a glass plonked onto the table in front of me. "They were out of Spotted Cow, so I got you something called a Booyah." Aaron touched my shoulder, then slid onto a chair. "The bartender said it's similar. Hey, what is it?"

"It's nothing. Sorry."

"Everything okay?"

"It was Kristen." I hesitated. "She's trying to convince me to meet her in Sydney for six months of backpacking."

"*Really.*"

"Yup. I know she misses me. Plus, I think she doesn't like being so far from . . . well, everyone."

"And how are you feeling about it?"

I pursed my lips. "I told her it's not a good time. 'Cause work is going well and, like, socially . . ." I gestured at the table, our two pint glasses standing tall, then blushed. I didn't add the third big reason: Kristen and I traveling together kept ending in bloodshed. "But she keeps asking about it."

"Oh man, I didn't want to influence you, but dude. I'm so relieved." He laughed and swiped up his beer, and my stomach flipped.

"I'm glad you're relieved." The warm bubbles in my chest rose, cautiously hopeful.

He nodded, thinking. "Weird she'd try to steal you away from me. But I guess, like, hoes before bros."

"When she pitched it, she didn't exactly . . . know about you. *Yet.*" My voice was slow and stretchy, a tape at the wrong speed.

He started to laugh. "And why's that?"

I swallowed. "I've gotten my hopes up a lot for things to turn into nothing. I told you I haven't seen anyone seriously in a while—shit, not that we're serious—I just mean . . ."

He grinned at me, eyebrows high, waiting for more.

In a rush: "Just because I didn't want to jinx it, you know? There's nothing worse than telling your friends all excitedly about a new guy and then having it fizzle out. And then they're asking you about it and you feel foolish." Well, there definitely were a few worse things. Kristen and I knew all about them. "But anyway, then I did tell her about you. On our last night. And she's so happy for me! But I guess she's pretty stoked on her backpacking idea. Can't blame her for trying, right?"

He stretched his arm around my shoulders. My whole body lit up under the weight. "Got it. Well, tell her you've got a boyfriend. That's why you don't want to move."

I couldn't keep the smile off my face. "Boyfriend, huh?"

"Kinda feels like it, right?"

I looked away when the eye contact got too intense. "It kinda does."

"Good. Just don't become a vagabond *right* right now. I suck at long-distance."

"I won't. But she's having trouble taking no for an answer. She can be intense when she wants me to do something with her. Hell, she's the reason I had so much fun at Northwestern—I definitely wouldn't have, like, gone skinny-dipping in Lake Michigan if it weren't for her."

His eyebrows lifted. "Now, *that* is something I'm sad I missed."

"I'm sure." I sipped my beer. "I think she's just hurting. I'm having a hard time being a good friend."

"Hurting how?"

Kristen in our hotel suite, Paolo's blood freckling her jaw: *He attacked me.*

"I mean, she's lonely. She has friends there, but not a *best* friend. Anyway, I wanna hear about you! What did I miss? Are you working on any cool projects?"

"Oh, nothing interesting." His hand slid from my shoulder to the back of my neck. He hit me with a soft-focus stare, then kissed me. I thought my heart would pound right out of my chest—and for the first time in forever, it was out of elation, not fear.

Boyfriend. He'd called himself my boyfriend. He'd claimed me as his girlfriend. For so long I'd been afraid to hope for it, and now it was happening, it was real, it was better than I'd dreamed. I set my palm on his squared-off jawline, pressing into the stubble there, and kissed him back.

I broke away first, with a shy giggle. "Hi, boyfriend," I tried.

"'Sup, girl," he joked back, then threaded his fingers through mine. "Hey, tell me more about Kristen. I should know more about my girlfriend's best friend."

My nervous system sped up, like someone had turned a dial. "She's the best. Totally bold and adventurous."

"I like how you two get yourselves into trouble together all over the globe." He lifted our hands and inspected my nails again. "Still dirty! I still want to hear about this epic hike."

No. Alarm washed through me, rinsing away the warmth. How could I be in a serious relationship when I kept losing my shit?

"It was, uh, kind of a mess. We got lost, wound up fighting about it. Worst part of the trip, really." I quaffed at the sudsy beer. My other hand, still in Aaron's, now felt clammy and cold.

"Whoa, all right. We don't have to talk about it. What else happened on the trip?"

I set my glass down. "You're so sweet to ask, but I'm kinda sick of rehashing it. And I care about your life! What's new?"

He leaned back easily. "Workwise, this big package-design thing just fell through. They decided to find someone on this site where artists bid on work. Cheapest labor wins."

"Yikes. Aren't those designers devaluing the work for everyone?"

He shrugged. "I get it, people need to get food on the table. And I'm lucky, I've always got the café."

"Man, nobody can ruffle you, huh?"

He grinned. "I don't see the point of thinking everyone's out to get you."

Like I do. Paolo's family, the dawning realization he wasn't where he was supposed to be. Local cops, an investigation launched.

"I like how you see the world," I told him, and gulped my beer.

WHEN THE BARTENDER announced it was last call, Aaron and I walked over to his apartment hand in hand. I was determined to keep Chile tucked away, out of sight, out of mind. His roommate wasn't home so we dropped onto the couch in the living room, and his record player cloaked the rabble of noisy bar patrons stumbling home below his windows.

For a few minutes, it was fine—exciting, fun, making out on the sofa with that swirly feeling of mutual attraction. But then I moved to climb onto his lap and my hand found his rough arm, and it hit me like a cymbal crash: Paolo's bicep cold under my fingers; Sebastian's sinewy back as we dragged him uphill. They were *real*—nightmares incarnate, acts that, though justified, could land us in jail.

I'd stiffened without realizing it, and Aaron touched my shoulders. "You all right?"

"Sorry—guess I'm a little on edge."

"What's up?"

I twisted and dropped onto the couch next to him. I longed to tell him, to open up about what was really wrong . . . but I couldn't. "Just kinda in my own head. I swear it has nothing to do with you."

"Okay. You wanna talk about it?"

Then suddenly I was crying, tears spilling down my cheeks while another part of me broke off and watched in horror: *Get it together, Emily, before you scare off your new boyfriend.* "I'm sorry!" I blurted out. "I know I'm being weird."

"No, it's okay," he replied, but his eyes registered bewilderment, alarm. He didn't exactly deny it—I *was* being a weirdo. He stood and hurried away, and my heart plummeted. Well, that hadn't taken long.

"Here!" He reemerged with a box of tissues, and one made a zipping sound as I yanked it from the top. "C'mere. It's okay." He sat next to me and wrapped me in his arms. "What's going on?"

I'd kill to be able to tell him—I'd give anything to just let it out. Instead I reined in the tears and pulled away. "I'm so sorry. It's not you at all. I should . . . I should actually start heading home, though."

"Oh. Okay." He looked wounded. "Can I walk you to your car?"

"No, thanks so much, but I'm fine."

But as soon as I got outside and turned the corner, I regretted my decision. The block was empty now, blackness pooling between the sallow streetlights. I was wearing leather boots with stacked heels, which produced a steady clop-clop-clop against the sidewalk. I tromped down the street under a thicket of tree branches, their buds protruding like goosebumps, and made my footfalls as quiet as possible. Literally tiptoeing around, trying to get home unnoticed. Something moved behind me and I gasped, but it was just a shadow in the beam of the nearest streetlight, a woman crossing the road fifteen feet away. Finally I flung myself into my car and locked the door.

On the drive home, winding through deserted city roads, I thought again of my footsteps, the cursed clomp of my boot. The giveaway that kept me from skulking through the night, unbothered. The irony: I'd been thrilled when Aaron noticed me, and when, tonight, he called me his girlfriend. But on the street, I tried to creep past any other male gazes, ghostlike. That's womanhood, I suppose, both craving and feeling repulsed by attention.

And not just from men. Take my parents—I skimmed past them like floaters in their vision, a refraction of light in the retina. It wasn't until college that I began to see their disinterest for what it was: emotional neglect. And yet a dude on the street moaning, "Mm, good *morning*," as I passed could curdle my stomach, sour my mood. Which was worse, being invisible or being seen? It was exhausting:

the ego, the desire to be noticed—even admired—always dilating and contracting, flapping open and crumpling closed, over and over and over.

What did I look like to Sebastian when he backed me against the wall, pinned me in place? I pulled into my driveway right as the awful highlight reel looped: a crash of fury and adrenaline as Sebastian's flesh yielded beneath my teeth; Kristen with the floor lamp; *Stop. Stop. Stop.*

The sudden give when his body left our arms and tumbled toward the blue-gray water below.

God, I was broken. Tears pricked my eyes one more time as I climbed toward my front door.

Poor Aaron.

He had no idea what he'd signed on for.

CHAPTER 13

"I feel like I shouldn't be here."

Adrienne Oderdonk, LMFT, was in her late fifties or so, with curly gray hair and kind brown eyes. A nondescript therapist in a nondescript building with pediatricians and realtors and dentists dotting the directory near the front door. She smiled serenely. "And why's that?"

"I guess I . . . got the message that therapy is for the weak." I'd grown up with negative knee-jerk reactions to it, in fact. When, fifteen years ago, a cousin had switched careers to get her PsyD, my dad had sneered at the concept over breakfast.

"Shrinks are charlatans," he'd said, as if deeming water wet. He shook open his newspaper and turned the page. "Charging two hundred bucks an hour to listen to suckers talk about their *feelings*. But hey, more power to her."

"Do *you* think it's for the weak?" Adrienne asked.

"Well, I'm here because I think I should be stronger, so I guess that confirms it." My laugh was like a bark.

"Let's try to keep 'should' out of the conversation."

"Right." I took in the spiral-bound notebook on the side table next to her, the clock ticking down our fifty minutes together. The box of tissues on the coffee table, anticipating snot and tears.

Priya had recommended Adrienne, and I'd skulked into her waiting room like a kid sent to the principal's office. I felt weird about going to a therapist after Kristen warned against it last year, but I wasn't sure I had a choice: I was almost thirty, in my first grown-up relationship, and on the brink of screwing everything up.

"When you say you want to be stronger, what do you mean?" she asked.

I looked away. *Strong enough to stuff my panic into a box. Strong enough to get through the day—an hour, even—without a slap of fear that Paolo will be found. Strong enough to hear a ringing phone and not freeze up assuming it's the Chilean police.* I'd looked into it after Cambodia—though there was no guarantee the U.S. would extradite me, if I was charged I'd have my face in the news, my passport flagged. My life ruined.

"Uh . . . more in control of my emotions, I guess. Like . . . like other people are." By *other people,* of course, I meant Kristen. What was I doing here? I couldn't tell her the truth: that it seemed likely, even inevitable, that we'd be caught. Kristen had been the mastermind last year, and of course her plan worked—we got away with it. But in Chile, I'd been in charge, and I was shaky and shortsighted, my confidence feigned. Any day now, they'd triangulate Paolo's last known whereabouts, his very visible night out in Quiteria. What's the proper way to ask a therapist to assuage your realistic concerns?

Answer: Tell her about another realistic concern. "So, last year, I . . . I was attacked, during a hookup, and I had a rough time recovering."

"I'm so sorry that happened to you."

"Thanks. I—I was a mess at first, to be honest. I could barely get through the day. But my best friend, she lives in Australia, but even so, she was there for me every single day during that period. Piecing me together until I started to feel like myself again. But then . . ."

Adrienne was fixing me with the kindest, most intense listening face.

"Last week, *she* had a similar thing happen to her. While we were on vacation together. And now I want to be strong for her, but . . ."

"Wow, Emily. Seeing her go through that must be pretty triggering."

I bit my lip. With enough time and Kristen's support, I'd sealed off the horrific Sebastian incident with a satisfying *thump,* like closing the lid of a coffin or a book's heavy back cover. I'd gotten back to my life and doubled down on my friendship with Kristen. But to suddenly reconceive of that once-in-a-lifetime nightmare as not so one-time-only . . . now Sebastian was back in the corner of my vision, and the feel of his cool, dry skin was mingling in my mind with Paolo's hairy flesh.

Paolo—they might be unearthing him this very minute.

"Did you report the attack?"

"We didn't, no." A beat. "Neither one."

Adrienne nodded. "What's often hard for survivors is that there's no closure. The perpetrator gets off scot-free, and you're left knowing he's still out there."

Alarm bells, red flashing lights: Sebastian wasn't roaming the streets, unpunished—Paolo, neither. Could she tell I was holding back? Was she testing me? *Why the hell are you here, Emily?*

"What's going on? I see the wheels turning." Adrienne tapped her temple.

"I'm . . . really nervous, honestly," I said. "I'm not even sure how therapy is supposed to work." Lord, I was an idiot. I'd had some vague, half-baked idea that Adrienne could teach me to control my anxiety over being caught—some magical technique for containing the fear. And that sorcery would allow me to act normal around Aaron, to deserve his affection, to be likable—*lovable*. I'd smooth things over with Kristen, too, and from there on out it would be nothing but flowers and rainbows, a life as beautiful as a cruise-line commercial. But it was like Kristen had said: Therapy doesn't work like that. Now I was dancing around the real issues, wasting Adrienne's time and making myself look dodgy.

"Tell me about this friend—the one you want to show up for."

I ran Adrienne through the basics.

"What's interesting to me is that when people are experiencing trauma, they tend to go inward," she said. "They're not thinking selflessly because they're just trying to survive. And yet you want to work on being a better friend to Kristen. Why do you think that is?"

Crap—she could see right through me. "Well, Kristen's done so much for me. I feel like I should—I mean, I *want* to become less of a taker and more of a giver. I want to step up."

"Has Kristen said she wishes you were doing more?"

"Not exactly," I said. Kristen seemed . . . weirdly fine. Did she really not need me like I'd needed her? I'd sent her a certificate for a massage at a Sydney spa, then an Uber Eats gift card with a note about getting herself some comfort food, but her thank-yous were upbeat and a bit gobsmacked: *Aw, you didn't need to do this!*

"What's going on with the rest of your support system?" Adrienne asked. "Family, other friends? A partner?"

"I'm not close with my family," I admitted. "Just Kristen—she's like my sister. And I don't have a huge gaggle of friends; I'd rather have one ride-or-die than, y'know, a million acquaintances. But also, I just started seeing someone. It's . . . super new, but yeah. He's great." I hooked my ankle over my knee and blinked at the tiny lotus flower there. It felt like eons ago that Kristen and I had gotten these.

"Can you tell me about him?"

I relaxed, told her how we'd met, how Aaron only put me on edge because he seemed too good to be true. How he was the first guy I'd really liked in five whole years, the first one I could see a future with. How different things felt with him, but how whenever we started to make out I froze up.

"Your face lights up when you talk about him," Adrienne observed. "Even when you're talking about putting walls up. It's nice to see."

I looked away, a closed-mouth smile tugging at my lips.

"You said he's the first guy in five years—who was the last one?"

"Oh, I don't think about him much." I waved my hand. "His name was Colin, we met on OKCupid. At first I thought things were going really well—we had great chemistry, he was totally my type, all that. But then, after a few months, shortly after he met my friends, I realized he was kind of . . . possessive, maybe. He and Kristen butted heads. And, you know. Love me, love my people."

Colin had flickered back into my consciousness a few months ago—a suggested friend on a new app I'd downloaded. While everyone else in my life had given me their vague, blanket approval of him at the time ("He seems great; glad to see you happy!"), Kristen had been the one to look closely and ask questions. One night she'd pointed out that his irritated response to my canceling plans "reeked of a personality disorder."

"And then no one for five years," Adrienne prompted.

"No one serious, no."

"And does . . ." Her eyes flicked to the notepad in her lap. "Does Aaron know you survived a sexual assault last year?"

"Oh, like I said, I wasn't . . . raped. He just—"

"It was sexual assault, Emily." She let it hang in the air for a second. "If it was unwanted sexual contact, that's sexual assault."

Tears sprang into my eyes again. "I guess. But to answer your question, no, he doesn't know about it. I don't talk about it."

Her eyebrows jolted. "Except with Kristen."

This is Joan. She's the best friend a girl could have.

"Of course," I said, right as the clock hit 7:50.

DRISHTI YOGA HAD always been my happy place, a point of refuge.

But now I wasn't sure.

It was a sunny, spacious spot with the scent of palo santo sugaring the air. In the front window, crystals and cacti had been artfully arranged, and I flicked my mat open on the studio's smooth wood. Priya appeared as I was carrying a tower of blankets and blocks over from the wall, and the props tumbled to the floor as she gave me a one-armed hug.

Back in college, Kristen had introduced me to yoga—I had her to thank for that. I loved it: cued breaths so slow they stretched my lungs like weather balloons; the fierce concentration required for even the simplest asanas. After Cambodia, my yoga studio had been my church. I'd feel tears brim in the deep ache of Pigeon Pose or in Camel Pose's brave unfurling, and in that moment I'd believe that maybe, maybe I could someday let it all go.

Could I really start the entire healing process . . . again?

Priya whipped off her sweatshirt to reveal a swath of rippling abs. "I invited my friend Tim, from Gethsemane," she said, straightening her mat next to mine. She meant the church, not the garden. "Hope that's okay."

"Of course! Have I met him?" Priya attended a huge Episcopal church in Bay View, and all the Gethsemane folks I'd met at her parties seemed fun and artsy.

"I don't think so. You'll like him." Priya was always inviting folks to things, mixing groups, happiest in a thrumming cocoon of other people. She strode to the front window to take a picture of the plant-and-rock vignette. I envied her effortless Instagram aesthetic, still lifes she elevated into art.

It had been a week since the incident in Chile, and it crept into my mind as I moved and flowed, my quads quivering. I imagined my fear of someone finding Paolo trickling out in my Ujjayi breath, my salty sweat. As my hamstrings finally, *finally* gave up their week of soreness in Staff Pose, I pictured Aaron sitting across from me, the two awful incidents hanging between us like a hologram. In Bow Pose, balancing on my belly, I felt something deep inside my abdomen tightening, taking form like a heat pack snapped into a solid. When we eased onto the floor and the class moved on, I lay still, waiting for my eyes to blink dry.

After Savasana, as we sat cross-legged, the instructor went off on a woo-woo tangent: *You are divine consciousness that has chosen to become human, because consciousness needs form to evolve and explore.* I cracked my eyes open and Priya and I exchanged a smile.

On the sidewalk after class, Priya said goodbye to Tim and then checked her phone. Her face lit up. "This is your friend, right?" She held up her screen and I squinted at the comments below her picture of Drishti's window display. Kristen was an Instagram lurker, following others but never posting photos of her own, so it took me a moment to recognize her handle. *So pretty—Emily was telling me about this place!*, it read.

Guilt surged through me. I hadn't contacted Kristen today—I'd been reaching out less, reasoning that she didn't seem to need me, that she always brushed me off when I asked if she was okay. Our phone calls felt awkward and strained as I struggled to discuss anything other than Sebastian and Paolo . . . or Aaron, since I figured she didn't want to hear me blathering on about my new relationship. Now, when something funny caught my attention, I sent it to Aaron, not Kristen. Which was shitty of me, right? Pulling away from her after she'd been there for me?

"That's her!" I managed, looking away from Priya's screen. *How weird.* The rock in my belly from class re-formed, sharper than ever.

BUT I DIDN'T hear from Kristen that night, either. A naggy part of me kept whipping myself—*bad Emily, you're avoiding your best friend*—but in the evening Aaron and I caught an indie horror movie at the Oriental, his arm slung around me in the cinema's red-velvet core. We spazzed out at the jump scares and he kissed my cheek when the credits rolled, and though we didn't spend the night together, during the date any thoughts of Kristen were a distant flicker.

It was the longest silent spell Kristen and I had ever had, and when I woke on Sunday—her Monday, on to the next work week—without a text, I felt a strange push-pull: relief plus guilt, respite plus shame. I pictured Kristen in her own bedroom on the bottom of the world, realizing—accepting—that I couldn't put her back together.

What's more, I began to think we really might get away with what we'd done. There'd been nary a mention of a missing backpacker in the news. My nightmare was five thousand miles away on a desolate slash of mountain, and the only person who knew about it was almost twice as far from me, and the wall I'd been building between us was growing firm. Aaron and I were in a relationship now and I was putting the past behind me. I still loved Kristen, and maybe someday she'd forgive me, but I couldn't count on it. Didn't deserve it.

Because my strongest feeling, the one hanging like a dome over all the others, was an intense desire not to speak with, reach out to, or even *think* of Kristen. It would be one thing if we could freaking *talk* about what we needed to talk about. But she'd barred the topic from our phone calls, citing security concerns, and anyway, she didn't seem to need me, she wasn't crumbling like snow the way I was after Phnom Penh. In fact, she was acting like it never happened. I thought dully that I should try harder, be a better friend, but I was like a person standing at the shore of Lake Michigan at the New Year's Day polar plunge. As much as I wanted to want it, I stayed rooted to the sand.

It was hard enough to keep up our friendship overseas; there was a seventeen-hour time difference, different schedules and seasons, lives of our own. Other friendships had ended—or at least taken a step back—over much, much less.

I brushed my teeth and pulled a comb through my hair. Acceptance was seeping into my lungs, little vapors. It had finally gotten through to Kristen that I wouldn't bow out of my life in Milwaukee to backpack with her. Aaron texted right then, and I let the fantasy unwind: Maybe this time next year I'd be planning a getaway with him. Or even a solo trip—if the yoga teacher was correct, wasn't it my *duty* as a human being with eyes and legs and a beat-beat-beating heart to experience things, to explore? All the hand-wringing about women *tempting fate* by going on adventures, how it was *our* responsibility to protect ourselves . . . wasn't it simply a way to keep women's lives small? To keep us cowering at home, controlled, contained? Perhaps I'd visit somewhere less exotic but just as incredible—a train voyage around central Europe, say, or a road trip to a national park out west.

I froze at the melodic chime of my front door. I glanced down the hallway at the light slanting in from the windows, and the doorbell rang again.

I slipped down the hall and pulled the door open a few inches, then went rigid. My ears crackled and shock whooshed through me. It was a blustery day and wind jolted between my front door and the world outside.

"Emily Donovan." Kristen took the door in her hand and opened it the rest of the way. She smiled wide. "Surprise."

CHAPTER 14

A dream—this had to be another dream, like the sunrise-on-Lake-Michigan one, defying the laws of physics, of linear time. Kristen was in Sydney this very minute, glaring at her annoying boss, buying autumnal vegetables, pulling sweaters from her closet for the impending winter. Her world was so unlike mine. She couldn't be on my front porch in Milwaukee, Wisconsin.

"I've missed you!" Her suitcase thumped to the concrete as she pulled me into a hug. I wrapped my arms around her too and was surprised to find her solid. The hug filled me with warmth and I squeezed our hearts together, breathed into her neck. *Kristen is here.*

"What are you . . . how are you here?" I said into her jacket.

She giggled. "How do you think? Sixteen-hour flight to L.A., four-hour flight to Chicago, bus to Milwaukee, Uber from the station." She let me go and grabbed her bag. "So, needless to say, I'm exhausted. You gonna let me in?"

I opened my mouth and then closed it, instead giving my head an incredulous shake. I held the door wide and she pushed past me.

"You should see your face right now! Picture a compilation video of the world's greatest surprise-party reactions. You're like a *GIF.*" She squeezed my shoulder as she passed.

"Kristen, are you okay? Are you having flashbacks or anything? I'm so glad to see your face." I gave her another hug, more urgently this time.

"Honestly, I'm doing great! Especially now that I'm reunited with my bestie." She paused in the entryway. "Was this gallery wall up last time I was here?"

I stared at her: *Does not compute.* Was I still asleep? The last time Kristen was in town was . . . two Christmases ago? "I guess you haven't seen it. Where are you staying?"

"I'll stay at my grandparents', don't worry." They lived in Brookfield, a suburb twenty minutes inland.

"Did you want to stay here?"

"Hmm, as tempting as your miniature sofa and leaky air mattress are . . ."

I followed her into the kitchen. "Well, let me know if you change your mind. I know your grandparents are . . . difficult."

"Thanks! Yeah, we'll see." She helped herself to a glass of water.

"How long will you be in town?" I smiled and tried again: "How long do I get with you?"

"I'll tell you the whole story once my brain turns on. Ugh, I'm so happy to be home. Spring is so nice here—after a *real* winter, not like Australia."

I gawped at her for a moment. "I can't believe it, Kristen! You're like a mirage." I wiped my palm across the air in front of me.

"I know." She giggled. "And you probably have a ton going on and I don't want you to clear your schedule for me or anything. I just really wanted to surprise you. There are so few genuine surprises in life these days, you know?"

I blinked at her. Was she serious? I considered two dead bodies quite surprising. The kind of shock that made me hope the rest of my days would unfold without my encountering the unexpected. Still, my chest gushed with how glad I was to see her.

"Real talk, Kristen. I was in a bad place after Cambodia last year. How are you doing?"

She gazed out the window. "I think I'm better at compartmentalizing than you. Since I went through some shit growing up."

I nodded. Her parents, dead in a house fire—orphaning her like Bruce Wayne. Pity and guilt mingled and rose through my throat. "God, I'm so happy to see you, Kristen. All I've wanted this last week is to have you here, to be able to talk about everything you went through."

"Aww, babe! Hey, do you have any coffee?"

"I can make some." I stood and yanked a spoon from a drawer. Our rhythm was all off, Kristen batting away my attempts at real talk like a ninja. I pitched a few scoops of coffee into the machine. "I can't believe you spent all that time on planes again just a week later. I'm not sure I ever want to travel again."

"Well, sixteen-hour flights are the norm for me these days."

I focused on clicking the carafe into place. My movements felt choreographed, like stage directions: *She clatters around, making coffee.* "You don't have to be okay, you know," I said. "What happened in Cambodia, it—it ripped me open, it left me confused and scared and raw. I couldn't . . . well, I don't have to tell you what a mess I was."

She watched me, nodding sympathetically. This was all wrong; she shouldn't have to comfort me. She was here, right in front of me—the exact thing I'd been wishing for since I got home. But I didn't feel better. With a pang, I wondered if the distance between Kristen and me had been a blessing: a long and narrow but viable path toward healing. Now I felt myself sliding the opposite way like someone dragged by the heels.

"But you got through it," she said. "And I will too. Especially now that we're together again." She smiled wide and then stifled a yawn.

"I'm glad you're doing well. But you must be exhausted." I glanced at the clock on the microwave—Aaron and I were meeting for brunch in less than an hour. "I can't wait to catch up, but I also don't want to keep you from sleeping."

We were good at this—navigating each other's bodily needs while in foreign lands, deprived of our usual routines. But she shook her head: "Seeing you is giving me a second wind. Are you up to anything right now?"

"Well, I actually have brunch plans. But we can hang out after?" So much brightness in my voice, sparkly and citrus.

"With who, Aaron?"

"Actually, yeah. I think things are going . . . really well." For once, I knew what I wanted: to end this awkward reunion, to smile and feel good with Aaron, and then to try again with Kristen later, when she'd caught up on sleep, when things between us weren't so . . . off. But then I made a stupid gamble, because I figured there was no way, no *way* she'd want to go out in public after a sixteen-hour flight and a four-hour flight and a bus ride and an Uber: "Want to join us for brunch?"

"I'm going to take a ninety-second shower," she replied, already rising from her seat, "and then I'm yours."

ON THE DRIVE to the restaurant, Kristen was relaxed and chatty, jabbering about the flight, her creepy Uber driver, how her grandparents had been weird about her impromptu visit since they were trying to turn her bedroom into a workout studio and had already shunted all her things to their cabin Up North. I tried to listen, but my mind raced: Sure, Kristen had always been energetic, eager to hang out, and quick to get over things, but . . . but wasn't this behavior bordering on sociopathic?

Or was it all an act and she was doing even worse than I'd let myself imagine? I should've felt *relieved* that she seemed so unperturbed, but instead I felt trapped. Her joviality baffled me—like we hadn't buried a body a week ago, like it was all in my head. I felt weak, broken in comparison. Why was she so goddamn cavalier?

"If you're tired, I'm still happy to take you to your grandparents'," I said. "We can get together after you've gotten some sleep."

"Ugh, no—I'm putting that reunion off as long as possible." She turned and grinned at me. "What, you trying to get rid of me?"

Well, yes. "God, no! Just wanted to give you an out. That's a *lot* of travel."

"Don't worry, I'm not too sleep-deprived to get a read on this new boyfriend of yours."

She's going to meet Aaron. What will she think of Aaron? The thought was so loud I almost zoomed through an intersection, slamming on the brakes when I registered Kristen chanting, "Red light, red light, red light!"

I'd texted Aaron while Kristen was in the shower, so when he spotted us from the restaurant's front window his face registered delight, not surprise. He waved and I forced a grin.

"Is that him?" Kristen clutched my arm and I flinched.

Surely she recognized him. Surely she'd found him on social media—she'd found Priya, after all. "Yep, that's the guy!" With every ounce of energy inside me, I managed to make my voice cheery.

There were handshakes and hugs, and when Aaron kissed me, heat plumed across my cheeks. A hostess led us to a spot inside a bay window. The café, a farm-to-table joint in a refurbished home, was noisy and bustling, diners speaking louder and louder to be heard over one another.

"So Emily didn't tell me why you're here!" Aaron scraped his seat toward the table. I leaned forward—I hadn't gotten an answer yet either.

"Yeah, so, I got made redundant. So now everything's up in the air. My former boss, the one here in Milwaukee from before I transferred—she's fighting hard for them to find me another role in the company, so who knows what'll happen. But for now, I had all these airline miles and I realized I wanted to be here. Near the people who matter to me." She beamed a radiant smile my way.

"Woof, I'm sorry," Aaron said.

"That's awful! Kristen, I'm so sorry." I felt my eyebrows stretching toward my hairline, eased them back down. "So you might be home for good?"

"I don't know yet. It all depends. I can't live in Australia without a work visa, obviously."

Wow. My insides did something complicated. On the one hand, this was exactly what I'd been hoping for: I could Have It All, the new relationship *and* the best friend I could confide in and cry with and hug as I worked through the horror of Chile. Someone to whom I could voice my fears of being caught—speaking without censorship and basking in her confidence, her care, the way she made me feel like my most badass self.

And yet—something was off. She'd only been here an hour, but I felt it, like we were broadcasting on different wavelengths.

But it was probably just her jet lag bumping up against my inse-curities. "I'm really sorry you got laid off." I reached out and grabbed her hand. "That sucks, even though you hated that job."

She shrugged. "Thanks. But you're right, I did hate it. Maybe this is the best possible outcome."

"When did it happen?" I asked. A child shrieked behind me. A pulse of paranoia: Did her boss find out what we did? Did some-thing give us away? "You were just talking about taking a sabbatical at work."

"I know! It *just* happened. So now that whole plan is up in the air." She turned to Aaron and said brightly, "Although I don't know why she'd even think about leaving you! Aaron, Emily only told me a tiny bit about you. You met at the coffee shop where you work, right?"

The waitress appeared, a red-cheeked teenager with her hair in a pretty French braid. She took our orders and sloshed coffee into our mugs—mismatched china on patterned saucers.

Aaron poured cream into his and two fat white dots splattered onto the table. He told Kristen the story, smiling and relaxed, and then she asked him what else kept him busy, and he good-naturedly told her about his freelance graphic-design projects, and I smiled and looked proud but internally I cringed. I felt foolish for keeping him secret for so long—how could I not see that would hurt him?

Kristen sat up straight. "So I'm sure Emily told you all about our trip to Chile."

My fingers jolted—just enough for the glass inside them to slip through and crash to the table. Rivulets of orange juice streamed toward the table's edges and dropped directly in Aaron's lap. The glass rolled away and shattered on the floor, a jangly crash. We jumped up and pressed our napkins on the puddle, and a waiter rushed over with a dishrag, and the entire restaurant turned to stare at us, silent, judging.

"So sorry," I murmured as we scraped our seats back up to the table.

"I was just talking about Chile," Kristen prompted. "I assume Emily told you about our adventures?"

Someone came by with a dustpan, and I apologized again as he crouched and swept.

Denial was one thing—denial was one way of dealing with trauma. But to actively bring it up?

"Oh yeah." Aaron's eyes flicked to me. "Seemed like you guys had a little too much fun. She was out cold for, like, five days after."

"I imagine she would be," Kristen said.

"Yeah, we did a lot of running around and hiking," I cut in, my voice high.

Kristen smirked. "Exactly. So much hiking. Have you been to South America?"

Aaron shook his head. "I'm a cold-weather kinda guy. I turn bright pink after two minutes in the heat."

Kristen chuckled. "We went through about ten gallons of sunscreen."

"Doesn't even help. I'm like . . . a shrimp. Pasty when they're raw, but toss 'em in a hot pan and suddenly they're the color of flamingos."

"Y'know, I've always liked cooking things that change color when they're done." She set her mug down with a clink. "It's like a magic trick. Like those purple beans that turn green when you cook them."

"What's wild is that shrimp turns pink to tell you it's done," he replied, "very handy. But chicken, right? It starts out pink . . . and turns white."

"Somebody get this man a nature show," Kristen cracked, and they locked eyes and laughed. My best friend and boyfriend hitting it off—this was supposed to be the dream. Instead I felt my insides tighten and crackle.

WHEN KRISTEN WENT to the bathroom, Aaron placed his hand on mine and stroked my knuckles.

"Can I ask you something?" he said.

"Of course."

"Did something . . . happen in Chile?"

The room fell silent and I felt a tunnel, hot and tender, starting at my throat and rushing downward, widening like a shotgun shell.

My voice a caw: "What makes you say that?"

"You seem so tense."

I stared at his smile, his thin lips in a kind *U,* and forced myself to breathe. My chest had tightened, as if my asthma were acting up. *In. Then out.* The dreamy yoga instructor from Pisco Elqui murmured in my mind: *Your smile powers your corazón.*

"It's totally nothing."

He shook his head. "You don't have to tell me if you don't want to. But I'm sure you guys'll figure it out. She clearly has a lot of love for you." He leaned in. "I'm sure it'll all be okay."

How lucky he was to be able to say that. To trust that nothing bad could ever happen. To never know the weight of a body in his arms, the way the flesh slid over the tendons and bones.

I played with the sticky maple-syrup container. "Kristen and I are fine," I said. "She's just—"

"Kristen, hey!" He cut me off as she reached the table.

"Hey there! Did they bring the bill?" She sat and lifted her Bloody Mary, a pint glass filled with viscous red liquid. She sipped until the straw gurgled and then plunked it on the table, and my stomach turned.

I couldn't help thinking it looked like Paolo's blood pooled on the hotel floor.

CHAPTER 15

"Sorry I, um, freaked out and spilled OJ all over everyone."
Kristen buckled her seatbelt. "Oh, it's fine. Most of it ended up on Aaron."

I backed out of the parking spot. "Right. But I guess I was . . . caught off guard? By your bringing up Chile."

Her eyebrows squeezed. "Why *wouldn't* I bring up Chile?"

I sputtered, unable to answer.

"You're talking like *I'm* the one acting weird. But *you're* being weird." She dug a water bottle from her bag and unscrewed the cap. "Hey, so Aaron is great. Not the kinda guy you normally go for. I'm surprised."

She hadn't eased up on this campaign, not for a second: Everything Is Fine, I'm as Upbeat as Ever. How was she so good at this?

"Yeah, he's kind of a hipster," I said. "But he's a great guy."

"I'm glad. Maybe different is a good thing. Since you seem to pick bad apples." She chugged some water as the assessment thudded into me. "I mean, no judgment. I do the same."

I glanced her way. She wasn't wrong: Ben the Abusive. Colin the Jealous. "Well, I know I can count on you to give me your honest appraisal."

"You know it!"

We paused at a red light and time stood still. "Hey, I don't want you to think I'm abandoning you or anything," I said carefully. "You'll always be way more important to me than any dude."

"Oh, I know that. Take a left at the next light. God, I hate coming here."

I hadn't driven to Nana and Bill's house in years, but my hands on the steering wheel remembered the way. Left at King of Kings, the big brick church and grade school with a marquee on the front lawn: MEN'S FELLOWSHIP & BIBLE STUDY 7 PM. Right onto Beaumont, a fat Dead End sign staked into the corner, and then straight through to the cul-de-sac bulging out of the road: Nana and Bill's elegant home on the left, a gaudy turreted mansion on the right, and a California-style ranch between them, its driveway flanked by stone-pineapple-topped pillars. The castle-like monstrosity on the right had been built over Kristen's childhood home—the one she shared with her parents before they were killed in a house fire. I'd always found it odd and a little sadistic that her grandparents stayed put: Living with them meant she was always two doors down from the site of that tragedy.

Nana and Bill's house was enormous, bigger than I'd remembered, with brownish brick and a peaked roof, windows gazing down at me like watchful eyes. Two massive maple trees framed the driveway and a row of bushes fringed the front door, and all of them had that about-to-burst spring look: crimson kernels clustered on the maples' boughs and lime-green puffs poking out from the bushes. Normally I loved spring, that period of rebirth, but against the tawny lawn and imposing house, the flora looked defenseless, preemie.

"Do you want me to help you carry your stuff in?"

"My grandparents are going to insist you come in and say hi. They're probably waiting by the door. Consider yourself warned."

"We're gonna go be social?" I raised my eyebrows. "Aren't you exhausted?"

"I'm hanging in there. C'mon."

We headed for the front door. Kristen had spent her teen years here, at a high-performing public high school that went to state for bougie sports: golf, tennis, soccer. Kristen had been on the poms squad, a postgrad discovery that delighted me to no end. (It was a dance team that used pom-poms, she informed me, and nothing like cheerleading.) In college we'd rolled our eyes at the girls who rushed sororities, eager to fit in. Picturing teenage Kristen high-kicking to Justin Timberlake was strange at best.

Kristen rang the doorbell, and for the umpteenth time that day, I steeled myself. Nana and Bill always put me on edge. Sure, they were friendly in that folksy, generic way. But I couldn't quite square my impressions of the nice, slightly snobby senior citizens I'd met with the remarks Kristen had made about them. How Bill had told her, smiling, that she'd never last in advertising. How he'd read her honors thesis ("Female Political Representation and Labor Force Participation in Thailand") and handed it back to her with nothing but a few passages underlined in the Limitations section, as if demonstrating his agreement with everything her dissertation *didn't* do. It was hard to imagine these publicly pleasant people acting so dismissive in private.

The door swung open and there they stood: Bill tall and round, Nana small and birdlike. They gave Kristen and me curt hugs.

"We picked out a bottle of Merlot," Nana announced, and I thanked her. Apparently we were doing some day drinking. "I'll grab us glasses."

Bill gestured me into a living room (family room? They looked identical and sat directly across from each other), and I sat. There was that awkward group exhale as we all smiled and looked at one another and wondered whose turn it was to speak. *Aren't you going to ask Kristen how her flights were? Aren't you excited to see your granddaughter for the first time in over a year?*

Bill broke the silence: "How was brunch?" I got the feeling he didn't really care.

"It was great!" I nodded eagerly. "We went to Evie's, near the casino? Solid French toast." I cleared my throat. "And how are you doing? It's been at least two years since I've seen you, right?"

"That long?" Bill made a puffing sound.

"We heard you had a nice time in Chile," Nana broke in, expertly clutching our topped-off glasses in a four-leaf clover pattern. "You girls are so brave, traveling around in a foreign country like that."

She leaned over to hand me one and I avoided her eyes, my heart suddenly racing. Would I ever be able to speak casually about our trip?

"Careful—Emily has butterfingers today!" Kristen called out. She winked, actually *winked*, and I felt myself blush.

Bill ignored her as he disentangled a drink from the others. "Yeah, we heard all about the little mountain towns you found in Chile. And all the—what's it called?"

"What?" Kristen asked, plucking a glass of her own. She looked unperturbed.

"The liquor you gals were drinking—pico?"

"Pisco!" I nodded. "Delicious stuff." I tried to catch Kristen's eye, but she was sipping her wine calmly.

"I get so nervous about you girls doing all that traveling on your own," Nana said. "I didn't even have a passport until I was in my forties—and I certainly wasn't going anywhere without Bill here."

"Yeah, we both caught the travel bug," I replied. Could they see it on my face, the panic, the blood I could swear was visible as it drummed against my temples? "But, um—what about you? What's new?"

"You didn't travel until your forties because you had Dad when you were twenty-one," Kristen said to Nana, ignoring me. "If Emily and I had eight-year-olds, I doubt we'd be cavorting around the Elqui Valley either."

"That's true, I was busy being a mother." Nana pursed her lips, as if she'd tasted something sour.

"Well, thank God we're busy visiting pisco distilleries instead of changing diapers." Kristen raised her glass high and I cringed again— why couldn't she set aside her resentment long enough to move the subject away from Chile, where we'd left a body in the ground?

"Nana and Bill, have you been traveling—enjoying your retire-ment?" I glanced from one to the other.

"Oh, they haven't gotten rid of me yet." Bill shrugged a shoulder. "How would they run Czarnecki Chemists without the Czarnecki?"

"You haven't retired!" I brightened, glad for the new topic. "I thought Kristen mentioned a retirement party at some point." Czar-necki Chemists was a local chain of pharmacies—doing well, im-probably, in a sea of Walgreens.

"Right, 'cause he said he'd quit the minute he turned seventy-five," Kristen said. "But apparently, quote, 'retirement is for the lazy.' "

"The man broke out in a cold sweat anytime anyone used the R-word," Nana added, her voice light. "I think he keeps working so that he doesn't have to be home with me." She grinned and jutted her skinny elbow toward him. This dynamic I knew from my own par-ents, before they'd finally split: self-deprecating humor, *Oh, isn't it funny how we can't stand each other.*

"Well, dear, somebody's gotta support your penchant for wine-tasting," he volleyed back.

But she just chuckled. "Oh, I've been retired since the day Kristen finished college. I have no trouble filling my days. But we're boring—tell us, Emily, what's keeping you busy?"

I set my glass on the coffee table, next to a thick black book that I suddenly realized was a Bible. King of Kings, where Kristen had gone to school, leaned fundamentalist, conservative Protestant; her dad had been super involved in the community—girls' basketball coach, deacon on Sundays. She'd switched schools after her parents had died, but Nana and Bill had continued to attend weekly services there.

"Oh, you know. Work is good—I'm at Kibble, it's a start-up? That makes fancy, organic cat food?" Bill and Nana nodded blankly. "It's fun; I'm learning a lot about the start-up world."

"The problem with start-ups is that they're just trying to make enough of a name for themselves to get bought out." Bill shrugged. "There's no long-term planning."

I smiled and sipped my wine, but his comment burned. This was what Kristen was talking about: always right, always confident, with a touch of criticism prickling beneath his words.

Nana turned to me: "Are you seeing anyone special?"

"Yeah, we just had brunch with him." Kristen smirked.

"It's—it's really new." I closed off the topic and everyone looked around uncomfortably.

A drilling noise pierced the air, and Bill rolled his eyes. "The house next door, they've had workers tromping around the yard for months now. You know the one, with the stupid pineapples," he said to me, pointing. I felt the air shift; Kristen had gone very quiet, and Nana regarded Bill with something twitchy and furious in her eyes. I wanted to fold up, shrink down to a tiny rectangle like a tent.

"Now, remind me," Nana tried, "do you have siblings?"

Didn't they have any questions for Kristen, whom they'd raised—whom they hadn't seen in so long? I shook my head. "An only child, like Kristen."

"And your parents are still in . . . Minnesota, was it?"

"That's right. My mom is. My dad's in Iowa."

"So you don't have any family here!" Nana said it with something like horror.

"Nope! I'm doing my own thing in Wisconsin, I guess."

I liked it here; after eight years, Milwaukee felt like home. It had many of the things I'd loved about Evanston, the town around Northwestern—old, pretty homes and picturesque lighthouses, with just enough of its own offbeat identity to make it feel far from Minneapolis, and a better fit for me. Milwaukee had a dash of the backwoods and bizarre: kooky out-of-time dive bars and schmaltzy speakeasies tucked in among bone-white museums and broad, aggressively hip markets. And the lakefront—that beautiful lakefront. Every spring I vowed to spend more time there, reading or swimming or picnicking or flying kites with friends' children. And every year, summer sped by and the leaves began to blush before I'd thought to make the short drive to Bradford Beach.

AN HOUR LATER, I began the lengthy and time-honored process of expressing my thanks and attempting to leave. I followed Nana into the kitchen, clutching my empty glass and the untouched bowl of nuts she'd set out.

She whirled around. "I want to exchange numbers in case you

ever need anything." She handed me her phone, which felt naked and sharp without a case. "Email too. We should have done this a long time ago. I know you're all set up here, but since your parents are so far away." Her eyes flickered. "Just in case."

IN MY CAR, I sat still for a moment, my breath traveling in droplets onto the windows and dashboard. Even *my* parents gave me a cursory hello when I saw them in person; Kristen's grandparents barely seemed happy to see her. And vice versa—the dislike between them was palpable.

Also. The way that the mention of Chile didn't bother Kristen— her almost aggressive casualness, the laid-back lean and unhurried, unworried timbre of her voice set me on edge. She'd brought it up at brunch with Aaron, and she hadn't led the conversation away when Bill broached the subject. Meanwhile, I was so anxious about getting caught that even a mention of the trip made my fingers shake, my teeth chatter.

Chile. The image appeared as if projected onto the windshield: Paolo's legs on the floor, sneakers turned up toward the ceiling. Blood in a big jammy oval a few feet away.

Sebastian's head against the cheap metal leg of a bed frame in Cambodia. Blood speckling Kristen's feet.

Stop. Stop. Stop.

I started my car, cranked the radio. When it was loud enough to drown out my thoughts, I drove away.

CHAPTER 16

I lifted the heavy globe, stuck my fingers inside. Like jabbing my nails into the holes of a human skull. I took a few steps and let the bowling ball slip from my grasp. It hit the alley with a satisfying crack, then curved toward the edge, narrowly missing all ten pins.

"Gutter ball!" Aaron called, and I turned to give him an exaggerated shrug. He was reclining in the booth, legs crossed, an old-fashioned held high, and I felt a warm rush at his relaxed air, how comfortable he was no matter the setting.

"Take two," I replied as the machine spit my maroon ball back onto the rack. It clacked against Aaron's like they were marbles for giants. I lobbed it a second time and though it arced to the left, it managed to send eight pins tumbling.

"That's more like it!" Bowling had been Aaron's idea; I hadn't been since high school, and I had to admit there was something analog and satisfying about it, the clatters and whirs and Rube Goldberg–machine mechanics of it all. Hideous oxfords, strong drinks in flimsy cups, the familiar smell of floor wax and fried food and shoe disinfectant. I slid onto the plastic bench and Aaron squeezed my knee before standing.

I hadn't seen Kristen since our strange day-date on Sunday, but I'd relaxed a bit since then. She was just jetlagged, I decided, and off her game. She was still my best friend, the one who knew me better than anyone else in the world. We'd fall into our old, familiar groove soon.

What's more, slowly, incrementally, my fear of being connected to Paolo's murder was withering. I'd checked the stats the night before: In the United States, 40 percent of murders go unsolved. Some arithmetic, then: That meant that detectives threw up their hands at almost seven thousand murders a year—seven thousand cadavers with no origin story, no clarity around the instant they went from human to body. And *that* meant there were thousands, maybe millions in the aggregate, of people walking the Earth this very moment who'd gotten away with murder. And surely most felt guilt, shame, regret like a cold sprinkler that spread out inside them. But they didn't turn themselves in or hang themselves with a confession blazing nearby.

Perhaps they relished the new lease on life, vowed to try harder, do things better from that day forward. *Forward*. Because we're three-dimensional creatures, stuck on a one-way timeline and unable to redo the past. The conclusion gave me some comfort, which was perhaps a bit sick: I wasn't alone, and I had no choice, really, but to roll on forward, smooth and steady.

Watching Aaron swagger toward the lane and sweep the ball bang down the center, his red-and-blue shoe a millimeter from the oily wood, I marveled again at the two-facedness of it all. *Does this make me a sociopath?*

Aaron followed me home afterward, and whenever I saw him in the rearview mirror I felt a stirring in my hips. He was so uncomplicated and good, straightforward and kind. And he wanted me. After all the dating-app jerks who'd turn hot and cold like a miserable shower; after those wasted years with Ben, who dangled conditional love like a carrot outside my cage; after the months with Colin, whose ugly side seemed to blink on like a light; here was Aaron, happy to see me, eager to spend time with me.

In my apartment I gathered some glasses and a bottle of wine. I'd cleaned earlier in case he came over, but I'd left it just messy enough for it to look casual, like I hadn't tidied up. I connected my phone to the Bluetooth speaker and cued up something sultry, a husky female singer tickling sad piano chords. Then church bells in the background, a dissonant fade-out.

I leaned against the sofa's arm and arced my knees over Aaron's lap. He stroked my calf.

"Can I ask you something?"

He took a sip of wine. "Of course."

"Were you raised religious?"

A flick of laughter. "Yeah, Methodist, but my parents never seemed serious about it."

I nodded, thinking. "And are you glad you had that?"

He cocked an eyebrow. "You asking if I want to raise my kids with religion?"

"Oh God, no," I spat out. "It really did sound like that, didn't it? I was just—"

"It's cool, Emily, relax." He ran his fingers over my leg again, higher this time, along the jeans' inseam.

I hurried to explain: "I was thinking about it after seeing Kristen's grandparents the other day. They still go to the same church she went to as a kid. One time she told me her faith made it so much harder for her after her parents died, because her mom wasn't a Christian. So Kristen thought she went to hell."

"Jesus." He shook his head. "How'd they die?"

"In a fire. She was twelve. So sad."

"That is sad." He thought for a second. "Was it, like, a freak accident? What started the fire?"

"I don't know, what starts any house fire? Faulty wiring or something?"

"That's awful." He drained his glass. "Well, I dunno about the heaven-and-hell stuff. I never really cared about the Methodist moral code, but it was nice being part of a community."

A moral code. My earliest associations with goodness and justice hadn't come from a sacred text but from careful observation of what garnered approval . . . or at least didn't draw my parents' ire. Sex, too, lacked a pall of morality—starting with Ben, what to do, when, and with whom had all come down to what made sense to me, what felt right.

Screw Sebastian for trying to take that away from me; what I did with my body was my decision, all mine. I sat up and reached for Aaron's jaw, then pulled him gently toward me.

"Well, hello." His tone bordered on giddy, and I smiled against his lips.

I ruffled his hair, flicked my head toward the bedroom. "Just be gentle, okay?"

And he was, his lips and tongue and fingers soft, and he paused to stamp my neck with kisses and ask, again and again, "Is this okay?" Every time I felt the faraway panic begin to flare, I watched his face, the uncomplicated kindness there, and breathed until it subsided. Breathed louder, harder, both of our breaths rhythmic and sultry, until all that existed was the feeling, deep and tender and raw.

After a freeze-frame of stillness, he slid his hand across the sweat on my back.

"That was amazing," he murmured, and gave my ass a cheerful slap. He padded into the hallway, and I listened to the minor melody trickling out of the living room.

I slipped into a kimono and sat on the edge of the bed. I felt sexy and wild, and I congratulated my body on finally cooperating post-Cambodia. I smoothed my tangled hair and turned on a lamp, then headed for the bathroom as soon as I heard him come out. As I neared, the music abruptly dropped out, replaced by the handbell-like chime that signaled a new text.

I'd dropped my phone on the coffee table earlier, and now I flipped it over. I scanned the screen twice, my stomach scrunching and crumpling like a sheet of tinfoil.

Two missed calls from Kristen, ten and fourteen minutes ago, when Aaron and I were in bed.

And just now, a text: "I need you."

CHAPTER 17

"Everything okay?" Aaron paused in the kitchen's doorway, brow wrinkled.

I looked up. My brain skittered ahead: *I should call her. Wait, no.* She'd purposely said nothing. That meant it was about Cambodia or Chile—definitely not something I could discuss in front of Aaron.

Or, hell, on the phone at all.

"What is it?" He crossed to me and I dropped the phone to my side.

"It's Kristen," I said. "She's— I'm so sorry to do this, but I have to go see her."

"Now?" He shook his head. "Is she okay?"

I ached to tell him, to open my mouth and let the truth spew like poison. *You were right about something happening in Chile. And in Cambodia, before that.*

My arms crossed over my belly. "Yeah, she's . . . going through something right now."

"Oh right, she just got laid off." I must've looked startled because he added, "Or something else? Sorry, I know it's none of my business."

"No, I'm sorry. To be all vague and to suddenly run out on you." I looked around. "You can stay, if you want? Dunno how long I'll be there."

"That's all right, I'll head home." Aaron lifted my chin and kissed me sweetly, his lips soft. "See you soon?"

A folding feeling in my chest, a desperate desire to blow Kristen off and sink back into his embrace. I pressed my eyes closed, steeled myself. "Of course."

I CALLED KRISTEN from a button on my steering wheel as soon as I got on the freeway, which I had all to myself at midnight on a school night. *I need you.* I flicked through the possibilities like a channel surfer: Something had happened with our Cambodian secret—maybe the body had been recovered, bloated and waterlogged, or someone had uncovered something in the hotel, some evidence we'd missed. Or—more likely—it had to do with Chile, the fresher cover-up, one that hadn't yet stood the test of time.

Or maybe it was so much simpler than that. Maybe she was finally freaking out the way I had after Cambodia, without upheaval at work and her last-minute trip to Wisconsin to distract her. Maybe it was all sinking in—the attack, the dawning horror of what she'd done to defend herself, and all those nightmarish hours afterward. *Aw, Kristen.* My love for her oozed from my heart like an egg's soft yolk.

"Hi!" She picked up right before it went to voicemail. She sounded . . . chipper.

"Kristen, hey. I'm on my way."

"You're what?"

"I'm coming over. I figured you . . . that isn't what you meant?" I switched to the right lane and slowed.

"Oh, I had a stupid fight with Bill at dinner and then I couldn't sleep and felt like talking. On the phone."

The baseball stadium sparkled on the left; I was still closer to home than to Brookfield. "Got it! I totally overreacted. I thought you meant . . . like, you *needed* me."

She laughed. "Girl, you know I always do!" A crunching sound. "Are you close? You can still come over! Sorry, I'm working my way through a bag of chips."

I slid onto the off-ramp, deflated and—though I knew it wasn't fair—irritated. "It's so late, I better not. But what happened with Bill?"

"He was giving me shit about getting laid off. Zero sympathy. As if he has any idea how these things work—he inherited his dad's company." More munching. "I know you understand what the job market's actually like for millennials."

"Totally. I'm sorry, Kristen. That sucks. He just doesn't get it." Ugh, if I'd known she didn't actually need me, I would've let Aaron spend the night—I wanted to text him, check if he'd consider heading back, but my phone wasn't in its normal spot in the console. "And it's keeping you awake? A job loss is . . . big. It merits grieving."

"I'm not, though. Grieving. Screw Lucas and that godforsaken job." She swallowed a mouthful of chips and her voice grew clearer. "It's just weird not knowing what the future will hold. I guess that's why I called you. You're my rock."

"I'm here for you," I replied, suddenly guilty that I was only half listening—that part of my mind was focused on catching Aaron before he turned his phone off and climbed into bed. At a red light, I hunched and groped around the footwell on the passenger side.

"And it was so nice to catch up in Chile," she went on, and I was so surprised my foot slipped off the brake. I whipped upright and flung my weight on the pedal. "All that uninterrupted conversation, you know? And, Em, I feel like we haven't talked that much since. No Kremily dates."

Kremily—I hadn't heard that one since before she moved away, the cheesy portmanteau we'd made up at Northwestern (our friendship was, we figured, easily as legendary as Kimye or Speidi).

"We definitely need some one-on-one time," I said. "I've been worried about you."

"Don't *worry* about me, just hang out with me!" There was a giggle in her tone. "Tomorrow?"

"Crap, I can't tomorrow." I had therapy, and felt another spear of guilt that I was hiding this from her. But . . . but we're all allowed to keep a few things private. "Friday?"

"Wait, what are we doing for your birthday on Thursday?"

"I'm . . . well, shoot. I made plans with Aaron before you were here. We're just staying in—I don't feel like doing anything huge this year."

"Got it." She sounded so sad, and a cringe went through me. I reminded myself that it was okay to have plans with my boyfriend. It was okay to not invite her too. But then her cheer rebounded: "'Nothing huge,' noted. Yes, ma'am."

"I'm serious, Kristen. I hate surprises."

"Then good thing you love me. Anyway, I'll let you go."

I bid her good night and, in a rush, tried Aaron: straight to voicemail.

At home, I got ready for bed with my brow knit, my mouth downturned, feeling I'd disappointed everyone. I almost laughed at my stupid reverie at the bowling alley—such hubris, thinking I could let my guard down.

Someday, I'd no longer lie in bed at night cataloging all the details, the reasons we'd be caught: witnesses at the leafy bar, the shallow grave, our footprints in the dark, the light of a window as we thrust shovels in a shed. Someday, those hours on the mountainside would take on an eerie, cinematic quality, like a horror movie I'd seen.

But definitely not today.

PRIYA PLUNKED A cup of coffee on my desk and I jumped.

"I could tell you needed it."

"Aw, thank you. That obvious?"

"Absolutely." The seat next to mine was empty and she dropped into it, spun lazily. "So what is it? Hangover? Insomnia? Your period?"

"D, none of the above." I finished an email and turned to her, my voice low. "I had a late night. Aaron came over."

A dramatic gasp. "It *was* D! Emily got some D!" She slid her foot beneath her and leaned forward. "How was it?"

I blushed, thinking of his lips on my hip bone, kisses as soft as butterflies. "It was good. Hot."

"Oh my God. I don't know how I'm going to look him in the eye at Mona anymore." She flashed her brows. "Good way to drum up business at the café. Keep you up all night so you're desperate for caffeine."

"You're ridiculous. And he didn't even stay the night."

Her eyes widened. "He just *left*? Like, wham, bam, thank you, ma'am?"

I shook my head. "My friend Kristen called, and I thought she wanted me to come over because she was freaking out, but by the time I figured out it was a false alarm, Aaron was . . ." I trailed off. Why was I telling her this? Priya didn't even know Kristen; she certainly didn't need to hear about Kristen's tizzy, real or imagined.

Mercifully a co-worker shambled over with C-suite gossip, something about Russell-the-wunderkind getting drunk and sloppy with a potential investor. I nodded as he spoke but couldn't listen. I felt like I was in a weird love triangle, with Aaron and Kristen each tugging on an arm.

I need you, she'd texted. Not *Please call me* or *Can we talk?* Or even *I miss you.*

As he spoke, my co-worker ran his palm over the back of his neck, past the nubby ponytail there, and I thought of Paolo again, his black ponytail matted in blood.

My stomach roiled. The thing about Kristen was . . .

I needed her too.

"ARE YOU EXCITED for your birthday?" Priya plopped into the seat across from me and tugged the lid off her salad. We were at a lunch spot that specialized in bowls—grain-, greens-, and noodle-based.

"I am!" I shook hot sauce onto my food. "It should be low-key. But I feel like my friend Kristen is plotting something." I tore the wrapper from my bamboo silverware. "I hate surprises."

"You *hate* surprises? Why?"

The question, ironically, caught me off guard. I took a bite and chewed thoughtfully. "I guess 'cause a surprise is, by definition, out of my control. I want to be able to trust that . . . that things and people aren't suddenly going to change." I shrugged. "I love travel and new experiences and finding new restaurants, things like that. But I'm not a go-with-the-flow kind of girl. Although I wish I was. More laid-back and . . . spontaneous or whatever." Everyone liked those kinds of women—women who were *down,* who were *game,* who were *cool.* They put everyone at ease and shushed the Nervous Nelly hissing, *Is this safe? Is this smart? Do we really want to be surprised?*

Maybe guys liked those women because they reaffirmed the men's worldview: *Nothing bad can happen to me.*

"What do you mean by not wanting people to change? 'Cause if you think about it . . ." She popped open her seltzer and shrugged. "Everyone's changing all the time. It's like, the only thing you *can* count on."

Was I talking about Kristen? Just last week, I was coming to terms with our friendship getting a downgrade—accepting that nine thousand miles and not one but two horrific experiences would nudge us apart. And then she'd shown up and my heart had swelled at the sight of her, tenderness and relief that she was here, that I could finally be real with the one person who knew what we'd been through. But that surprise had gone sideways too: Things between us still felt stilted.

"Maybe I'm more worried now that I have Aaron—like, things are good, so I have more to lose," I said. "I told you about Colin, this guy I dated a few years back: At first I thought he was sweet, but then my best friend pointed out that he was starting to act possessive. And then there's my high school and college boyfriend, Ben. I thought he was one way and he turned out to be . . . bad news." I unfolded a napkin. "It caught me off guard. So that's probably why I like to, you know. See down the road ahead of me."

"That's right. Weren't you going out with Ben for, like, a million years?"

"Ha—four. His family basically adopted me." I stabbed a piece of broccoli. "He and his parents and his little brother—they all genuinely enjoyed spending time together. It was mind-blowing."

Priya tapped her nails against the can of seltzer. "Unlike your parents?"

"Damn—you're starting to sound like Adrienne."

"Sorry! I love talking about people's families. It's fascinating."

"It's fine. I'm just not sure my parents are all that interesting."

"They're divorced, right?"

"Yep! They split when I was fifteen." Mom had been the one to tell me, calling me into the kitchen and barely looking up from the sizzling pan she was stirring on the stove. She'd finished the conversation with: "You need to be on your best behavior because Dad and I are going through a tough time right now."

"And now you're in your first committed relationship in forever." Priya pointed her fork at me. "And you have no model for a healthy relationship that lasts. God, children of divorce are such commitment-phobes. You know I'm one too, right?"

"Tell me about your folks. They're in Madison, right?" It felt nice, opening up to Priya about something other than personal gossip, our co-workers, the news. But her words had prodded open an old, deep trapdoor of insecurity. What if I wasn't capable of making things work—with Aaron, with Kristen, with anyone?

Luckily, I had therapy that night in which to dissect it.

"It sounds like this is a real source of anxiety for you." Adrienne seemed so calm and present, like she never left this chair, remaining rooted while clients wafted in and out.

I snorted. "It's kind of a cliché: My parents split, so now I'm scared of being in a serious romantic relationship."

"If you were to make a pie chart of all the things that make you anxious, how big of a chunk is this?"

My pulse sped and throbbed in my neck at the reminder. There was a huge stressor I was avoiding in therapy, by far the largest slice of the pie: Paolo's flesh rotting under a few inches of dirt. Bloodstains smeared across the floor and shower curtain. Potential witnesses at the bar, the hotel, the long road back in the dusky predawn.

But we're focusing on my relationships here.

"Well, it's a bigger chunk now that Aaron and I are officially together." I futzed with my necklace. "It's weird, part of me feels like getting close with Aaron means abandoning Kristen. Even though there's no reason I can't have a best friend and a boyfriend."

"Why does it feel like abandoning her?"

"She's . . . I told you, she's like a sister to me. She's all I've needed for so long."

"All you've needed," she repeated. "Do you see why that's a lot to put on any one person?"

"You think I'm too dependent on her?"

"I'm not making judgments about you. Or about Kristen." She leaned back. "But I want you to think about what a healthy support system looks like. One that's . . . diversified. The way you talk about Aaron, it sounds like he's a really positive person in your life."

I gave a fervent nod.

"That's great, that there's another person you can count on. And of course your new relationship is going to shake up your and Kristen's dynamic. It's normal and healthy for friendships to change, but there's often some pushback."

I pressed my lips together. "I think you're right." I could feel my face contorting, crumpling around the ugly fear: I'd be a bad girlfriend to Aaron and a bad friend to Kristen. I'd wind up sad and alone, with guilt bloodying my insides and nightmarish memories staining my days.

"I don't want to screw things up," I said. "I *hate* screwing up." *Jesus, of all people to be running around with two homicides in their past . . .*

"Would you call yourself a perfectionist?"

"Oh, one thousand percent. Even as a kid, I was such a goody two-shoes. All my report cards said, 'a pleasure to have in class.'"

"So not much of a rebel? Even as a teenager?"

I winced—today, I was still a model citizen, except for the two enormous stains on my record. "I got in trouble with my parents sometimes," I admitted. "Especially my dad. He could be . . . unpredictable."

As a child, I seemed to attract their attention only when I did something wrong, often without realizing it. One of my earliest memories was of singing "This Is the Song That Doesn't End" at the top of my lungs as I ran up and down the stairs, a three-year-old whirling dervish. I can still remember the bright, sharp confusion as my father stopped me in my tracks and spanked my tiny buttocks. The memory filled me with steamy shame, too tender-hot to tell Adrienne.

"And your mom?"

I scraped at my fingernails. "We got along okay. When they split up, I thought maybe she and I would become close. But over time I started to see how she . . . she wasn't really in my corner either. When I moved out, I kind of realized I didn't need them. Like, I was forming my own family. With people who actually cared about me. Like Kristen."

Closer than a sister, the only one who loved me unconditionally. Who'd risk her life for me, who'd sacrifice her own sleep and well-being to nurse me through my pain.

My insides contracted: I should've kept on driving west last night, I should've continued on to Brookfield just to give her a hug. How selfish of me, turning around to try to get Aaron back in my bed.

Adrienne set her pen down. "Do you believe you need to be perfect to deserve Kristen's friendship?"

Guilt streamed through me. "I mean, she's a pretty perfect friend. We're already . . . kinda mismatched with how good she is to me."

She pursed her brow. "I don't know Kristen, so I'm not saying this is going on." She flipped over her notebook. "But in some relationships, Person A seems like they're doing more work than Person B, but Person A *wants* it that way. They like being the caretaker, so it serves them to keep Person B in that needy role. Does that resonate for you?"

No way. The thought filled my belly with discomfort: Kristen keeping me down, finding pleasure in my helplessness. "I really don't think Kristen and I are like that," I said loudly. "We both want the other person to feel strong. And, like, there are times when I've had to prop her up too." Like those lonely hours in the Elqui Valley, the night when I'd champed up and taken charge as death hovered in the air around us.

"Okay." Another serene nod. "Perfectionism keeps coming up when you talk about your relationships. Do you agree?"

"Totally. It's so destructive. Kristen has pointed out how self-sabotaging my perfectionism can be."

She peered at me for a moment, then glanced at her notebook. "It's common among children of parents like yours. But it's dangerous, tying your worth to never making a mistake. Can we try a visualization exercise?"

I nodded, unease brewing in my chest.

"I want you to close your eyes and picture the worst thing you've ever done. A time you were anything but perfect. Really picture your past self going through the motions. Take a minute to . . ."

Her voice faded as the scene cued up around me: Sebastian yanking his hand away from my mouth, shock in his eyes as blood dripped from his palm where I'd bitten it. The relentlessness, the fury in Kristen's gaze as she took Sebastian down. *Stop. Stop. Stop.* Blood, so much blood, surging all over the floor, more than a single skull should hold, like his head was a jug of sloshing wine.

It's happening. My lungs were collapsing, deflating, balloons with the air leaking out. My heart beat wildly, my fingers clawed at my purse—lungs on fire, a single thought blaring like an emergency alert system: *AIR, AIR, AIR.*

I shoved my inhaler into my mouth and pressed hard. *Ahhh.* With the second dose, I noticed Adrienne had stood and was looming over me, her face twisted in concern.

"I'm fine," I told her, snapping the cap back onto the mouthpiece. But did either of us believe it?

CHAPTER 18

I woke up on my birthday with butterflies in my stomach—excitement, yes, but anxiety too. Not because I was thirty (still young, whatever) but because I had a feeling Kristen had planned something unexpected. The apprehension was like orange-red coals, threatening to ignite. What had she said about women's intuition? We see things men miss?

I flopped onto my side and unplugged my phone. A deluge of birthday greetings on Facebook; texts from both parents as well as some friends. A video from a high school pal, still up in Minneapolis—her twin toddlers shouting, "Happy buff-day, Emiry!"

Nothing from Aaron, oddly. Or Kristen. Yet.

I padded into the kitchen and started up the coffee maker. As it brewed, I turned on NPR: A Missouri man had thrown acid on a congregant outside a Sikh temple. Horrible. *A nut job,* my mom would say with a shake of her head. And, okay—not healthy, I'd give her that, not emotionally controlled nor self-actualized. But what if monsters walk among us and they *aren't* nut jobs? Sebastian was a seemingly normal guy who grew angry, so angry, he could have killed me. Anger isn't a mental illness. Maybe regular people do terrible things all the damn time.

The doorbell rang and I opened the door to a skinny guy in cargo shorts, holding a package out in front of him. The box had a moist, loamy smell and I spotted the branding on top: Burleigh Blooms.

I smiled as I carried it into the kitchen and hacked at the tape, then pulled out a bundle of white calla lilies, as smooth and crisp as luxe hotel linens. Had Aaron sent these? That'd make him the first boy to do so since Ben, back in high school, when he showed up at our six-month anniversary with a mammoth bouquet from the grocery store. I fished around for a card and pulled it from its navy envelope.

Surprises may not be your thing
But since you were not answering
My plea to make some birthday plans,
I took it into my own hands.
So finish breakfast and your joe,
Head to work, and off we go. —K

I had to hand it to her—though I hate surprises, I do enjoy a riddle. Kristen knew my brain so well, hers and mine were like the matching halves of a heart necklace. "Breakfast and joe"—that was the clue, a granular detail in a singsong prelude. I set my empty mug in the sink and flung open my cabinets, then my fridge, rifling around my dishes, inside the smooth bag of coffee grounds, under an egg carton's lid.

Nothing—and I had to get to the office. I leaned over the sink, the counter digging into the heels of my hands.

PRIYA IS WAITING

It was faintly visible in the bottom of my dirty mug, tiny block letters like something printed out. I plucked out a plasticky disc and ran it under the tap, and the words grew clearer: invisible ink. Nerves bristled up my spine. How had Kristen known I'd use this mug today? And, Jesus—my chest froze over—how did she get into my kitchen to plant this?

A soft *thwock* behind me made me whirl around so fast, the rug skidded beneath my feet. A single flower had rolled off the counter and landed on the tile. It lay there in its sculptural beauty like a white flag, a dead dove, a Calatrava memorial to the dead.

I rubbed my temples. It was going to be a long day.

. . .

RAIN SLAPPED THE windshield as I drove to work. No matter how many times I changed lanes, I was always caught in a big rig's wake, pounded by a torrential rooster comb. On the radio, a calm-sounding reporter announced that a man had been arrested in a sex trafficking case. Police found zip ties and duct tape in his car, she intoned, right as my tires began to hydroplane. I sailed ahead, my heart a sudden snare drumroll. The wheels found purchase and I lingered at a stop sign.

Zip ties and duct tape. Who would do that? What went through his head as he drove to work, supplies rolling around in the trunk?

I paused in the lobby, wet and wilted.

"Hi, Jeffrey," I called to the guy at the security desk. He had a rind of gray hair and hangdog eyes. "Really coming down out there."

But today, as with every day, he didn't reply. I plodded toward the elevator, a puddle unspooling on the floor behind me.

Up at my desk, Priya trotted over with a massive cupcake. "Happy birthday!" she cried, presenting it with both hands.

"Thank you! Is this my next clue?"

Her impish smile confirmed it.

"So it turns out I didn't even need to find the first one." I peeled back the wrapper. "And drink coffee mixed with mysterious invisible ink."

"Kristen told me to bring this right over. In case you didn't find the first clue." She pressed her palms together. "This is fun—I haven't done anything like this since my sorority days."

"Which was all of, like, two years ago." I pulled apart the cupcake's base and plucked something waxy from its center. A folded slip of parchment paper—Priya leaned over my shoulder to read it:

Already, she's Kibbling through her epic day!
Out on Rogers, Mona's assembling nutty lattes.
Will they get her order right
And make a beverage to delight?

"All right, so you're here at Kibble," Priya proclaimed, arms crossed, "and Café Mona is on Rogers Street, and that's where you always get a latte. Are you supposed to go there next? Ooh, thanks!" She took the cupcake half from my outstretched hand.

"Maybe? It seems a bit obvious. And I don't get *nutty* lattes—I get oat milk. Shut up." We giggled at my milk snobbery. I reread it. "The rhythm is weird too. With the first two lines."

Russell cruised into the office, thick blond hair bopping.

"I should probably at least turn on my computer," Priya said.

"Same. Hopefully this can wait." I tossed the slip of paper onto my desk.

"I want play-by-plays—this is the most exciting thing that's happened at work since a bad batch of spinach sickened cats aaaall over the Eastern Seaboard." She flourished her palm.

"Oh God. Let's hope my birthday does not end with cat diarrhea."

I answered some emails while polishing off the cupcake. When I picked up the scrap again, sugar zapping through my blood, I almost laughed aloud:

Already, she's Kibbling through her epic day!
Out on Rogers, Mona's assembling nutty lattes.

The first letters of the first words: A-S-K-T-H-E-D-O-O-R-M-A-N. I grabbed my building pass and headed for the elevator.

Jeffrey leveled a blank, rheumy stare at me instead of answering, then shuffled over to his desk and produced a small stuffed animal. It was a cat—black and white and a few inches tall. I thanked him and turned it over in my hands, looking for more. Kristen and I both liked cats, but we had no special associations with them. My job at Kibble—was that the clue?

Upstairs, the toy's shiny black eyes watched me as I worked. The scavenger hunt hovered over my shoulders: Kristen and I hadn't communicated in code like this since college. Was there a deeper implication here?

A text from Kristen: "Happy birthday, my beautiful friend! How's your day?"

I hesitated for a second, then wrote, "Thank you! I cannot believe you went to all this trouble, you puzzle-making genius!" I picked up the cat again.

This time, I noticed that what I'd taken to be a blue collar was actually a thin strip of fabric. I unwound it (like a noose, I thought, or a garrote) and spread it across my desk.

Oh hey, the Fourth exciting clue! // Soon you will get your proper due. // Yes, now the showboating must end // Before I over milk this trend. // You've shown a lotta logic here // The ending is now drawing near.

"Get your proper due," "showboating must end," "ending drawing near" . . . what did it say about my general emotional state that it all sounded ominous?

Priya popped by, her cheeks flush with excitement. She furrowed her brow at the blue snippet.

"I have no idea," she announced, leaning back. "Y'all are too fancy for me."

"It's weird that Fourth is capitalized, right? That's gotta mean something."

"It *is* weird, since otherwise there aren't really any typos. This too." She pinned the strip under her finger. "'Over milk'—that should be hyphenated."

"It's an odd phrase, 'over-milk this trend.' You don't really milk a trend." I stared for a second, feeling the pieces slide into place the way the pins align on a picked lock. I grabbed a Sharpie and scratched at the fabric:

Oh hey, the <u>Fourth</u> exciting clue! // Soon you will <u>get</u> your proper due. // Yes, now the show<u>boat</u>ing must end // Before I over <u>milk</u> this trend. // You've shown a <u>lotta</u> logic here // The ending is <u>now</u> drawing near.

I chuckled. "Get oat milk lotta—latte—now. The fourth word of every line."

Priya clapped her hands. "Go see your man!"

I made her promise to cover for me, then skidded out onto Rogers Street. The rain had stopped and the sun squinted between the clouds. I was almost to Café Mona's door when I remembered Aaron wouldn't be there—he mostly worked afternoons.

Well, crap. Did I have to find another clue inside the coffee shop? Inside, I paused and pictured Kristen hanging out here before planting the next riddle, inside my beautiful, impenetrable Café Mona—slung across the mismatched chairs and lumpy sofas, wrapping her fingers around their fat, chipped mugs. It felt incongruous, a mismatched collage.

Aaron *was* there, ensconced in a green armchair and buried in a book. A smile stretched across his face as I headed toward him.

"Well, if it isn't the birthday queen!" He stood to kiss me, then wrapped me in a hug. My shoulders eased and my heart rate slowed. "Having a good day?"

"Yep!" I sat. "I'm several clues deep into Kristen's scavenger hunt. Did she loop you into it?"

"Sure did!" He leaned forward. "What are the other clues?"

I pulled them out of my purse one by one; Aaron kept shaking his head, astonished. He'd been the one to plant the invisible-ink circle inside the mug and slide it to the front, I learned. Not Kristen.

"And come to think of it, this clue was foolproof too." I handed him the blue strip. "If I didn't catch the doorman bit and took the cupcake one literally, I'd still end up here. Kristen thought of everything."

"What, does she think you're not as smart as her?" The joke hung in the air for a moment. The scavenger hunt did feel a little like a tacit declaration: *Nobody knows your brain like I do.* But no, it was a labor of love, nothing more. Not a reminder that she would always outwit me, always have the upper hand.

Aaron held out a small, neatly wrapped rectangle. "For you!"

"This is so sweet! I thought dinner was the gift." Aaron had offered to cook for me that evening—candlelight, cloth napkins, the whole nine yards.

A shadow flashed across his eyes, and then he shrugged. "I couldn't wait!"

A white box, creamy and smooth. I lifted the lid, then peeled back a fold of gossamery paper.

The room fell silent. All I could hear was my heart beating in my ears.

Because what was inside was impossible. It had been stolen from my bag that awful night in Quiteria, Chile.

Inside the box was the green leather wallet.

CHAPTER 19

My fingers sprang open and the box clattered to the floor, tissue paper crinkling. I gasped and lunged for it; Aaron did the same, and our heads bonked near our knees.

"Sorry! I'm such a klutz." I set the box on my lap and held the wallet. On closer inspection, it wasn't exactly the same. The zipper was different, the card slots vertical instead of horizontal. Still: freakishly similar.

"It's so my style," I said, which was true, and forced a smile. "Thank you so much, Aaron."

"Kristen helped me pick it out!" he said. "She said you got pickpocketed in Chile. That sucks—you didn't tell me that."

A rush of cold, like a tap turned on in my chest. What else had she told him? "I was embarrassed—I left my purse open in a bar like a dummy. But this is so thoughtful and perfect. Thank you."

"I'm glad you like it!" I could tell he didn't totally believe me. I leaned in for a kiss.

"Did you look inside?"

"Oh God, are we not at the end yet?" I unzipped the wallet and nosed my fingers into each compartment. There it was: a crisp dollar bill with Kristen's tiny cursive across the front. I read it aloud:

Before we conclude this, I just have to ask:
Who handles the handler's masterful task?
Who debeards the barber and cooks for a cook?
Who buries a digger and steals from a crook?

Who makes up a barrister's ultimate will?
Now seek out the person who just fits the bill.

My breath caught in my throat and I was momentarily speech-less. Buried bodies. Stolen wallets. Wills for the dearly departed. Friends and families and next of kin spangled across South Africa and Spain, begging for clues to the young men's whereabouts.

But Aaron mistook my horror for puzzlement. "Sorry, can't help you—I can't even do a sudoku. An *easy* one."

I chewed on my lip. "It's kind of morbid, right? Burying and stealing and writing wills?" My heart thumped in my wrists and neck.

Aaron plucked the bill from my hand. "It's sorta like, 'Don't bullshit a bullshitter.' It asks who does *the thing* for whoever does it professionally." He pointed. "Cooking for a cook, making up a law-yer's will. Wouldn't that just be, like, another cook? And another lawyer?"

I felt it snap into place. "Let me see that again." Aaron watched, grinning in anticipation. "Oh right, duh. 'Who debeards the barber.' It's a famous logical paradox: If a barber . . . that's it, if a barber exclusively shaves every townsman who doesn't shave himself, who shaves the barber?"

He furrowed his brow. "Not the barber?"

"He can't, because he only shaves men who *don't* shave them-selves. So there's no solution—a paradox. It's a thought exercise. Kristen and I learned about it in this philosophy class we took. I forget what it's called."

But Aaron had his phone out. "Is it Russell's paradox?"

"That's it!" I met his high-five. And then the final realization clunked. "Oh my God. Russell. My boss, Russell. Do you think I'm supposed to talk to him?"

Aaron's shoulders shook with silent laughter. "Well, would Kris-ten have the balls to call him up? Tell him what to do?"

"She would." The box with its pretty green ghost inside slipped off my lap again, and I caught it before it hit the ground. "She absolutely would."

BACK AT MY desk, I hesitated. Aaron had procured a wallet and along with it, some intel on Chile, compliments of Kristen—the story of the pickpocket, something I'd kept from him. What would crop up in this conversation with my boss?

I lingered in the doorway of Russell's glass-fronted office, then gave the frame a timid knock. He started, then broke into a grin.

"Word on the street is it's your birthday!"

"The rumors are true."

"Well, happy birthday. Big plans?"

I shook my head. "Just dinner tonight. And . . . a friend of mine set up a cute treasure hunt for me."

"Kristen! She is one convincing lady. And a great friend, because she got you a day and a half off."

I was quiet for a moment. "Wait, what?"

"Your weekend starts now. Don't tell the others or everyone will be wanting the same treatment. But if you keep an eye on email tomorrow, we'll call it work from home." He winked, and I continued to gawp.

"So . . . I should go home?"

"I think Kristen has bigger plans than that. But yeah, get outta here. Enjoy your birthday." He waved and turned his attention back to his screen.

Bigger plans? Aaron was making me dinner tonight; I'd agreed to hang out with Kristen tomorrow, Friday. And things with Kristen were still so . . . strange, especially the way she zipped off like a dragonfly whenever I tried to talk to her, head-on, about Chile. Trepidation stirred, with white-hot guilt on its heels: *Kristen planned this big, intricate treasure hunt because she loves you. Whatever she's got in mind, it's probably awesome.*

I called her as I traversed the parking lot. "Dude! What on Earth did you say to Russell?"

She giggled. "I just reminded him what an asset you are to the company. Are you on your way home?"

"Leaving now."

"I'll be waiting for you!" she cried, then hung up.

A LEXUS SUV hunched on the curb in front of my apartment, and little blossoms from a dogwood tree powdered the windshield. Kristen climbed out as I stepped into the warm air.

"Happy birthdaaay!" She threw her arms around me.

"Thank youuuuu," I sang back. "I can't believe you got me out of work! What's the plan?" Was this it, the climax of her intricate plot?

"We're going Up North!" She opened her palms to the sky. "To Nana and Bill's lake house! This is gonna be so fun!"

It flashed before me: a broad cabin with floor-to-ceiling windows, set low on a spit of land jutting out into Lake Novak. The house was built from pines stacked like Lincoln Logs, with a vast, vaulted atrium and bedrooms in a ring on the second floor. I'd visited with Kristen a few times in college and shortly after, and had mostly forgotten about it since.

My mouth hung open. "We're going *now*?"

"Yep!" Kristen waved toward the Lexus. "Bill let me borrow his car. I know how much you love it there."

She was right, the whole area made my heart smile: winding country roads etched into thick forests, a jumble of lakes with just a few miles between them, like they were holes poked by a giant. Ancient evergreens stretching hundreds of feet toward the sky, maples and oaks filling in all the negative space.

But right now, my chest was compressing at the thought. A finch overhead stopped singing and swooped onto the hood of my car, and the fear crystallized: Was it really a good idea for us to leave town together? Lately, traveling as a duo had led to chaos—as if the two of us, untethered from our homes, were a beacon for cruelty.

And anyway, I had plans with Aaron tonight.

"I was actually supposed to—"

"Don't worry, I talked to Aaron. This weekend, I have you all to myself!"

"Oh! Was he . . . okay with that?"

Her face darkened for a second, like it was on a dimmer switch. My stomach twisted as I wondered what tone she'd taken with him, what she'd said in conversations I wasn't privy to. Sharing the pickpocket story, guiding him toward a look-alike wallet. Informing him that his plans were canceled, that I'd be *hers* on the night of my birthday. But then she grinned. "Of course. He is truly such a sweetheart." She gestured toward my front door. "Let's get you packed, yeah? Beat rush hour?"

I stared at her. Too long. I thought briefly of pushing back, of saying no, of suggesting we set out tomorrow, not today. But I knew I couldn't resist. Surprises were like mine shafts and I'd just stepped into one; the only path was downward into the chilly dark.

LAKE NOVAK WAS three hours north of Milwaukee—two on I-43 and then another on country roads, passing through tiny downtowns that were like knots on a string. Black Creek, Bonduel, Cecil, Mountain, each a sudden burst of supper clubs, hardware stores, and ugly bars, beer signs crowding the windows. We stopped for burgers and frozen custard ("Get the peanut-butter sundae—it's your birthday!") and watched billboards roll by as strip malls and fast-food joints turned to undulating fields of corn and soy and wheat. The journey tugged at my sense of déjà vu, and with a sickening punch I figured out why: We'd been just like this, Kristen in the driver's seat, the road unfurling out front as rows of crops ruffled beside us, when we made our way to Quiteria.

Having Kristen here in Wisconsin should be a dream, but I couldn't relax. Our togetherness felt like playing with fire, like flicking a lighter closer and closer to a cloud of gasoline. What if fate struck a third time? What if a handsy guy attacked her and we were disposing of a body once again? Much as I hated to admit it, I was glad she was staying with her grandparents and not with me. Grateful for the fifteen-plus-mile cushion.

I sent Aaron an apology for pushing back our plans, and he replied with a run of "Have fun!" texts—he was either fine with my ditching him or faking it well. At first it seemed odd that he'd given Kristen his blessing, but then I realized he didn't have much of a choice: Could the brand-new boyfriend really say no to the best friend since college? Kristen had turned on men for much less.

Like Colin. I hadn't felt as strongly about him as I did Aaron, but I'd liked him in that zippy, belly-butterflies way, and found myself mentally crocheting our coupledom into the future: spring picnics, summer weddings, hayrides and pumpkin patches, elegant holiday parties. I'd introduced him to Kristen, excitedly, and she'd seemed to like him too.

Until he and I had our first fight. It was over text, and while other friends to whom I'd sent the screenshots told me to give him the benefit of the doubt, Kristen had taken a very different stance: "Oh, *hell* no." Though her proclamations stung, I'd felt grateful for the lack of pussyfooting and soothed by her solidarity; after all, if the roles were reversed, she'd want me to give it to her straight. And so I'd ended things with Colin. Confident it was the right call, because she'd never steered me wrong. But now . . .

I opened my texts, tilting my screen away from Kristen in what I hoped was a nonchalant lean, and for the first time in years I pulled up my final exchange with Colin. My eyes widened as I reread it: Was that what it had always said? Colin had asked if we were still on for drinks, with some cute emojis, and I'd unthinkingly said I was too swamped with work. He'd replied with sad faces, some frustration that I hadn't given him more warning (*Why didn't I give him more warning?*), and I'd disappeared for ten minutes—I could picture it now, polling friends, crowdsourcing my next move, my heart thrumming like a hummingbird—and then I'd replied with a weirdly formal text: "Colin, your anger and lack of respect for my time are unacceptable. Please don't contact me again."

Now my cheeks flushed as I scanned his shocked, confused replies. I'd felt so confident sending that, using Kristen's suggested language almost verbatim. In hindsight, I'd sounded like . . . well, I hated the sexist term, but I'd sounded like a crazy bitch.

Abruptly, the rolling fields yielded to dense woods, so we were tunneling through the trees. I looked at Kristen and took a deep breath. *Relax, Emily.* Maybe I was still remembering wrong. Maybe there was more context, more telltale signs of possessiveness than the text transcript showed—it'd been five years, after all.

And hey, this was exactly what I'd wanted: uninterrupted time with Kristen, the chance to reconnect, to discuss all the things we'd shoved under the rug from Chile and Cambodia. Plotting a treasure hunt, involving my friends, planning a weekend away—it was all so kind, so selfless, so Kristen. So why did I feel so uncomfortable? The satellite radio cut out, dropping the pop song Kristen was singing along to. She lifted her phone from the console.

"Here—cell service is gonna go in and out, too, but I have a ton of music downloaded." She held it out. "DJ's choice."

I was perusing artists when a text came through, a flash of green and jolt of vibration, so that I couldn't help but read it. I stared at it in confusion and felt my pulse ticking in my hands and ribs. It was from someone Kristen had put in her phone as Cindy Broker:

Kristen: Congratulations, Grand Management Services has approved your application for 450 Parkland Lane #2. When would you like to come into the office to sign the lease?

450 Parkland Lane. I knew exactly where that was.
I passed the For Rent sign every day.
It was a block and a half from my apartment.

CHAPTER 20

"You just got a text," I said. "From your . . . broker?"

"Oh my God, what'd she say?"

I read it aloud, then looked over. Kristen was beaming as we whipped around a curve.

"I didn't want to tell you until it was final," she said, "but I'm officially moving back!"

"Whoa!" I stared out the windshield. On the side of the road, a cloud of flies furred a flattened raccoon. Eventually I shook my head. "So your old boss wasn't able to get you into another department?"

"Y'know, I realized I'm done with Sydney."

"Wow." I snatched my water bottle from a cup holder. "What are you gonna do for work?"

"Well, now she's trying to figure out a way to bring me back into the Milwaukee office!" Kristen flashed an openmouthed smile my way, like this was amazing!

"Wow," I said again. Sudden sunlight tore into the windows; the trees here were snapped in half, all jutting out the same way. They looked like broken bones.

"Tornado," Kristen said, following my gaze. "Last summer. Hundred-mile-an-hour winds."

"Jeez." I looked at her. I was happy, truly, but not in the uncomplicated way she was. I so desperately wanted to match her excitement level. I wanted to sit my emotions down and bully them into compliance. "I can't believe you're moving back!"

"I'm ready for a change. I did almost two years in Australia.

People don't understand how far it is from everything. Even Asia is, like, fifteen hours away."

"Damn." I nodded. "Well, that's great, then!"

"And wait till you see this place I found—it's so cute and so close to you!"

"Awesome!" Why were things so *weird* between us right now? What I wouldn't give to regain the feeling of closeness we'd had in Chile, pre-Paolo, the two of us together in a safe, warm womb. I wanted it the way I'd wanted to fall back in love with Ben all those years ago, before he hit me—when the biggest problem was that I felt nothing. Now, all I felt was a heavy, hovering anxiety.

Relax, Emily. With a little patience, we'd get through this rough patch and go back to being Kremily. She and Aaron would grow close, too, and my Milwaukee life would feel complete.

And this weekend in the woods? It would be good for us, a perfect place to start.

Kristen cleared her throat. "Hey, you ever gonna turn on some tunes?"

"Right, sorry." I chose an album, something appropriately upbeat and celebratory, and we wound through the forest without passing another soul. Maybe we really were the only people alive.

WE PARKED ON the broad, flat pad near the street, then clambered down a path carved between tall trees—fat firs and slim birches and ragged-barked popples. Pine needles crunched under our feet as we approached the front door. Behind us, the lake was magnificent: rippling and alive, reflecting the bloat of moss-green foliage directly across from us.

Kristen fumbled with the lock and then heaved open the front door. The smell hit me like an old song: pleasantly musty, sweet pine and funk. She began opening blinds, and as sunshine soaked the interior I took in the antler chandelier, the green-and-cream-striped sofa, the stack of logs and old *Bon Appétit* magazines piled by the stout woodstove. She insisted I take the largest bedroom, the one with a soaking tub in the en suite bathroom. She took her usual room down the hall.

"And watch out for rabbit poop," she called as I unzipped my bag. "In the closets and stuff. Apparently a family keeps getting in and making a mess. I wanna kill the little assholes—they ruined these gorgeous moccasins I gave Nana for Christmas."

"Aw. Bunny just wants a nice Airbnb," I murmured to myself.

We changed into bathing suits and dragged lawn chairs out to the boat dock (not to be confused with Grandpa's Pier, on the opposite end of the property). I followed waves with my eyes, watched them scatter around lily pads, get punctured by reeds. An azure bluet dragonfly, pretty as a piece of turquoise, landed on my knee and cocked its head. *This is going to be great,* I thought. *And having Kristen down the street will be wonderful.* I needed to stop girding my loins around her. Don't we elicit whatever we anticipate?

"This place is so healing," I said, glancing her way. "I feel like it's already helping me release some stuff. From Cambodia. And . . . Chile."

She was quiet, the only sound the waves slapping against the dock. Would she *fiinally* open up about it?

"You know what else is good for that?" she said. The lawn chair creaked as she rose from it. "Wine. Let's run to the grocery store before it gets too crowded."

She strode toward the cabin, shoulders loose, hips swaying. Like someone without a care in the world.

AT THE LAKEWOOD Supervalu, we zoomed around the aisles, joking as we piled things into the cart. We tossed supplies for s'mores atop a case of spiked seltzer, nestled bottles of wine among the fixings for burgers and brats. Kristen selected two T-bone steaks from the case: "A dinner fit for the birthday queen."

Back at the cabin, we chitchatted as we put the groceries away—mundane stuff, purposely avoiding anything about Chile or Cambodia this time. It felt so normal that for a second I forgot about the past, the rough-skinned men who'd attacked us, the lives we'd snuffed out, the people who were looking for them, for us. I felt a sudden, swooping ache for how our lives had been, the friendship we used to have. It felt like homesickness.

"Oh my God, what's wrong? Why are you crying?" Kristen dropped a loaf of bread and rushed over to me.

"I've been so worried. About you, about being caught . . . about everything." My voice teetered and I swiped at my cheeks.

"Aw, Emily, it's okay! We're not going to get caught."

I snuffled. "It's not just that."

She gazed at me, her eyes tender.

"I just . . . you've been acting so *normal*. Like this huge and terrible thing didn't happen. How are you so . . . fine?"

For a moment she stared at me, lips taut, pink emerging on her cheeks like a Polaroid developing. Then her nose quivered, catlike, and glassy tears dripped.

"Oh, Emily." She cupped her hands over her face and dropped into a kitchen chair.

Whoa. "Kristen, hey. You're not alone in this."

"Aren't I, though?" She pulled a napkin from the holder and blew her nose, a long, ducklike honk. "You don't even— I don't know what you want me to do. How I'm supposed to act. I can't go back in time and do things differently, Em. I can't make it all go away. And the way you look at me ever since then—the way you're looking at me *now*, like I'm a monster, like the sight of me makes you sick. It was an *accident*. I never meant for it to happen the way it did. I hate myself, Emily. I hate myself for putting us through that again, and you hate me too."

My stomach plummeted. I lunged around the table and wrapped her in my arms. "Kristen, listen to me: I don't hate you. I don't. I wasn't . . . I'm not calling you a monster, I'm not saying it's all your fault." I rested my cheek against the top of her head. Her hair smelled autumnal, like sunflowers and scalp.

"It's not fair." Her voice was so watery, I could barely make out the words. "When *you* were the one who was attacked, we did what we had to do, period. But now that it's *me*, suddenly you're . . ." She trailed off.

My guts twisted. "You're right. I'm so sorry. You're right." A tear rolled off my cheek. "But I wasn't fine after Cambodia either. And I'm not fine now. You've been so calm, like nothing happened. Like we didn't experience this majorly traumatic thing. I was starting to, I don't know, question my sanity or something. Like we were on totally different pages."

"Well, I'm not fine! Clearly." Her trunk shook with sobs. I could feel relief sweeping through me, prickly sweet, like Champagne.

So Kristen felt everything too. Kristen was also steeped in guilt and horror, scrabbling through the days just like me. Her calm confidence, that dismissive air—I saw now that it wasn't gaslighting; it was her being strong for me, because she felt responsible. How unfair would it have been for her to quiver and quake and confess to me that she thought we'd both be caught, when it had been *her* attacker, *her* hand around the wine-filled weapon? She had no choice but to reassure me. Suddenly the weight of how I'd been treating Kristen clobbered me. Kristen, an assault survivor, no less.

We cried together for a few seconds, then sat up and let the sobs turn to shy laughs.

"We're okay?" I asked.

She nodded and wiped her eyes. "We're okay."

"And, Kristen, thank you so much for making this trip happen. And the whole treasure hunt, obviously. I'm sure it took a lot of work on your part. It's magical being up here and I'm—I'm so glad to be here with you."

She smiled. "You're welcome. I'm glad we're here too."

I glanced beyond her. "Should we finish putting the food away?"

"We definitely should." Kristen giggled again, the sound wet and rickety, and as I headed for the fridge she fitted an album in the old record player, and as Fleetwood Mac lashed its way into the living room, Kristen danced over to me, and as we sang along with the chorus, crooning into the walls of our big pine box that we could still hear you saying you would never break the chain, something popped between us like a cork, and in its place rushed sweet relief.

LATER THAT NIGHT, our bellies full, we sat on Grandpa's Pier and watched the sun sink behind the tree line, painting the clouds orange and red in a final hysterical blaze. I was so relieved, I kept tearing up: Finally, *finally*, my psyche had stopped yanking away from Kristen, my oldest, purest friend. We sipped our beers as the water turned to oil, then became too dark to see. But I could hear what I could no longer view—waves percussing the dock's metal legs, the lonesome warble of a loon, bullfrogs like plucked strings on a bass guitar.

"Oh, I have something for you." Kristen's voice skimmed over the water, a puck on a rink.

"*More* surprises?"

"Just me being cheesy." She pulled an envelope from the pocket of her hoodie. I shined a flashlight on the card inside: a pretty, painted flower motif, HAPPY BIRTHDAY visible in the corner.

> *Dear Emily,*
>
> *HAPPY BIRTHDAY! It's hard to believe we've been friends for 10+ years. I can't imagine my life without you—in a way, I guess I owe those douchebags in our Stats 101 class a thank-you. I'm so proud of the smart, strong, independent woman you've become. And I count myself so lucky that, after 2 years apart, we'll finally live in the same city again!*
>
> *I've been thinking back to those late nights when we'd sneak out at 4 or 5 am and splash in the water and then watch the sunrise over Lake Michigan together. Remember that? When we'd feel like we were the only ones awake in the whole world. When we'd feel like not just Evanston but the entire world was ours. When we would dry right off— perfectly, boldly ourselves.*
>
> *XOXO,*
> *Kristen*

*PS If you ever forget how amazing you are, you know
who to call. Because I never, ever forget, and I'd be honored
to count the ways.*

PPS Last line of the day, promise! ☺

"Aw, Kristen!" I stood to wrap her in a hug. "This is super sweet.
It's been a great birthday."

"Even with the surprises?"

"If surprises get me to paradise, then sure."

Out on the water, a fish jumped, *bloop.* "I was thinking about
how it felt at Northwestern—like we were in our own little world,"
she said. "Figured it was time to bring back the riddles."

"Clever. And hey, I'm glad to enter my thirties with a reminder
that we're huge nerds."

We watched distant headlights curve around the far side of the
lake.

"I'm getting eaten alive by mosquitoes," I announced, and she
followed me inside.

I hadn't looked at my phone in hours, but when I did, it couldn't
find cell service. "Hey, Russell said I should be on email tomorrow,"
I said. "Do we have to drive somewhere for Wi-Fi?"

"No, we have a thingie now. A hotspot." She ducked into the
hallway, and I heard her fumbling through plastic. She returned and
tossed the gadget my way. "But we only get a limited number of gigs
a month. So you can't stream a movie or anything."

I waited for it to connect, then sifted through all the birthday
wishes. There was a peculiar note from Nana, sent only to me:

Dear Emily,
*How are you doing at the lake? I just wanted to make sure
you're comfortable. Kristen has been acting a bit strange lately.
Please don't hesitate to call me if you need anything.*

That was alarming enough, but then another email, one from
less than an hour ago, made my vision swim. A discordant hum

whooshed in my ears, shrill and wrong, like the sound of an orchestra tuning up.

It was also from Nana, and it was sent to Kristen and me.

"This is why I think you're so brave with all your travels," it read, followed by a URL. I tapped the link with a shaking finger.

It was a CNN article, Paolo's smiling face at the top. The headline: BACKPACKER'S REMAINS FOUND IN REMOTE CHILEAN VILLAGE.

CHAPTER 21

"Hey, did you want to make a campfire tonight?" Kristen called. She'd stuck her face into the freezer so her voice echoed. "We bought ice cream, but we could also do s'mores. I'm great at building fires. But we can wait until tomorrow."

When I didn't answer, she smacked the freezer door closed and whirled around. "Did you hear me? We should probably get more firewood, but—"

"Kristen." I dropped my phone on the table, *thunk*. "You need to see this."

"What is it?" Her nose wrinkled. "Did someone you used to hook up with send you a birthday text? I hate when dudes—"

"I'm serious. Check your email."

She squeezed her eyebrows, then snatched her phone off the kitchen counter. I watched her face as she read: expressionless.

"Well, shit."

I reread the email. "Do you think Nana knows?"

"Knows what? That we're stupid girls who travel to faraway places and are lucky to still be alive?" She rolled her eyes. "The obnoxious thing about Nana's performative *concern* is that she isn't actually worried about me—she'd be glad to say 'I told you so' if something happened. It's just another way for them to criticize me." She raised a naggy finger. "'Look at you making stupid decisions, and no surprise, I was right and the world is dangerous and you're not a functioning adult.' Typical." She flopped into the chair across from mine.

"Wait, that's not even my point. Paolo. Was freaking *found*. Doesn't that disturb you the tiniest bit?"

Kristen stared at me, stock-still, then cocked an eyebrow. "Let's turn our phones off."

"Kristen, for Christ's sake, no one is listening, we're in the middle of nowhere with crappy reception, and—"

"Phones *off*." She said it firmly, calmly, like I was a little kid having a meltdown. I slowed my breathing and knew she was right. Siri was always listening, always ready to pipe up and hook us into the grid.

"Not till after we read the article," I said.

"Fine."

The body of a 24-year-old Spanish-American backpacker who went missing after months of traveling around South America has been found, according to police. Paolo García was last seen in Puerto Natales, a city in Chilean Patagonia, on March 27.

On Wednesday, police confirmed to CNN that a body found by police in Arroyito, a remote area in Chile's mountainous Elqui Valley, was his.

On Thursday, Chilean National Police told CNN that they had completed an autopsy overseen by an American consular official. Police have not released information about the cause of death but confirmed they are treating the investigation as a homicide.

The García family is now working to bring Paolo's body back to the United States, police said.

"Right now we are grieving and desperate for answers," said Rodrigo García, Paolo's father and the owner of Castillo Development, a Los Angeles real estate development firm. "The police must figure out who did this and make him pay."

Paolo García was born in California but spent most of his life in Barcelona. He had dual citizenship in the United States and Spain.

García was regularly out of touch for weeks at a time during his travels, so it's unclear how long he was unaccounted-for before his family reported him missing. The man's personal effects, including his passport and wallet, were not with him, so local teams are investigating where in the area he may have stayed, according to Spain's Agencia EFE news agency.

On Wednesday, Paolo's sister Elena García said her brother wanted to live life to the fullest. Paolo had been saving up for the trip for years, and he was "very excited to see new countries and meet new people," Elena said.

The last time they spoke was on March 23, when Paolo messaged his sister to say how amazing his trip was.

"He wanted to explore the world, to live life without regrets," Elena said.

I looked up. Kristen was still reading, stone-faced.

Each revelation was like a bass drum, struck. *Boom:* Paolo was American. *Boom:* Paolo came from a wealthy family, one with the resources to not stop until they'd gotten justice. *Boom:* This news might grip the nation, handsome Paolo as the next photogenic Natalee Holloway. *Shit.*

And Paolo had a family. A sister. *Jesus.* Now they weren't shadowy stand-ins in my imagination; they had names, voices, lives. Suddenly all I wanted was to google the sister, learn everything I could about this poor sibling-less Elena, jam my thumb onto the bruise. Why isn't there a term for someone who's lost their brother or sister? There are orphans and widows and widowers. This seemed worse.

Finally Kristen stopped reading. She blew a breath out through pursed lips, then tapped her screen.

"What are you doing?" I asked.

"Replying to Nana. Then my phone goes off again. Yours too."

"Christ." I held down the right buttons, then tossed my dead phone onto the table like it disgusted me. "It's a lot, right?"

"It's not ideal."

"Not *ideal*?"

"Nothing about the autopsy. The cause of death or state of decomposition. And now they'll probably start asking around in all the touristy towns. I still think we're fine, since he hadn't even had time to check into a hotel, but—"

"He's *American,* Kristen. The freaking American consulate is involved."

"I know—I can't believe he didn't mention that."

"He had a *sister.*" I slapped at my phone. The guilt I'd been holding back breached the dam and gushed into my stomach. "He had a *family.* And they're grieving, Kristen. Because of us."

She looked bewildered. "Hitler had a mom too. That didn't make him less terrible."

"They found him! It took them less than two weeks! And his family's loaded! We're so screwed."

She looked right at me, holding eye contact even as my gaze flitted around the room. "Emily, it's fine."

"How is it fine?" I realized my breath was high in my chest, tight and quick. My throat felt like it was shrinking and I stood, rummaged in my purse, and closed my lips around my inhaler. Began the sweet countdown from ten to one.

"Are you okay? You want some water?"

"I'm not okay." I sat down roughly. "How are you so calm?"

"Because we were smart. Because we did everything right." She splatted her palm onto the table. "They found him in a town we were never seen in. *We* don't even know exactly where we were. And the body must have deteriorated—they don't know exactly when it happened. There's nothing tying us to it."

I wanted to believe her. But she hadn't been the one to spearhead this operation. And when *I* was the one in charge, something always went wrong. "How do you know we did everything right? You were freaking out the whole night!" I counted the loose ends on my fingers: "Someone could have seen our car, or seen us getting the shovels or putting them away—there was that light. Or someone remembers us from the bar. Or maybe we left something of his behind in the suite—it was dark, and we were hustling. We didn't even have proper cleaning supplies. Or, or what if the rental car had built-in GPS or satellite tracking or something, and they can track where we—"

"Emily." Her hazel eyes bored into me, so calm and earnest, greenish in the evening light. "Those things aren't true. We didn't leave anything in the suite. Nobody was tracking our car. And no one saw us doing anything. But even if they did, you're forgetting the most important reason I'm not worried."

My eyes felt like storm clouds—heavy drops threatened to fall. "And what's that?"

She lifted my phone and held the dark screen out to me at face level. I frowned at it, then shook my head, confused.

"No—look into it," she said. My focus shifted to the ebony mirror, streaked with oil and with a spidery crack webbing out of the left corner. Then my focus slipped one level deeper, and I saw the image, like a Magic Eye picture: myself, my own face, young and sweet-looking. We used to joke that while Kristen had Resting Bitch Face, I had Resting Happy Face—strangers always stopped me to ask for directions, and men on the street never told me to smile (instead finding other egress for their harassment). I understood: This was not the face of a murderer. I rolled my lips inward and leaned away.

"Now, we'll turn our phones back on and you'll check your work emails and that's the end of that. Okay?"

Her nonchalance unnerved me, and repulsion fluttered in my torso. But the urge to strain away from her felt different this time. Less primal, more cerebral.

I gazed at the antler chandelier, then nodded, because there was nothing more to say. But for once, her confidence wasn't reassuring. It felt obstinate, unearned.

And it couldn't drown out the loudest line from that article, the phrase already looping in my brain: *desperate for answers.*

Kristen, of all people, should know that desperate souls stop at nothing to get what they want.

CHAPTER 22

I woke early and blinked into the filtered light; birdsong wafted through the open windows and I closed my eyes again, savored it, knowing something bad was brewing, too, though I didn't remember what.

I couldn't hold it off for long, and my eyes snapped open at the frigid thought: Paolo's body, policemen like ants poring over the Elqui Valley. The land out there did look like anthills, come to think of it. Fox-colored and sandy. Perhaps to the right-sized giant, the Andes were little mounds teeming with two-legged insects.

Last night I'd briefly considered asking Kristen to take me home, but that wouldn't accomplish much; Kristen was the only one who could commiserate, and I'd rather be despondent here at the lake than in my darkened apartment. Now I tossed off the covers; there was nothing to do but go on with my day. I'd carry my coffee out to Grandpa's Pier. Bring some reading material, something to occupy me when thoughts of Paolo inevitably popped and frizzled in my mind.

As the coffee maker burbled, I perused the wooden bookshelf in the living room. An entire section was devoted to religious titles: devotional Bibles and books by millionaire televangelists and a dog-eared copy of *The Purpose Driven Life*. A bound workbook of daily devotions from King of Kings, the church where Nana and Bill were congregants, with a large crucifix on the cover. I thought back to my conversation with Aaron—how he'd liked the built-in community. My own brushes with organized religion had been minimal; when I went to the occasional youth-group outing at the local megachurch in high school, it was more out of yearning for new friends than interest in a higher power.

I'd liked most of what I'd picked up during those youth services, though—how Jesus hung out with sex workers and lepers, all his Zen-like kōans about turning the other cheek, giving a man the shirt off your back, not pointing out the speck of sawdust in someone's eye when there's a log in your own. He seemed like a cool guy, nonjudgmental. Very different from how Kristen described King of Kings Lutheran Church and School. What a name.

I found a Stephen King (ha) book in the back and stepped outside. Small ferns bowed along the shaded footpath, giving the site a Jurassic feel, out of time. I paused to dig a pebble out of my shoe and grabbed a tree trunk for support. It was a pine, its pretty skin cracked and valleyed like a pan of crinkle-top brownies, and so old the lowest boughs were a few feet over my head.

I spotted something on the bole of a tree a few feet deeper into the forest. Squirrels scattered as I picked my way over to it. Around hip height, there was a change in the trunk's texture:

KC

+

J̶R̶

At least, I *thought* it was a JR. A heart enclosed the carving and I sank my finger into it. It looked old and weather-beaten; I'd been to this cabin perhaps a half dozen times and I'd never noticed this before. Kristen Czarnecki . . . and a pair of letters viciously crossed out, hacked at with an ax or saw. A childhood crush? I made a mental note to ask about it and headed for the dock.

Johnboats dotted the lake, olive green and boxy. I reclined on a dew-slick folding chair and listened to the sounds of morning: wind rattling the reeds and lush boughs overhead, the splashy *kerplunk* of lures hitting the water, the sucking smacks of water lapping at the dock. A critter—a chipmunk, maybe, or a mouse—skittered through the brush behind me, and a fish jumped opposite a fisherman's line, ruffling the smooth reflection.

What a disconnect. The outside like visual Valium, my insides prickling with dread.

Stop. Stop. Stop.

I heard the slap of the screen door, and then the crunch of Kristen making her way down the path. She appeared, mug in hand.

"Morning!"

"Thanks for making coffee." She eased into the seat next to mine, careful not to spill her brimming cup. I studied her as she took a sip and gazed out at the water. So unbothered by last night's revelation, as if this were normal, learning that experts just excavated the body you buried. My stomach contorted. God, for one glorious, glimmering moment yesterday, I had convinced myself that Kristen and I were on the exact same page. Couldn't we time-travel back to that?

We watched the fishing boats for a while. Someone caught a pearly rainbow trout, and the shouts of the men in the skiff sounded as if they were mere feet away. Funny how lakes do that—warp the dimensions of everything around them.

"What is *that*?" Kristen stared at the air just above her shoulder, seemingly at nothing. Then I spotted it: a caterpillar, perhaps an inch long, squirming like a worm on a hook. Tufts of white fur sprang from a black body.

"It's a hickory . . . something. Pretty rare in the Midwest, I think. Hey!"

Before I could stop her, Kristen lifted a twig and sliced it through the air above the caterpillar, sending it tumbling to the dock.

"Why'd you do that?"

She looked genuinely confused. "It was stuck in a spider's web."

I groaned. "Kristen, it was trying to spin a cocoon. That was its own silk."

She leaned over and searched the deck for it, then shrugged. "It was probably going to turn into an ugly moth anyway."

I didn't tell her she was right.

. . .

Clouds rolled in, gray-blue and engorged, so we headed into town. Kristen parallel parked with confidence, then rooted around for an umbrella in the back seat. Through the rain-spattered windshield, I took in the businesses along the main street: a café, a pizza joint with beer signs glowing in the windows, an improbable barber-and-computer-repair-shop combo. Kristen led us up the front steps of a refurbished home, and the front door jangled as we stepped inside Second Chance Antiques.

Silvery light filtered in from the bay windows, spotlighting swirls of dust. I took a shallow sip of air; the dankness needled at my asthma, and my chest constricted like a corset yanked tight. Second Chance was a wonderland of junk: a labyrinth of tall shelves piled with old dishware and '80s Happy Meal toys and fusty board games. I lifted a dusty jade elephant and searched for a price sticker—Priya collected elephants.

"I remember coming here as a kid." Kristen poked a porcelain poodle, inspected the pink bows at its ears. "My mom always let me pick something out. She knew the owner, Greta, who's the *real* antique."

"I didn't hear you come in!" A tiny woman materialized between the shelves, her voice high and brittle. She shuffled toward us in white orthotic sneakers, her cloud of dyed black hair bobbing.

"Greta! It's me, Kristen Czarnecki!" Kristen opened her arms and Greta made two laborious blinks, as if her eye muscles were old and tired too. Then her eyebrows shot up and her mouth crinkled into a grin.

"Kristen! You look more like your mother every day." Greta buried her in a hug, so I couldn't see Kristen's reaction.

Greta spotted me and frowned. "Well, hello," she clucked suspiciously.

"This is my friend Emily!" Kristen presented me with both hands, like a game show host. "She's visiting from Milwaukee with me."

"You know who she looks like? What's-her-name." She stared hard at Kristen, as if she could figure it out via osmosis. "That friend of yours. The one who was always up here with you when you were little girls. Jamie."

"I can't believe you remember that! Jamie, that's right. She *does* kinda look like her." They both turned to me, appraising. I felt an uncomfortable ripple deep in my abdomen.

Greta screwed up her lips, thinking. "That girl, Jamie, I always thought—"

"How are things at the store?" Kristen's interruption wasn't as smooth as she hoped, and my antennae went up. Greta looked confused, then grabbed Kristen's hand. "Oh, y'know, fine. And you've been somewhere far away, right? Australia?"

"Yep, Australia! Greta, you are sharp as a *tack*."

"It's running the shop. Keeps me on my toes." She tapped the side of her head, then gazed at me. "I'm eighty-four years old. Can you believe that?"

I made a grand show of my surprise. To be honest, I would've guessed she was in her mid-eighties, but I admired her immodesty.

"I hope I'm half as badass as you when I'm eighty-four," Kristen offered.

"Language, Kristen." Greta creased her crinkly brow. "Well, how long are you girls in the North Woods?"

"Just through the weekend. Oh, but I'm moving back to Milwaukee!" Kristen pressed her hands together. "I found an apartment in the Fifth Ward."

"I'm not surprised. Wisconsin has a way of pulling folks back. People try to leave, but it never sticks." A phone began ringing in the back of the store, and it took Greta a moment to notice it. Finally she shuffled off and Kristen and I went back to browsing.

After a few minutes, Kristen announced she was going to the coffee shop next door, and I headed to the register to pay.

"You're enjoying your time with Kristen?" Greta asked as she wrapped the stone elephant in newspaper.

"Yes! It's so beautiful up here."

"You gave me a real start. When I saw you with Kristen? I thought you were her little friend Jamie, all grown-up." She smoothed a long piece of tape on top.

I smiled, unsure how to reply.

She leaned forward. "But of course, you couldn't be. That would take a miracle."

I chuckled uncomfortably, the way you laugh when a man in power makes an off-color joke. "What do you mean?"

She handed me the newsprint bundle, and with a spasm of fear, I thought of the melted clump of Paolo's belongings. Paper wrapped around our darkest secret. And the people in L.A. who'd give anything to uncover it.

"You know what happened to Jamie, God rest her soul."

My chest clenched up. No way. No *way* that, in addition to Sebastian and Paolo and Anne and Jerry Czarnecki, Kristen's childhood friend was . . .

I narrowed my eyes. "I'm sorry, what?"

She twisted her mouth into a sad smile. "If Jamie walked into my store, well." She shrugged. "That would mean I was seeing a ghost."

"So, who's my doppelgänger?" I kept my voice light as I set a pot in the sink and turned on the tap. Greta hadn't had any more details to share, just murmurs along the lines of "That poor, sweet girl." I couldn't believe Kristen hadn't mentioned a dead close friend. God, she must've been the unluckiest kid alive, tested like Job while the people closest to her dropped like flies . . .

"No, use the filtered water. And don't forget the beer."

"Beer?" I glanced at her.

"Eight years in Wisconsin and you still don't know how to cook a brat? Typical." She dug around in the fridge, then emerged with a brimming Brita and a can of MGD. "For cooking. The good stuff is for drinking."

"And here I was about to boil them in tap water like a Neanderthal." I refilled the saucepan carefully. "You didn't answer my question. The friend I look like?"

"Jamie. I can't believe Greta remembered her name. It's been over fifteen years." She passed me a Spotted Cow Ale. "You don't really look alike. Other than both having dark hair."

"And she used to come up here?"

"Mm-hmm. We were best friends when we were kids."

JR—the hacked-out initials in the carved heart. "You both went to that Presbyterian school?"

"Lutheran. Presbyterians are wild by comparison." She took a sip of beer. "We went to school together, yeah. But we knew each other our whole lives. Our parents were friends even before I was born; they lived in the house between us and Nana and Bill."

Aha, so Jamie grew up in the California-style house with the fat stone pineapples. But why was Kristen leaving out the biggest detail—the fact that Jamie was no longer alive? I kept pushing: "Are they still there?"

Her eyes darkened. "No, they moved away. Hey, did we remember to pick up lighter fluid?"

"We did, it's by the door." I gave her one more chance: "So what happened to Jamie?"

"Nothing good." Kristen crossed to the wood-burning stove and swung its metal door open. I waited for her to go on, even out of decorum, as the awkwardness jelled. At last she sent the door squealing shut. "We're low on firewood."

"You know what's weird? When I was checking out, Greta made it sound like Jamie had . . . died." The word splatted into the space between us, so indelicate.

Kristen was almost to the door, and she froze. "Yeah. When we were kids. There was . . . an accident." She tugged at the doorknob. "I'm gonna light the charcoal and chop up some wood for later. Watch the brats." She snatched up a hatchet and some lighter fluid on the way out and let the screen door bang behind her.

When I carried the sausages out after her, she was swinging an ax gracefully, muscles taut, brow furrowed in concentration. There was something catlike in the way she kept dismantling the hunks of wood, slicing and rearranging and going back for more.

CHAPTER 23

The red drop hovered and then sank, dispelling into soft swirls like clouds in coffee. No, like blood in water. Like the matted clumps softening and slinking away from Sebastian's skull in Tonle Kak River.

How did Jamie die? My mind kept returning to it, a kid's tongue slipping into the wet hole of a lost tooth. But Kristen had made it clear she didn't want to discuss it.

She gave the jigger another shake, then pushed the bottle of Campari aside. "People think you're supposed to shake negronis over ice, but they're wrong," she said. "You just stir it."

Kristen had taken up cocktail making in Sydney, a self-taught venture involving triple sec, homemade bitters, and not one but two kinds of vermouth. Fortunately, Nana and Bill kept a fully stocked bar in the cabin's finished basement. We'd already sampled her old-fashioneds and manhattans and were feeling a bit loose. She dropped in the orange peel and handed me my cocktail; our glasses kissed, and I took a sip.

"You're right—I love it." Herbaceous and rich, like drinking rubies.

"I still can't believe you've never had a negroni." She flopped onto the sectional sofa next to me. "I thought Milwaukee's, like, a world-class city."

"Well, Barker Tavern is still serving the prix fixe." A few bucks for a shot of Jameson, a can of PBR, and a loose cigarette tucked into the tab—a local staple.

"Got it. So there hasn't been much of a reason to branch out."

The cheery demeanor, jokes tossed off like fluff in the wind: Less than twenty-four hours after we'd read the article, Kristen seemed to be doubling down on her insistence that everything was fine, that life was normal, that we had nothing to do with all that. Denial as a coping mechanism: It wasn't how I'd handled my post-assault life, but at least I could understand it. Until yesterday, everything *was* fine—in the sense that no one was after us. But now? As Paolo's wealthy father vowed to bring his son's killer to justice?

Kristen slid her hands around the glass, leaving fingerprints in the dew. "It's so weird to be up here without Nana and Bill. I feel like we're teenagers sneaking illicit drinks in the basement."

She kept doing this, too, introducing topics of conversation so I wouldn't have time to bring up Paolo. But I knew distressing her wouldn't help matters, so I angled for more info on Jamie: "You got to bring friends up as a kid, right?"

"Yeah, in the summer. My room had a trundle bed, which we thought was the coolest thing."

"And you brought Jamie?" When she nodded: "It must have been nice having a friend here. I say that as a fellow only child."

"It was so fun! We'd make up elaborate water ballets in the lake. Like, standing on inner tubes and flopping off in unison. Then we'd get mad when the other messed up the choreography." A peal of laughter. "Or we'd take the canoe out. Me in the back, steering, of course. I'd get so bossy."

I smiled. "That tracks."

"We were like sisters." Kristen sighed. "I miss her."

"I'm surprised you haven't mentioned her before."

"Oh, I definitely have."

"To me? Nuh-uh—I'd remember."

"I for sure have. I remember telling you about my bestie and neighbor, like, multiple times over the years."

"No way." Had she? Had this mysterious Jamie simply slipped past my notice on earlier mentions? I'd always thought Kristen had had a lonely childhood, like me. It'd be one thing if they'd simply drifted apart, but . . . Lord, a dead best friend felt like something I'd know. "I saw some letters carved into a pine tree. Were those her initials, all hacked out?"

Kristen's voice frosted over: "Yeah, I did that a long time ago."

"How come?"

She peered down at her drink, at the red moon trapped in her tumbler. "Let's talk about something else. Like how glad I am to be out of Nana and Bill's house, oh my *God*. I can't wait to move in to my own apartment. The past is so in my face in Brookfield."

There was something there, something beyond grief about her friend, but I didn't want to poke too hard. "Yeah, everyone regresses when they go home," I said.

"Nana asked if I'd be back in time to go to church with them on Sunday. Like they're still trying to save my soul." She took another crimson gulp. "I think the only time they really liked me was when I was, like, ten years old and Christianity was my entire identity."

"You called yourself a Jesus freak, right?" I teased. We'd had those what-were-you-like-as-a-kid conversations, wondering in hushed awe what would've happened if we'd met just a few years earlier. I myself had embodied the nerd trifecta: marching band, chess club, debate team.

Something flickered in her eyes. "Oh yes. Proud Jesus freak right here."

"Speaking of, didn't you say all your childhood stuff is here in the cabin?"

"Yeah, good memory. They stuffed it in the unfinished part so they can turn my bedroom into a gym." She gestured toward a door breaking up the green-plaid wallpaper, then grinned. "What, you want to see pictures of me in cross necklaces at church fundraisers and everything?"

"Kind of!"

She chuckled, but I felt it, a shift in the air pressure. "Oh, I don't feel like digging back there."

"C'mon, I want photographic proof that you were on the poms team."

"No. I don't want to see that stuff." Her words were sharp and the moment froze up, all awkward.

"So, you were saying," I murmured. "Your grandparents still want you to go to church?"

"Totally. Praying the Holy Spirit will enter me yet. I'm kinda shocked they're still holding out hope—hell, I'm almost thirty—but I guess if you believe what that conservative synod teaches, the logic holds up." She shook her head, amazed anew. "When I went to school at King of Kings, in religion class I would pray—out loud, every single day, from kindergarten on—for my mom to become a Christian so she wouldn't go to hell. I was terrified, and I suppose that's how Nana and Bill feel about me now."

"God, you poor thing. Why would they send you to that school with only *one* Christian parent?"

"Right? I didn't realize how messed up it was until they were long dead."

Oof. I rubbed her shoulder and she sipped her Negroni self-consciously.

"And then when they died, I could see my devotion for what it was. For all the talk of Jesus being my shepherd—it was the first time I realized I was a sheep." She swallowed. "And it felt horrible. Like I'd been lied to every single day. But I guess it was ultimately freeing. Like: Now you have no power over me."

She always talked about her parents at the cabin; being Up North made her sentimental, Lake Novak's clear water a sluice for childhood memories. I knew her parents' deaths had brought her fanatical youth-group days to an abrupt end. But this conversation felt . . . different. "I'm—I'm sorry you had to go through that, Kristen. I really am."

She tilted her cocktail and the ice jingled. "Power is a funny thing. You know how they say that the opposite of love isn't *hate,* it's indifference? Like, we're looking at the scale all wrong." She tapped her nail against the glass. "I think it's the same thing with fear. The opposite of fear isn't safety. It's power."

I peered at her. I wasn't sure I agreed—I'd give anything right now for the assurance of safety when it came to our crimes. The promise that no one would arrest us, besmirch our good names, extradite us, or try us in the court of public opinion.

Well, and. Even if I *could* secure that kind of bubble wrap, it wouldn't protect me from a lifetime of fear. Fear of verbal abuse, of emotional blackmail, of careless misogyny designed to make me feel small. All the acts of casual violence I attracted, expected, thanks to my designated gender.

"Can I have a hug?" I asked, suddenly sad for us both. She set down her glass and pulled me into her. She stroked my hair, the way she had in Chile, when asthma attacked me like a rabid dog.

WE BUILT A campfire before bed, both of us lost in thought as the wood snapped and sputtered. I held my marshmallow over the glowing coals, rotating the stick until I'd achieved a uniform ochre. But Kristen plunged hers into the flame, turning it into a torch and then gazing at the tiny inferno so it was reflected in her eyes.

Years ago, we'd been right there, sitting around the campfire on Novak's verdant edge, when she first told me what had happened to her parents. It was the summer before junior year, a moment seared into my brain.

"My mom wasn't even supposed to be home," she'd said, her tears reflecting orange, like lava. "The night of the fire? It's so messed-up. She was supposed to be up in Door County with her girlfriends, and I was gonna go to a sleepover because I hated being alone with my dad." The injustice had brought tears to my eyes too. "But Dad wasn't feeling well, so she stayed home. Ugh, it makes me so *angry*."

I'd shuffled my camping chair closer to hers, then grabbed her hand. We'd been so young, still—twenty years old and newly close. "So you were home? That must've been so scary."

"It was terrifying. The smoke alarm woke me up and I tried to run into the hallway, but the doorknob burned my hand." She clutched her palm to her chest, as if she could still feel the white-hot pain. "I opened my bedroom window and climbed onto the huge maple tree there—I'd done it a million times before. And then I ran over to Nana and Bill's."

As she described the rest, it played in my mind like a scene from a horror film: Young Kristen screaming and jabbing at the doorbell until her grandparents finally woke and let her inside. Nana and Bill physically restraining her as the fire trucks arrived. She'd thrashed and hollered, begging to be let back into the blaze so she could find her parents in the choking blackness. But the fire had trapped them in their suite. They were burned alive, unsalvageable like the house that collapsed around them.

Now, seventeen years after the tragedy and almost a decade after Kristen shared the memory with me, she poured water on the camp-fire so it bubbled and hissed, and we bid each other good night.

Hours later, I stared at my bedroom's slanted pine ceiling, unable to sleep. Crickets scratched and rattled outside the window; a fat insect or possibly a bat thumped into the screen. I counted, then counted again. Like if I added it up enough times, I'd get a different answer.

Kristen's parents. Jamie, whose brief life Kristen had kept from me. Sebastian, then Paolo.

Five deaths in fewer than twenty years.

I'd thought we attracted violence when we got together, some-how pulling in the energy of chaos, of poor decisions and awful dudes. And I trusted Kristen, I knew her soul, knew she was loving and good. But it was the kind of thought you can have only in the woolly shame of the middle of the night: *God, that's a lot of death for someone so young.*

I thought back to Nana's email yesterday: *Kristen has been acting a bit strange lately.*

And Kristen's words in Chile: *We see things they miss.*

I yanked my phone from its charger and turned on its flashlight. I tiptoed past Kristen's room and eased myself down one creaking set of steps, then paused at the top of the basement stairs. Why are basements so creepy, even when they're refurbished? I flicked on the light, pulling the door closed behind me before the beam could scatter. Awake, alert, I stalked through the den and reached for the door to the unfinished section.

One, two, three, four, five. Five lifeless bodies, families grieving, psyches stopped too soon. I knew all about the last two—I knew they were self-defense, a case of wrong place (okay, wrong head-injury placement), wrong time. If I just knew more about numbers one through three, I could quiet this trickle of treason, of suspicion. Kristen and I were 100 percent counting on each other to keep our secrets safe. I needed to know what I was dealing with. *Whom* I was dealing with.

I pulled the knob and blinked into the darkness. *Okay, this part is legit scary.* I groped around for a light switch but caught nothing but shelving units to the right and left, cobwebs detaching to coat my fingers. I swept my phone's light across: work bench, rowing machine, table saw. And more utility shelves topped with bins and boxes. There—a bare bulb hung from a beam in the ceiling, ten feet away.

The cement floor was cold on my socked feet, and when I pulled the light's cord I saw movement, a scattering. I spotted a massive millipede disappearing beneath an old wooden chest and pressed my hand to my thrashing heart. Just bugs.

Where to begin? I rifled through the nearest shelves, tilting boxes to read their labels, tipping dust into my lungs. The furnace clanged on and a scream caught in my throat. After a few minutes I found the right boxes, newer than the others, in an alcove behind the boiler: KRISTEN BEDROOM.

I dragged the first box into the rec room and plopped onto the floor, then cringed at the loud hiss the tape made coming loose from cardboard. High school and college stuff, English papers and random playbills and concert stubs, a certificate awarded to the pom team's MVP. Too recent—by the time Kristen was in high school, her parents and best friend were already dead.

With the second box, I hit the jackpot—here was Kristen in her tween years, skinny-limbed and red-faced with a mouthful of braces. I pulled out a stack of thin King of Kings yearbooks. There were two sections for every grade, perhaps forty students per graduating class.

I flipped toward Kristen's grade, eager for answers. I was finally going to lay eyes on my double, the mysterious Jamie R.

But in the edition from the year Kristen's parents died, someone had scribbled out Jamie's face, angrily, infuriated black ink that ripped through the paper. Like someone full of rage had gone at it with a ballpoint pen. I turned to the group photos—choir, math club, the Christian Discipleship Award—and everywhere Jamie's face had been was now a snarl of black. What the hell?

I rummaged around in the box and pulled out a stack of photos, and the trend continued: smiles and pink cheeks and bright eyes and then the black gashes, scrawls wherever Jamie's head should be. What had this . . . Jamie Rusch done to piss young Kristen off? I grabbed my phone, knee-jerk, then remembered there was no service here without the hotspot on.

I couldn't find anything about Jamie's death, the mysterious "accident" Kristen had referenced. Nothing about Kristen's parents either. I sat back on my heels. *It could still be a fluke.* Maybe Kristen really did attract accidental death the way a brown banana draws fruit flies.

I took a few pictures of the photos and the yearbook—I'd google Jamie later and didn't want to forget her last name. As I was packing everything back into the boxes, I heard a groan above me, somewhere north of the drop ceiling. My pulse ticked up—time to go.

In the basement's ugly back, I slipped the boxes onto a rack and hurried over to the utility light. I gave the space a final glance, then went rigid: Something in the corner had moved, something alive in the darkness. I fumbled with my phone and beamed the light that way, and two shiny eyes stared back.

A tiny mouse, rigid with fright. I didn't notice my surge of frosty fear until I was already laughing.

. . .

IN THE MORNING, I asked Kristen to turn the hotspot on, but she waved me away. "It's Saturday," she pointed out. "We can be off the grid."

"Don't you think we should check if there are . . . any developments? In Chile?"

She carried her coffee mug to the sink. "I'm not worried. Hey, I'm gonna go for a run."

After she left, I ransacked the closet where the hotspot had been the first night, but it wasn't there. I dug through drawers and cabinets, peeked at the floor near all the power outlets. I groaned in frustration. Why was she cutting me off?

I climbed the path to the parking pad near the street—a higher elevation, so maybe I could get a signal. I got a goofy text from Priya and two sweet ones from Aaron, and I wondered again if he was annoyed that Kristen had steamrolled his dinner plans. But I couldn't get enough bars to reply, let alone load my email or read the news. Frustration jolted down my arms. Who did Kristen think she was?

When she returned, red-cheeked, I called her over from the picnic table. "Can you please go get the hotspot? Please. I'll feel so much better if I know there's nothing in the news."

She rolled her eyes, her chest still heaving from the run, and disappeared inside. I followed her and watched her unplug it from an outlet in the downstairs bathroom—one of very few I hadn't thought to check.

"Why were you charging it here?"

She shrugged. "Why not?"

She handed it to me and then marched back outside with a yoga mat under her arm. I clicked the link in Nana's email and, head buzzing, searched for any related news—but there was nothing.

I exhaled. I started to reply to Aaron but couldn't figure out what to write—I felt like such an impostor, a terrible girlfriend masquerading as an honest one. As a *good* one, one who wouldn't hurt a fly.

I set my phone on the counter and went outside. I found Kristen on the boat dock, moving gracefully through a yoga flow. I watched her for a moment; a few yards out, an otter's head erupted from the water, and its little eyes regarded me before sinking back under the surface. Like he knew.

"Care to join me?" Kristen called, from Side Angle Pose.

"That's okay."

She shifted into Triangle Pose. "All good on the Internet?"

"Um . . . I guess so." I gazed up at the distant tree line, where a bald eagle was carving long ribbons through the sky.

"What is it?" She folded her mat in half and walked over.

"It's nothing."

"Did you find something?"

"No! I . . . forget it."

"What?"

I crossed my arms. "I just . . . hate having this secret. It's like a wall that keeps me at arm's length from everyone."

"But *we* don't have that wall. We're in this together." She leaned against a tree. "You can talk to me."

"I *can't,* though. Every time I bring it up, you change the subject. You shut down."

She sighed. "I'm sorry. That wasn't intentional. But . . . what is there to talk about? We can rehash it a million times and stress ourselves out, but that won't change anything. I thought we both wanted to move forward?"

"I do, but . . . it's keeping me from getting close to other people too. It's just . . . it's tough, okay?"

"I know it is." She placed her palm on my forearm and I pulled away.

I sighed. "It was different after Cambodia."

She tilted her head, listening.

"It was awful, but with enough time—and your help, obviously—I could kind of put it in a box and go back to my old life. I could stop thinking about it all the time, I wasn't . . . reminded of it or anything. And I didn't have anyone to . . ." I trailed off.

Her eyes widened. "What? Go on, then."

I shook my head. How could I explain it? I wanted to let my guard down around Aaron, but I felt the secret cutting through our fledgling relationship like a sickle through grain. A pang of self-disgust followed: how gross, thinking that having a boyfriend made me a better person than her. More eager to be authentic.

Her eyes turned red and filled with tears. "I risked *everything* for you. When I saw you needed help in that hotel room in Cambodia, I didn't even think—I just acted, because you're my best friend."

It hung between us, and she didn't need to say the rest: *I saved your life—I killed for you—and this is how you repay me?*

"I told myself you'd do the same for me," she said, her voice low. "But I thought it'd never happen to me—I'd never be attacked, no guy would ever try to hurt me. And then when it did, in Chile . . . I wish I could take it all back, Em, I do. But I thought we were in this together."

I started to cry too. "I'm sorry, Kristen. I just wish we could tell someone."

"But why? So you can relieve your guilty conscience and then spend the next ten years in jail? Think about that—no, I'm serious, picture it. You want to spend your thirties in a women's prison in, like, Fond du Lac?"

I hesitated, so she finished the thought: "Do you want *me* to spend my thirties there too? Because it's all or nothing."

I shook my head vehemently. She reached for my hand and threaded her fingers through mine. She swung our fists together, like we were kids playing Red Rover. Together, a wall, an impenetrable force.

"I know it's hard," she said, "and I'm sorry we're in this position. But it will get better. I know it doesn't feel like it now, but it really will start to fade, like it did last time." She snuffled again. "When my parents died, and then Jamie, I didn't think I'd ever get over it. And I was kind of right—you don't move on and never think about it again. But things . . . shift. Life becomes this new trajectory where these are the circumstances, and life goes on. Does that make sense?"

I nodded.

She heaved a heavy sigh. "I'm sorry that the sight of me makes you feel bad."

"Kristen."

"I am. I dunno what else to say. You're not— I'm not saying you're being mean or unfair or anything. I really am sorry."

"Hey now." I shot her a meaningful look. "I'm sorry you've been feeling that way. I just don't like being evasive with Aaron. I like him a lot." I gave my head a quick shake. "I want to be open with you, okay? No secrets."

She cracked a smile. "Girl, you're the one who's being weird. I'm an open book." She pushed past me. "I'm gonna grab some of those seltzers, and then we're going swimming! Can you add some air to the floatie?"

She strode up to the cabin, stepping over roots and rocks, moving as smoothly as a lynx. Her words echoed in my mind: *I thought it'd never happen to me.*

Two dead backpackers, a year apart. Two dead parents, killed in a fire. One dead best friend, killed in some kind of accident. So much death.

I thought of the article again—Paolo's handsome smile, the merry texts to his sister. His father's solemn vow.

Another echo in Kristen's voice: *I told myself you'd do the same for me.*

CHAPTER 24

A mosquito whined in my ear, high-pitched and screechy, tiny nails on a chalkboard. I swatted at the air and pulled the strings of my hoodie tighter. It was cold out here, colder than I'd expected. Compared to Milwaukee, we were only a few hours closer to the North Pole, but here the air chilled as soon as the sun slinked away.

"Did you see that one?" Kristen pierced the sounds of night: throaty frogs, chittering crickets, the tinkling gurgle of lake water around the pier's metal legs.

"Crap, I missed it."

"It was a good one."

"Damn." This was Kristen's second shooting-star sighting since we'd picked our way out here twenty minutes ago, our flashlights nosing over the root-strewn path. Even with my crummy night vision, I could tell the popcorn sky was spectacular: pinpricks of light stretching from the trees' lumpy tops to the far side of the lake. On the narrow pier, we'd splayed on our backs, heads almost touching, legs in opposite directions.

"Maybe I should turn around and face that way," I said.

"No, they were both right over us. Oh look, there's a satellite." The silhouette of her hand blotted out the stars, and I tracked the dot across the sky: a freckle of white moving steadily, determinedly west. I lost it where the stars marbled into a creamy band. The Milky Way, the edge of the galaxy, as Kristen had explained during her two-minute astronomy spiel, alongside the Big and Little Dippers and Orion's brilliant belt.

A swishing sound, and a cluster of stars blinked out. "What was that?"

Kristen snickered. "A bat, most likely. You know way more about wildlife than I do."

"A bat—must be." I willed my heart rate to slow. It was so peaceful out here, and beautiful, but also isolated and rustling and remote. Terrifying in its own small-town way.

"My parents used to tell the story of how a bat got into the cabin," she said, "long before I was born. I don't even think they were married yet. They used to throw these epic parties here, and somehow a bat came in through the fireplace."

I stayed quiet.

"It's not even that good of a story. You can tell it must've been really funny at the time, but in the retelling there was just a lot of yelling and grabbing weapons and running around. I guess the women were worried about it flying into their hair, so my mom told everyone to put, like, pots and colanders on their heads."

We both laughed, and the sound rolled around the lake before dying out.

"Well, I love it. That's some quick thinking on your mom's part."

Kristen let out a *hm,* somewhere between a laugh and a sigh. "She was awesome. You would've loved her."

"Definitely." A breeze made the treetops whisper. I pulled my sleeves over my hands and tucked them under my armpits.

"Dad avoided us when we were up here—he just wanted to fish—but Mom would play with me all day long," she went on. "She'd set up obstacle courses in the water: around the sandbar, touch the reeds, that kind of thing. In retrospect, she just wanted me to be a strong swimmer."

A memory from my own childhood dilated: I was four or five and when my mom was too sick to take me to a neighbor's pool party, I'd begged my dad. The pool was rectangular and teeming with kids, and I jumped right into the shallow end, which came up to my shoulders. I was thrilled to be there, amazed my dad had agreed—shocked that my pleading had, for once, worked. As my tiny feet skimmed the floor, I lost track of how far from the edge I'd strayed. Without warning, the pool's bottom slanted away, and I was hopping, coughing, finding it harder with every second to keep my head above water.

Just as the panic peaked, salvation: A mom, one I didn't even know, was suddenly in the water too, clutching me in her arms, murmuring, "It's okay, you're okay." She was fully clothed—a tank top and jeans. I clung to her neck and looked around for my dad and felt a rush of relief and love when I saw the strangled worry on his face. The warm feeling popped like a blister on the car ride home: As I shivered atop a damp towel, Dad said gruffly, "You shouldn't go in the pool if you can't swim. That woman had a beeper on her—you ruined it." That night I got a spanking for causing a scene.

"Or she'd scrounge together craft supplies," Kristen continued dreamily. "One time we made toy sailboats out of chunks of two-by-fours and poked 'em all the way along the shore."

In the stillness we heard a loon's sudden tremolo, three warbling notes.

"I miss my mom," Kristen said, her voice almost a whisper.

"Aw, Kristen."

Another beat. "Last year I missed the anniversary of her death. Isn't that weird? I thought of it two days later. It felt like I'd betrayed her. Erased her existence." She choked out a bitter laugh. "And then my next thought was 'Oh right, Dad too.' They died the same goddamn day—November 10, 2001. And I was *glad* to not have thought about him for so long. Manipulative prick."

My heart stung so hard I pressed my hand over it. "I'm sorry, Kristen. I'm sorry." I wondered if it was easier for her to talk about this while facing the sky, both of us cloaked in darkness. But why tonight? Was it the Sazeracs we'd sipped after dinner, or something deeper, something coming to a head? "Do you think . . . is this something that's been coming up more for you lately?"

"I don't know."

"Maybe it would help to talk to someone," I said. "You've mentioned how much your therapist helped you back then. Have you looked her up? Maybe she's still practicing."

"Lydia Brightside—she was a character. Maybe you're right. Or maybe I'm just . . . feeling sorry for myself. Which is not like me, you know. I hate the wallow."

"You do! Rarely do you let me indulge in pity parties. It's why . . ." I was going to joke, *It's why I keep you around.* But the tug in my gut had returned, the desire to distance myself from her—at least until I had more answers. About Jamie, about her parents, about her baffling indifference to Paolo's body being exhumed. "It's one of many reasons you're unstoppable," I finished.

The silence swelled around us, mixing with the cold and pressing into our skin. Another mosquito zipped past my ear and I sat up.

"I'm freezing," I announced. "I'm ready to go inside."

"I'm gonna stay out here a bit longer." I couldn't see her face, but her voice was rickety and small.

As I headed for the cabin, fear slipped beneath my porous skin. My flashlight made only a pathetic globe of safety in the dark; beyond it, Lake Novak faded into a blackness so consuming, I couldn't be sure the rest of the world hadn't disappeared.

I was almost at the door when my flashlight clipped some shivery motion. I jumped and searched in the dark, and a trapdoor of horror opened inside me when I found it: Beneath a pall of flies, a dead rabbit lay on its side. Its neck was gashed and bleeding red-black.

Kristen's words returned to me: *I wanna kill the little assholes.* And with the audio, a visual, Kristen's confident hatchet swing.

No. I took an involuntary step backward. My sandal clipped the edge of a fat root, and suddenly I was soaring through the air. My arm banged into a tree and I clawed at its bark as I fell to the ground. I sat there for a second, waiting to see what hurt. Then my ankle erupted with pain.

"Kristen!"

My cry scattered through the trees, reverberated around the lake, rose toward the umbrella of stars.

I cleared my throat and tried again, deeper this time. "*Kristen!* I need help!"

I listened so hard I could feel my ears straining. The crickets answered, then a few errant frogs. A lonely owl—no, maybe it was a coyote.

No, a wolf. I looked around, nerves thrumming, like my blood was on fire.

"Kristen?"

No reply. I trained my flashlight on my ankle, prepared to see the area purple and gray and shiny-taut. But there was nothing there, nothing to show I'd fallen.

A hand grabbed my shoulder and I screamed.

"You scared the hell out of me." I pressed both palms into the pine-needle ground.

"*I* scared *you*? I thought you were inside! I almost peed myself when I saw someone out here. Do you mind not shining that in my face?" Kristen covered her eyes and I lowered my flashlight.

"I was yelling for you." I couldn't hide the crossness in my voice. "I fell and hurt my ankle. How did you not hear me?"

"Oh my God." Kristen dropped to her knees and inspected it. "I'm sorry! I had my earbuds in. I did a guided meditation on the dock."

"It really hurts."

"I bet it's a sprain. Those suck." She hoisted herself up and slid her arm under mine. "Let's get some ice on that. Here, I've got you." Putting weight on my leg triggered a blast of menthol cold. "Lean against me. Let's go."

Kristen set me up with my foot on a chair, a bag of frozen peas resting on top. She gave me two ibuprofen and rustled up a first-rate first-aid kit, with an old tube of arnica cream and an anemic-looking Ace bandage, which she looped across my ankle and fastened with two clips, their hooks sinking into the fabric like fangs.

"Did you see the rabbit outside?" I asked as she repacked the kit. "I don't know what would do that to it."

"Probably a coyote," she replied without looking up.

I glanced down at my ankle, bound like a mummy. "You're probably right."

KRISTEN WENT TO bed before me, and I stayed curled on the couch, in the dome of light beneath an antique lamp. Moths throbbed against the window screens. My brain clicked and clattered, a wooden roller coaster ascending its hill. What had happened with Jamie that pushed Kristen to deface her yearbook and destroy the carving? How could she remain so blasé about the discovery of Paolo's body? And our conversation on Thursday, when she'd briefly convinced me she was as shaken as I was—why did that now feel like a trick, a trap?

I hobbled to the kitchen counter and turned on the hotspot—this time I'd plugged it in myself. *Jamie Rusch:* My heart hammered away as I spilled her name into a search bar on my laptop.

I scanned the results hungrily, then felt the Earth lurch, spin off its axis. I clutched both fists to my lips.

An accident, Kristen had told me. An accident had claimed Jamie's life.

But it wasn't true.

In the very same month that Jerry and Anne Czarnecki died in a raging fire, young Jamie had killed herself.

And Kristen, formerly her best friend, currently mine, had lied about it.

CHAPTER 25

Jamie Leigh Rusch Memorial Fund—the website looked good, professional, even, with a black-and-white photo of the grinning girl that stayed stuck in place as the text over it scrolled. An extremely upsetting metaphor: Jamie, forever trapped at twelve while the rest of the world moved on. She was awkward in that preteen way, with spindly bangs and a shy smile and skin as shiny as a newly waxed car. I squinted at the photo—she did look like me. Same brown, wavy hair and full brows.

In blue, near the top, the fund's motto: *Raising mental health awareness and serving the greater community.* Then all the phrases that made the cause of death clear: "ending stigma" and "access to mental health care treatment" and even a bit about changing our language, "brain illness" instead of "mental illness" and "died by suicide" in lieu of "committed suicide." An embedded video near the bottom showed Jamie's parents speaking at a big black-tie fundraiser, and I watched it with the sound turned off. Then I clicked on Gallery, expecting photos from past fundraisers, but—oh, God—it was photos of Jamie.

Jamie as a bonny baby, with apple cheeks and a button nose. Jamie as a toddler, holding a drippy ice-cream cone with something like reverence. Gangly school-age Jamie with a basketball tucked under her arm. The last photo centered on junior-high Jamie in a silky green basketball jersey and shorts. Her teammates held her up on their shoulders: adolescent girls cheering and smiling at her, all braces and frizzy hair and bodies in the extreme, some tiny and compact, others stretched-out and gawky. Oh, what an age: broad, sudden swings from baseline, our largest deviations from the mean right when we'd kill to be quote-unquote *normal.*

Kristen had been very into basketball back then, too, so I scanned the faces one by one. My heart jumped when I found her—while all the other girls were gazing up at Jamie, who'd presumably sunk the winning basket, Kristen was in the back, eyes uncertain, staring straight into the camera.

I found Jamie's obituary: survived by her parents, Thomas and Jennifer Rusch, and a little brother, Luke. Found dead on November 24, 2001. Two weeks to the day after Kristen's parents died.

Her best friend and both parents had died in the same month. And she'd never mentioned it.

I scrolled to the bottom of the page and saw that the address for the memorial fund was in Las Vegas, that wacky man-made oasis. I googled the elder Rusches; the mom was in marketing, the dad a realtor in Henderson. Far from their Wisconsin dwelling, the pineapple house between Kristen's first home and Nana and Bill's mansion. The Mojave Desert is another spot where there are hardly any shadows, sun-splashed by day and moonlit at night. The kind of place where you could bury a body but the stars, all those floodlights, wouldn't keep it in the dark for long.

Kristen had kept this from me. I knew about her childhood pet (Green Bean the guinea pig), the time she broke her wrist showing off on a swing set, and the ridiculous Easter-themed play she'd written in fourth grade, which her classmates had dutifully performed. I should've heard about the loss of a close friend, and whatever bad thing led to those angry black scribbles, now hidden in a basement's silty dark.

A thought I'd almost but not quite had when the birthday treasure hunt had reached its dramatic conclusion: *Is it really a good idea to be alone in a cabin in the woods with Kristen?*

A floorboard creaked above me and I flinched. Why did *everyone* who got close to Kristen wind up dead? The sudden house fire, a horror-movie cliché . . . a chill radiated across my shoulders as I started to type in any details I could remember, anything that might lead to news articles about the blaze that killed her parents. But before I could hit Enter, the Internet sputtered out—I'd burned through all five gigabytes. I closed my laptop and sat in the dark while night sounds pressed in around me.

WE ROCKED IN our seats as the road swerved through the trees. Kristen was taking it too fast, accelerating as we snaked around hairpin turns.

"Why is it so twisty?" I asked, clutching the handle on the door.

"They had to carve the road out around all the lakes and swamps and ridges up here," she replied. "It's actually hillier than you'd think. Like here, it's a crazy drop-off if you go off the road." She gestured my way.

"So how about slowing down?"

"I've driven here a million times." She careened around another corner and the seatbelt tugged at my neck.

I took a deep breath. "Hey, so I wanted to ask you about your friend Jamie."

She squinted through a patch of sun. "Didn't I say I don't want to talk about her?"

"Well, I googled her. I was curious to see if she looked like me." A ham-fisted lie, but the best I could do. "And I saw that she . . . died by suicide."

"That's right." Camo-like shadows rippled across her face from the sun peeking through the trees.

"I thought you said it was an accident."

She shot me a raw, strangled look. "Because it's painful for me. Okay?"

"I'm sorry. I really am. I know she was like a sister."

"Yeah." She shook her hair out of her eyes. "You know, if someone said to me, 'Do you think a twelve-year-old could stand it if both her parents died, and then her best friend since birth killed herself a few weeks later?' I'd be like, 'Obviously not.' But here I am. Here we are." She turned to me. "It was really hard. Losing her. I don't ever want to go through that again."

She stayed that way for a beat, watching me. Unease billowed in my torso.

"I can't even imagine. What . . . what happened?"

She shrugged. "No one knew how much she was hurting. Not even me."

"Was she depressed?"

"Guess so, yeah."

"God, she was just so . . . young. For someone that age to . . ."

"It's more common than you'd think." She swallowed. "Remember how we both used to love *The Virgin Suicides*? 'Obviously, Doctor, you've never been a thirteen-year-old girl.'"

We burst out of the woods and onto a country road, with a bar on one side and a dingy gas station on the other. At the last second, Kristen took a sharp turn and pulled up to a pump. "It'll be cheaper up here," she said, before snatching up her purse and slamming the door.

My brain was like minnows in a pail: Thoughts crisscrossed and swarmed and bumped into one another. Was Kristen being weird about Jamie, or was I the one seeing menace in the wholly explicable, as Kristen kept insisting? Was Jamie's death really a suicide, or had Kristen had, well, *something* to do with it . . . and was I an awful friend for thinking that? Then there was the next stepping-stone in logic, something I'd never allowed myself to face head-on: Could all this death mean that . . . that the night with Paolo—?

Kristen opened the car door before I could finish the thought. She jabbed a button on the dash and the radio bellowed on. As we pushed back into the forest, I replayed our conversation in my head. All Kristen's talk of losing Jamie, how she couldn't go through that again . . . what was *that*?

Presents rattled in the back seat: the stone elephant for Priya, nifty beer glasses made from old bottles for Aaron. A nice Merlot blend and a card thanking Nana and Bill for letting me celebrate my birthday at their cabin. I'd sent Nana a polite reply to her email, thanking her for her well wishes and asking what she meant by the line about Kristen acting "a bit strange lately." She hadn't replied. It was odd—in her email, she came across as more concerned about *me* than her own granddaughter.

We soared past open fields with machines creeping across them like giant metal insects. Anxiety mounted as we approached the freeway and then thundered down I-43. Closer to Milwaukee, to civilization, to real life. Here the mystery surrounding Paolo's death felt even truer—here it was a news point, not just a distant, passing item that blipped over the transom and meandered away like a satellite traversing the northern sky. I pictured Los Angeles cops waiting at my front door, the neighbors watching like dull-eyed cows.

That night, back in my own bed, I dreamed of beestings and bat bites, tiny pricks in my smooth, tender bark, setting off a cascade of pain. I woke up sweating and began unwrapping the elastic encircling my leg. I pictured it as the bandage uncoiled: a bloated white ankle, the skin of a corpse, plus a slash of squid-ink black streaking down one side of my Achilles tendon. But when I peeled off the final inches, the ankle looked the same as always.

CHAPTER 26

"I feel . . . scared." My fingers were moving of their own accord again, the thumbnail scraping the skin below each tip. "Like, this intense fear that flares up when I least expect it."

Adrienne nodded gravely. "What does that fear feel like?"

I raked at a notch in my pinkie nail. She hadn't asked the question I dreaded most, because I'd need to lie: *Scared of what?* Of the L.A. police uncovering something we'd left behind. Blood on the hotel floor, a nugget in the pile of ashes we'd abandoned in the fireplace. Fingerprints on shovels. DNA in the trunk.

Or, take your pick—I had plenty of options, plenty of bad memories like bogeymen to keep me awake at night. Like that awful night in Phnom Penh. Kristen's eyes flashing as she swung the lamp and took Sebastian down. *Stop. Stop. Stop.*

"I feel it in my chest," I said, "like the beginning of an asthma attack."

The clutch in my ribs had plagued me throughout dinner the night before. Aaron and I had had our belated birthday meal; he'd wanted to cook everything for me, but I'd insisted on making it a co-celebration, since he'd just picked up a coveted design project. I told him about the cabin, about roasting marshmallows and watching satellites skate across the sky. I turned the tale of how I'd twisted my ankle and yelled to a silent, unlistening night into a slapstick comedy, dorky and cute.

I omitted a few things: My dreamlike, phoneless showdown across the kitchen table with Kristen. The mutilated rabbit that appeared in the dark. Digging in the basement in the middle of the night, angry scribbles where Jamie's face should be. Like the news broadcast in an airport—edit the feed to limit hysteria. It was exhausting, keeping a lid on the fear. It threatened to crumple my lungs and give me away.

"What do you think is triggering it?" Adrienne asked.

There it was. A sliver of ivory nail pulled free.

"I'm still . . . uneasy with Kristen being back here." I couldn't tell her why, but deep down I knew the answer: I was beginning to question if I could really trust her. Which felt surprising and strange and wrong—historically, Kristen was synonymous with safety in my mind.

"Why do you think that is?"

I shrugged. "She's still acting like everything's fine. Which is one way to deal with something scary, but I worry it's an act. Like, she's keeping it all inside where it could go off like a bomb."

Adrienne nodded. "And what makes you think she's keeping it in?"

For starters, she refuses to even acknowledge *the wealthy developer teaming up with the LAPD to find us.* Her behavior when we'd found the CNN article had been so bizarre that a part of me kept whispering, *Was that insincere?*

"She just seems . . . off. Normally she's a joy to be around—she's intoxicating, you know? But since she came back, things between us seem strained. And Lord knows I wasn't myself after I was attacked, so I'm not judging her for it. But it's like she's aggressively happy or something—fake."

Adrienne tilted her head. "It's notable, how much time we spend talking about Kristen's emotions. Do you think you might be prioritizing them over your own?"

"It's not that," I spit out. But then I sighed. "I know she cares about me. And I . . . it's not wrong to be worried about my best friend."

"Of course not," Adrienne replied, and my defensiveness slackened. She crinkled her brow, gathering her thoughts. "So, Kristen acting 'aggressively happy' puts you on edge. It makes you feel *more* worried about her and focused on how she's doing." She waited until I nodded. "And you've said she's super smart. And in tune with your emotions, right?" I nodded again. "So, I wonder if maybe she . . . she *knows* she's having this effect on you. I'm not even saying it's intentional, but maybe it's a way to sort of maintain the power balance in the relationship. Remember when we talked about how when a friendship changes, someone usually pushes back?"

Nausea in my belly, like a bud unfurling into a fat, prickly leaf. I wanted to tell Adrienne she was wrong, but combined with all the alarms boinging around my head since the weekend, well . . .

"I always told myself Kristen was all I needed," I admitted as a tear trickled past my nose. "And I do love her, I do. But now that I have other people in my life—now that I have Aaron . . ." I snatched up a Kleenex. "I feel so guilty saying this. Like it's a betrayal."

"It's okay, Emily. Anything you say here is between you and me."

A loud, slow exhalation. "I think she wants me all to herself." I didn't know it until it was out of my mouth, and then it was true: "Like, she planned this birthday trip even though I told her I already had plans with Aaron. Just informed him she was taking over and he'd have to wait."

"Did you let Kristen know that that bothered you?"

"Of course not. She was just trying to do something nice for me."

Her eyebrows flashed. "Some people would say that hijacking your birthday plans is not respecting your boundaries."

Tears brimmed again as the truth lapped at my mind. Unavoidable. Irrefutable. *Kristen's love looks a lot like control.*

"What happens when you think about talking to Kristen about this stuff head-on?"

It felt . . . unfathomable. "I just hate confrontation," I said.

"That's fair—conflict is uncomfortable. But sometimes bringing things into the light can actually help, right?" I stared at her miserably, so she continued. "Let's step back. When you were a kid, what happened if you tried talking to your parents about something they did that upset you?"

I shook my head. "I didn't."

"You didn't. Period."

"Well, I learned not to at a young age." I stared at my hands. "Because if I spoke up, I got in trouble. They were in the because-I-said-so school of parenting."

"Wow, Emily." She nodded solemnly.

Something flopped in my breast, something deep and raw and spiky. I pictured my dad's furious eyes, the sudden shock of a spanking when I had no idea I was misbehaving. How the pain cut off my singing mid-word. "I don't want to talk about it, if that's okay."

"Of course." She waited as I blotted my cheeks. "Let's go back to Kristen steamrolling your birthday plans with Aaron. How did he feel about that?"

"He said it was fine. But would he tell me if it wasn't?"

"What do you think?"

A beat. "He's just so *nice*. Maybe that's making me uneasy too."

"That's a reason to feel scared?"

I squirmed. "I think things are going really well. And now I'm waiting for the other shoe to drop. For the past to come back and haunt me." For the universe to punish me for all the lies—the universe or the Los Angeles police.

"So you're afraid that him treating you well makes it more likely that things won't work out."

I ducked my head away.

"Do you think that's true?" she asked.

"It's not rational, no."

She dropped her notebook onto her lap. "Remember how I used to be a lawyer? My job was to get the jury to look at the evidence objectively. Cognitive behavioral therapy is kind of the same thing: You examine your thoughts like a scientist so you can challenge the ones that don't hold up. So let's look at this fear, this belief or, or thought pattern you've noticed. Just because a feeling is *real* doesn't mean it's true."

THAT WAS THE lesson Adrienne hoped I'd take away from the session. Because she thought my fears were irrational, that a body *hadn't* been exhumed, that there *wasn't* a group of armed professionals actively tracking me down. But that evening, I saw her advice in a new light: Be a scientist. Be like an attorney, build the case. I now knew Kristen was controlling, pulling the strings whether she meant to or not. And clearly *something* had rattled my lizard brain during my time at Lake Novak—enough to make me doubt that I could trust her.

One, two, three, four, five dead bodies. My subconscious kept counting, kept scraping at our friendship like an art restorer chiseling the grime off the truth.

The question at hand: Was Kristen a bystander with links to multiple deaths through a series of unfortunate coincidences . . . or was there something more at play?

My stomach clenched and bile scalded my throat. The hugeness of the accusation swooped through me and jangled my balance. I dropped into my desk chair, breathing hard.

A part of me, tucked under my consciousness, had been circling this question for *weeks*. I'd held back, policing my thoughts, unwilling to state it so directly. Because the implications were devastating: Kristen, my oldest and closest friend, the only one who saw the ugliest parts of me and loved me anyway, who loved me *unconditionally,* might be a murderer. But I couldn't ignore the evidence sloshing against me like a pounding surf: the bodies, all those bodies. Coincidence didn't produce that kind of pile. I felt suddenly cold, and my arms and jaw began to shake.

Focus, Emily. I breathed deeply and imagined all my feelings, heartbreak and horror and disbelief and fear, crumpled down into a little ball, like the lump in the fireplace after we burned up Paolo's things. That's what was at stake—arrest, murder charges, our futures ruined. I had to know if I could trust Kristen. I had to know if she was truly safe.

Had Kristen killed anybody? That was the big question: not self-defense, not accidental death, but murder. The questions below it popped up like goosebumps. What had happened to her parents? To Jamie? Was her takedown of Sebastian an isolated incident? And what really happened the night Paolo died?

Something hysterical frothed up through my throat and came out as a moan. *Focus.* If this were an issue at work, the next step would be coming up with action items and carrying them out, one by one.

First, I read everything I could find on the fire that killed Kristen's parents, which wasn't much: a few sentences in the local paper, noting only that the cause was undetermined; obituaries for both parents, Jerry and Anne, plus a plea for donations to a charity in lieu of flowers. I searched for *Kristen Czarnecki* and *2001.* Then her grandparents, one by one. I was slightly surprised to find that Nana's real name was Tabitha, which felt just as made-up as Nana, but otherwise, no bombshells.

Who could help—who could tell me the truth about Kristen? Jamie was dead. There was Nana—I thought back to her strange, suspicious email, and to the end of that odd drink at their enormous home. Nana in the kitchen, nervously jamming her phone into my hands. Perhaps she was an ally, eager to help but unable to say more. I tried calling and hung up when her voicemail clicked on. I replied to my unanswered email, too, a polite, "Just following up!"

I drummed my nails against the space bar, thinking hard. Wait—there was someone else Kristen had opened up to, someone who knew the whole story. My mind went blank for a moment, and then it blazed out of my fingertips and into Google: *Lydia Brightside, therapist, Wisconsin.* Her headshot smiled at me from the top of the search results: a woman in her sixties with short reddish-gray hair, small eyes, arms folded in what was clearly the photographer's suggested pose. So it wasn't an alias, a name crinkled by Kristen's memory.

The first link was a bio on the website for something called Westmoor Behavioral Services:

> *Lydia Brightside, MD, PhD, is a board-certified pediatric psychiatrist with a subspecialty in Conduct Disorder Treatment. She serves as founding executive director and chief medical officer for Westmoor Behavioral Services. Dr. Brightside has more than four decades of experience studying and developing*

unique pharmaceutical and pioneering therapeutic interven-
tions to treat behavioral disorders in children and young
adults . . .

Huh? I navigated to the center's About Us page:

Founded in 1995, Westmoor Behavioral Health is a leading
residential treatment center in Wisconsin for children and teens
struggling with developmental disorders and mental and be-
havioral health issues.

This . . . didn't sound anything like the grief counseling I assumed
young Kristen had undergone. But maybe Dr. Brightside was in private practice as well? I found her CV on an academic website and
scoured her work history—nope, she'd worked exclusively at Westmoor Behavioral Services since cofounding it a quarter century ago.
Was Kristen keeping even more from me than I thought?

I pulled the center up on a map: It was about two hours from
here, in a semirural area dappled with lakes.

In college I'd donated plasma a few times, and while most of the
process didn't bother me—the prick, the waiting, the marbled bruise
and wooziness afterward—there was one sensation I spent the whole
forty-five minutes dreading. I'll never forget the feeling of plasma-
stripped blood flooding back into my veins, a snaking rush of un-
pleasant cold, like frozen lightning.

And that's exactly how I felt when my eyes sank below the map
to the user reviews. Coldness tearing through everywhere blood
should be.

No one comes here except by court order, the first one read.

And then the real upshot: *This is where judges send kids who are*
too rich to go to juvie.

Juvie. My God. Was her time there related to the three deaths
circling her head like horseflies at that age? Was she a danger to herself and, more terrifyingly, others?

If Kristen had been involved in a juvenile court case, the records would be sealed. But who would try to prosecute her? What did she do that would land her in an inpatient clinic, meeting regularly with Wisconsin's preeminent expert on "conduct disorder"? Perhaps she started acting out as she grieved her parents' death: anger, despair, and survivor's guilt all churning with the hormones of puberty. Maybe she clapped back at teachers and mouthed off to her grandparents. But would that land her in a bougie alternative to a juvenile detention center? That seemed more like the proper treatment for a child who'd . . .

I flashed to it, Kristen at the lake house, bottle of lighter fluid clutched in her hand. *I'm really good at building fires,* she'd said. And: *My mom wasn't even supposed to be home.* No way could twelve-year-old Kristen have . . .

My heart raced. This couldn't be a coincidence. And if it meant what I thought it did—if the answer really was "Murder, Kristen, yes"—then, God, what did that say about our last night in Chile? Hell, what did that mean for *me,* right now?

In a rush, I created a throwaway email address and contacted Westmoor under the guise of being a grad student researching psychiatric care in the state. Just general sniffing around. Nothing specific about Kristen.

A jolt as I hit Send, and then I sat back, feeling unseemly.

The next morning, an email was waiting for me from Westmoor Behavioral Services.

Dear Ms. Schmidt,

Thank you for your inquiry. To answer your questions, Westmoor does not accept insurance and therefore serves a very selective community. We work closely with the Wisconsin court system to identify minors who would benefit from our inpatient services; families cannot check a patient in without a referral. Westmoor's mission of providing a safe, supportive environment for children with severe behavioral issues is unique in the state, although we see similar models in other regions.

"Severe behavioral issues"—so it was true. Young Kristen was diagnosed with this as a child. But surely she didn't spend weeks or months in an institute?

But then my eyes widened:

In regards to Dr. Brightside's history, she has seen patients at Westmoor exclusively since the center opened in 1995. She is not in private practice, and full-time resident patients at Westmoor are her only clients (in addition to group therapy with parents, siblings, etc.). I've attached a PDF of our brochure. Please let me know if I can be of further assistance.

And there was my answer.

A handful of years before she befriended me outside an econ class, Kristen—Kristen who felled Sebastian with a lamp and then calmly hatched a plan to sink his body, Kristen who swung a bottle of wine so hard it reshaped Paolo's skull—had been locked up in a center for emotionally disturbed youths.

Shit.

CHAPTER 27

LOS ANGELES FAMILY OFFERS $1 MILLION REWARD IN HOMICIDE INVESTIGATION

The family of Paolo García, a 24-year-old backpacker whose remains were found in a remote Chilean village, is now offering a $1 million payout to anyone with information that leads to an arrest.

While holding a framed picture of her son, Fernanda García pleaded for justice for him. Fernanda says on April 25, she received a phone call informing her that the body of her son, Paolo, had been discovered by local police in the Elqui Valley, a mountainous region in northern Chile. That call would shatter her life.

"It breaks my heart that he was taken away from us," Fernanda said.

Fernanda and her husband, Rodrigo García, CEO of the Los Angeles real estate development firm Castillo Development, expressed hope that a $1 million payout would incentivize witnesses to come forward. García was last spotted at a crowded restaurant in Puerto Natales, a port town in southern Chile, on the night of March 30.

"Someone must have seen something," Rodrigo said. "The money won't bring him back, but he deserves justice."

Almost four weeks passed between when Paolo was last seen and when his body was found on April 25 in a shallow grave about 25 meters from the road in Arroyito, a sparsely populated agricultural town in northern Chile, according to reports. Police confirmed that an autopsy had been performed, but no additional information on the cause or time of death has been released.

Paolo was described as a fun-loving and gregarious young man who was finally fulfilling a dream of traveling the world. Born in California, Paolo grew up in Barcelona, Spain, where he enjoyed playing tennis and cooking for friends and family. At the age of 16, he was diagnosed with thyroid cancer, and his parents say that beating the disease left him determined to travel and engage with people all over the world.

If you have information that could help detectives, call Los Angeles Police or text the tip to 637274.

I was at work, digging into my sad salad and scanning the news almost on autopilot, when I saw the headline. My stomach roiled, threatening to expel the limp greens I'd already swallowed. *Shit.* This was bad; this was very, very bad. My heart beat faster and faster as I read, *badum badum badum,* until it seemed to be convulsing like a person in the final throes of suffocation.

Nothing like a million dollars to jog people's memories. God, there were so many potential witnesses whose paths had braided with ours, a big tangled knot: The cars we passed on our predawn drive home to the hotel. The waiter at the patio bar, our fellow patrons, the bartender who watched me freak out and blubber and screech, in English, that my wallet had been stolen. Christ, we were nothing if not memorable. Oh, plus—whoever had turned a light on as we clanked the shovels and flashlights back into the shed. The whistling custodian who took a photo of us in our bathing suits— had he noticed we'd moved his tools? Had the hotel's housekeeper wondered why the shower curtain was hung up differently? *Way to keep a low profile, morons.*

And, Jesus. Tennis player, amateur chef, freaking *cancer survivor?* This made Paolo real; this made what we'd done, even in the name of self-defense and -preservation, more odious. Until now, I could see Paolo as subhuman—Sebastian too—and lock them in a mental jail cell: BAD MEN. Not: bad men with hobbies and loved ones and pasts. Nausea bolted up through me.

"You signed up for yoga, right?" The Slack message from Priya felt like an intrusion, far too mundane for the emergency on hand.

I was about to bow out, but hesitated. Normalcy—I had to maintain it, had to go through the motions lest anyone think anything was wrong. I had a schedule to keep; Aaron and I were grabbing dinner after my class. And anyway, Drishti Yoga had served as my temple after Cambodia, the key to calming me down—better to vinyasa than to sit at home, reading the article over and over. I closed the browser window. "I'll be there."

SHORTLY BEFORE SIX, Priya hoisted her mat over her head and slung the strap across her chest: Artemis with her quiver of arrows. I had a missed call from Kristen and texted that I'd try her later. There was, I realized, nothing in particular for us to *do.* In the past, I'd have sought out Kristen's reassurances: *We're fine, we were smart, no one's looking for us.* Now, after all I knew about her past, the dead bodies studding her personal history, I just wanted to stay as far away from her as possible.

At the studio, Priya made a beeline for the locker room while I waited to rent a mat. My ankle felt better, but this was my first class since the injury. I stepped into the changing room and stopped short.

At first I thought I was hallucinating, the way I'd seen Paolo at baggage claim all those weeks ago.

But no—it was her. Priya and Kristen were standing inside, half-changed, heads bent over a phone.

"Kristen?"

She looked up and grinned. "Priya said you guys love this teacher!"

"I— Hi. I didn't know you were coming."

"Kristen was telling me about the private yoga class you took in Chile," Priya added. "I wanted to see the instructor she was talking about."

"I found her on Instagram. I'm obsessed with her." Kristen went into a spot-on impression, her fake accent thick: "Keep your knees *suave* . . . now we bow to the sky."

I smiled back but felt my eyebrows knit. Why draw attention to where we'd been, and when?

Priya turned to cram her stuff into a locker and I gave Kristen a WTF look. She responded with a scrunched brow and shake of her head: *What is it?* Another woman burst into the changing room, banging the door against the wall, and we hustled to get ready for class.

In Warrior 3, I found my balance, tough and firm, but next to me, Kristen wavered and then fell, brushing my outstretched arm and knocking us both over in the process.

Then, in handstand practice, Kristen kicked her way up as if she had something to prove. She stood there calmly, palms as feet, blood rushing to her face but her expression determined.

KRISTEN AND I had parked near each other, so we shuffled down the sidewalk together. As soon as Priya was out of earshot, Kristen turned to me.

"What's going on? You're being weird."

"*I'm* being weird?" My fingers flew to my collarbone.

"Do you not like me hanging out with Priya?"

"It's not that," I said, though it kind of was. I started walking again. "Did you not read the news today? The family's offering a million-dollar reward. We're screwed."

"Hey. Do we need to turn our phones off?"

I stared at her. "You're seriously gonna make me turn my phone off when you were just telling Priya about Chile?" Heedlessness followed by paranoia—the whiplash set off more alarm bells.

"What, about the yoga studio?" She grinned. "You haven't told people about that? Maribela was awesome."

We stopped in front of my sedan. "I don't think we should be drawing attention to the fact that we were there at that exact time."

She rolled her eyes. "If we're trying to act normal, news flash: Talking about yoga *at yoga* is normal."

"I guess, but—"

"Em, no one is drawing a line between us and that," she interrupted. "Here, if you want to keep discussing let's at least toss our phones in your car."

I complied, slamming the door with gusto, then turned to her, fists on hips. "You're being reckless."

"What, you think Priya is going to see the news and, like, call the FBI?"

"I know, but—"

"Hey, I've got a hot tip." She held her hand up like a phone. "These two women I know, sweet girls, law-abiding. They were in that same region of the world as that backpacker sometime last month, so you should probably send a SWAT team. A million dollars, please."

"I *know*. It's not logical." I shook my head. "You should read the article. It's terrifying."

"Fine, but it'll probably just result in a deluge of false leads. If anything, it proves they've got nothing. And if they do miraculously get as far as talking to us: Yeah, we chatted with him at a bar, there were a ton of people there, I made out with him, he left, never saw him again. He was a *vagrant,* Emily."

"But someone could have seen us . . . loading the trunk, or putting the shovels back, or, or maybe we didn't clean as well as we thought in the suite or the rental car . . ."

"No one knows anything but us. You and me." She narrowed her eyes. "Unless you've told anyone. Like Aaron?"

A sparkler of fear in my chest. "Of course not."

"Emily." She settled her hands on my shoulders. "We need to stay calm and stick together. Now is not the time to freak out and start acting weird." She glanced at a gaggle of teenagers ambling past. "Okay? We got this."

I nodded, because it felt like the right thing to do. But in truth, I couldn't shut myself into my car fast enough. I watched her reach the corner and disappear behind an office building.

I had to face the facts: After Chile, Kristen and I had fundamentally opposing ideas of what Paolo's death meant for our friendship. Even now, with the walls closing in on us, I could only see it as a reason to cut all ties. But Kristen saw things differently. And Kristen was used to getting what she wanted. In life, and especially from me.

I saw it again, Paolo's legs on the floor. Toes upturned like a stargazer.

And Kristen's eyes, pleading and wild.

Emily, she'd said. *We have no choice.*

I CHECKED MY email when I got home, and felt a cold jab when I saw one of the senders: Casa Habita, the hotel where we'd stayed in Quiteria. The spot with the charming wood-burning stove and extra-thick shower curtain. I clicked on it as nausea curled:

> *Dear Ms. Donovan,*
> *Thank you for your recent stay at Casa Habita. I contact you regarding the unfortunate death of an American tourist in this area. At the request of the local police, all hotels in the region are asked to contact all visitors who stayed in the four weeks past. If you saw anything or have information about Paolo García, reply to this message please and we will connect you with the local policeman. Thank you.*

Crap. We'd paid in cash, but I'd been the one to fill out the reservation form at check-in, since it was in Spanish. I texted a screenshot to Kristen with nothing but a question mark, and she replied imme-diately: *Nope, don't remember anything. But that is a long span of time—who would?*

Who would? *Who would?* Alarm shot up through me and I sti-fled a groan. Then I saw the time and jolted; even if I left now, I'd be late for dinner with Aaron. Dammit, why was I always behind on things these days? Life was moving too quickly, jerky and unnatural, like an early black-and-white film. I ran to my car and backed into the street, then whipped through a yellow light.

At the next intersection, I breathed deeply. I had to relax, had to seem normal with Aaron. Had to not total my car in my distracted rush to meet him. Getting killed in a collision right now—my vital organs mangled by metal and plastic and upholstery and glass—would be a little too on the nose.

A hell of a way to add to Kristen's body count.

I DIDN'T FEEL like talking about her, but Aaron was insistent. It was sweet, in a way—he asked how things were between Kristen and me, and when I blanched at the question, he grew determined to help.

"Is she jealous that you're spending time with me?" He dabbed his mouth with a napkin. He looked so cute: fresh from the shower, his shaggy hair combed back, handsome in a slim button-down and jeans. "I thought when a woman gets into a new relationship, her friends give her, like, two months of intense couple time before they expect to see her again."

I sighed. "It might be partly that. She moved home and I wasn't sitting around, waiting for her with open arms and a wide-open cal-endar." I pushed my plate of penne alla vodka away. Aaron had picked out a hole-in-the-wall trattoria with homemade pasta, and I was dousing my feelings with carbs. "You know this is my first real relationship in forever. She's not used to having to share me."

"Well, then we'll invite her to hang out with us more! I don't mind." He twirled linguini against a spoon. "The more the merrier."

His openness, his cheer—two of the big reasons I fell for him. But in this particular equation, they couldn't save us. I swallowed, hating what I had to say next: "She's kind of . . . judgy of people I date."

He cocked an eyebrow and grinned. "Fine, but be honest. Have any of them been as undeniably charming as me?"

"Of course not!" I tried to match his smile. All night, I'd been distracted and distant, unable to keep up with his jokes.

Kristen's words echoed between my temples: *You seem to pick bad apples.* And my grateful response: *I know I can count on you to give me your honest appraisal.*

"Let me put it this way." I picked at the crust on my bread plate. "You know when a friend starts dating someone who, deep down, she knows is bad news? So she keeps him away from her friends because she thinks they won't approve?" Aaron had several close female friends, so I knew he could relate. His eyebrows rose and I rushed to finish the thought: "This feels like that, but inverted. I *know* you're amazing and I don't want her to tell me otherwise."

"So she doesn't think I'm amazing?" His glasses reflected the candlelight. I couldn't tell if his eyes looked wounded behind them. My heart squeezed.

"She likes you!" I shook my head. "It's not personal. She doesn't think anyone is good enough for me."

"She's not wrong. You are way out of my league." He pulled a hunk of bread from the basket and chuckled. "I have no idea what you're doing with me."

"Shut up. You're the best." I grabbed his hand, then raised it to kiss his knuckles. "I mean it, Aaron. I really like you."

"I dig you too." He squeezed my hand. "All right, as long as you're not hiding me from Kristen out of, like, shame. Which I would *totally* understand, to be clear." He waved away my protests. "Naw, it's sweet that she has super-high standards for her friends."

"I guess that's true. It's nice that she cares." I leaned back. "My parents just say vague things about how I should probably 'settle down.' "

"Ooh, have you told your parents about me?"

"No, not yet . . . but please don't take that personally, 'cause I don't tell them anything." *Settle down*. It's the same thing we tell a fussy three-year-old—stop making noise, stop annoying me. Make yourself someone else's problem. "Wait, do your parents know about me?"

"Sure do! Just that I'm dating someone new. They're not, like, driving down from Appleton to meet you tomorrow."

A waiter scooped up our plates. Aaron excused himself and I sipped my jammy wine as if I could drink in his sweet words. They reached my belly and sat there, sparkling.

I hoped I'd convinced Aaron, made him see that Kristen's whole not-good-enough-for-Emily thing was just a front. It was about keeping me all to herself. I was only now realizing how wide her territorial streak really was.

But wait. Whether it was conscious or not, I'd been keeping Kristen away from Aaron from the start. Even in Chile, before he and I were a couple, I hadn't mentioned him—I'd only brought him up on the last night. I'd told myself it was because I didn't want to jinx it, but it was more than that.

A distant thought began to form, like a thunderhead rolling in.

When I did tell her about Aaron, something changed. And I hadn't done it delicately—I'd rolled the announcement into my rejection of her plan for us to backpack together.

The thought sailed closer, larger, taking shape.

I heard it as she must have heard it: *No, Kristen, I won't go along with your plan. No, I don't want to spend half the year with you.* And, in the same breath: *There's someone special, someone I'm choosing over you.*

I could sense its shadow now, the last millisecond before the revelation slid into place.

It made a terrible kind of sense: Kristen was used to getting what she wanted. She saw Aaron as a threat. And she'd do anything to bind us together—to create another secret, the one thing I couldn't ever tell him, a wall separating him from me. From *us,* Kristen and myself.

My God. *She'd do anything.*

Aaron returned and I rearranged my face into a smile.

"Did they bring the dessert menu?" he asked, spreading the napkin over his lap.

"Not yet." I crossed my legs and the lotus flower tattoo on my ankle winked up at me.

"I THINK THERE'S something wrong with Kristen," I said, then blanched. "Er, wrong with our friendship."

Adrienne nodded and waited for me to go on. It was nice of her, fitting me in for an emergency session, but now that I was here I realized I couldn't actually voice any of my fears. Finally she said, "Wrong how?"

"Maybe our relationship isn't super healthy," I said. "I always thought of her as protective, like, she always had my back. But now . . ."

The pieces were all coming together. Evidence accumulating. Bodies piling up.

A trail of failed relationships—even some female friendships, now that I thought about it—in my wake.

"The way she talked me out of dating certain people in the past . . . I think you're right, I think she's possessive." Possessive and possibly dangerous. A hell of a combination.

"I remember you brought her up when you told me about your last boyfriend," Adrienne said. "Colin, right?"

I pressed my fist to my lips. "That's right. Everyone liked him—everyone but Kristen. She pressured me to end things with him, but when I look back on the relationship, he didn't do anything wrong." I shook my head. "I don't want the same thing to happen with Aaron."

I can't let her near him. I thought it so quickly, so confidently, it shocked even me.

"So you're trying to break the pattern this time," she said.

"Right. But I don't know how. I'm . . . the idea of getting out of the friendship scares me."

Of course I couldn't mention everything riding on our alliance. The slayings that yoked us together. The ghosts of the rough-handed backpackers hovering between us.

"What do you think will happen if you set some boundaries?"

There was a soft thump in the hallway and we both turned toward it. My heart vroomed as the fears whorled: Though it wasn't logical, I pictured cops breaking down the door and violently arresting me for murder. My life ruined, my cozy, rose-colored future snuffed out like a candle. My world collapsing.

And then the thoughts climbed higher, a key change: *I'm afraid of my skull collapsing, cracked like an eggshell by blunt-force trauma. Or my lungs collapsing in a deadly house fire, singeing from the inside as smoke fills every air sac.*

"That was probably the next client looking for the bathroom," she announced, turning back toward me. "So you were saying. You're ready to set new boundaries?"

I nodded. "I want some distance. I don't want all our baggage coming between Aaron and me."

"Simply acknowledging that is huge." Her fingers brushed the side of her clipboard, then dropped. "I keep doing that."

"What happened to your notebook?" That's what felt odd about today's session: In place of the typical spiral-bound pad was a sheath of printer paper stuck to a clipboard.

"Oh, it's somewhere in my back office."

I tilted my head. "So it's missing?" She'd assured me that all we talked about, everything she jotted down, would remain confidential.

"No, I—I didn't see it when I got here, but I was running late and didn't want you to wait." She leaned forward. "So. It's going to take some strength to change the dynamic. Because she's going to push back, and you, too, will be tempted to return to what's comfortable."

I nodded slowly. "I know. But things are different now." Now I had Aaron. And now the scales over my eyes were thinning by the day. "Aaron and I started dating while Kristen was in Australia. And things were *great*. Our relationship didn't feel fragile until Kristen showed up in Milwaukee."

Had she flown all the way to Wisconsin to come between Aaron and me? After all, she'd materialized on my doorstep, *abracadabra*, just a week after I told her about him and, in the same breath, said no to her backpacking pitch . . .

A new thought popped: God, was it really a coincidence that she lost her job the second our trip ended? Or had she *quit* her job and switched to plan B when she noticed I wasn't calling her every hour, like I had after Cambodia? When she realized I was diving headfirst into a new relationship—one that might really go somewhere with her nine thousand miles away, unable to call the shots? When she figured out that the ties of fresh trauma hadn't bound us together like she'd hoped?

Adrienne scribbled something on her printer paper, then tapped the pen's cap. "You've done a lot of great work in just a few weeks," she said. "Deciding to stand up for yourself is huge. It takes an enormous amount of bravery, especially since it sounds like Kristen won't let go without a fight."

Stop. Stop. Stop. I was an idiot. I *knew* what Kristen was capable of—I'd seen it firsthand.

Her gaze vaulted to the clock on the wall. "That's all our time for today."

I gathered my things and said goodbye. Alarm was sweeping through me, growing in speed and intensity. Maybe I was being paranoid—maybe this was all a huge misunderstanding, and I was misinterpreting Kristen's innocent gestures as some scary *Single White Female* shit. But if my terrifying hunches were correct, sweet Lord, I needed to avoid her—and keep Aaron far away from her too. This wasn't the kind of thing we could talk out: *So, Kristen, you killed another man and moved halfway around the world to make me yours alone, huh? Does that mean I should fear for my new boyfriend's life?*

I trudged down the hall to the waiting room. Someone was hunched over their phone on the sofa there, and I gave a bland smile without making eye contact. My hand had just grasped the door-knob when the stranger spoke.

"Emily?"

My heart dropped. I froze and turned slowly, first my head, then my whole body.

Kristen raised her eyebrows and smirked. "Well, hello."

CHAPTER 28

*S**he is stalking you.* It's what my brain spit out first, a warning, the same low voice that pipes up when you pass a group of leering dudes or walk too close to the edge of a cliff. *Back off. Run away.* Fight or flight, cortisol and adrenaline conspiring to keep you safe.

She frowned and gave a little laugh. "What are you doing here?"

"What are *you* doing here?" It came out as defensive, and I swallowed hard.

"I'm seeing a therapist. For an intake." She glanced down the hall, then at me. "Priya recommended her. I didn't realize you were going here?"

I dropped onto a seat. "Priya told me about this place too." I tucked my purse onto my lap. "Are you seeing Adrienne?"

"Um . . ." She glanced at her phone for a moment, then nodded. "Adrienne Oderdonk? It's going to be hard for me to not accidentally say 'Badonkadonk.'" She cracked a smile. "I finally took your advice. You've been telling me to see someone and I figured as long as I'm, you know. Careful with my words, it's okay."

I thought, *You lie.* I thought, *You're so tidy at explaining things away.* But instead I said, "So we're both seeing a therapist in secret! So Midwestern of us."

"I know! Hashtag-stigma." I heard Adrienne's door open down the hallway and stood to leave. "Well, good luck."

"Text me later," she called.

I was almost to my car by the time the other details fell into place: Adrienne's missing notebook; that faint *thunk* outside the door. And how, just a few days ago, I'd confessed to Kristen that I wished I could come clean, unburden myself of the truth about Sebastian and Paolo. Had Kristen figured out I'd be here and somehow confiscated notes from my session to check what I'd told Adrienne? To scan for anything incriminating, make sure I wasn't skating too close to the truth? Or had she followed me to the therapy practice, skulking in the shadows and then pressing her ear to the office door? *Calm down, Emily, you're being ridiculous.*

But what if I was right?

BUT I HAD to be wrong. Paranoid, ridiculous Emily. As I spooned pasta into a bowl and carried it into the living room, I replayed the conversation in my head. Kristen kept popping up where she didn't belong—my yoga studio, my therapist's office, my front door. It was ironic: I'd felt gutted when she'd moved to Australia, but then I'd built a life for myself here. And now she was ramming herself into every part of it.

Kristen texted a hello as I cued up a show. Commercials at the beginning, employee pricing on SUVs and laundry detergent tough enough for toddlers' stains. Mundane stuff for women with families, women with ordinary lives. Women without a browser history checking if their best friend was just a bit murdery.

"How'd it go tonight?" I hit Send, saw that she was typing back.

"Pretty good. She said she'll refer me to someone else in the practice. Conflict of interest."

I sent back a question mark, and she added, "She figured out I was the Kristen you talk about."

A scattershot spray of fear. *Shit*—if Kristen wasn't already worried about my blabbing, she would be now.

I spent a while rewording my text, trying to get it right. Finally: "Got it. I hope that doesn't make you feel weird—I'm extremely careful about your/our privacy. But of course you come up, you are my best friend! ☺"

"I figured."

A silence, no little typing dots, and I couldn't think of anything to say either. After a moment I jumped up from the couch, shook out my hands, and lifted my phone once more: "Will you go again? With a different therapist?"

"Not sure yet. It was an intense session."

Intense. I swallowed. "Adrienne's a pro."

"She seems smart."

I stared at it. It probably just meant *Adrienne is intelligent, she's good at her job.* But it could also mean: *I don't like her. She's smart enough to read you—to read between the lines.*

"I'm glad you gave it a shot. Super brave and awesome of you." I added a few clapping emojis to underscore my point.

She was typing on and off for a while, and then a longish text came through: "We'll see if I go again. I had to make up an excuse bc Nana and Bill would be so judgy about it. But thanks, and you too. Hey, remember what I said in my birthday card. Read it, remember it, believe it. We're in this together." She finished with a heart.

I thought it over, then decided she was talking about that PS: *If you ever forget how amazing you are, you know who to call. Because I never, ever forget, and I'd be honored to count the ways.* I responded with a kissy emoji and dropped my phone on the couch.

I turned off the TV show halfway through, unable to concentrate. Thoughts were churning, swirling like vultures. Who could I trust when I couldn't trust my best friend? Could I count on her to keep us both safe? What would she do if I didn't remain attached to her like a barnacle? Would she hurt those I loved?

Or would she . . . the thought made me ill, it was so repugnant, so verboten, more repulsive than incest or pedophilia or any gut-level taboo: Would Kristen kill me if things didn't go her way? I thought of her pointed stare when I asked about Jamie—*I don't ever want to go through that again.* I let out a whimper. For so many years, I'd seen Kristen as a constant, her love as undeniable as gravity. Now it was clear that she was more of a loose cannon than I'd realized. And that that cannon just might be zeroed in on me.

Focus, Emily. I had to review the evidence, come up with a plan. I dropped my bowl on the coffee table and marched into my room. The email from Westmoor was still open on my computer. I loaded the pictures I'd taken of Kristen's yearbook and photos, the ones with poor Jamie's face scribbled out. I pulled up the scant articles I'd found about the fire, about Jerry and Anne Czarnecki's untimely end.

There were options I hadn't exhausted yet, avenues I hadn't explored. Like Nana—I'd try harder, see what she'd offer up about her granddaughter's mental-health history. Or I could call Second Chance Antiques and beg Greta for more stories.

But when I snatched my phone off the sofa, Kristen's text still stared back at me: "Hey, remember what I said in my birthday card. Read it, remember it, believe it. We're in this together."

Something had been bugging me about the card—it read a bit stiffly, especially toward the end. Less like how Kristen normally talked, and more like one of her . . .

What had I done with it? I dug around in the pile of mail on my kitchen table, then found it in a tote bag in my bedroom:

Dear Emily,

HAPPY BIRTHDAY! It's hard to believe we've been friends for 10+ years. I can't imagine my life without you—in a way, I guess I owe those douchebags in our Stats 101 class a thank-you. I'm so proud of the smart, strong, independent woman you've become. And I count myself so lucky that, after 2 years apart, we'll finally live in the same city again!

I've been thinking back to those late nights when we'd sneak out at 4 or 5 am and splash in the water and then watch the sunrise over Lake Michigan together. Remember that? When we'd feel like we were the only ones awake in the whole world. When we'd feel like not just Evanston but the entire world was ours. When we would dry right off— perfectly, boldly ourselves.

XOXO,
Kristen

PS If you ever forget how amazing you are, you know
who to call. Because I never, ever forget, and I'd be honored
to count the ways.
    PPS Last line of the day, promise! ☺

"Last line of the day"—why not "last clue" or "last surprise"
or similar? Because she was referring to the last line of the card,
the one that sounded a bit wonky. I ran it through her usual codes
and had it in seconds. *"Dry right off—perfectly, boldly ourselves. X"*
D-R-O-P-B-O-X.

My pulse surged, pushing out against my fingers and throat.
Dropbox—we occasionally used the hosting site to share files, mostly
trip photos siphoned from our digital cameras. The URL of her
Dropbox account filled in automatically.

My heart had reached my ears now, whooshing like the surf, like
a deafening snare drum. I scanned through the folders there: work
stuff, camera uploads, dated subfolders bursting with pictures from
some of our earlier travels. And then my breath caught: There was a
new folder, created on my birthday, labeled *Chile.*

Relax, Emily—it's probably just, duh, photos from Chile.

But we hadn't shared our photos from that trip, hadn't created a
shared album and compared shots. I steeled myself, then clicked.

There was another folder inside, this one labeled *Phnom Penh.* A
squall of hysteria rose through me and I crouched over, prepared to
vomit. What. The hell. Was this.

I clicked again, and a pop-up appeared: *File is password-*
protected. Beneath it, a field with a blinking cursor. I tried *Emily,*
Quiteria, Paolo, Sebastian. I thought about texting Kristen, but fear
held me back. Could she tell I was trying to access the file now? That
I'd realized I hadn't completed her little treasure hunt?

I grabbed the card, pressed it open at the spine.

PS If you ever forget how amazing you are, you know
who to call. Because I never, ever forget, and I'd be honored
to count the ways.

Counting—that was the clue. And come to think of it, we hadn't met in Stats 101; it was Statistical Methods in Economics. The card was riddled with numerals, and I underlined them hastily:

HAPPY BIRTHDAY! It's hard to believe we've been friends for 10+ years. I can't imagine my life without you—in a way, I guess I owe those douchebags in our Stats 101 class a thank-you. I'm so proud of the smart, strong, independent woman you've become. And I count myself so lucky that, after 2 years apart, we'll finally live in the same city again!

I've been thinking back to those late nights when we'd sneak out at 4 or 5 am and splash in the water and then watch the sunrise over Lake Michigan together. Remember that? When we'd feel like we were the only ones awake in the whole world. When we'd feel like not just Evanston but the entire world was ours. When we would dry right off— perfectly, boldly ourselves.

I input the numbers, breathing hard, and hit Enter.

My shoulders slumped. *Incorrect password; please try again.*

I returned to the card one more time. *Screw you, Kristen, for taking what I thought was a sweet sentiment and turning it into a riddle. Like this is all a game.*

Aha—relief like a key slipping into a lock. *When we'd feel like we were the only ones awake in the whole world.*

I tried the combination again, this time with a 1 at the end. I smiled, almost *clapped,* when the file began to download.

I watched the progress bar slide to the right, then opened it eagerly.

It filled the screen. It took me a moment to make sense of it, the dizzying colors, overexposed whites and blacks and colorful blobs at funny angles.

And then it took form. The blobs were lanterns, strung across a busy street. There were people everywhere, bustling to and fro, but in the center were two shapes, clear and crisp in the swirling night scene.

One of them was Sebastian, handsome and alive and smiling as he touched my waist. The other, of course, was me.

CHAPTER 29

My fist flew to my mouth as my feet scrambled beneath me, pounding down the hallway and making it to the bathroom just in time. It all came up, dinner and more, deeper down into me, the bitter bile of my true insides. Sweat and tears and snot streamed out, too, and then I leaned against the tub, eyes closed, chest heaving.

That night. *That night.* I'd pictured that moment so many times in my mind's eye, a split second after Sebastian and I had agreed to go back to the hotel, when a sudden flash had blinded me. I'd always thought it was an accidental photobomb, that we were in the background of some stranger's vacation photo, and if the right person noticed and connected the dots, I'd be screwed. There it was, in vivid color: proof that I'd been with Sebastian right before he went missing.

But . . . Kristen. Kristen had taken it. Kristen had had it all along.

It was a threat, then. A reminder that she had dirt on me. I glanced around for my phone, then remembered it was all the way in my bedroom. But she'd been coy in our text conversation tonight, walking the knife's edge between sweet and suspect. Something like, *Remember what I wrote in the card, believe it—we're in this together.* If I go down, you do too.

I gathered my energy like it was something I could mop up off the floor. On shaking legs, I staggered to my room. The photo was still staring out from my screen and I X'ed out of it. Christ, she'd had it for over a year. She hadn't deleted it back when we promised not to leave a trace. Instead she'd been waiting to deploy it. As what—collateral? Blackmail?

Another violent shudder rushed through me. *Shit.* She'd set this mousetrap on my birthday, an entire week ago. Right before I began to wonder if I should sever ties from her for good.

As if she'd *known*. Claws out. She whipped out the trump card, the proof that I'd never, ever be out from under her thumb.

There was something else thrumming beneath the horror, something brighter, and it suddenly boomed into the forefront: I was oddly satisfied, almost *thrilled,* to have my answer. I wasn't paranoid, and my anxiety hadn't been unfounded. Was Kristen deranged? Disturbed and manipulative, at minimum. She'd killed Sebastian; she'd killed Paolo. Why was I twisting myself into a knot debating if that made her a killer?

The doorbell rang and I stared in the direction of the front door, alert as a meerkat. I flicked off the light and crept into the hallway, hoping whoever it was would give up and go away.

But they rang again. I stood very still and listened as someone thumped on the door, then tried the knob, an insistent jiggle.

My phone chimed in my bedroom and I scuttled toward it—having my phone on my person wasn't a bad idea. I swiped it off the desk and saw Kristen's new text: "I can see you turning lights on and off, dummy," plus a laughing emoji.

I sucked in air and breathed it out. *Okay, Emily. Okay, okay, okay.* I tucked my phone into my back pocket and waltzed to the front door.

"Hi!" She hugged me, car keys jangling in her hand. "I stopped by my new place to take measurements and thought I'd see if you're home! Wait, what's wrong?"

"I . . . I just threw up." I scraped my tongue against my teeth. "I think I ate some bad ricotta." I kept my hand on the door, smiled weakly.

"Oh my God. Do you want me to get you anything? Throwing up is the *worst*."

"Thanks, but I'm fine. I just want to lie down. I feel kind of . . ." Suddenly my head did feel swoopy, like I might pass out. The floor pitched beneath me and I grabbed the wall.

"Are you okay? Here." She looped an arm under mine. "Do you need a doctor? You look awful."

"I'm fine. I'm just gonna go to bed." As if someone had turned on a faucet, my hands were suddenly fizzing hard, tingling and twinkling on the inside. "Thanks for stopping over, but I—" The fizz rushed up into my skull and I doubled over, my shoulder pressed against the wall.

"Keep your head down. You're okay. Do you wanna sit?"

"I'm fine," I repeated, eyes squeezed shut. The frothy feeling was beginning to clear. I breathed in, then out. Hyperventilation, that's what was happening. Not enough oxygen to the brain, or was it carbon dioxide?

"C'mon, I'll help you to your room." She pulled me forward and I flashed back to that night at her cottage, her pulling me across a knotted terrain of branches and roots and rocks. Past the rabbit that only a madwoman would kill. I funneled all my attention into my left foot, then my right one. Rhythmic, like canoeing. Like digging a grave.

After a short eternity, we reached the edge of my bed.

"Thanks so much, Kristen. I'll text you, okay?"

"Feel better." She turned to leave and my eyes thudded closed. Already, my chest was loosening, the rush in my ears tapering. I would deal with Kristen later, when I'd had some time to think. For now, I had to protect myself.

I rolled onto my side and clutched my pillow, then froze—Kristen was still there, still in my bedroom. Standing over my desk, head down, her back to me.

"Jamie," she remarked, and her finger touched the scribble on the screen.

All the air rushed out of the room. Oxygen—there was none, a perfect vacuum.

She clicked the mouse. " 'Two Dead Following Brookfield House Fire,' " she read aloud.

Another click. " 'Dear Ms. Schmidt, thank you for your inquiry to Westmoor Behavioral Services.' "

Slowly, slowly, she turned to face me.

"Emily, what the *fuck*."

CHAPTER 30

"Kristen . . ."

Her eyes bored into mine. "What is this? Why were you going through my stuff? And why the hell were you talking to Westmoor?"

I kept opening my mouth and then closing it, like a fish dangling from a hook.

"What's going on, Emily? I'm sick of your lies. I'm sick of your *bullshit*." She swung her arm as she said it, sending my laptop and several pens crashing to the floor.

"I . . . I was just trying to find out . . . if . . ."

"What, you think I need to explain myself?" Lightning shot through her eyes. "Okay, fine. I had a fight with my best friend, and then, because I was twelve years old, I scribbled her face out in my photos. As for Westmoor, yes, I spent some time there after the violent and painful death of my parents and the suicide of my best friend in the span of a few weeks. I had a breakdown and needed psychiatric care. And I've been pretty goddamn open about it, considering it's still painful to talk about. I told you about Dr. Brightside."

"I'm— I just wanted to . . ."

She shook her head. "Wow. So this is why you've been avoiding me like the plague. God, I'm pathetic, trying so hard to make things right with you."

"Okay, if you're such a great friend . . ." I pointed at my computer, upside down on the floor. "Then why the hell are you blackmailing me with a photo of Sebastian and me together? That I needed to solve a damn *riddle* to find? What kind of devoted best friend does that?"

Her mouth dropped open, then emitted a scoff. "You think I'm *blackmailing* you?"

"We said we'd delete everything from the trip! And I did!" I was gaining steam now. "You lied to me . . . for a *year*."

"Christ, Emily, think about what you're saying." Her palms splayed. "How was I supposed to know what would happen next? I took it because he was hot and you rarely bring guys home and I thought you'd thank me later."

She looked so earnest, with the frustrated energy of a five-year-old who needs you to know she's telling the truth. But . . . but this was more of her skillful manipulation, right?

"Then why keep it? Why set it up for me to *find,* for Christ's sake?"

"Because I was scared." She clutched her hands together. "You looked ready to crack, Emily. I was so scared of what you might do."

I flicked a tear away. "So why send it now? How is that not blackmail?"

"I sent it because you kept talking about telling someone. How much you wanted to be open with your new boyfriend or whatever. It's not blackmail, it's . . . a reminder. That there's a photo tying Sebastian to you. I never, ever want to use it. But I needed to make you see."

What the hell kind of logic was that? I shook my head. *She's lost her damn mind.*

"And also, wow, the nerve," she went on. "What did you think? That I'm this bloodthirsty psychopath?" She took a step toward the bed, and I scrambled up into a seated position. "You, of all people."

After all I've done for you . . . after I killed *a man to save your life.* I braced to hear it, heart pounding.

But instead, she crossed her arms. "After what you did to Sebastian."

I stared at her for a moment. "Wait, what?"

"Don't play dumb. I watched you kill him."

Beneath me, the bed slanted, a boat on rocky seas.

"What are you talking about?" Kristen had hit him with a floor lamp, swift and hard, sent him sprawling onto the floor. But that wasn't what killed him; that just drew blood, knocked him off his feet. And then . . .

"Are you kidding me?" she yelped. "You wouldn't stop kicking him. I had to pull you off him."

Stop. Stop. Stop. Blood trickling like paint down the floor lamp. Behind me, Kristen's eyes wide, thunderstruck. Blood mottling her hands, her wrists, her shoes.

"No." I shook my head, then heard my voice rise into a shout: "No! That's not how it happened. I . . . I had to stop you."

Sebastian's head on the floor, nestled against a leg of the metal bed frame. I'd looked into Kristen's furious eyes, and then detected motion before I could even process it.

Three kicks, four, blood staining the metal leg and pooling into the cracks in the laminate floor.

"Stop. Stop. Stop."

Finally I'd heard Kristen's pleas, distorted as if we were underwater, scuba diving in the deep. Crying, begging me to stop. And I'd turned, grabbed for her. She lunged toward him, murmuring in horror, but I dragged her away and into a hug, and we'd leaned against each other, shaking.

"No," I said again, weaker now. "That's not how it happened. You're . . . confusing me."

"That's exactly how it happened." She reached the edge of my bed and stopped. "You killed Sebastian and I'm the reason you're not in jail for it."

CHAPTER 31

You killed Sebastian.

No. This wasn't true. It couldn't be. This was classic gaslighting—messing with my head, screwing up my memories with the deftness of a grifter. Or a magician, *poof*—Kristen had made her culpability disappear. My stomach twisted like a towel wrung dry.

But I had to stay alert, I had to be safe. Strategic, for once, like her. And the safest distance between Kristen and myself was as many miles as I could manage.

"Okay," I said. "Clearly I'm not thinking straight. I—I told you I looked into Jamie when we were Up North. You said your old stuff was in those boxes." I pressed my damp palms into the comforter.

"I can't believe you went through my things," she replied. "Such a violation."

"I'm sorry. I really am. I forgot about it until . . . well, finding that photo of Sebastian and me sent me into a tailspin. I guess it was, like, a psychological defense to seeing the picture and just kinda losing it. I went down a rabbit hole."

"A rabbit hole of what—researching the fire that killed my parents? Contacting my old therapy center? What are you even accusing me of?" Shiny tear tracks ribboned down her cheeks.

Shit—my defense made no sense, not when I'd contacted Westmoor days before finding the Dropbox photo.

But Kristen seemed too worked up to notice. "I don't know what to say. That someone I love and trust would even *have* these thoughts about me . . ." Her hand slid to her midriff, as if I'd stuck a knife there. "I can't tell you how hurtful it is."

Guilt pulsed through me, hot shame infusing the cold fear. "I'm sorry."

She pressed her fingertips to her forehead, then heaved a sigh. "I'm gonna get going."

Preteen Kristen scribbling out her best friend's face. Checking into a facility for help with the squall of grief. She'd put forth such a convincing argument, such a consistent account. My head was spinning too quickly to decide if I even bought it. For the moment, I was still scuba diving—treading water until I could figure out what to do next.

"I'm not going to tell anyone," I said. Her gaze jerked my way. "About Chile or Cambodia. I swear. We're in this together, and I don't want either of us kissing our lives goodbye." I rolled my legs off the bed and rose. "I'm serious. I just want to move on. So don't worry, okay?"

I crossed to her and she flinched as I neared. I stood awkwardly, my hands hanging in front of my chest, and finally she shrugged.

"Get some rest," she said. "I'll let myself out." I watched as she grew smaller and smaller in the hallway and disappeared into the foyer. She closed the door with a *thunk*.

I lay corpselike on the bed for a long time, watching light from passing cars streak sideways along the wall. I thought about the photo of Sebastian and me. Why had she saved it, led me to it? Her explanation made sense at first glance, but it didn't hold up to scrutiny. It was like a star so dim that it disappears when you look right at it. She'd called the picture a *reminder*. But if she sent it to South African authorities—even if she included my name—I could toss Kristen under suspicion too. She'd been to Westmoor; she was the one with a record. Would she really be that self-destructive, blowing up both of our lives like an extremist with a bomb strapped to her torso?

My mind vaulted back to that night in Phnom Penh. All those

times I'd replayed it, the flash in Kristen's eyes, her lunging *her* leg back and then swinging it into his body . . . but no, now that she'd pointed it out, another voice was calling bullshit on that account. That wasn't the real memory, just one I'd inexpertly pasted on top. Brains can do that, rewrite an ending—funny organs obsessed with self-preservation, with making oneself right. Now I could flick back and forth between the two scenarios, fake and real, the kick coming from *her* foot, from mine. Like a picture search in a children's magazine. Scenario A and Scenario B: Spot the difference.

Right? Or was Kristen manipulating me? Maybe she knew if she said it confidently enough, if she looked at me hard like I'd lost my mind, I'd believe her. I'd convince myself I'd done it.

So much power. So much confidence. *Confidence*—that was another item on the list of traits the modern woman is supposed to exude. Not vanity, not Kardashian bluster, but a deep fearlessness, Lizzo Vibes, Beyoncé Power. Big Dick Energy. It was another trap: They want us fearless but also fearful, our swagger faltering when a passerby tells us what he'd like to do to dat ass. When a man pins you against the wall like a butterfly on a board. I'd felt so scared, and then, just as suddenly, so angry. I'd wanted to make Sebastian afraid. I wanted him to hurt like he'd hurt me.

Now the best thing I could do was act on a thought I'd had earlier: *Get away.* Put as many miles between myself and Kristen as possible so that I could think, dammit, without the constant fear of her popping into the frame. And I'd bring Aaron with me, lest she have any ideas about eliminating the inconvenient obstacle between her and me.

So I called him. Told him I needed to get away for the weekend, begged him to find someone to cover his shifts at Café Mona. I looked up travel deals as we spoke and one city called out to me, needled at my sense of déjà vu, though I wasn't sure why. All the sunshine, maybe. No shadows in which to hide.

Aaron promised to see if he could get off work, and we hung up. Panic stretched inside me: What if he couldn't? What if he backed out now? Would I book a solo trip, grab my things and run so that . . . what? I could sit in a hotel room and fixate over that murky night with Sebastian, alone?

Stop. Stop. Stop. An hour ago, I'd felt so sure it was in my voice. I pressed the heels of my hands against my eyes, pressing until a spray of lime shot out against the black of my eyelids. Like the Northern Lights.

Finally, finally, my phone vibrated on the coffee table. All of my cells jumped a millimeter toward the sky.

But it wasn't Aaron. It was Kristen, of course it was Kristen, always Kristen, Kristen, Kristen.

She'd texted, "I've been sobbing in my room all night. I can't believe you."

Shame swooped through me and I unlocked my phone to reply.

And then I paused. A commercial on the TV was blaring, an annoying jingle about the best wireless network.

Get away. It had been echoing in my head all evening. And yet I was about to engage, knee-jerk, and start the cycle all over again.

I set my phone back on the table. Picked up the remote next to it, cranked up the volume, and settled into the soft sofa behind me.

AARON TEXTED AS soon as I stopped thinking about him: "Wen can cover for me. LET'S DO IT." Several celebratory emojis, confetti and champagne. I closed my eyes and grinned, pulled the phone against my heart. *Thank God.*

But as I opened the booking site, doubts crept in. I'd have to pretend to be normal—not just normal, *excited*—twenty-four hours a day, as Aaron and I wandered the reddish streets and watched the sun dip over distant mountains and ate meals together, breakfast, lunch, and dinner.

He texted me his birthday so that I could book our flights: *God, I don't even know his birthday yet.* Would we travel well together— would he find me gross? What if I got hangry or sick or snappish or stressed? What if we got into a huge fight?

A fight. With Aaron. In our own oasis, a jumble of glass and steel in the middle of the sunbaked desert.

And then a new thought padded in, as sly and unassuming as a cat.

Is Aaron safe with me?

I WOKE TO a string of texts from Kristen ("Can we talk?" "I really think we need to talk." "Are you ignoring me?") and muted the conversation before I even got out of bed. As I neared my desk after a meeting, I saw that my phone was ringing. I was about to snatch up the handset when I realized it was Kristen, one of the few numbers I knew by heart. I jabbed around in the phone's settings until I found the Do Not Disturb function.

"It's been ringing off the hook for the last hour," the designer kitty-corner from me announced.

"Sorry about that." My stomach tightened like a fist.

I was vacant-eyed in meetings, quietly replaying Sebastian's final moments: Was that Kristen's foot bashing into his ribs, or mine? If it was the former, why could I see it so clearly, feel the heavy thump of my toes meeting his flesh? Toward the end of the day, as I passed the floor-to-ceiling windows, an eerie feeling washed over me. I swiveled my gaze to Rogers Street below. Kristen would be out there, I *knew* it—facing the window, hands in her pockets, solemn and staring and still. The shot in a horror movie stamped with a sudden, dissonant chord.

I scanned the sidewalk through the budded boughs of trees, over the fruit-tree petals stippling the cement. There was a teenager, an old man with a cane, a frazzled-looking woman with a baby strapped to her bosom.

I turned and hurried on. Kristen wasn't there.

ON THE DRIVE home from work, my heart pounded at every red light. She'd stopped calling and texting around two, and this was worse, the sudden silence so loud it sizzled against my eardrums. I held my breath as I turned the last corner onto my street, braced to see Kristen out front.

But there was stillness, empty space. Even the birds closed their beaks as I let myself in, locking the door behind me. I was partway through yanking down the blinds when I started to laugh. Here I was, cowering in my own home like Kevin freaking McCallister in fear of my supposed best friend. The friend with whom I'd just spent four days in a remote cabin in the woods. *Look what's become of you.*

Then I got a text from Kristen, the first in almost four hours.

My rib cage locked up and my fist flew to my mouth. *Bad.* This was very, very bad.

It was a screenshot of the tip line for the South African Police Service. Her caption: "Don't think I won't turn over that photo."

CHAPTER 32

I called Kristen immediately, head pounding, jaw juddering like a jackhammer. The first ring cut out after a moment, and then we were both on the line, breathing at each other.

"So that got your attention," she said.

The lies dripped out of me before I even had time to think—excuses, placations, supplications to please please please not be so mad at me. Natural as slipping out of a foreign language and into my mother tongue. "I'm sorry I missed your calls, it was so busy at work today, and I wanted some time to really think about what I wanted to say—"

"Just stop." Her voice cracked. "Do you have any idea how awful I've felt for the past twenty-four hours? How deeply you hurt me?"

A javelin of guilt went through me, followed by a groundswell of indignation. My Achilles' heel, the chink in my armor, the soft belly that made me curl up like a pill bug: *You hurt me.* Over and over, Kristen found it, exploited it, wielded it like a weapon. Like a bottle of Carménère wine, held aloft.

"Kristen, look," I said softly. "I'm sorry I hurt you. But the photo of me and Sebastian—"

"We really need to talk." Her voice was a machete, slicing off my words. "Can you come over?"

"What?" My chest tightened. "We're talking now."

"You know what I mean. In person."

"We're talking right now," I said again. "I have a lot to do tonight. I'm going out of town tomorrow and I need to pack. I don't see why either of us should drive twenty miles—"

"Because I don't think this is a conversation we should have on the phone." She didn't quite clear her throat, but the *ahem* was implied.

I slammed my hand onto the couch cushion. Had Kristen always been this paranoid? Her insistence on squeaky-clean search histories and turned-off phones had always seemed sage—and in stark contrast to her cheerful chatter about our travels. The Instagrams she showed Priya, the easy patter with Aaron. *She* was the one acting brazen, like she wanted to get caught.

Now she sounded like a wild-eyed conspiracy theorist, quivering under a space blanket and tinfoil hat.

"No one is listening, Kristen. No one is freaking tapping the phones of a couple of thirty-year-old white girls in southeastern Wisconsin."

She scoffed. "What, you think I'm crazy? Do you think your phone just *happens* to only be listening when you say 'Hey, Siri'? That it couldn't hear every single word that came before?" Her voice had a quivering intensity, like a hunting bow pulled taut. "Or, or do you think it's a *coincidence* that after someone mentions, like, a museum during a phone call, you start seeing ads for it? Think about it, Emily. Don't be stupid."

She had a point, but still I rolled my eyes. "Well, you sound pretty damn sketchy right now. If they weren't listening before, they sure as hell are now."

"Stop. This is serious. Just stop, please."

Stop. Stop. Stop. I wished I could set up something like a police lineup, have her read the line in a hysterical pitch. Had it been *her* larynx vibrating that night, or mine? The thought rammed me in the gut and I curled over it, my palm on my stomach.

"Come over," she pleaded, "or I'll come to you. I don't want to send the photo, but . . . you're not leaving me much choice."

"That's how you want to handle this?" I said. "That's the kind of friendship you wanna have?"

Silence, a long one, two cars playing chicken on a dark country road.

"I'm saying this because I actually care about our friendship." Her tone was gravelly, preternaturally calm. "And you left me no choice."

"Kristen—"

Now her words tumbled out, one lightning breath: "Be here in twenty minutes or I'm sending the photo. Don't test me." And then she hung up.

I FLEW DOWN I-94, gravity building in my chest as if I were a meteor hurtling toward Earth. The air was steely and cold, with a charged, loamy smell, and the halos around oncoming headlights were obelisk-shaped, blurring my vision.

I began to change lanes and a semi blasted its horn, sending spiky adrenaline through my limbs. I swerved and gripped the wheel, then watched the Mack truck cruise by. The driver honked again, as if to further admonish me, and I cried out, my frustration mingling with the big rig's basso honk.

I kept seeing the photo in the windshield, the bright headlights reminiscent of that camera flash, the bang of brilliance as Sebastian and I stumbled toward his demise. Sebastian, blond and broad and overexposed. Sebastian, who was still missing, his body food for sea creatures at the bottom of Tonle Kak.

Kristen's voice, a whisper: *Sebastian, whom you kicked until his skull yielded.*

No. The exit sneaked up on me and I jolted into the right lane, slamming on the brakes as the ramp deposited me at a red light. My heart beat in time with my turn signal. Tick-tock, tick-tock, tick-tock.

I passed the darkened peak of King of Kings, and its stained-glass windows caught my headlights as I turned. Inside Nana and Bill's subdivision, a glint of eyes watched from the curb: another rabbit, its black eyes protruding from the sides of its head. Was it a warning, a portent of doom from the hacked-up animal I'd seen Up North? I never did figure out what kind of predator left axlike gashes in the neck of its prey. The rabbit turned and scurried into a copse of spindly trees.

At Nana and Bill's, I parked at the end of the driveway and spotted a figure in an upper window, watching me climb toward the front door. A rinse of fear at the sight of her—my best friend, my co-conspirator, my biggest threat. The silhouette turned off the light, dissolving into darkness, and when I steeled myself and reached for the doorbell, Kristen was already there, pale-faced and red-eyed behind the storm door.

"Hi." I stood hunched, unsure whether she'd go in for a hug. Finally she held the door open for me instead. I hung my thin jacket on a hook inside.

"Can you leave your purse out here too?" She pointed at the foyer's bench, and I rolled my eyes. Satisfied that the government wouldn't be listening in on two girls having a heart-to-heart in one of their childhood homes, Kristen led me to her bedroom and closed the door behind us.

Her bed and dresser had been shoved into a corner, and several expensive-looking cardio machines were scattered like sculptures around the rest of the room. A weight bench crouched next to the closet, each dumbbell a gleaming weapon.

She plopped onto her bed, then whisked up a tissue and tossed it into a nearby trash can. The bin was already half full, physical evidence of her grief. Her hurt looked so genuine, so tangible. The appropriate response to learning your best friend has been investigating whether you're a monster. Doubt prickled anew.

"Should we talk?" I sat on the corner and ran my palm across the smooth duvet.

She curled her knees to her chest. "You only came because I said I'd turn over that photo."

Yeah, no shit. "I came because I care about you. That made me realize how much you really needed to talk, like, ASAP." I swallowed. "Because you wouldn't send that photo and my info to the South African police, right? You know that if someone called me in for questioning, I could name you too."

She chewed on her lower lip. "But the evidence . . . it only leads to you."

"What are you—" But then the truth rocketed through me. In Quiteria, I'd filled out the hotel check-in forms and handled the car rental. The photo from Phnom Penh was of Sebastian . . . and me. It was my name on all the forms, my face in the photo. It would be her word against mine.

I could claim she'd been involved, sure.

But I couldn't prove it.

My vision blurred and gravity shifted. I breathed deeply until the room righted itself: *Focus, Emily.* I tapped her shin. "Tell me what you need—I want to make things right."

Kristen heaved an unsteady sigh. "It's such a mess," she said. "I keep having nightmares that a bunch of guys with guns bust into my bedroom. Or that we're back in the Elqui Valley with people chasing us around those hairpin turns. And sometimes . . ." She cried for a few seconds, tears plopping onto her blouse. "Sometimes I dream I'm back in our suite and Paolo is . . . that I couldn't stop him. It's so scary, Emily. I thought I understood what you went through in Cambodia, but I was wrong. It was so much worse."

I was frozen, every nerve on high alert. Was she referring to the attempted assault? Or . . . or what came after, when she wrapped her fingers around a bottle of wine?

"What was worse than you thought?" I asked, my voice gossamer-thin.

"The . . . the trauma, I guess. That moment when he shoved me and my head hit the wall."

Kristen exhaled with a constricted sigh, *ujjayi pranayama* in yoga. "I was scared in a way I've never been before," she went on. "It's like it changed me, irreversibly. You know how someone can drop acid and have a bad trip and then they're just *different* from that day onward?"

"And that's what it was like? An acid trip?" I needed her to clarify: Was she talking about the frightened instant or the one that followed, the one where she swung the bottle like a club?

The thought jabbed at me: *If killing Paolo left her this rattled, she* couldn't *have been the one to kill Sebastian . . . could she?*

"That moment of fear," she said, "it's like it marked me—*defined* me. And, you know what, it *has* made me paranoid. All I see are dangers now. Fear of everyone I meet. Fear that . . . that the people I trust are gonna turn on me." She smoothed her palms down her thighs. "I thought I was keeping my shit together, keeping my whole world under control. I even went to a therapist. But then"—here her voice wobbled—"then I realized you'd been, like, *investigating* me behind my back. Like I'm some kind of freak."

But you threatened me, I wanted to say. *You hoarded an old photo and left me breadcrumbs so I'd find it when my own fear bordered on paranoia, after a year of telling me we couldn't risk keeping any evidence around.* But I knew that saying this would buy me another hour on this bed, supplicating at Kristen's feet. I needed to slap a Band-Aid on her ego and get the hell out of Milwaukee.

"I'm sorry you saw that," I said gently. "I was spiraling and grasping at straws, you know? The photo you showed me—er, wanted me to find—it threw me." I shook my head. "I'm sorry you've been feeling not like yourself. I went through that last year too. It does get better with time, but . . . I get that, feeling raw. I want you to be okay." I patted her knee.

"I thought you were here for me." She dabbed a tissue under her eyes.

"I am!"

"No, you're leaving me."

"Just for the weekend." I glanced at her. "We'll both be thinking more clearly after a day or two, right?"

A beat. "Where are you going?" When I didn't answer, her voice grew more insistent: "Who are you going with? Aaron?"

"I'm going to Phoenix for a few days. With Aaron, yeah. I . . . I can't be a good friend right now. And I want to be. Can you understand that? It's not about running away from you. I just need a change of scenery."

A wet sniff. "I thought you had my back."

"I do. And you have mine. But you of all people know how healing travel can be, right? It's a reset. And then once I'm back, we can start fresh." Not true—I'd use the time away to distance myself from Kristen, to create boundaries where there were none. I felt the lies buzzing in my sinuses, swelling like Pinocchio's nose.

Another moist inhalation. "I'm so lonely right now," she said. "And scared. And you're the only person on Earth who knows the full extent of why."

The full extent—what proportion of the truth did I actually see? What had happened in our hotel suite when Paolo was alone with Kristen? Whose foot had connected with Sebastian's body a year earlier? What really happened to young Jamie? And was the fire that killed Kristen's parents really a random house fire . . . or had someone set it, watching a pinprick of light fork and race through the house like white-hot dominos?

"I'm right there with you," I said, because I didn't know the answers to any of my questions. Only Kristen did, and my freedom—my *life*—hinged on her wanting to protect me. "I know it's tough, but we'll get through this. As long as we don't do anything stupid." *Like turning over an anonymous, incriminating photo:* I thought it so hard I imagined she could hear it, accomplice ESP. "You're brave as hell, Kristen. I've always been in awe of your courage. And how calm and smart you are in the midst of a crisis. I'm—I'm just trying to channel that. With a couple days of us not talking. I'm trying to be brave like you, okay?"

This did it. Of all the tricks I'd tried, the sticks and carrots and honey-gooey words I'd lobbed her way, this was what convinced her.

"I trust you," she said. "I don't get it, but I trust you." She rolled off the bed. "I want to show you something."

My heart thudded as she rummaged in a dresser drawer. *Please just let me go,* I silently begged.

She lifted a cloth sack and pulled out what appeared to be a crumple of newspapers. She peeled back a layer and stared at its center.

"We're really in this together." Then she tipped it my way.

At first, I thought it was a big, dark rock, the kind you crack open to find the geode inside.

But then a part of it caught the light. I spotted words on the lumpy surface, a flash of blistered plastic.

I'll take it, she'd said as the air in our suite eddied with smoke and the acrid smell of burnt plastic. *I'll toss it when I get home.*

But she hadn't. She'd kept it, more collateral. Before me was a fossil: the molten remains of Paolo's journal, phone, passport, and wallet.

CHAPTER 33

"**O**h my God. You said you'd get rid of this."

"I kept it in my suitcase. It made the flight here with me."

My eyes bulged. "But why?!"

"It's . . . it's like the photo. I don't plan to show it to anyone, obviously. But I wanted you to see."

She's out of her mind. But I nodded serenely. "I'm sorry I made you doubt me. But we can trust each other. We *have* to trust each other."

She stuffed the lump into its bag. "Can we please do more talking as soon as you're back?"

"Of course," I lied. I inched toward the door. "I should get going. You're okay?"

She pulled me into a tight hug and cried into my shoulder. There was muscle memory there, a deep-seated urge to tuck my chin toward her neck, to feel our forearms pulling in tandem. When I let her go, I had the flickering thought that this felt like a goodbye—an ending I'd been seeking for the better part of a month now.

But as I plodded toward the stairs, a pit of shame opened inside me. There was a reason I kept repeating my farewells, aiming for a clean cut but then watching the skin scab and purse together, uglier and uglier, every time. There was a reason I kept going back, a sad-eyed addict begging for another hit.

As I passed by the living room en route to the front door, my gaze fell on the Bible still centered on the coffee table. With a sudden pull in my chest, I got it: the reason people crave religion—the confidence, the superiority, the assurance of what's right. The yearning for someone to tell us what to eat, think, and do. Simple answers to complex questions and the certitude that there's nothing to be afraid of, that it'll all work out in the end. The opposite of fear.

As I scooped up my purse, a creak above me made me freeze, ears pricked, heart staccato. *Time to go.* I glanced behind me, then heaved the front door open and hurried out into the night.

I MADE IT to my car and sat slumped in the front seat for a long time. Everything was wrong. Kristen had told me to jump, and I'd responded, "How high?" I'd comforted her, patted her shin, wrapped her in a tight embrace. I *must* be getting something I craved, or else I wouldn't be here now, gazing into the black tunnel of Nana and Bill's street when I should be home and packing for Phoenix. Why was it so freaking dark? Why weren't there any streetlights in the suburbs?

A sudden knock made my entire body jerk—I pressed a hand to my sternum and breathed hard, the horror movie watcher who didn't see the jump scare coming. Nana's face floated in the window, her eyes and cheeks gaunt in my dome light's glow. I rolled down the window and she cracked a nervous smile.

"You forgot this." She held out a clump of fabric, and it took me a moment to recognize my jacket.

"Oh shoot, thank you." I dropped it onto the passenger seat.

She lingered. "I thought I'd missed you. But then I saw your car."

She wanted to tell me something. Days earlier, I would've leapt at the chance to ask about her spooky email, about Westmoor, about young Kristen and her dead best friend, poor Jamie in the pineapple house I could just make out next door. But now the strongest impulse, deep in my hips, was to get the hell away from here.

"Is everything okay?" She said it in a rush, like she thought I'd whir the window closed and drive off, tires squealing.

I froze. "You mean with Kristen?"

Something flashed in her eyes. "She's been acting, er, a little upset. I guess it's got Bill, you know, on edge. And me as well." Her eyebrows shot up. "Not that it's about us! But I'm concerned for her. And you." Nana glanced behind her and I caught the look again. Fear, bright and glinting, both tiny and vast. Toward Kristen? Or— a new thought sparked, the conclusion I would have jumped to first under any other circumstances—toward Bill?

"Nana, why do you ask? What's been going on at home?" She stared at me, and hastily, I added my knee-jerk courtesy: "If you don't mind my asking, that is."

"It's been a bit of a zoo, having everyone under the same roof." She peered up at the house, its windows like unblinking eyes. *I just wanted to make sure you're comfortable,* she'd emailed on my birthday. *Kristen has been acting a bit strange lately.*

"Is there something you want to tell me, Nana? Is something wrong?"

She ran her tongue across her lips. She'd just taken the sharp in-breath of someone about to blurt something out when—

"Nana!"

A hand dropped onto Nana's shoulder and we turned to see Kristen's smiling face. How had she gotten here without us seeing? How long had she been standing there?

"Emily forgot her jacket," Nana announced, too loud.

I gestured toward it with a flourish. "And since I missed Nana inside, I was just saying hi."

Kristen nodded. "I thought you were in a hurry, so I was surprised to see you out here with someone. Thought I'd investigate."

"Just your old grandma!" Nana's voice was a singsong.

"Well, thank you for keeping me safe from all the dangers of Brookfield," I cracked, and Nana chortled. "Anyway, I should let you go. Kristen, we'll talk soon, okay?"

"Happy travels," she replied, her smile shifting into a smirk. "Be safe."

KRISTEN HAS LOST *her mind.* Was Nana safe? Was there something I could do? Would any of my loved ones be in danger while I was out of town . . . Priya? The thought looped as I drove the tree-lined roads past looming colonials, broad Tudors, neo-classicals with grand white columns in the front. No flashy McMansions here: Kristen's neighbors were classy and smug, convinced that nothing bad could happen to them, not behind their moats of landscaped gardens and neatly trimmed bushes.

I wasn't being fair—I was simply jealous, the envy like a stent in my heart, pushing against it from the inside. These people paid their mortgages, cut tuition checks, debated whether the Vitamix was worth the splurge. They weren't wondering if someone they knew was deeply unhinged. If the police were hot on their trail. If the walls, professionally painted in a pretty shade of eggshell, were closing in on them by the second.

With the exception of one. I flashed to Kristen again, crumpled on the bed, used Kleenex piled like snow in the bin at her feet. No way was that an act. Right?

At a four-way stop, I burst out of the subdivision and onto a main road, and I realized I'd been holding my breath.

The flicker in Nana's eyes: I'd recognized it with a surge of solidarity. I felt it myself so many times a day, bursts so tiny and sharp and expected and, and *normal* that I barely registered them: just the usual accompaniment to walking or eating or smiling or not smiling or showing a little skin or wearing a poofy parka or simply existing with a female form.

I merged onto the freeway and accelerated hard. My pulse picked up speed along with the sedan as I flew past the grounds of the Wisconsin State Fair, the baseball stadium, the three glass domes of the botanical garden, latticed like bugs' eyes. When my exit appeared, no one wanted to let me in and I had to jam on the brakes, then dart in front of an SUV who pretended not to see my blinker.

In the rearview mirror I saw the driver's angry upturned palm, a what-the-hell gesture. As if it were my fault for taking up three-dimensional space, for having volume and mass and density.

And then I did the thing I never, ever do. I lifted my middle finger and waved it above my shoulder, so that he couldn't miss it. For a moment I felt powerful, but then at the next light he pulled up next to me and rolled down his window to let out a stream of obscenities.

I stared straight ahead and, as my heart pounded in my rib cage, pretended not to notice.

CHAPTER 34

My stomach tightened when Aaron's car pulled into my drive-way. I waved and rolled my suitcase outside, then turned around to lock up.

I jumped as two hands encircled my waist, then smiled as he nuzzled my neck.

"Hello, you," he said.

"Hey there." Our foreheads touched and I closed my eyes. Oh, how I wished I could give in to the feeling, melt into his arms. "You excited?"

"Let me take that." He grabbed my suitcase and I followed him to the car. He hit a button and the trunk flew open and bobbed at the top. Something in its angle, the gaping maw, brought me back to that moment in Chile, when we were sweaty and sore from digging a shallow grave and ready to face the unthinkable horror of producing a body for it. The rental car's trunk had bounced in the same way, like it was laughing at us.

He closed it with a *thunk* and shot me a crooked smile. "I brought us chocolate croissants again. Hope you're hungry."

"So sweet! Thank you." Just like in the airport weeks ago, when I hadn't known I'd see him. His shape emerging near baggage claim, hitting me like a thunderclap.

We set out under a silvery sky. "It's supposed to rain here all weekend," he announced, drumming his fingers to the garage rock he'd put on. "Hopefully it holds off until we're in the air."

"Yep." It took a huge amount of effort to reply. This trip might've been a horrible idea. "Thank God we're going somewhere sunny."

My phone was ringing again, and I rooted around in my bag. A number I didn't recognize, one with—oh God—too many digits.

Aaron glanced my way. "Everything okay?"

"Yeah, no, sorry, I— Let me check one thing." I tried to keep my fingers from shaking as I googled the country code of the incoming call: Chile. *Shit*. Plus two new texts from Priya, a reply to my late-night plea to steer clear of Kristen while I was away; she'd sent back a string of question marks, followed by "WTF? Everything ok?"

Aaron gestured at the dashboard. "Hey, this reminds me: I packed some THC gummies."

"Huh?" I glanced around, bewildered, then realized he was talking about the stonery song on the radio. "Oh. Great! You're not . . . afraid to fly with it?"

"Nah, it's in my dopp kit." He waved his hand and I stared at him, my envy so thick I felt it seeping out of my pores: not a care in the world, nothing to worry about. *The opposite of fear isn't safety*, Kristen had said. It's knowing you'll always be in charge.

The song finished with the unhinged *shrawww* of an electric guitar, and the peppy morning-show DJs sprang into action:

So, Dave, I'm sure you've been hearing about this twenty-four-year-old backpacker whose body was found in Chile.

Oh, everyone's got a theory. Last week I heard someone say they thought aliens were involved, since that region is famous for its UFO activity.

What I can't get over is that the parents are—

"You know what's wild?" Aaron pointed at a speaker. "This dude disappears, probably got himself twisted up in some shady shit. Drugs or whatever. But no one wants to say that—it's gotta be aliens who are responsible, nothing he could've done. 'Cause he's a dude. Like, remember Natalee Holloway? It was all: *Well, why did she leave her friends? And why did they let her go off with a guy she didn't know that well?*"

It was like all my cells were firing at once and I coughed, an ugly bark, then flipped to a different station.

"Sorry," I said. "It just freaks me out. Thinking about . . . scary stuff happening to tourists."

"Naw, that makes sense. I know you *just* visited there."

I willed myself to say something, anything else, but I couldn't. Finally, he sealed off the topic: "Well, nothing to worry about in the mean streets of Phoenix."

AARON ATE A gummy before boarding and fell asleep shortly after takeoff. I didn't want to risk growing (even more) paranoid while in a tin tube improbably sailing through the sky, so I didn't partake. Solo travelers flanked us on either side, a beefy guy in a Packers hat next to me and a businesswoman next to Aaron, tapping away on her laptop.

The Chilean number hadn't left a voicemail, but it had called again while we were on the tarmac. I pressed my fingers against my lips, as if to keep from screaming. I thought of Sebastian in Cambodia, his calloused palm against my mouth. Adrenaline coursing through my arms, muscle tissue firing as I fought against his grasp. The penny taste of blood when my teeth closed around his flesh. Had a bit of it come out in my mouth? Had I spit it out in a glob of bloody phlegm as he swore and pulled his hand toward his heart, or had I invented that detail now, in hindsight? The brain is an artist, after all—remixing, shape-shifting by the minute. Editing the feed so that I could convince myself that *Kristen,* not me, had kicked his trunk, forced his head up against the leg of the bed.

We hit some turbulence and the captain turned on the seatbelt sign. Aaron stirred and went back to snoring, but the woman to his right gripped her armrests and gasped when the plane made a belly-flipping dip. Another rustle of concerned murmurs as the plane jerked again, hard enough to make the tray tables jump.

Turbulence had never bothered me. It was just the plane hurtling through pockets of wind. Me, I preferred to obsess over realistic fears.

Aaron nestled his head on my shoulder, and I leaned my cheek on his silky hair. My eyes flicked to the screen next to me, where Baseball Cap was flipping through stations of live TV with an aggressive tap, one surely felt by the woman in front of him. He stopped on CNN and I read the ticker crawling along the bottom, an endless feed of fires and invasions and shootings. Above the scrolling headlines, two literal talking heads, a Barbie-esque woman and a man with a handlebar mustache, were discussing an entirely different topic.

And then I saw it. It sucked me down like an open hatch in deep space.

The headline snaked across the screen, right to left, so quickly I thought maybe I'd read it wrong, transposed the letters, conjured up the string of words I feared the most. I felt cold all over, my shoulders and jaw and hands all tensing, and Aaron sat up in his seat and slumped in the opposite direction.

I whipped out my laptop and jabbed at the On button; the hard drive seemed thick and logy as it booted up, different screens appearing and wheels turning languidly. After what felt like hours, I connected to the inflight Wi-Fi. Another short eternity as I waited for CNN.com to load.

I had to scroll down to find it, my eyes devouring the endless headlines, the blue-tinged photos of politicians and pro athletes and health crises and brutal devastation.

And there it was, eight bolded words on the left-hand side, in code.

WITNESS COMES FORWARD IN SEARCH FOR BACKPACKER'S KILLER

CHAPTER 35

Los Angeles police are focusing on a small farming town in Chile as the last known location of a young man killed while backpacking, and law enforcement officials from several countries are aggressively searching for his killer.

On April 25, the body of Paolo García, age 24, of Barcelona, Spain, was found near Arroyito in a shallow grave about 25 meters from the road, according to reports. He had been missing for approximately four weeks before his body was found. Although a suspect has not been named, a witness claims she spotted García in Quiteria, a remote mountain town, on the night of April 13.

"I can't believe it. We met in a crowded bar and talked about meeting up for a stargazing tour the next night, and I was surprised when he didn't show up," said Tiffany Yagasaki, a British woman who was also backpacking through South America. "I didn't think about it again until I saw his photo in an article about his body being found. It's so shocking—he seemed friendly, and everyone at the bar was just chatting and having a good time."

"This is our first real lead," Los Angeles Police Captain Miranda Sedivec said in a statement. "We're grateful to Ms. Yagasaki for coming forward with vital information, and we encourage anyone else who can contribute to the investigation to do the same."

On May 1, the García family offered a $1 million reward for information about their son's death. The family's lawyer declined to say whether Yagasaki's cooperation was related to the reward.

Quiteria, a small village with a population of 800, is primarily agricultural. It also welcomes thousands of tourists, mostly in the summer months (December through March), due to its scenic location in the Andes Mountains and its abundance of distilleries making pisco, a white-grape brandy. García's body was found about 38 kilometers from Quiteria.

Friends in Barcelona described García as a fun-loving young man with a taste for adventure and a love of meeting new people. He was also a thyroid cancer survivor who participated in fundraisers to bolster cancer awareness and research.

"He could talk to anyone, anytime, anywhere," Valeria Ramos, a friend from university, told Spain's Agencia EFE news agency. "He could walk into a room full of strangers and make them all smile."

If you have any information, please contact the Los Angeles Police.

Tiffany Yagasaki—she must've been one of the two female backpackers we'd seen at the restaurant, then again at the bar. An internal wail—*Oh God oh God oh God*—Tiffany and I had talked at the bar, had drunkenly grown chummy while Kristen flirted with Paolo a few yards away. Did she remember us? Had she told anyone? But the most devastating detail was in the first line, of course: *Law enforcement officials from several countries are aggressively searching for his killer.*

I had to tell Kristen. Without saying something stupid, obviously, something suspicious or incriminating.

I'd tell her to look at a newspaper—that wouldn't look shady, would it? Although if anyone triangulated our whereabouts that April night and then combed through my messages later . . .

I could feel it, the paranoia, growing inside me like a tapeworm, threatening to strangle my viscera.

A code—I'd do a simple one, one she'd quickly grasp but that no one else would notice. Checking again that no one around me was watching, I typed it out, then went back and filled in the words:

Hey Kristen,

I've been thinking about the last letter I sent. Just wanted to add that Raquel truly is a

dramatic wench—rude & myopic. Look, that bitch made even Alice grow speechless.

—Emily

Writing it stilled my racing thoughts, slowed my heart rate. The hard enter in the middle of the email, the meticulously crafted second line . . . Kristen, whose brain I'd once joked was practically fused to mine in a conjoined-twins situation, would know to read the last letter of each word in the second line: *Check the news.* I pushed my hair off my face and hit Send.

And then I realized I had no idea what I expected her to *do.* I was on a plane. I'd quite literally left her blubbering in her grandparents' palatial home. I slipped my laptop into my bag. Though Chile was the more immediate concern, my thoughts flowed back to Cambodia.

For over a year, I'd been working hard to keep the images out of my head. Like an app running in a phone's background, some part of my mind was always whirring: *Keep it buried, keep it buried, keep it buried.* Buried like Paolo's body under the tawny dirt. Buried like Sebastian's body in Tonle Kak River.

I'd felt so numb that night—this I remembered clearly, a visceral memory of my senses shutting down. With Sebastian's wound still oozing blood, Kristen had yanked me into the bathroom and turned on the shower, letting steam bead and drip on the mirror and walls and flimsy shower curtain. I shook and shook, my shoulders like a jackhammer, my teeth chattering so hard they rattled my skull, they addled my brain, aren't you never supposed to shake a baby because the brain will boing around inside their head? That's what was happening to me as mist settled on my eyelashes, as vapors floated in translucent curls, as Kristen held my shoulders and pushed her forehead against mine.

I jumped ahead to another scene, also wet and wan. My legs were like jelly and not just from the nerves this time: Together we'd dragged Sebastian up the short but steep hike to a lookout point, a cliff over the foamy waters of Tonle Kak. Thanks to the pollution, the night sky had an eerie yellow tinge to it, like bile. We'd visited this spot two days before, when it was pocked by tourists, young folks like us staging selfies at the cliff's edge. I'd read aloud from our guidebook, taking on a newscaster voice, all arm flourishes and enthusiasm.

This spot was nicknamed *suicide ridge,* and we took turns trying to pronounce the many diphthongs and plosive consonants of the Khmer expression. Legend had it that this was where women, married or betrothed but miserable about it, had once loaded their pockets with shale rocks from along the path, then hurled themselves into the water below; though the forty-foot drop would likely do the trick, the heavy stones ensured they'd drown as planned.

We'd thought nothing of it that day, but in our hotel room's bathroom, mist swirling and our skulls smushed together as if we could co-cogitate through osmosis, Kristen brought it up again. Or had I been the mastermind, the evil genius? Suddenly the boundaries between us were growing threadbare.

A *ding* and the captain turned off the seatbelt sign. No—I had to stay focused. Kristen was the dangerous one, not me. Even if you removed Sebastian from the equation, Kristen was still the one with a trail of dead bodies in her wake, from the time she was a kid: both parents, Jamie, and now Paolo. One's an anomaly, two's an unfortunate coincidence—*maybe.* But four? Four's a freaking *trend.*

Aaron crossed his arms and scooched down in his seat. I steeled myself and then traveled back in time once more, back to that night in Cambodia, the air clogged with bugs and moisture and smoke from distant trash fires. It pressed around us like bad breath as we stumbled up the hill, Sebastian's feet dragging behind us. We crammed stones into whatever pockets we could find in his clothes: against his belly in his tucked-in shirt, inside the waistband of his shorts.

Touching his skin, cool and clammy even in the body-temperature air, sent waves of revulsion through me . . . but, if I was honest with myself, there was something oddly satisfying about it, too, the weights violating the man who'd tried to violate me. I'd been so angry when I wrestled free from his grip. I'd almost enjoyed plunging my teeth into his palm, putting him in his place. I'd felt so furious that when I saw him on the ground, his head bumped up against the bed frame . . .

Sick. All sick and sickening thoughts. Next to me, Aaron scratched his nose, nestled his cheek against his horseshoe-shaped pillow. *I love you.* We hadn't said it yet, but thinking it was like a prism of clarity in the murk of my psyche. My affection for him bulged, followed by a ferocious, crackling fear at the thought of losing him. What would Kristen do if she somehow got her hands on him, jealous as an ex-lover? Or, equally threatening: What would happen if he learned about the skeletons in my closet? The *literal* skeletons in my hands, one stuffed into the trunk of a rental car in Chile, the other dragged up a hill in Cambodia?

Wait—how did we get Sebastian over the cliff? I waited for an image to arise, a fade-in. There: Kristen and me rolling his body toward the ledge, feeling gravity take hold, slowly at first and then with mounting vehemence, like a roller coaster cresting its first giant hill. We'd stepped back and waited for the splash—it felt like an eternity, something was wrong. But then we heard the wet crash, the river gratefully accepting our sacrifice. We'd both leaned way over and peered into the water, but any glimpse of Sebastian was already lost to the foamy rush.

This isn't helping. None of the relentless remembering was bringing me any closer to answering the critical question: Who killed him, Kristen or me? It was a strange sensation, like worrying about the future, projecting what might go wrong, only I was fretting about the past. *Am I dangerous, even now?*

No—I was a kind person, a good person, living my little life. I loved animals and nature and yoga and pizza. I set my hand on Aaron's and he flipped his palm and wove his fingers through mine.

The woman next to him peeled her eyes off her laptop and glanced down at her seatmate, at our interlocked fingers. I thought of how we must look to her: a good-looking, comfortable couple traveling together—not even ruing our middle seats, so in love were we. I'd wanted this for so long. Aaron made every second warmer, safer, happier.

Traveling together—suddenly the magnitude of this endeavor hit me, how we'd be together 24/7 for four entire days. Together when I came out of the shower, nose and cheeks ruddy, hair tangled, face bare. Together when my blood sugar plunged and I got cranky and short. Together when I ate too much bread and felt gassy, my abdomen distending like a balloon. We'd had sleepovers, sure, but this felt different. Momentous.

I'd been so focused on running away, I'd almost missed what I was running to.

I nuzzled my head against his shoulder, then closed my eyes.

No, not to. *With.*

CHAPTER 36

No one was waiting to arrest me at the jet bridge. No one paid attention to us as we strolled through baggage claim and found the car-rental desk, and I looked around in astonishment: *Nobody knows.*

Phoenix was orange-brown and sunbaked, with the dry, crumbly quality of cheddar that's been sitting out on a cheeseboard all day. It was hot, too hot, the sauna air catching in my lungs. Aaron didn't complain as we loaded our bags into the back of a rental, but his forehead dripped like a glass of iced tea.

No new voicemails, but now I was getting a call from a number with an L.A. area code. L.A., where grieving parents offered a million dollars for intel about their son. L.A., where a dead man's father probably had the police department wrapped around his wealthy pinkie. Where a family mourned a son who outran cancer but not the wrath of my best friend. I turned on Do Not Disturb and slipped my phone into my bag.

We churned around the airport's loops, then shot out onto the interstate. We were in a mammoth, tanklike, gas-guzzling black SUV—the only option left with our last-minute booking.

"So I wanted to talk to you about something."

I looked at Aaron sharply. "What's that?"

"Um, I'm not sure how to say this." *Oh my God oh my God oh my God.* "Kristen called me yesterday."

Deep breath in, deep breath out. "What'd she say?"

"It's— I dunno. It was bizarre. She said she's worried about you."

"Oh boy. Did she say why?"

"She used the word . . . *unstable*." He blushed. "Sounded like she thinks you're on the verge of a breakdown or something. She wasn't sure you should be traveling."

"Jesus Christ." I glanced at him. "And you're just telling me this now?"

"Well, I didn't want to lead with it."

I squeezed my eyes shut. "You know that everything she said is bullshit, right? I'm fine."

He didn't reply. Beyond him, the tangerine moonscape billowed past his window.

"Aaron."

"That's not all."

I was going to explode. Something was detonating in me, about to erupt all over the dashboard.

"What'd she say?" I tried to make my tone blasé, eye-rolling.

"She said . . ." He cleared his throat. "She said the reason you've been kinda . . . stressed-out since you got back from Chile is that something happened there. Where you hurt someone or something? By accident. She didn't go into details."

My face went slack. *No no no no no.* By the time I noticed I wasn't breathing, it was too late to act shocked or confused or scornful or anything, *any* emotional mask that might point to my innocence.

"In a quarter of a mile, turn right," the GPS intoned.

"Aaron." My voice sounded squeezed and I shoved it deeper into my chest. *Breathe, Emily.* "You know that I'm fine, and that Kristen and I haven't been on the best terms. So this is just her trying to manipulate you. Okay?"

He eased around the corner. "So, I'm Team Emily, eleven times outta ten." A car pulled out in front of us and he made an *ope* sound. "But you have seemed kinda out of sorts these past few weeks. Or am I way off base?"

My brain scrambled, a rat in the bottom of a pail. Should I flip the script, insist that *Kristen* had been the one to hurt someone? Deny the violence altogether? Make up another reason I'd been acting strangely? But I was so tired of lying—so sick of trying to act normal when it was all probably about to come crashing down around me.

I'd made up my mind, then. I'd tell him the truth.

"I'm sorry I haven't been completely honest with you," I said. "Something happened with Kristen, and it's been weighing on me."

He waited, listening.

"First of all, no, I did not hurt anyone in Chile. That's a lie, I swear to God. Please believe me."

He nodded at the windshield. "I believe you, yeah."

"Something . . . happened back in Cambodia. A year ago? Something bad." I swallowed hard. "I was, um, attacked. It was a . . . a sexual assault." I stared down at my lap but could feel him tense up next to me. "It was really scary. Obviously. But Kristen walked in on us and that—that stopped it." Still the truth. Just a redacted version of it.

"Oh my God, Emily. I'm so sorry."

"Thanks." Tears gathered and I turned toward the window. My sunglasses bulged in the side-view mirror.

"Did you report it? Were you hurt?"

"No, we just—we just got out of there. We left town, went to Laos for a couple days. We were both pretty shook up." *Edit the feed to limit hysteria.*

"Shit." He placed his hand on mine. "I'm glad you told me. And I'm really, really sorry that happened to you. Ugh, it makes me so mad." He shook his head again. "Who would do that?"

I sighed. This was the problem with good guys—they simply couldn't fathom how awful so much of their cohort could be. "Thanks. So yeah, that was really tough. And I thought I was getting over it, but then you and I started dating. And I realized I hadn't *really* processed the attack. You know how I kinda—clammed up with you a couple times."

"Aw jeez, I hope I wasn't pressuring you, or—"

"No, no, you were great. You *are* great." I squeezed his hand.

"You made me realize how much I wanted a real, adult relationship. But seeing Kristen in Chile . . . I told you how she tried to talk me into leaving Milwaukee and traveling with her."

"Right. And you said the other day, she's always weird about your boyfriends."

"Exactly. She's tried to, like, poison my brain with past relationships. I think she wants to keep me for herself. Like, I had this college boyfriend, Ben, and he *did* suck, but Kristen was the one who talked me into breaking up with him. And then there was this guy, Colin, a few years ago. It seemed like things were going really well, and then Kristen convinced me he wasn't a good guy, even though in retrospect he didn't do anything wrong."

"Yikes." He switched lanes and passed a station wagon with a shaggy dog gazing forlornly out the back.

"I think that's why she sees Chile as the turning point," I went on. "Before that, she always had me all to herself. Until now. Until *you*. And I knew she'd try to plant seeds of doubt." I tipped my head back. "But she's still doing it. Driving a wedge between you and me. She couldn't get to me, so she's trying to get to you."

That last night in Chile, when I told her about Aaron—that was the catalyst, the beating butterfly wings that led all the way to this hurricane. That's why she picked out Paolo, that's why she orchestrated the whole gruesome night: She went balls to the wall to bind us forever, to create one shared experience that put us in our own snow globe, apart from the world. She acted shell-shocked and helpless as I hatched a plan to deep-six the body. She watched with glee as I plotted to bury her mess like a time capsule, a ticking bomb.

And then—come to think of it—once I'd signed on, once I couldn't turn back, once it was clear her plan was working perfectly, she'd reclaimed her usual role as the foreman. She demanded I survey the area while she drove ahead; she presided over the handling of Paolo's body. *She knows it's the one thing I can't tell Aaron, the thing standing between us, and she loves that.*

But then I threw a wrench in her plans: I pulled away.

I gazed at Aaron, his wrist hooked casually over the top of the steering wheel. My heart rate vroomed. How far would Kristen go to right the ship?

The hotel appeared and Aaron pulled into the lot. He put the engine in park and turned to me with his most earnest face. "I'm sorry, dude. That all sucks."

"Thanks. I just needed some space from her. And Arizona is nothing if not space, right?"

"Oh, for sure. And hey, I'm stoked to be away from the ol' grind and here on, you know. Mars." He gestured out the window, where the clay-colored ridges resembled a sci-fi comic book. "But I'm glad you told me. I knew something was up." He drummed his fingers against the parking brake. "You can always talk to me. We all have shit we don't feel like talking about. And that's fine! But . . . I've been down that road before, relationships where she—or I—wasn't willing to let that guard down, you know? And just be real."

I nodded slowly. It was one of those weird, high-def moments when the conversation is so real, so important, you're almost detached, floating a few feet above it.

"See, here's what's cool." He yanked the key from the ignition. "You want space, you want to get away—I get that, I've done that, I've dated people who've been like that. But usually that means they run away from *me*." He tapped his sternum. "And you insisted we head west! Together! Makes me feel like a million bucks."

My voice was round and shy as I said: "I always feel happier around you."

I glanced his way and saw his chest puff, his eyes shine. So I knew I'd said the right thing. But what I thought first was: *Right, because I wasn't running away from* you.

THE HOTEL WAS on the outskirts of town. A faded mural of southwestern motifs spread across the wall behind the check-in desk, and the blue and tan blankets draped over the armchairs looked filched from a yoga studio. Aaron gamely complimented everything in sight, snapping photos and pointing out details, as if he could sense my disappointment. God, he was kind.

On the elevator ride, a wave of exhaustion hit me. I raised an eyebrow. "Those gummies still accessible?"

The room was a bit more promising, with broad windows and a slim balcony facing a crumply mountain we eventually identified as Camelback. Bristly, moss-green trees dusted the flat expanse between us and the mountain ridge, and the thought spilled out before I could cork it: *This reminds me of the Elqui Valley.*

There it was—the downward rush of THC, like a choir of Gregorian chanters sliiiding an octave down. A whole bunch of monks. What a funny thought: Silent monks opening their mouths to sing, to give their vocal cords a workout, to let the sound waves crash and echo around them. Also, that's a funny word, monk. *Monk.* What was I just thinking about?

Oh, right: how very kind Aaron was. And beautiful, kind Aaron wanted to hold me, to kiss me, to make me feel safe. *Safety*—what did we call it? The opposite of fear? The thought warmed me and I crossed to the wardrobe, where he was diligently sliding his shirts onto hangers. I slipped my arms around his slim waist and kissed his neck. He turned around, his grin matching mine, and then meeting mine, and then our mouths were moving together in a slow, interesting tango, and then our fingertips and soft skin and all our bodies' corners, inner and outer, concave and convex, moved like one.

It was all feeling so good, stretchy and wide and endless, until the awareness of Kristen, of Sebastian and Paolo and the LAPD began to build in my mind like charged particles, like the sudden viridescent blare of the Northern Lights, and when I gasped it was out of panic, panic like I'd never known, panic that I'd never, ever, ever be free from my nightmare.

Afterward, we lay spooning in the tangled sheets, watching out the window as the crooked horizon grew umber and then politely faded into the background, black.

"I'm starving," he announced, propping himself up onto an elbow.

"I'm . . . I might be too high. I'm feeling a little . . . anxious."

"Oh no, I'm sorry. About what?"

About Kristen leaking the photo of me and Sebastian, maybe even sweetening it up with an anonymous tip about its connection to Paolo's case. Or sending in the molten lump, Paolo's license number still visible, along with my home address. About the calls I keep getting from Chilean and Los Angeles numbers. About the cops breaking down the door, throwing me on the ground and maybe hurting you, too, in the commotion.

"It's like—I get to the end of a breath and I worry that I'll forget to take another," I said, which was true. "Or that I'll never have the energy to get up again." It was a lesser concern, but still it registered: I needed to pee and the bathroom was fifteen feet away, and how, hooooow would I ever cross the distance?

"Aw, babe. Guess these gummies are pretty strong for a newbie. What do you need?" He brought me water and found a nearby spot with takeout pizzas. He woke me to say he was going to pick up his order—the only thing I remember before morning. In my dreams, I saw the mama rabbit, her neck so hacked her head clung by a flap of white-red skin. She kept trying to hop but instead limped and hobbled and zigzagged closer and closer to the edge of a Chilean cliff.

WHEN I WOKE, Aaron was out on the balcony, frowning at his iPhone screen. He was deep in a photoshoot with a tiny gecko that clung to the glass, loving the attention. He stepped inside and asked how I was feeling, but all I could say was that I needed coffee. Suddenly, being here felt ludicrous. Where would I be safe? Should I leave the country, hide out in Canada, hope that no one would extradite me?

"I didn't see a coffee maker," Aaron said. "Should we grab breakfast downstairs?"

Normalcy—I had to maintain it, had to fake it. So I brushed my teeth and stepped into some clothes. I'd failed to plug my phone in, and it had died; with a flare of anxiety, I jabbed the charger into the wall and walked away right as the Apple symbol appeared on the screen.

The sight of food made my innards turn: shiny green apples, one of those conveyor-belt toasters, a cauldron of oatmeal with brown sugar and raisins in canisters nearby. I forced down a banana as we sat on the deck, squinting into the sun and paging through a book of local hiking trails. Walking sounded nice, moving through wide-open space when it felt like cardboard walls were pressing in on me from every direction. We selected the lowest-hanging fruit, and I relaxed at having a plan—a three-mile loop that began just a block away from the property, following a country road and then branching off for a final ascent. "Rewarding views" from a portion along a steep ridge.

As Aaron rose to refill his Styrofoam coffee cup, I allowed myself a dreamy moment: What if this could become our lives? Not scraping peanut butter from tiny plastic tubs near an ugly lobby, but living somewhere new, somewhere beautiful. A fresh start totally distinct from Kristen, the past; here, with the sun stamping our table and lizards flicking by our feet, I could almost convince myself that the madness of the months since Cambodia existed on another plane, a different dimension, with no bearing on this one. Maybe this was Arizona's magic, all that talk of vortexes and UFOs and the connection to the stars: Here, no one could touch us.

We marched inside and prepared for our trek—snacks packed, sunscreen applied, dorky baseball caps perched on our heads. We were halfway through the lobby when a voice made me freeze.

"Emily!"

Aaron whipped around next to me, but I stayed still as an ice sculpture, fragile as a flake of snow.

"Emily." It was louder now, closer, and a vault opened up inside me, down and down and down. *No.*

A hand on my shoulder. Like it was a needle and I, a soap bubble, iridescent and doomed.

I turned and blinked at her. *Pop.*

"I came as fast as I could," Kristen said. And she pulled me into a one-sided hug.

CHAPTER 37

*POLICE RELEASE SKETCH IN APRIL SLAYING OF
SPANISH-AMERICAN BACKPACKER*

*Los Angeles investigators, working with Chilean officials,
released a composite drawing in an effort to track down a
woman they suspect is connected to the death of a Spanish-
American backpacker last month.*

*Paolo García, 24, was in the middle of a year-long backpack-
ing trip around South America when he disappeared. He was
last seen on April 13, and his body (identified by dental records) was found in a shallow grave in Arroyito, a farming area
in northern Chile.*

*Police released a sketch of someone believed to be involved.
That person was described as a white female in her 20s, about
5 feet 6 inches tall, with brown hair and a North American
accent.*

*The death of García, who lived in Barcelona but had dual
citizenship in Spain and the United States, made headlines on
multiple continents and sparked an international manhunt,
with García's family offering a $1 million reward for informa-
tion that leads to an arrest.*

*Anyone with information on García's murder or the person of
interest is urged to contact Los Angeles police.*

CHAPTER 38

My lips pursed to ask the inevitable: *What are you doing here?* Then I started to laugh. Of *course* she was here. I'd asked her that exact question multiple times over the last few weeks. Always when I'd let my guard down, when I'd just begun to relax. She'd have some reasonable-sounding explanation, for sure. She'd be confused and hurt when it was clear I wasn't thrilled by her sudden appearance. Lather, rinse, repeat.

Aaron asked it for me, his voice bright but baffled. "Kristen, holy shit! Aren't you in Milwaukee?"

Her eyes flicked toward mine. "I took a red-eye. Just landed. Emily . . . told me she needs my help."

"What?" I blurted. Now we all three looked mystified, a Bermuda Triangle of bewilderment.

"Your email . . ." she said with a meaningful frown.

"How did you find us?" Aaron asked.

"Aaron was . . . posting photos. With tags."

"I— What about my email made you think I was telling you to come here?"

She wrinkled her nose. "I thought that's what your message meant? You said no contact and then you . . . you contacted me." She shook her head and laughed bitterly. "Well, if this isn't some bizarro codependent power play . . . Jesus, Emily."

"*Excuse* me?"

"Whoa, let's all take a breath." Aaron had that panicked look on his face, as if some mysterious and ancient female ritual were about to begin.

"No, it's true, Emily. You say jump and I say how high."

"I never told you to come!"

"That's *bullshit*." Her voice rang out and the din of the lobby disappeared. I noticed fish-eyed stares from the woman behind reception, a mom with a straggling toddler, a sunburned couple on their way to breakfast.

Kristen glanced around. "Maybe we should discuss this in private."

"Should we go back to our room?" Aaron held up his key.

No way was I locking us in a room with this woman. They both gazed at me, their eyes pleading. But for such different reasons.

And then it was very clear what I needed to do: protect Aaron at any cost. Her desperate call to him last night hadn't had the effect she'd hoped; it hadn't made me hers. What would she do to get him out of the picture now? Who knew what she was capable of?

I did. I was maybe the only person who did. "Aaron, why don't you head back upstairs?" I gestured into the lobby. "Kristen and I will have a chat."

"You sure?" he asked, and I nodded. He pressed his palm onto my waist as he passed. I watched the elevator swallow him up, and panic fanned out in my chest.

"Should we go outside or something?" Kristen glanced around. "I really don't want to talk about this here."

"No. No one's listening. We're talking now." I strode to a sofa and she shuffled after me. I waited for her to say something, and when she didn't, curiosity got the better of me: "Where's your bag? Where are you even staying?"

"Here. They've got my suitcase, but the room won't be ready for a few hours."

"Oh." An awkward beat. "You . . . you really shouldn't have come."

"This is ridiculous. You send me that goddamn cryptic email telling me to check the news, and so I see the article about a witness coming forward and I have a heart attack, obviously, and I run to you because all you've been saying for weeks is that you need some-one to talk to and you're freaking out."

I frowned. "So you came because you thought I was going to tell Aaron?"

"No, I came because you're my best friend." She opened her hands, exasperated.

We stared at each other, our gazes forming a single laser beam. She gave her head a disgusted shake and muttered, "You say jump . . ."

Well, how's that for irony: We both thought the other had us at her beck and call.

Kristen leaned forward and murmured, "Don't look, but the woman at the front desk is staring."

"Probably because you're making a scene."

She stood. "C'mon. I need to stretch my legs."

I watched her go, my pulse pounding in my ears. She got to the door and turned to stare at me, an expectant dog impatient to be let out. "You . . . you don't want to be alone?" I asked.

"I didn't fly two thousand miles to be alone, Emily."

I slid my hand into my backpack and realized, with a crashing sensation, that I didn't have my phone—it was still plugged in up-stairs.

As if she could read my mind, she held up her own cell. "You want me to turn this on and send that stupid photo?"

This time nobody turned, no one gawped at the break in deco-rum. Because Kristen was so good at this: making the malicious sound innocent, incidental. For all anyone knew, she was just teasing me about a drunken snapshot from our younger days.

Which was the truth, in a way.

Hopelessness swelled, an urge to wail and keen and beat my fists on the homely hotel rug. Instead I followed her to the entrance. The automatic doors slid open, a gasp of hot desert air. Kristen took a few steps and then looked back, her hazel eyes feline and inescap-able. I saw her as a mountain lion—face calm, ears pricked, gazing over her shoulder at me with the soft knowledge that I had no choice but to follow.

The hotel dumped us directly out on a busy six-lane road. Kristen turned right and stepped onto the cracked sidewalk. At least we were still out in the open here; a short way down was a strip mall with a nail salon and barre studio and Chinese restaurant. Funny how now I *wanted* us to be exposed, for people to see us.

"We need to just come right out and say it," she announced. "This needs to stop."

"I agree." Sunlight pressed hard on my scalp; a bead of sweat skidded down my spine. "Well, wait. What are you referring to?"

"This fighting, this tension—everything I say or do, you interpret in the worst possible way. It's suffocating." She walked with purpose, and I realized we were nearing the trailhead Aaron and I had picked out over breakfast.

"Well, maybe if you didn't keep dangling that photo from Cambodia over me, we could both relax. And now the, the *glob* of Paolo's melted IDs and stuff? It's messed up."

She stopped marching and turned to me. "Well, maybe if you didn't always seem one step away from losing your damn mind and blowing up our lives, I could get rid of them and still sleep at night. With the knowledge that my best friend wasn't about to betray me."

"Kristen, listen to what you're saying. *You're* the one threatening to betray *me*."

She scoffed and took off again. The trail marker emerged on the road, a weather-beaten sign with a map covered in squiggly trails and warnings of every kind: pack water, don't litter, watch out for pumas. If you see one, make yourself big and tall and loud.

The first chunk of the trail was next to a gravel road. I'd go no farther than the big bend up ahead, I decided—not one step more. We climbed in silence for a moment.

"You are relentless, you know that?" Kristen cried. "You're the most selfish person I've ever met. I've done *everything* for you, and it's like the more I try to be there, to put your needs first, the more you turn away. Like I disgust you. I don't know what you want." She whirled around to look at me. *"Tell me what you want."*

"I want Paolo to be alive!" I roared. The trail, flanked by cacti, had opened to a wide ridge on one side, and my voice echoed across a canyon. "I want to undo everything we've done. I want . . . I want Sebastian to be alive." Tears rushed into my eyes.

Kristen's eyebrows shot up. "He *attacked* you."

"I know, but . . ."

I saw it then, my foot hammering against his ribs again and again and again. Without ambiguity, without doubt. I saw what I'd done. *Stop. Stop. Stop.*

"I didn't have to kill him." I lowered my chin and the tears broke free. The parched earth near my feet sucked up the drips.

Kristen placed a palm on my shoulder. We were too close to the edge, I realized. It was the kind of twisty mountain road you'd drive with your heart pounding, your eyes stretched wide to let it all in, your knuckles on the steering wheel white and bloodless.

"Yes, you did. He was a bad man. You had no choice." Slowly, slowly, she brought her free hand up to my other shoulder. She pushed down a bit, like a coach giving his star player a pep talk. "But this is the problem. We're bound by what we've done. As long as we're both here and, and free—we're both indebted to each other. There's no way out."

I was trapped. What flitted through my head in that moment wasn't Ben's harsh shove all those years ago, his arms right where Kristen's were now and then the sharp push, the echoing clang of skull against wall. It wasn't Sebastian's hands, either, one against my mouth and the other mashing my wrists into the wall, rendering me as panicked and helpless as a moth in a net.

Instead I flashed to my father's hands, huge against my tiny frame, grabbing me so suddenly my little legs were still midstride and then smacking my bottom in one swift, discombobulating move. A casual spanking, an automatic, unthinking motion, like hitting the

Off button on a noisy toy. I didn't even have time to stop singing the song I'd learned from *Lamb Chop's Play-Along.*

Joy turned to captivity. Agency turned to impotence. Contained, controlled, trapped under the thumb and other fingers of a force who saw me only as the end of a preposition. Daughter *of.* Result *of.* Cause of noise and mess and annoyance, disturbing the air molecules around us.

Wrath rose up through me, a huge neon plume.

"No way out," Kristen repeated.

She began to close her eyes, a deliberate blink, and the second stretched out, slow motion. I saw it with clarity, like we were psychically connected again, our neurons firing in sync. This was her villainous monologue, the moment when she explained to me—to *herself,* to the viewers of the movie she envisioned as her life, in her twisted mind—why she needed to kill me. I'd set it up for her, teed up the perfect climax: Here we were, on a cliff not unlike the one we'd found in Cambodia—only here there was no water underneath, only craggy rock. Above us, a wide-open sky and orangey mountains in every direction. A landscape thousands of miles from Chile's Elqui Valley, but the set pieces were nearly identical.

Her eyelids were halfway down now, almost covering her pupils. I caught it in her gaze, the tragic inevitability. To kill me was the only way forward. Acceptance.

But she'd forgotten something. She'd miscalculated.

Yes, she'd been the one to kill Paolo, justified or not.

She might have killed her parents and though I didn't know how or why, she'd had something to do with her best friend Jamie's death.

And yes, Kristen had been the one who'd devised a scheme to launch Sebastian's limp body off a cliff, lower than this one but just as deadly.

But I'd been the one to kill him.

All that energy, all the emotional labor and assaults on my nervous system and, and all the internal battery power I'd funneled into fear: fearing the world, fearing men, fearing my unstable best friend, mercurial and destructive.

I saw with piercing lucidity that I'd had it all wrong. *They* had it all wrong. A laugh rumbled through me, light and clear.

I was a killer; *they should fear me.*

As Kristen's eyes squeezed closed, I raised my hands to her collarbone. And in the glint of the morning sun, I pushed.

CHAPTER 39

Her eyes snapped open as her body tipped back; her arms remained outstretched, palms cupping the air instead of my shoulders, so she looked like a zombie or a stiff-limbed action figure toppling over, *thunk*.

No, a cartoon: Her arms and legs flailed, outlined in rich cerulean sky. Clouds of dust and clods of sandy dirt puffed from the ground as she staggered away from me. Her eyes found mine in the hovering split second before she dropped like a stone.

A split second. They call it that because it's like a hatchet, the moment when life cleaves into Before and After. In the hanging silence, the weight of what I'd done rushed through me with a wide, downward *whomp*.

They say your life flashes before you right before you die, but in that instant, as Kristen's death wafted before us both, what crashed through me was all the good times we'd had: splashing into Lake Michigan, the water brisk on our bare skin; studying for econ finals late into the night, crunching through tall bags of Pirate's Booty and laughing until our sides hurt; getting ready for nights out in Milwaukee, borrowing each other's lipstick and earrings and spangly tops; unforgettable experiences in Uganda, Vietnam, even Cambodia.

Even Quiteria. "That's us," Kristen had said, pointing toward the horizon. "See those two little stars? You can tell."

And I'd squinted at them, understanding. "You're the one on the left, the pinkish one."

And she'd clutched my arm, giddy and free. "I was going to say the same thing!"

A voice in my head, almost a whisper, wiser than my own: *This isn't you.*

The spell broke and I rushed to the cliff's edge. It took me a second to spot her—the top of her head was a few feet down, and she was gripping a withered shrub.

She looked up at me, her eyes like bright marbles: "Emily, please!"

I flung myself onto the dirt and reached for her. My fingers didn't come close and she whimpered, unwilling to let go of the plant. Her toes scuffed against the dirt, trying to find purchase, but they just slid along the sloped earth.

I kneeled and whipped off my backpack, then slammed my belly back into the ground and dangled the rucksack from its top loop. Kristen ducked as the dirt and rocks I'd disturbed tumbled over her, and then she looked up again, eyes wild.

"Grab a strap!" I screamed. Dust and stones dug into my other arm, my knees.

She groaned and made a swipe for it. "I'm gonna fall," she cried. Her free hand clawed around the shrub again, and she leaned her face against the hill, breathing hard.

I pressed my own cheek into the ground and hung the bag as low as I could, letting out a groan.

"Lower!" she shrieked, and I felt my arm grow another inch, my whole body one tensed muscle, superhuman, like the mom who lifts a car to free her child.

The cotton loop jerked and I tightened my knuckles in the nick of time. "I've got you," I called, then rolled away from the ledge, away from the drop, away from the danger, feeling Kristen's weight coming with me. I spun onto my side and her hand appeared, a dramatic *thwock,* the exhausted but triumphant smack of a reanimated corpse emerging from the grave.

"Help me!" she choked out, and I scrambled back to the edge. I reached for her other hand and she flailed, her nails skinning long lines into my wrists. Then we grabbed each other's forearms, two death grips. I leaned into the road, gravel tumbling, both of us groaning with the effort. She heaved her knee up with that CrossFit-toned core, and I pulled her onto the trail.

"Kristen." We both got to our feet, facing each other. It was a marker of trust, I decided in one of those microsecond calculations, that she remained with her back to the hill, confident I wouldn't push her again. I heard something behind and to the right of me, a low hum under the birdsong and rustling breeze, but I didn't turn to look; our eyes bored into each other's.

"Emily." Blood leaked like tears from a scratch on her cheek. Her sweaty forehead had converted reddish dust to mud, a sheen of ochre. The hum grew louder, closer. "I can't believe you did that."

"I—I didn't mean to," I said, knee-jerk. Then I realized what that tone in her voice was: admiration. "Er, I don't know what came over me."

The hum was almost a roar now, climbing in pitch, and I realized it was a car, racing up the road we'd taken here. I flicked my gaze that way, and Kristen reached out and touched my biceps, gently pulling me away from the car, closer to her. She leaned her face in tenderly and her mouth approached my neck, my jaw, and finally, my ear.

The car tore around the corner and I could just hear her murmur over the engine: "Well, I do."

She paused exactly long enough for confusion to bang through me—her timing was precise, intentional. She shoved hard, and I stumbled back, directly into the vehicle's path.

I screamed and flung my arms over my face, but the driver was quick: A squeal of brakes and the crunch of tires, and the SUV lurched to the side, spraying me with gravel and a gust of gas-scented wind. It careened toward Kristen and, behind her, a forty-foot drop and an endless chasm of negative space.

I peeked out between my forearms, and the pieces snapped together all at once, the sudden realization like a gong crash. *Thrilling,* the dopamine gush of Figuring It Out, of solving a brainteaser or one of Kristen's riddles or the last clue in a tricky escape room.

Eureka: The SUV was our rental.

The driver was Aaron.

And as I watched, frozen in horror, my best friend, my boyfriend, and the car I'd rented as part of a package Orbitz deal all toppled, headfirst, over the cliff.

CHAPTER 40

AUTOPSY RESULTS REVEAL SLAIN AMERICAN BACK-
PACKER DIED OF HEAD INJURY

Paolo García, the 24-year-old Spanish-American backpacker
whose remains were found in a remote mountain region in
Chile, died from blunt-force trauma to his head, according to
an autopsy report exclusively obtained by The Gaze.

The forensic autopsy, which was performed in Chile and over-
seen by American officials, identified fractures in the skull and
subarachnoid hemorrhage—ruptured blood vessels in the fluid-
filled space around the brain—denoting a fatal head injury.

According to the report, toxicology tests on a sample of
García's vitreous humor—the jelly in the globe of the eye—
also revealed the presence of Rohypnol in his system at the
time of his death. No other superficial injuries or internal
abnormalities were recorded, although decomposition left
medical examiners unable to analyze other factors.

While a spokesperson from the Los Angeles Police Department
did not respond to a request for comment, García's father,
Rodrigo García, says this leaves more questions than answers.

"For Paolo to be drugged, hit on the head, and buried in the
middle of nowhere—it just does not make sense," he says. "He
was the nicest kid. He never hurt a fly."

CHAPTER 41

The numbness came next, my brain shrinking inside my skull so that my body could take over, moving on autopilot. I sprinted back the way we'd come. Flagged down a car, begged the curly-haired woman inside to call 911. I wanted her to drive me back up, but a dispatcher told her it might block emergency services. So I jogged up the hill, asthma plucking at my lungs, and peered bravely over the side.

There were tire tracks, a half shade darker than the dirt, carved into the steep earth. Flattened shrubs and a mangled cactus, its geometric limbs snapped off at funny angles. A few stories below was the SUV, its hood squashed, its body corkscrewed so that it rested on the passenger's side. It was so still, like a mural, the Arizona sun glinting off the glass and steel. If Aaron was wearing his seatbelt, he might have survived.

But then I spotted Kristen's legs. They were all I could see, the rest of her under the SUV's grill—legs unfolded like the Wicked Witch of the West. Like Paolo's hairy legs, poking out from his own blood-soaked backpack. They were tawny and toned and hairless, shiny in the light, with gray sneakers still laced up at the end.

And they weren't moving.

My screams echoed around the canyon and returned to me, as if the land had rejected them. *This is your fault,* the orange hills seemed to say. *Why should we absorb your pain when you brought this on yourself?*

Distant sirens blotted out my howls. Fire trucks appeared and I thought crazily of the fire, all those years ago, of Kristen's kind mom and mean dad and the forking flames that killed them both. So much noise and chaos, the song that doesn't end—there was a deep, rhythmic thwocking now, too, a drumbeat, no, a helicopter, all of it getting louder and louder, drowning out my thoughts.

A cop sauntered out of a squad car, too casual, and asked me if I was the one who'd called 911. I can't remember his face, even though I stared right at it, but after a few seconds I said yes, and he said they'd like to take me to the station, just standard procedure, to ask some questions and get my statement. He was kind, his voice calm and reassuring, and so I agreed, because of course I wanted to help.

The police station was generic, like a movie set. He brought me into a room and offered me water, a bag of chips, and weak, tepid coffee. I sipped at the water, my hand shaking like a maraca, as I tried to explain what'd happened. Just on the mountainside, just those critical fifteen seconds there, since I was confused and too distracted (*oh my God oh my God are they dead are they okay*) to get into the backstory.

I told it backward. Kristen went over the ledge because Aaron swerved the SUV toward her. He swerved because I was in the road. I was in the road because Kristen and I were talking, and I didn't know a car was coming. We were on a walk together because we needed to talk. As for Aaron . . . well, I didn't *know* why he drove out after us. Truly, I had no idea. The cop kept telling me I was doing a good job, and I kept interrupting to ask how Aaron and Kristen were. He asked for my name, my number, my home address. I was so rattled I had to think hard, suddenly debating if I'd switched the numbers in my own zip code.

Finally he volunteered to give me a lift to my hotel—he was so kind and self-assured, "You're doing great, I'm sure you're eager to get out of here"—but I asked him to take me to the hospital instead. The next few hours reside in my memory as a murky movie montage: sitting in a waiting room, asking everyone and no one if my friends were okay; reaching for my phone again and again, realizing with a squirt of cortisol that I didn't have it. I was untethered, a helium balloon that could float up into the stratosphere and pop without anyone noticing.

As the day began to wane, the ER's doors slid open and ushered in a puff of hot air. A couple rushed inside. They reminded me a bit of my parents: thinning hair and crinkled eyes, but with the slim frames and expensive glasses of those who won't give up their coolness without a fight. They glanced around, then hurried up to the front desk.

The woman behind it, whose hair was a beautiful tower of corkscrew curls, looked up at them with the same unimpressed glare she'd given me. I tilted my head, listening hard. Something about this stylish couple prickled at me, beyond their passing resemblance to my folks. Why did they look familiar?

The woman opened her mouth and the world stopped.

I froze and listened harder, in disbelief, with that same sense of corked time as when something wakes you in the middle of the night and you listen, listen, *listen,* waiting to see if it happens again.

But luckily for me, the receptionist made them repeat themselves, and this time there was no mistaking it.

"I'm Jennifer Rusch," she said—Jamie's mother. "We're here to see Kristen Czarnecki. She's our goddaughter."

CHAPTER 42

I elbowed my way up to the desk.

"I'm Kristen's friend," I announced. "Have you heard any-thing?"

"She's in emergency surgery." The receptionist glanced up from her computer. "We won't have updates till she's out of the OR."

"When will that be?" Jennifer Rusch and I said in unison.

The receptionist knitted her fingers together. "Can't say."

The Rusches turned to me, their eyes wide. "What happened? What do you know?"

"She— There was an accident. Can we sit down?" The room below me was tilting, the way the earth sways when you get off a carnival ride.

Thomas—I remembered their names from the memorial website with sudden certainty, Thomas and Jennifer—gestured toward a cor-ner of the waiting room.

"Sorry, how do you know Kristen?" I asked, even though I knew. What I meant was: What are you doing here?

"We used to be next-door neighbors," Thomas replied. "We were close with Kristen's parents. We live in Las Vegas—Kristen's grand-father called and we drove straight down. They're on a flight here now. The doctor who called them said Kristen's in critical condi-tion."

I was tingling everywhere, shock sparking me from the inside. I'd assumed it, intellectually—I'd seen her lifeless legs at the bottom of the canyon. But hearing it now ignited my grief, like gas fumes catch-ing fire.

"They didn't want Kristen to be alone," Jennifer added. "We hadn't heard from Bill in probably ten years. But I guess we're the only people they know within driving distance. They didn't . . . none of us knew she was here."

"It's awful." Thomas's hand swept over the nape of his neck.

Jennifer frowned at me. "And you're her friend? You came out here together?"

"Not . . . exactly." My voice cracked, a hair's breadth away from sobbing. "I'm Emily Donovan, and I live in Milwaukee. I was—"

They interrupted with self-introductions, Tom and Jenny, and we resisted the urge to trade nice-to-meet-yous.

"So, my boyfriend and I came out here last night. And this morning Kristen . . . surprised us."

"Surprised you?" Jenny repeated.

I nodded. "I didn't know she was coming. She's living with Nana and Bill." I shook my head, unable to organize the pieces. "And you're their old neighbors. Jamie's parents."

Jenny paled as Tom turned fire-engine red, as if the two shared a single blood supply.

"How do you know about Jamie?" Tom demanded.

I rubbed at the bridge of my nose. "Kristen told me about her— she said they were best friends."

A look zapped between them.

"Who are you again?" Jenny stared as if she'd only just noticed me.

"I'm Emily. Kristen's friend." My stomach roiled and my voice bubbled with reflux. "My boyfriend was in the car accident. He's in surgery now too." I closed my eyes and the scene ran beneath my eyelids again: the front of the car plunging into Kristen, and then the entire mass pivoting downward, a roller coaster at the tippy-top of its hill.

"Wait, your boyfriend was in the car with Kristen?"

"No, he—he was driving the car that hit her." Their brows lifted. "I think he was coming to get me, and then there was . . . an accident. It was a mountain road, with a drop-off on the side. He went over it and—and the car took out Kristen too."

A stunned silence. Tom dropped his elbows onto his knees. "Why was Kristen on the side of a mountain road in Phoenix?"

This was it. I took a deep breath, steeled myself. "She had just pushed me. Into traffic. She didn't know it was my boyfriend driving, and she certainly didn't think he'd turn the wheel in time. But she . . . she pushed me."

Another glance flickered between them. I searched their faces: alarm, horror, disgust, check, check, check. Noticeably absent: surprise.

Why would she try to kill you—that's the question I expected next, that I was bracing for, my mind running a million miles an hour. It didn't come.

It was now or never. "She followed me here. It was nuts. I was trying to get away from her, but Aaron—my boyfriend—posted a photo with a location tag, and she flew out here like it was nothing. And then she made it sound like *I* was the one who wanted her here, like it'd been my idea. She's . . . I think she's unhinged." I shook my head and smeared at my tears. "I'm sorry—I heard you say she's your goddaughter. I know how weird it sounds, but it's the truth."

They were silent, stone-faced. A doctor appeared, a stethoscope slung around her neck, and asked for Mr. Meuleman's family. I darted over and met her skeptical "You're family?" with a blank nod. I knew from the front desk that someone had contacted Aaron's parents, at least.

"I won't beat around the bush—the surgery was a success," she announced, and I melted with relief. "That said, it's going to be a long journey to recovery. He has a broken nose and multiple facial-bone fractures, two broken ribs, hemothorax—that's a pocket of blood between the chest wall and the lung—and a shattered patella."

"But he'll be okay?" My voice was hoarse.

She nodded. "It'll take some time and some physical therapy, but we expect him to make a full recovery."

"Can I see him?" I asked.

"Right now he needs to rest. We'll let you know when he can have visitors—I'd guess two, three hours at most."

I thanked her and she bowed her head before striding away, onto the next emergency, the next accident, the next mangled body clinging to life by a caterpillar's gossamer thread. One flick of a twig and we'd lose 'em, *snap*. I sat back down by the Rusches, abruptly exhausted.

Still, questions fluttered. This was my chance—the universe making the intro I'd been too chicken to send when I found that memorial website.

"Can I ask you a little more about Jamie?"

Tom cracked his eyes open while Jenny squeezed hers shut.

"I'm sorry, I'm sure it's painful to talk about. But . . . there's some stuff I've been trying to piece together. About Kristen. And I bet you could help."

"I don't think this is the time," Tom said, so loudly Jenny jumped. "We should stay focused on waiting for news about Kristen."

"Of course. I'm sorry." I blushed all the way down to my toes.

They got out their phones, froze me out with their swiping and tapping. Jenny approached the front desk again, then returned and announced they wouldn't know anything for another few hours at least. I shifted around, trying to get comfortable in the stiff-backed seat. I'd abandoned my backpack on the road, so I had no money, no ID, nothing.

"Do you need a phone?" Jenny frowned at me. "Do you want to call your parents?"

I shook my head. "I—I don't even know their current numbers. And I lost my bag in the accident." Panic whooshed through me and I blinked back tears.

"Aw, it's okay!" Jenny leaned forward. "Look, where's your hotel? I can give you a lift—you should probably pick up some stuff for when your boyfriend wakes up, anyway, right?"

I nodded at Jenny gratefully, and she swatted her husband's arm. "Give me the keys."

"You're leaving?"

"It's Hotel Rosita," I blubbered, and she entered it into her phone.

"That's only fifteen minutes away. We'll be right back, Tom."

I followed her out, feeling Tom's eyes on our backs the entire walk to the door.

CHAPTER 43

"You know, I get why Tom doesn't want to talk to you." We'd been driving for a few minutes when Jenny abruptly turned off the radio. NPR, something about police brutality in India.

I gazed straight ahead. "I truly don't know what Kristen is doing here. Like I said, I was trying to get away from her. Because she scares me."

She sighed. "When I look at you, I just see Jamie. You even look a tiny bit alike."

"So I hear."

She glanced at me, then back out the windshield. The sun beat onto her face in a golden rectangle, but she didn't flip down the visor. "Tom can't understand why I kept in touch with Kristen either. He's only here because he didn't trust me to drive the four and a half hours in my emotional state. But I care about Kristen. I can't help it. Even if she is bad news."

I watched strip malls scroll past the window. "I've been learning that. That Kristen's bad news. I've been trying to put the pieces together and . . . and figure out what was really going on with her, with our friendship." I glanced at Jenny. "I've been wondering what happened to Jamie for a while now. Would you be willing to tell me?"

"Jamie died by suicide." Her voice cracked, but then she regained her composure. "But before that, Kristen had her wrapped around her pinkie."

She took an off-ramp, trundled onto a frontage road.

"They were best friends practically since birth. When we moved into the neighborhood, Jamie was only a few months old and Anne was pregnant with Kristen, so we grew close right away." She reached out to turn the air-conditioning down, and I saw her fingers shake. "At first, I was thrilled that the girls got along so well. But as soon as they hit third or fourth grade, I started to worry. Kristen was always pushing Jamie to misbehave: 'Come on, don't be a baby, steal this candy from the cupboard or pocket this lipstick from the drugstore.' Whoa." She braked and tapped her horn at a BMW suddenly gunning around her. "The weirdest thing was, Kristen was always doing naughty things and then trying to convince Jamie *she'd* done them. Once I heard crying and rushed into the playroom, and Jamie was sitting there with her beloved American Girl doll in one hand and its head in the other. Kristen claimed that Jamie had ripped it off, but when I asked why, Jamie said she didn't know." Her knuckles were strangling the steering wheel, tighter and tighter. "Even after I'd sent Kristen home, Jamie stuck to her story. But when I checked the nanny cam, Kristen had decapitated the doll, not Jamie. Weird, childish stuff. But I wondered what was making her act out."

The revelation swept through me. Kristen had been gaslighting people since she was young. Jenny figured it was just a little-kid quirk of Kristen's, but I knew the truth; I knew Kristen was still at it, decades later. Scrambling my memories, accusing me of acts she herself had committed. *Don't play dumb—I watched you kill him.* How easily she'd convinced me.

At least I was certain now: Kristen had killed Sebastian. *My* shouts had been the drumbeat, a desperate plea as she kicked the life out of him: *Stop. Stop. Stop.*

"And was . . . was the bullying the reason Jamie . . . ?" I couldn't finish the thought.

Jenny shook her head as we bumped into the hotel's parking lot. She pulled into a spot and turned off the car, then leaned her brow against the steering wheel and sobbed.

I touched her shoulder gingerly. "Do you want to go inside, or . . . ?"

She shook her head again. "I need to finish saying this or I'll never get it all out."

The car was already heating like a pot of water on the stove. "Um, is there any way we could turn the AC back on?"

"We have OnStar. When the car's running, it records everything."

It was so like Kristen—practical yet paranoid, sensible yet absurd. I nodded and unbuckled my seatbelt.

"Jamie was being abused," Jenny said, fighting to keep her voice under control, "by her basketball coach. Kristen's father. She didn't tell anyone, but she wrote about it in her diary, which I found afterward."

My stomach lurched. "Oh my God. I'm so sorry." Kristen's asshole father—he wasn't just an asshole, he was a predator, a child molester. Had he abused his daughter too? She'd said she hated being alone with him. I'd spent so much time wondering what lay beneath her dark compulsions; I'd questioned whether Kristen was a run-of-the-mill sociopath or maybe a vulnerable child cracked open by her parents' death or her grandfather's casual tyranny. But if her own father had modeled a cycle she couldn't help but reproduce—bullying, gaslighting, violence—well, it didn't justify anything, but it might help explain it.

"I'm so sorry, Jenny. I don't know what else to say." My heart seemed to be folding in half like a soggy paper plate. Poor Kristen, poor Jamie, poor anyone else who got in that awful man's way. It was no wonder Kristen hadn't had any serious romantic relationships in all the years I'd known her.

"Thanks." Jenny battled the tears for a few seconds, then went on. "Her diary said something else too. She'd . . . she thought the only way to stop the abuse was to kill him. She was so young—she just wanted it to end. She—she thought it would be okay because he was a Christian, and that meant he'd automatically end up in heaven."

Now I was crying too. Steam from our hot breath and tears crept up the windshield, closing us in.

"She did it on a night when she thought only Jerry would be home. Just waltzed right in and did what she thought she had to do. Only, Anne was home—Kristen too." She wiped her trembling hand beneath her nose. "But Kristen saw her. Ran after her, all the way to our house, screaming. It woke me up, but I—I thought I was dreaming." Her sobs shook the car as fog climbed into the windshield's center, hazing out the hot world outside.

"I don't know how to say this," I ventured, "but I have to ask—are you sure it was Jamie and not Kristen who started the fire? If Kristen's MO was accusing Jamie of things she did herself—"

"No. I read her diary. Jamie came up with it all on her own."

"But if Kristen—"

"Kristen knew that Anne was home," she cut in, hunched over like a teenager. "Jamie didn't, but Kristen knew her mom had decided last-minute not to go away for the weekend. And Kristen would never hurt her mom. She loved her more than anyone in the world. When she—that night, when she gave up on Jamie and ran to Tabitha and Bill's, yelling so loud she woke me up, she was screaming one word over and over: *Mommy*."

"Oh my God." It fit, but I wasn't sure I could accept it—could Kristen, an agent of hurt and chaos, really have been adjacent to that tragedy and not directly involved? Or maybe her parents' death was the spark that ignited her cruelty. Perhaps she'd then guilted young Jamie into killing herself, or blackmailed Jamie by saying she saw her start the fire, or . . .

I glanced over at Jenny. She was curled like a question mark, silhouetted in the window, and for a flash I saw what Jamie would look like now, button-nosed and pretty. My heart sank. Could another twelve-year-old, driven to desperation, really have behaved as destructively as Kristen?

Just look how far she pushed you.

Jenny sniffled. "So Kristen screamed all the way to Tabitha and Bill's, and they called 911 and kept her safe. But she told them—she *knew* she'd seen Jamie in there, and though I never asked her, I bet she had some idea why Jamie would want her father dead. Oh God. Jamie used to go up to their cottage with them on weekends—I don't think I'll ever forgive myself."

A cry, then, so long and mournful I thought of the loon, its call echoing as if to channel all the pain of a broiling, dying Earth. I let my own tears stream over my neck, soaking into the collar of my dirty tank top.

"But we didn't know. We had no idea!" She disgorged a few more sobs. "And when Bill didn't demand an investigation, we thought what everyone else thought: The fire was an accident, a tragic, freak thing. But then Kristen rang my doorbell. God, I can remember it like it was yesterday. I opened the door to find her bawling. And in between sobs, she told me she'd seen Jamie leaving her house the night of the fire. She thought Jamie had started it. I didn't believe her, of course. I told her to leave."

She took a deep inhalation and pushed it out in a stream. Her breath was raspy, an odd accordion sound. "But then I read the diary. I couldn't tell Tom. Tom doesn't know—about the abuse, the arson, any of it. It would break him. Tom has no idea what that mother-fucker did to our daughter. God, sometimes I wish Jerry wasn't dead so I could burn him alive all over again."

The fury wafted off of her like heat. Tears streamed down her face and I could see the veins banging along her throat.

I reached out and touched her hand. She jumped, then sagged a little.

"I tried to speak with Bill in private." Her voice was furious and compressed, carbon pressed into a diamond. "He didn't want to hear it. Any of it. He didn't want to tarnish his memories of his son. I could have killed him then and there. He kept saying it was too late now, we'd both lost a child and accusing his son of pedophilia and my daughter of arson would only cause more pain. Plus, I'd have to tell Tom, and, and if we'd gone to the authorities to explain, the story would've been sensationalized in the press. The whole world would be looking at my beautiful daughter, pitying her, blaming her, calling her a victim, a murderer, looking for photos where she showed too much skin, picking her apart, tearing her to shreds. Tom and I were already at rock bottom—no way could we deal with that kind of pain. And for what? It wouldn't bring my Jamie back. It wouldn't undo what had been done. So we packed up and moved across the country, and . . . and tried to start over."

My heart felt like a cello, groaning a long, mournful note. Poor Jamie, poor Kristen. Poor Jenny and Tom.

"Kristen went to a mental-health center after that," I said, "an inpatient one, for minors. I thought it was basically in place of juvie for kids who'd done something wrong."

Jenny shook her head. "I didn't know that. But it doesn't surprise me that she had a mental break after all that trauma. Oh, that poor girl. I told you I didn't like how she treated Jamie, but . . . Christ, nobody deserves that. I can't imagine how that screws you up, long-term."

I nodded. "You didn't hear from Kristen again after that?"

"She friended me on Facebook a few years ago. After she gradu-ated. I always wondered about her, kept her in my prayers . . . Jamie loved her, you know. They were best friends. In a weird way, Kristen feels like the last connection to my Jamie." Her eyes turned steely. "My heart stopped when Tom said that Bill was calling today. I hate that Bill even has Tom's number."

I gave her hand a squeeze, and she looked down at it thought-fully. We sat in silence for a while.

"I'm sure you realize you can't tell anyone what I told you," she said. "Not anyone."

"I know." Sweat prickled on my forehead and dripped down my back. It felt like my whole body was crying.

"Emily."

I looked up. "Yeah?"

"Why were you trying to get away from Kristen?"

The car was almost unbearably warm now, sun beating in through the back.

"I'm not sure I can tell you," I replied. All the pieces were floating around now, swirling like dry leaves.

She swallowed hard, then bobbed her head. "Okay. But I doubt the Phoenix PD is going to like that answer."

The penny dropped. Jesus Christ. I turned to her, eyes wide. "You think if Kristen doesn't pull through, they'll charge me with her murder?"

"No." She clunked the car door open and the saunalike breeze mingled with our steam room inside. "I think they'll charge your boyfriend."

CHAPTER 44

Jenny's husband called as we were up in my messy hotel room. I'd taken a quick shower, scrubbing dirt from my skin while Jenny waited on a stiff armchair. I was yanking out clothes for Aaron and stuffing them into a tote bag when she lifted her phone and ducked into the muggy bathroom. When she reemerged, her face was grim.

"She didn't make it," she said. "Kristen didn't make it."

My heart dropped like an ice fisher plunging through a frozen lake, down into the inescapable cold, and I slumped against the wardrobe. I flashed back to that morning in Chile, the morning after, when Kristen and I stopped at a cliff on the drive out of town and screamed into the canyon below. I felt the same strange sensation now, something huge and sweeping, erupting out of me and up into the atmosphere. A mushroom cloud of power and sorrow. Something you could see from space.

"I'm sorry." Jenny touched my arm and I jumped.

"I'm sorry too," I said, and meant it. I hesitated. "What do we do now?"

"We should head back there. Tom said there are cops waiting to talk to you."

Cold adrenaline careened through me. My hand shook as I grabbed my now fully charged phone on the way out. I unlocked it while the elevator made its slow descent: texts and voicemails from Kristen, "You ok?" and "Stay strong my friend" and "I'm on my way," each one a stab to my gut. *Kristen.* As late as this morning I'd still been waffling, trying to decide if she was being inappropriate or if I was being too sensitive, too suspicious.

But that was before she shoved me in front of an oncoming car.

Well, in response to me pushing her off a cliff. Because she'd convinced me, erroneously, that I had it in me. That I was like her. That I could solve my problems by taking someone else's life.

Oh God. My stomach gurgled; my vision swam. The silver doors split apart and I took off through the lobby, sprinting past the automatic doors in time to vomit. I spat and spotted Jenny in the doorway, but she whirled around and dashed back inside. A moment later she reappeared with a cup of water, and she rubbed my back as I brought it to my lips.

"Little sips, not big gulps," she said.

"Thanks." I swallowed. "You're being so nice to me."

"Like I said." Her chin trembled and she looked away. "You remind me of my daughter."

I finished my water and followed her to the car, acid still burning my windpipe and tongue.

AARON WASN'T AARON. He was battered and bruised, his face bulging and purple like an overripe plum. The face of a fighter, a boxer. A Spanish-American man beaten to death by a beautiful American visitor.

My heart had pounded as I'd entered the hospital, but I hadn't seen cops anywhere. So I'd chanced it—sprinting to the surgery wing, asking a nurse there for directions to his recovery room. This felt like borrowed time, sand draining through an hourglass before everything blew up in our faces.

Again.

Gauze covered one eye, a watercolor wash of blue peeking out from the bandage, but Aaron opened the other and cracked a wide smile.

"Emily! How ya doing, babe?"

"I'm so glad you're okay!" I touched his hand. "How are you feeling?"

"They gave me painkillers, so . . . awesome." He swung his hand into a thumbs-up. "I feel as good as you look. Which is . . ." Now his fingers shifted again, forming the okay sign.

"A charmer, even on codeine!" I ruffled his hair. "The nurse said your folks are getting in this evening." I was praying they'd arrive before Bill and Nana, or that we'd be kept separate, the Czarneckis heading straight to the morgue—I couldn't face Bill and Nana today. Would they be sobbing and disheveled? Stoic and composed? Or, God . . . unflinching and, apparent only in the tiniest expressions, relieved that she was gone?

No. Kristen was their flesh and blood. They weren't monsters . . . they weren't like me.

"You're gonna meet my paaaa-rents," Aaron sang.

I smiled. "Exactly how I pictured it."

"You still haven't given me a kiss." He pouted, then pursed his lips.

I leaned down and gave him a gentle smooch. He sighed happily.

A nurse had informed me Aaron had no memory of the accident, no memory beyond grabbing his keys and pulling out of the hotel parking lot, and it seemed unfair to demand answers when he was drugged-up and loopy. Still, the questions burned my throat like bile.

"Can I ask you something?" I said.

"Sure!"

"Why did you leave the hotel and come after Kristen and me?"

He twisted his mouth, thinking hard. At least I'd know if he wasn't telling the truth—he didn't seem capable of lying right now.

"So, I knew you didn't want Kristen here," he said, "since we came to Phoenix to get away from her. But then, when you sent me upstairs, I checked my phone and saw an article that they'd released an image of a suspect in the dead-backpacker story. It was aaaaall over the news." His fingers winged out.

Shock foamed up through me, nearing my jaw, my face, my scalp.

There was a Wanted poster out there with my face on it? What, a police sketch? Surveillance footage?

"And I went, Whoa, that girl looks like Kristen. And then I remembered it was in Chile! And that you said that she's been acting cuckoo-banana-crackers!" He tapped his temple. "So I thought you might be in trouble. And I tried to call you, but your phone was in the room. So I was like, *crap*." He looked thoughtful for a moment. "Can I have some water?"

I poured him a cup from the bedside jug and helped him with the straw. He finished glugging with a satisfied "Ahhh."

"So you noticed I'd left my phone," I prompted.

"Right. And I ran back down and realized you were gone. I asked if anyone had seen you and this woman said she thought you'd gone outside. I ran out and couldn't see you but I still had the car keys in my pocket. Figured you couldn't have gotten far. I thought I saw your red backpack disappearing around the corner, so I hit the gas. And that's . . . that's all I remember."

"Wow. Thanks for coming for me."

He knit his brow. "Did I save you?"

"You did, Aaron! I'm so grateful."

"Good. 'Cause you're awesome. You're way out of my league." He laughed, a slow, Mitch Hedberg–like guffaw. He pursed his lips again, lifting his chin for another kiss, and I leaned over and stamped his forehead with a peck, aiming for a clean spot among the tapestry of bruises.

"Hey, speaking of Kristen." He squinted. "What happened to her? Is she okay?"

A nurse appeared in the doorway and Aaron greeted him, his question forgotten. No one seemed to notice my hand shaking as I waved goodbye.

HIS PARENTS LOOKED so much like him: Aaron had his father's lush hair and angular jaw, and his mother's sharp nose and pretty eyes. Their faces were contorted with fear, but Aaron seemed delighted to introduce us, quick to joke about his injuries. I wanted to spend the night at Aaron's side, but they were politely firm in that parenty way, so they dropped me off at the hotel and promised to pick me up at eleven A.M. sharp, in time for visiting hours.

But around ten A.M., I got a call from the police station. A bored-sounding woman asked me to come in again—voluntarily, she added, if I wanted to help. They'd pick me up in fifteen minutes. I hung up, my head swimming, already racked with what felt like a full-body hangover.

A different officer wanted to speak to me this time, a detective, and he gave me his condolences on the loss of my friend. He was friendly as well, but there was a wolfish quality droning right below the surface. My heart thudded; I blinked hard, trying to clear my fuzzy mind.

"We've been in touch with the Los Angeles police," he announced. "And we don't want to jump to any conclusions. But it seems that Miss Czarnecki matches the description of a suspect in an April slaying in South America."

He tapped a few things on his phone, then turned it to me: the police sketch, carefully penciled in, like the ones on TV. God, they'd nailed it, wise feline eyes and all.

"We ran her passport. She was in Chile with you in April, correct?"

Damn, that was fast. "Yes."

He put his phone away. "We know Miss Czarnecki flew into Phoenix separately. On a flight she booked last-minute. And several witnesses at the hotel saw the two of you fighting in the lobby right before her death. So let's go over the details together one more time. Since this isn't as cut-and-dry as we thought."

Suddenly it was blindingly clear, as bright as fresh mint, as crystalline and cold as a laser-cut diamond: They thought Aaron and I had killed Kristen to shut her up. God, now that I thought about it, every detail pointed that way—the evidence she'd cached linking me to the crimes in Chile and Cambodia, all her vaguely threatening texts, the way she plummeted to her death less than an hour after the sketch was released . . .

And no one had been there to see it. No one knew she shoved me into traffic first—that Aaron swerved not to hit Kristen but to *avoid* hitting me. All my insides contracted and a retch shot up my throat.

"We got investigators on the scene right away," he went on. "They'll be looking into the tire marks, the crash site, all that stuff too. And forensics will be taking a very close look at Miss Czarnecki as well—dirt under her fingernails, that kind of thing."

He took a sip of coffee. I reached for the water in front of me and then went cold all over. The detective saw it too: a patch of purply bruises on my forearm, clustered like a bunch of grapes. And scratches, too, angry red stripes, lined up like stretch marks. Battle wounds where Kristen had grabbed me as she clawed her way up the cliff.

And then I touched the flimsy cup and the last piece thunked into place. I'd pressed my mouth to a cup here yesterday, too, left behind wet pieces of my DNA.

Dirt under her fingernails. Or skin cells. Irrefutable proof that there'd been a struggle before Kristen plunged to her death.

"Am I under arrest?" I asked, my voice strangled.

The detective leaned back, eyebrows high. "Nope. This is just a friendly chat."

"Then I'd like to go now." I pulled my hand back. "Please."

We stared at each other, each locked in a frigid glare.

Finally, he shrugged. "Of course. We can have someone give you a lift to your hotel."

"I'd like to go to the hospital, please." When he didn't say anything: "Aaron's parents are waiting for me there."

"Sure thing. Maybe I'll see you there later." He braced his beefy hand against the table to push back his chair. "We have some questions for Mr. Meuleman too."

CHAPTER 45

Aaron looked clear-eyed today, more focused and alert. My heart twisted at the sight of him; I feared it was the last time he'd look at me like that, his expression warm and brimming with love. His parents gave me hugs (they were huggers!), and I tried to seem casual as I requested a few minutes alone with their son.

When they'd closed the door behind them, I glanced around—no cameras, at least none that I could see. I'd keep my voice low and hope for the best.

"Aaron, I need to tell you the truth," I murmured. "It won't be easy, but I need you to hear it from me first."

"What is it?" He stared at me, his eyes so full of concern that I thought I might disintegrate like a shooting star, which, after all, is just a lowly meteor that lost its way, burning up as it plunges into the atmosphere.

My throat tightened. I took a deep breath and braced myself.

And I finally, finally told the man I loved the truth.

It wasn't hard, once I got going. I started with Cambodia—how Kristen had felled Sebastian with a lamp, kicked his head into the bed frame while I howled for her to stop. How, afterward, I'd wanted to call the police, but she'd threatened me, too, forced me to clean up the hotel room, to help her dump his body over the ledge like a coin into a well.

How she'd manipulated me in the weeks that followed, nursing me from afar, convincing me we'd made the right call. Talked me into giving her another chance with a week in Chile, one where everything seemed normal again until that final night, when I came upon her and Paolo's body, and again, she forced me to abet her horrible cover-up. Since then I'd tried to cut her out of my life, but she kept upping the pressure. And then she tried to kill me. She nearly killed Aaron too.

"Listen," I concluded, my voice an urgent whisper, "we're in trouble. They think we killed her on purpose to shut her up—and they don't even know how bad it is, yet. Everything linking me to the two backpackers." I shook my head. "I'm so sorry I dragged you into this, Aaron. There aren't words for how sorry I am. But they think we were trying to keep her from talking. No one else saw what happened yesterday; no one knows you were just trying not to hit me."

He looked shell-shocked, his one exposed eye as wide as a sand dollar.

I touched his cheek. "Aaron, it's okay. I won't let you go down for this. You're there for me in a way Kristen never was—God, it's like the wool's been pulled from my eyes. All this time, I've been hesitating and holding back and doing whatever she told me, but that's over. I'm done."

"What are you—?"

"I'm going to tell them everything." I squeezed my eyes shut. "I knew it was wrong to hide those bodies, but I let Kristen convince me to do it. I'm done lying and I can't be the reason your life is ruined. So when the cops show up and ask you what happened, tell them the truth. Because I'm going to tell them the whole story, all the crazy twists and turns that brought us here. It's time for me to take responsibility. I—I love you, Aaron."

His face opened up. "I love you too, Emily." He batted his hand around for mine, and I grabbed it. "You can't . . . I can't lose you. Those other backpackers—I believe you; I know that was Kristen, but what if the cops don't? What if they . . ." He was crying, tears sliding over the bulges and bruises.

"Shh, it's okay." I leaned down and kissed him. "It's really okay. I won't let them charge you. It's time for me to come clean."

He sniffled. "Emily, you have to talk to a lawyer. Please, please do that for me. My uncle's a lawyer, he's a good guy. He'll help you find someone. I'm begging you."

I hesitated. I just wanted this to be over. I was so tired of running.

"*Promise* me." His hand gripped mine with surprising strength. "I won't say a word until then. I'm serious. I love you. If you care about me at all, you'll do this for me."

A nurse appeared in the doorway and told Aaron some cops had asked to speak to him. Aaron kept his eyes on mine as he asked the nurse to send them away.

CHAPTER 46

The Phoenix PD let me fly home after a few days on the condition that I stay in the country. In the meantime, they kept their mouths shut, building their case.

But Paolo's parents couldn't leave me alone.

Rodrigo and Fernanda García—they were the reason we were big news. A Wisconsin woman whose pretty face matched the composite sketch, killed by her best friend's boyfriend on a lonely stretch of mountain road, while the travel buddy—me—appeared to get off scot-free . . . well, I could understand why they couldn't turn away. The Garcías, armed with their fortune, were relentless: They held press conferences and vigils; they kept the pressure on Washington; they demanded extradition; they made #JusticeforPaolo trend internationally.

Goddamn Tiffany Yagasaki, the witness from the bar in Quiteria, identified Kristen and me both, and the news vultures went wild. Trolls tracked down my workplace, my personal email, my phone number, using every means and only the most colorful language to tell me I deserved to be raped or killed. Kibble quietly cut ties. I lowered my blinds and went into hiding as news crews idled outside my front door.

All the while I met with Deirdre, the lawyer Aaron's uncle hooked me up with, and she was a godsend—smart and thoughtful and always so lucid, not to mention beautiful, the picture of success in her tailored power suits and stick-straight bob. We walked through my backstory together, point by point, as she homed in on details that would help set me free. I learned about duress and self-defense and entrapment, opportunity to escape, reasonable fear for one's life—the legal case that *nothing* that happened in Phnom Penh or Quiteria was truly my fault.

The Garcías' incessant campaign was making life a living hell, so finally Deirdre crafted a letter to the U.S. embassy, recounting what Kristen had done in Chile. She outlined how Kristen had subsequently followed me to Milwaukee, how she'd brought a lump of Paolo's burned possessions with which to blackmail me, control me, keep me quiet. I read the letter over and over until the lines blurred and the words ceased to make sense. Phrases jumped out at me: *My client abdicates further involvement in the case* and *We consider the matter now closed* and *My client has confirmed she will not travel to Chile.* I laughed a bit at that last part. As if I'd ever return.

Someone leaked the statement, and the media attention crescendoed from a fever pitch to a terrifying roar. Reporters, already titillated by Aaron's involvement and the splashy car crash in the Sonoran Desert, swooned at the story. Trashy newspapers painted us as a murderous young couple, plotting to eliminate the only person who knew about my dark past. Blogs asked if Kristen and I were secret lovers, and one called Aaron and me Bonnie and Clyde, which made no sense—weren't they robbers?

But even as the news coverage intensified, Deirdre's careful wording did the trick; officers stateside stopped pandering to the Garcías over a case that was never theirs to pursue. It was the Arizona Attorney General's Office she was worried about—vehicular manslaughter, coercion, conspiracy. And I only cared about getting Aaron off the hook, innocent as he was. So we waited and watched. I wouldn't speak up until either Aaron or I was charged, she decided—but we'd be ready if that happened. I admired it, the swift computations in her own area of expertise.

Kristen and I had been so worried about the media circus, about being crucified by the court of public opinion, but now I was in the middle of it, surviving. She'd called it onto us that Arizona morning, inviting it in like a congregation crying out for the Holy Spirit. Twenty-four hours a day, I shut out the sunlight, moving around my dim apartment while a swarm of spectators loitered beyond the drawn blinds.

By the second month, it was getting to me. Aaron suggested I stay in his apartment while he recovered in a nearby hospital, but I needed space from him, as well, to sleep and think and grasp around at my feelings in the dark. Besides, I couldn't imagine the awkwardness of sharing a bathroom with his roommate or the pang of picking up his scent everywhere, just the ghost of him.

Eventually, I boarded the Amtrak to Minnesota for an indeterminate stint with my mom and her soft-spoken, self-conscious husband. They believed me, thank God, and learned to scan the driveway for the glint of cameras, to screen their calls for reporters. Every time we crossed paths in the hallway or kitchen, they seemed surprised to see me, as if I were a seldom-used appliance they'd tucked into the attic.

I gave Priya the house number since my cell service sucked, and one night she called a little after eleven to check on me. My mother was furious the next morning, admonishing me for disturbing her slumber, and the familiar guilt crackled in my gut. But for the first time, Adrienne's calm words came to me: *You're not responsible for other people's actions.* I told my mother it wouldn't happen again but that the mistake was Priya's, not mine. She clucked and walked away and I made a mental note to tell Adrienne during our next Zoom session.

Then, the following weekend, Mom made French toast for breakfast and asked, her voice gruff, what my Milwaukee friends were up to these days—her version of an apology. I accompanied her on drugstore and grocery runs, and one day she shyly proposed mother-daughter pedicures. And I thought maybe, without Kristen influencing me, isolating me, her voice mosquito-like in my ear, my relationship with my mom could change.

While I was away, Priya was on porch duty: Every few days, she swung by my apartment to collect the lavish flower arrangements stippling the porch. There were gift baskets, too, brimming with wine and snacks and chocolates, and Priya couldn't believe I didn't want them, didn't even want to see photos or hear about them. They were all bribes from cable news programs, begging me for an exclusive, a tell-all, thirty minutes of pouring out my soul. Priya took the comestibles to work, and my former co-workers snacked on the pleas of producers everywhere.

There was hate mail, too, and once, Priya arrived to find the word MURDERER spray-painted across my door. She called the cops, and my landlord, bless him, didn't try to end my lease on account of it. I felt myself building up immunity to the vitriol, the judgment. These people didn't know what really happened, all that Kristen and I had done. I never spoke up about Cambodia. I deleted the Dropbox photo, but Deirdre was unconcerned: No body, no victim, no crime, and even if the photo *did* surface on a search of Kristen's hard drive, it'd fall to Cambodian authorities to pursue it—and they had no reason to waste resources on two foreigners, American me and South African Sebastian. The revelation was disorienting and absurd: Now that Kristen was gone, I had nothing to worry about when it came to Phnom Penh.

I told Aaron the truth, but otherwise I kept the secret locked inside. It was ours alone, his and mine, like those sunrises at Northwestern, gulping up the dawn while the rest of the world was asleep. We got away with it. And in a weird way, it was a relief to be free from the assumption that I was "Minnesota nice."

Aaron quickly grew stronger, shattering the doctors' expectations. We texted most days, with the occasional FaceTime: I told him about the remote projects I'd picked up in St. Paul, and he gossiped about the nurses and orderlies and fellow patients, who was flirting with whom. He wanted to talk more, but I told him that while I was there for him as a friend, I needed to pump the brakes on our relationship. I had to make sure I wasn't trading one omnipotent idol for another, the way I had swapped Kristen in for Ben. For now, my decisions needed to be mine alone.

Nana and Bill's lawyer informed me I would not be welcome at Kristen's funeral—no surprise there. I imagined randos from her high school showing up in gray and black, titillated by the news trucks outside, the vague thrill of drama by proxy. I pictured Bill suspiciously eyeing all the "friends" Kristen had never made in her short lifetime. And Nana, her eyes at half-mast, knowing the truth. As if these years with her loose cannon of a granddaughter were simply borrowed time, a bizarre period before reality corrected itself.

Aaron wasn't welcome at the funeral, either, though it didn't really matter. Now that he knew the truth, he grieved with me for Kristen but also for Jamie and Sebastian and Paolo, for Kristen's young parents, snuffed out too soon. The hospital's psychiatrist helped him find a therapist to deal with the PTSD—his mind, it seemed, had glommed onto that moment on the mountainside, the second when his girlfriend appeared in front of the car—and he was improving, dealing, growing.

Summer rumbled through the Midwest: farmers' markets and baseball games, Fourth of July fireworks and the distant smell of brats. Aaron was released from the hospital with nothing but a cane for balance, and we joked about buying him a top hat and choreographing a soft-shoe routine. I laughed harder than I had for months.

In spite of everything, I missed Kristen—mourned for her, in that physical, achy way, as if every time I thought about her someone cracked open my ribs and poked at my heart. For a decade, she'd been my closest friend, my sister, the most important relationship in my life. But there was a tinge of inevitability to the grief, as if things had gone back to the way they were, as if she'd simply moved back to Australia. I sometimes slipped into present tense when talking about her, and I felt her in my friendships, my bond with Aaron, the callow closeness with my mom. Kristen's life and love and, yes, death had made me the person showing up in those relationships. Sometimes, for a moment, I forgot all about Phoenix, and in my mind Kristen was fine and funny and vivacious and beautiful, charming strangers in remote corners of the world.

THE NEWS CREWS lost interest, and I moved home. Arizona was still trying to drum up charges against us, but Deirdre was confident there wasn't enough evidence to make a case that Aaron and I had killed Kristen together. No one had seen us on that quiet patch of road, so it was our word against a dead girl's. Folks in the lobby at Hotel Rosita had seen Kristen scream at me and practically drag me outside, and it wasn't hard to find character witnesses poking holes in any theory that painted Kristen in an angelic light. In a particularly creepy twist, Kristen's former employer revealed that the company's Australian branch had fired Kristen *two weeks* before our Chile trip. Why? Because she'd assaulted her boss, Lucas, at a company outing. Apparently she shoved the tiny man into a shelf of liquor bottles following an altercation.

Another disturbing detail: Deep in Kristen's toiletry kit, tucked into her suitcase and left behind the front desk at the Phoenix inn, police found several vials of Rohypnol—the very same sedative Paolo had in his system. Likely not hard to obtain when your grandfather owns a chain of pharmacies.

I had no idea what she planned to do with the drug this time, but it meant that Paolo had been incapacitated by the time Kristen swung that wine bottle. It meant that every word she'd told me in that blood-spattered hotel suite was a lie. She probably thought no one would ever know about the roofies in his system, what with his body decomposing under reddish dirt. Apparently the eyes "resist putrefaction" better than blood. Kristen, with her horrifying compulsions, certainly hadn't planned on *that*.

The months ticked on. Fall blew in on a crisp, rustling breeze, then winter, the snow dreamy at first and then cold and unrelenting. Aaron moved in with me and we spent Christmas with his family, New Year's with a mixed group of our friends. His medical bills had reached ludicrous, almost hilarious figures, and patchy contract work had drained my savings. So we discussed. We figured it out, as we always did. We went with the highest bidder: almost five years' salary for thirty minutes with a cable news show. I'd been over the story so many times with Deirdre, I was pretty sure I could tell it in my sleep, from the minute Kristen and I hugged hello in an airport in Santiago to now.

Aaron and I held hands throughout the interview, taking turns sharing our story. He understood me so deeply. It was like we shared a nerve network, a brain.

IN JANUARY, NINE months after Kristen and I met up in Chile, Deirdre called with good news: Arizona had dropped the case. Aaron and I knew we had to celebrate—we'd been waiting for this moment for so long.

Two weeks later, Aaron's gaze found mine. We were in an underground club on a street lined with bars. Tbilisi, Georgia, was nothing like I'd imagined: a beautiful patchwork of tiled mosques and domed brick hammams and windy cobblestone passages, vines clinging to the cliffs around the city's broad river, and fortresses and castles peeking out from distant sepia mountains. And always wine, so much wine.

I pulled my wallet from my purse—the bag wasn't leaving my lap this time, no pickpockets for me, thanks—and ordered us another round of chacha, an alarmingly fiery grape brandy the locals drank by the boatload. The bar had vaulted brick ceilings, a mottled orange-white, and the feel of a dungeon; a bartender told me the space had once been home to covert government interrogations.

The night had just made the sudden lurch into shitshow-ery: People were smoking in the dark corners, a Turkish tourist ducked into the stock room with a waitress, and someone dropped a drink, the shrill tinkle cutting through the throbbing bassline. I plucked at Aaron's elbow, suddenly eager for quiet, for water, for the giggling tango of us tipsily rehashing the night and brushing our teeth before snuggling into our lumpy queen bed. Maybe we'd even find cheese-stuffed bread on the way home. It was everywhere here, golden and gooey, *khachapuri* on every corner.

But then a woman sat down next to me and, hearing my English, asked where we were from. She was Bulgarian, slim and angular, with a curtain of thick brown hair. She was based in London but had taken the year off to travel, chipping away at her savings while working her way north from Azerbaijan.

I scooted my stool back so that we could form a triangle. She was gregarious and engaging. And traveling alone, she said—moving slowly by bus, taking her time, without an itinerary or advance registrations. So brave of her, feisty.

"What did you say your names are?" she asked, her accent like a gently beaten gong.

"This is Dan," I said, and reached for Aaron's hand. When he squeezed it, I felt it all the way down to my heart, my groin, my soul. "And I'm Joan. We just love meeting new people."

ACKNOWLEDGMENTS

Thank you, reader, for picking up this book. What an honor, a joy, a goddamn miracle to picture you holding it in your hands right now. Thank you, thank you, thank you for choosing to spend your limited time and energy on this weird and dark adventure cooked up in a hotel suite in Chile. Without you, this story is just a big vat of words; you're a crucial part of the alchemy, the ingredient that makes the narrative come alive, and I'm beyond grateful. I hope something in these pages resonated with you. Thank you, truly.

This book wouldn't exist if it weren't for Jennifer Weber, my soul sister and beloved travel buddy, who lives in Australia now but has *nothing else* in common with Kristen, let the record show. Jen, who'd have thought our wine-fueled running gag in Pisco Elqui would lead to this? Thanks to Stephen Clarke, too, a backpacking stranger so kind and respectful and awesome that we could joke about murder within hours of meeting. Ha.

I hit the sibling jackpot with my sister, Jules, who is thoughtful and kind and creative AF. I'm so grateful to have you by my side. Thanks to Leah Konen, an excellent friend, brilliant thriller author, and world-class beta reader. I can't imagine my writing life without you. Thanks to Megan Brown, comrade on more world travels than I can count, not to mention supportive and loyal friend and thorough, lucid early reader. Megan, I can't wait to be exploring downtowns and charming strangers in faraway places with you again soon. Thank you to Danielle Rollins for the careful beta reads that didn't just make this book stronger—they made me a better writer. And thanks to Jennifer Keishin Armstrong for the thorough early read and for all the work dates, phone calls, and helpful texts; everyone needs someone like Jennifer to keep them centered in this wacky industry.

Erin DeYoung helped me get this book written in so many dang ways: Thank you, Sedi, for your careful notes, for troubleshooting phone calls, and for being an incredible friend. You have such a gift and I'm so grateful to have you in my corner. I'm in awe of you! Speaking of the DeYoungs, thanks to Ben for making me cocktails and patiently explaining concepts like extradition and duress (that said, all errors and wild stretches are, of course, my own). Thank you, Owain, for all the hugs and hilarious comments and epic sword fights. And huge thanks to all three for letting me escape to your beautiful home when I needed some space, metaphorically and literally. You're the best COVID pod anyone could ask for.

Everyone needs a healthy and varied support system (just ask Adrienne Oderdonk!), and I'm perpetually dazzled by and thankful for my crew, including Lianna Bishop, Megan Collins, Alanna Greco, Leigh Kunkel, Abbi Libers, Anna Maltby, Erin Pastrana, Julia Phillips, Melissa Rivero, Peter Rugg, Katie Scott, and many others. Love and thanks to Julia Dills, who cracked me up, listened to me gripe, and cheered me on as this book finally came together. You're the damn best (not to mention so smart, it scares even me).

Huge thanks to my rock-star agent, Alexandra Machinist, for fiercely and deftly championing my work and career. Three books in three years! Is this real life?! I'm so grateful to Lindsey Sanderson, too, for all the effort and help behind the scenes. And I'm the luckiest to have Josie Freedman helping my stories make the magical leap from page to screen—gosh, do I love working with all of you.

I can't fully express my gratitude for my editor, Hilary Rubin Teeman, a legit genius who honed this idea until it lived up to its potential. You're the most incredible collaborator and sage and cheerleader, yes, but I'm most in awe of your ability to whittle an idea to its sparking, zapping core. Caroline Weishuhn, I'm beyond grateful for your masterful notes and all the work you do to transform a Word document into a bona fide book. There aren't words for how much

I love working with publicity dream team Sarah Breivogel and Justine Magowan as well as marketing maven Colleen Nuccio. Please just picture animations of rainbows and sparkles and happy dancing hearts to accurately convey my feelings toward everyone at Random House.

When I pitched this idea, I had no idea that foreign travel would feel so, well, foreign by the time I wrote these words. Major thanks to the essential healthcare workers who tirelessly gave their all during a scary and stifling period. And thank you to everyone who stayed home and stopped the spread and trusted science. I'm praying that by the time you read this, travel won't still feel like a faraway dream.

Last but certainly not least, thanks so much to my loving family, especially Nagypapa and Nagymama, Uncle Tom and Cathy, and of course, my mom and dad. Love you.

ABOUT THE AUTHOR

ANDREA BARTZ, a Brooklyn-based journalist, is the author of *The Lost Night* and *The Herd*. Her work has appeared in *The Wall Street Journal, Marie Claire, Vogue, Cosmopolitan, Women's Health, Martha Stewart Living, Redbook, Elle,* and many other outlets, and she's held editorial positions at *Glamour, Psychology Today,* and *Self,* among other publications.

Andreabartz.com
Facebook.com/andreabartzauthor
Twitter: @andibartz
Instagram: @andibartz

ABOUT THE TYPE

This book was set in Sabon, a typeface designed by the well-known German typographer Jan Tschichold (1902–74). Sabon's design is based upon the original letter forms of sixteenth-century French type designer Claude Garamond and was created specifically to be used for three sources: foundry type for hand composition, Linotype, and Monotype. Tschichold named his typeface for the famous Frankfurt typefounder Jacques Sabon (c. 1520–80).